FAR HORIZON

TONY PARK

Quercus

First published in Australia in 2004 by Pan Macmillan
This paperback edition published in 2016 by

Quercus Editions Ltd
Carmelite House
50 Victoria Embankment
London EC4Y 0DZ

An Hachette UK company

A CIP catalogue record for this book is available
from the British Library

PB ISBN 978 0 85738 795 0
Ebook ISBN 978 0 85738 592 5

10 9 8 7 6 5 4 3 2 1

Printed and bound in Great Britain by Clays Ltd, St Ives plc

For Nicola

Acknowledgments

The man who provided me with the greatest assistance during the research of this book wants to remain anonymous. He was one of many Australian Army engineers who were involved in landmine clearance in Mozambique and he provided me not only with a wealth of detail about the dangerous business of de-mining, but also with descriptions and photographs of Maputo. To him, and the members of 17th Construction Squadron, Royal Australian Engineers, who shared with me the stories of their tour in Namibia, thank you. Any mistakes or exaggerations about the work of the Australian Army or the UN in Africa are all mine.

I researched and wrote *Far Horizon* while travelling in southern Africa with my wife in our old Land Rover. My thanks go to Dennis and Liz in Zimbabwe, who continue to care for and garage the truck in between our visits, and the many other friends and acquaintances we've made on our travels over the past eight years who all added to our knowledge of Africa and its wildlife. Gary Phillips from National Airways Corporation in South Africa helped with information about helicopters, and Dr Michael O'Flynn's stories of his work in Soweto's Chris Hani Baragwanath Hospital taught me more than I wanted to know about gunshot wounds. Again, any errors are down to me.

My mother Kathy, wife Nicola and mother-in-law Sheila all read and re-read early drafts and made editorial suggestions that proved sound. The book would not have got this far without them.

At Pan Macmillan I am indebted (forever) to fiction publisher Cate Paterson for her initial reading and suggestions, and for the deal; to Sarina Rowell and Glenda Downing for their sensible, no-nonsense edits; and to publicist Jane Novak for that first cup of coffee.

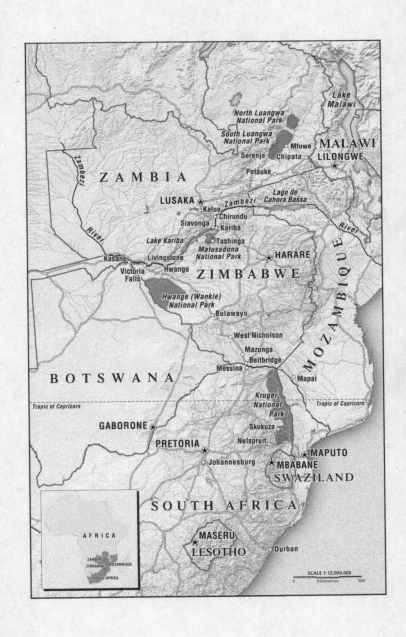

Lake
Malawi

North Luangwa
National Park

South Luangwa
National Park

Mfuwe

MALAWI

Serenje   Chipata

LILONGWE

★

Petauke

ZAMBIA

Zambezi

LUSAKA ★   Kafue   *Zambezi*

Chirundu

Lago de
Cahora Bassa

Siavonga

Kariba

Lake Kariba   Tashinga

Kasane   Livingstone

*Matusadona
National Park*

★ HARARE

Victoria
Falls

Hwange

ZIMBABWE

River

*Hwange (Wankie)
National Park*

Bulawayo

MOZAMBIQUE

West Nicholson

Mazunga

Beitbridge

BOTSWANA   Messina

Mapai

Tropic of Capricorn   *Tropic of Capricorn*

*Kruger
National
Park*

GABORONE ★

Skukuza

PRETORIA ★   Nelspruit

Johannesburg   ★ MAPUTO

MBABANE

SWAZILAND

SOUTH AFRICA

AFRICA

MASERU ★

LESOTHO   Durban

ZAMBIA
ZIMBABWE MOZAMBIQUE

SOUTH AFRICA

SCALE 1:12,000,000

0   Kilometres   300

Prologue

'Theron needs to speak to you.'

The voice on the other end of the mobile phone was South African. Normally its tone was friendly, jovial.

The man driving the truck said nothing, but swung the steering wheel hard, one-handed, to the left, bringing the bright yellow Bedford to a halt on the grass verge of the road.

He said nothing despite the flurry of questions.

'What is it? Did you see something?' asked one of the tourists from the rear cab. 'Why have we stopped?'

'Mike? Are you still there, Mike?' Rian de Witt said into the phone from his office in Johannesburg, four hundred kilometres away.

The driver ran his free hand through his long, dark hair, until it stopped at the band holding the strands in a ponytail. On the other end of the phone line he heard an ambulance siren in the background that brought back memories of the hospital where

1

she worked. As his mind raced he stroked his bristly jawline. Anything to stop his hands from shaking.

He looked out across the expanse of dry yellow grass, the plain spotted here and there with stunted, thirsty acacias. A bachelor herd of impala rams grazed a hundred metres off to the right. They barely paid any notice to the garish overland tour vehicle or the chatting passengers.

'Yeah, I'm still here,' he said. The accent was from half a world away, maybe softened a little after more than a year's absence from his native Australia.

Michael Williams was there in body, but his mind was across the border again, out past where the little antelope were grazing, over the Lebombo Hills that marked the border better than any line on a map. He was thinking of Mozambique.

'Where are you?' Rian asked, knowing what was going through the Australian's mind. Worrying.

Another pause.

'Mike?'

'Kruger. I'm still in the national park. Up north. Near Punda Maria. Mobile phone's only just come back into range again. What do you mean Theron wants to speak to me?'

'He didn't say, but he said it was urgent.'

Sarah Thatcher, a blonde-haired woman in the front passenger seat, realised the tour guide hadn't stopped because he'd seen a lion or an elephant, or a leopard. This was personal. Sarah's instincts were aroused. She reached for the notepad in the side pocket of her daypack, flipped it open and wrote the word 'Theron' on the blank page, shielding it from his

2

view. It might be nothing, but the way the colour had drained from Mike's face suggested the opposite.

He was normally so bloody laid-back. But she had been trained to observe and now saw how his shoulders were bunched and knotted, like a big cat tensing before a final leap. His stocky frame was tensed, the muscles on his nut-brown arms clearly defined, the khaki T-shirt blotched dark with sweat. Something in the truck's big diesel engine tick-ticked as it idled.

He said it was urgent. Mike felt his pulse rate climb. His left hand gripped the steering wheel now, so hard it started to hurt. The mobile phone felt like it might shatter in his right hand.

'When? Where?'

'You're supposed to be crossing from South Africa into Zimbabwe tomorrow. You still on schedule?' Rian asked.

'Yeah.'

'He wants you to report to the South African Police post at Messina, at the border crossing, tomorrow morning. I gave him your schedule and he said he'd meet you there.'

A hundred possible reasons. But why the urgency? 'OK.'

'Mike?'

'Yeah?'

'Are you really OK? Is everything all right, man?'

'I'm fine, the passengers are fine, everybody's fine,' Mike said, trying to sound relaxed.

He'd run away from the horror, changed his life, but he hadn't run far. Maybe, he told himself, he'd stayed in Africa because one day he might get a call like this one. He hadn't heard from the detective for a year and had nearly given up hope that he ever would. Or, he wondered, had he started to hope the call would never come?

The faces, the places, that lived in his nightmares had grown dimmer and appeared less frequently as the months marched on, but now, as he said his good-byes and switched off the mobile phone, they leapt back into horrible focus.

Twelve Months Earlier

1

'I am dying, Michael,' Carlos said. He folded the single sheet of cheap notepaper carefully in half, then placed it on the smoking embers of the campfire, next to the blackened kettle.

The day was warm already, even though the sun was only just emerging, red and threatening, above the tree line. The sun can be merciless at the end of the southern African dry season.

Major Michael Williams – he preferred Mike, but Carlos was always so damned formal – swilled a mouthful of lukewarm water from the plastic litre-bottle. He paused, just for a moment, before swallowing it. He felt ashamed, but he couldn't help wondering if his friend had drunk from the bottle as well.

Both men watched in silence as the paper slowly wilted and began to smoulder. The Australian tried to think of something to say that wouldn't sound pathetic.

'There are drugs. We can get them through the UN. You can live . . . for years.' He knew he had failed as soon as he uttered the words.

Carlos dipped into the breast pocket of the sweat-stained blue two-piece overalls that the African civilian United Nations de-miners wore in the field, and pulled out a crumpled packet of Zimbabwean Newbury cigarettes, the remnants of a carton Mike had bought him on his last leave. At fifty cents a packet there are few economic incentives to quit smoking in southern Africa. Carlos reached across, rising from the jerry can of diesel on which he was perched, and offered Mike a smoke. The army officer accepted, flicked open his Zippo and lit both cigarettes.

'This is Mozambique, not Australia or America. I am finished,' Carlos said, then dragged deeply on his cigarette.

He coughed as he exhaled. His cough had been bad for weeks and was getting worse. His eyes were deep in their sockets, his ebony skin stretched much tighter across his cheekbones than it had been when the two men first met in Maputo, five months ago.

They had been late leaving Maputo, the Mozambican capital, the day before and Mike had grabbed their unopened mail on the way out of the office. He had stuffed the letters in his daypack and had only remembered them this morning. He was sure they both knew when he handed it to him over breakfast what was going to be in Isabella's letter to Carlos.

Mike reflected that it had been he who urged Carlos to see Isabella for a check-up and a blood test. Now that the news both men dreaded had finally been delivered, he couldn't help feeling somehow responsible.

'I have the virus, Michael.' The smoke from the burning letter had obscured his face for a second or two. It was a tough enough admission for any young African male to make.

Mike had seen the condom advertisements and the billboards pushing monogamy, but it was all too little, too late. Every day the newspapers carried another story about AIDS orphans, anti-retroviral drugs and statistics. The statistics and projections were mind-blowing, almost unreal. Carlos was real.

The birds were coming to life as the sun turned the butterfly-shaped mopani leaves on the dense thickets of trees around them from pink to ochre, to gold. Despite his friend's terrible news there was still promise in the new day for Mike.

He thought of his own letter from Isabella as he prodded the fire with a rusted tent peg and then topped up the two coffee mugs with hot water from the kettle. Mike's note was on the same cheap hospital stationery, but its message, unlike Carlos's, was a lifeline.

'What does your letter say?' Carlos asked.

'Not much,' Mike lied. 'She's going to be at Mapai in a day or so. I was hoping to meet her there, but now . . .'

'I am not going to die today or tomorrow. You do not have to stay with me every minute.' White teeth lit his broad black face as he forced a grin for his friend's sake. 'I will take you there when we have finished surveying the minefield and you can travel back with her if you like,' he said, waving his cigarette in a vaguely Latin gesture to indicate the matter was solved.

Mike was excited because of his news, and, as a

result, also felt guilty. 'We have to talk,' Isabella had written in her spidery, barely decipherable doctor's hand, adding the date and time she expected to arrive at the mission clinic in Mapai, where she did volunteer work once a month. Perhaps, he mused, it was the confirmation of Carlos's illness that spurred on his thoughts. Whatever the cause, he now knew what he had to do, what he had to say to Isabella. Carlos was a good ten years younger than he was. A strong, articulate, educated young African man in his prime, who spoke more languages than any army linguist Mike had ever met. He had been a university-educated teacher before he became a soldier. Currently, as a civilian employee of the United Nations, he oversaw people who dug in the dirt of Mozambique for landmines. Now he faced a death sentence. Life shouldn't be this fucking hard, Mike said to himself.

'The doctor, she is the one for you,' Carlos said. He smiled, but Mike could see sadness in his dark eyes. Carlos turned his glance to the dying fire and flicked his cigarette into the hot ash.

Mike stood, shrugged off the faded grey T-shirt he had slept in and fetched his mottled camouflage shirt from the front seat of the Nissan Patrol. He ran a hand through his close-cropped hair and then buttoned the uniform shirt as he walked, trying to ignore the smell of stale smoke and dried sweat. He brushed a smear of dust from the circular blue and white embroidered United Nations roundel stitched to the armband on his right sleeve. Below the UN badge was an Australian flag and his country's name, stitched in white cotton. He was, as he realised every day, a long way from home. He scratched the stubble on his chin and decided that as he was in the bush he could forgo a shave for one day. Mike walked around to Carlos's side of the fire and laid a hand on his shoulder.

'We'll see Isabella together. She'll tell us what you need and we'll get it. I'll see to it, mate.'

Carlos didn't look up, and Mike removed his hand. The remains of their half-eaten breakfast, tinned herrings in tomato sauce wrapped in *pao*, the locally baked bread, sat cold and unappetising on a plastic plate on the upturned Manica beer crate that served as their table. Mike grabbed the last of the *pao* and shovelled the oily mess into his mouth. 'Let's go,' he said between swallows.

'I do not want to endanger your life, Michael,' Carlos said as the Australian busied himself loading their meagre camping stores and bedrolls into the back of the Nissan.

'Pass me the gas bottle. You're not going to endanger my life unless we start kissing, mate,' Mike said, in a lame attempt at lightening the sombre mood.

'You know what I mean.'

He was hinting at what all of them feared, deep down inside. All of those involved in the dirty, backbreaking task of cleaning up the remains of other people's wars. If one of them stepped on a mine, the other would have to treat him. There would be blood and there would be saliva and vomit.

'No, Carlos, don't worry about it,' Mike said. 'We'll see it through.' Mike knew this was an easy statement for him to make, as he only had a month left to run in

Mozambique of his posting with the UN Accelerated De-mining Program. After that, he would be off home to Australia. Or maybe even to Portugal with Isabella, if things worked out.

'Right, let's get to work,' Mike said.

Carlos nodded and drained his cup. They loaded the jerry cans and climbed into the Nissan for the short, bumpy trip from their bush campsite along a track one of the UN teams had been clearing of antipersonnel mines. The team had been called away two days earlier to destroy some mortar bombs found in a small village north of Mapai. They should have been back by now, but it had turned out the bombs were just the first items in a big cache of ammo left over from the civil war days, and they had been delayed.

Carlos and Mike had been warned that a party of politicians and journalists were going to be visiting their AO – area of operations – in a week's time. They had been tasked by Jake, their supervisor, to find some accessible places where they could safely show the VIPs what the UN teams were doing.

'All this for a PR stunt, eh? What a joke,' Mike said as he drove. Carlos stayed silent. Despite his complaining, Mike knew that glad-handing politicians and babysitting journalists was an important, if sometimes painful, part of their job. The recent pace of international events had taken the world's attention away from UN backwaters like Mozambique and the de-miners knew they were fighting for every cent of funding from a shrinking budget. The more publicity they could generate about their work, the greater

10

chance they had of staying in business until the job of mine clearing was finished once and for all.

Carlos's silence unnerved Mike. Normally the African was chatty, and ordinarily Mike would have been grateful for the respite. He hated mornings. Today, though, he craved his friend's banal questions about life in Australia and the other countries he had visited, or his musings on the league table of African soccer teams, which interested the Australian about as much as the game itself. Mike busied himself by turning on the Global Positioning System receiver mounted on the dashboard and watching the clever little gadget acquire a signal from three orbiting American satellites somewhere in space.

It was seven o'clock when they arrived at the track junction, where the mine-clearing team had stopped work before being called away. Carlos and Mike had arrived in the area the previous evening, but it had been too dark to carry out their inspection. They had camped overnight in the bush nearby.

Mike stopped the truck and pulled out the large-scale map of Mozambique from between the driver's seat and the console, and then pushed the *mark* button on the GPS. This gave him a readout of their position on the earth's surface, in latitude and longitude. He wrote down the coordinates in his green hard-covered army-issue notebook.

'Twenty-three degrees, twenty-seven minutes south, and thirty-one degrees, fifty-five minutes east. We're slap-bang on the Tropic of Capricorn,' he said, pointing at the first row of numbers on the screen. Carlos smiled politely, but said nothing.

There were no recognisable features in the dense mopani forest, but somewhere a few kilometres to the west of them was the border with South Africa and, on the other side, the world-famous Kruger National Park. About a hundred kilometres to their north, and slightly west, the borders of South Africa, Zimbabwe and Mozambique all converged. On the South African side, opposite where they were plotting the minefield, was one of the highest densities of wildlife in the world, but in Mozambique, the bush was all but devoid of large mammals.

They stayed seated in the Nissan, the engine ticking over in order to keep the air-conditioner running.

'Bloody shame to think about all those rhinos and elephants and everything else that used to be here,' Mike said, as he surveyed the bush around them.

'People starved during the civil war – and after it. They had to eat,' Carlos replied, not meeting Mike's eyes as he spoke.

Mike knew that the local people had snared and shot game to feed themselves, but others had turned to the poaching of bigger game, such as rhino and elephant, out of greed. He said nothing, though.

The only sign of wildlife Mike had encountered in Mozambique, apart from snakes and baboons, was the eerie whoop of the hyena, which could occasionally be heard in the bush at night. Recently, however, he had read that the fence on the South African border had come down and there was now nothing stopping all manner of dangerous creatures from wandering into areas like the one they were visiting, where their teams had been clearing mines.

Mike checked the map again. The area where they were working, an old hunting concession named Coutada 16 by the Portuguese, was to become part of a peace park or, to use the technical name, a trans-frontier conservation area. The peace park concept, he thought, was a good one. It envisaged cross-border national parks where animals could migrate freely and safely across Africa's international borders, and well-heeled tourists could pour millions of dollars into bankrupt economies. One of the envisioned 'super parks' would unite the Kruger park with Coutada 16, along with Gonarezhou National Park in Zimbabwe to the north. A great idea, but there were many obstacles to overcome before it would ever become a reality. Like landmines, for instance.

'Someone's taking this peace park thing seriously, otherwise why would we be clearing bush in the middle of nowhere?' he asked rhetorically.

'At times I never thought I would live to see peace in my country,' Carlos said as he wound down the window and lit a cigarette. 'You think it is sad about the animals, and it is, but think how cruel man is to man as well. Look at the landmines and the bombs we uncover. From all over Africa, from all over the world. First the Rhodesians chasing the Zimbabwean nationalists around our country – mining, bombing, shelling. Then the South Africans and RENAMO fighting us in FRELIMO. Landmines and bombs from Russia, Germany, Czechoslovakia, England, Portugal, South Africa . . .'

Mike said nothing, just nodded. He sensed the sad realisation that was sweeping over his friend, the bitter irony that he had survived so many years of war only to be struck down by an avoidable disease. Though still poor, Mozambique's fortunes had grown year by year since the end of the civil war between *Resistencia Nacional Mocambicana*, the Mozambique National Resistance, or RENAMO, and the *Frente de Libertacao de Mocambique*, the Front for the Liberation of Mozambique, known as FRELIMO. Former fighters from both sides had been working together to rebuild the country since the first multi-party elections in 1994, and while Carlos had lived to see his country at peace, he would not see it prosper.

When Carlos had finished his cigarette, Mike said, 'Remember, we're just here for a recce, OK? I want to make sure it's going to be safe enough to bring the politicians and the media this far into the bush.'

'I think you are impatient for your doctor's appointment, yes?' Carlos said with a wink.

Mike was pleased to see Carlos's spirits lifting, even if his levity was laboured.

Their local guide, an elderly Mozambican called Fernando, came into view, walking around a bend in the track. The de-mining team working in the area had praised his knowledge, eyesight and good humour.

Carlos got out of the Nissan first and spoke to Fernando for a while in Portuguese, the common national language of their former colonial masters. He translated the gist of their conversation for Mike. 'He was a park ranger before the war, working for the Portuguese. Then he worked as a hunting guide in Coutada 16 and now we pay him.'

Mike guessed his age at somewhere between fifty and seventy. Fernando had a cap of tight frizzy grey curls atop a face as weathered and lined as elephant hide. He had two teeth left in his top row and none in his lower jaw that Mike could make out. He was dressed in the tattered remnants of his old khaki National Parks uniform. His shirt was patched in several places and his shorts were frayed and held up with a knotted length of twine, but creases showed where both had been neatly ironed.

Fernando straightened his wizened body and saluted Mike as he stepped down from the Nissan. Mike noticed that the AK-47 at his side was obviously cared for by him as lovingly as his tattered uniform was by his wife. The rifle was probably as old as his clothes, but, like them, still did the job.

'*Bom dia*, Major,' he said. Mike returned his salute and the greeting.

Carlos and Mike left the Nissan and followed Fernando along the course of white plastic tape the clearance team had strung out to trace the cleared section of the minefield. Mike recalled from the team's initial report that the mines they had so far found were antipersonnel, Russian-designed and made in Poland in the 1970s. Nasty little bastards designed to take off a foot or shatter a leg below the knee.

Mike looked up and down the track and stroked his jaw thoughtfully. He wondered if he could usher twenty or thirty civilians, including pushy photographers and television cameramen, along the narrow path without any of them stumbling over the white tape.

'Mike, over here,' Carlos said. He was down on one

15

knee, at the extreme end of the cleared path next to one of the metal stakes that supported the white tape marking the corridor. He had a twig in his hand and was gently scraping the dirt in front of him.

'What is it?' Mike asked.

'PMN 2.'

Carlos got down on both knees now, lowered his head and gently blew the dust away. The smooth round pressure plate of the antipersonnel mine was gradually revealed.

'Nasty,' Mike said. 'Whichever of our guys drove the last stake into the ground didn't know how lucky he was.' The rusted metal picket was only centimetres from the mine.

'I'm going to lift it,' Carlos said, looking into Mike's eyes.

'No. Mark it and let's move on.'

Carlos held Mike's stare and shook his head. 'We can't leave it here, Michael. You know that. It is a hazard to our men, let alone the dignitaries.'

'Carlos, we're desk jockeys, for Christ's sake.' Both Mike and Carlos were trained de-miners, but their task as senior members of the UN mission was the planning of operations, not digging in the dirt. Mike's unvoiced concern was Carlos's emotional state in the wake of the news he'd just received. On the other hand, he wanted to convince Carlos that he still had a future with the UN team, despite his illness.

'All right,' Mike said, 'but at least let me get your protective gear.'

*

16

Mike checked the heavy diver's watch on his wrist. It was already nine. 'How's it going?' he called across to Carlos. Again, he felt guilty that he'd been lost in thoughts of Isabella – her perfume, her dark eyes, her slender legs beneath a short denim skirt – as he sat on the fallen log, smoking, while Carlos worked.

Carlos had found a second mine near the first and insisted that he should disarm that one as well. It was still in the ground in front of him, but he had cleared the soil from the pressure plate.

'Almost finished, but I am getting too old for this business, I think.' Carlos straightened his back, rose up on his knees and undid the Velcro fastenings of his armoured vest to let the air through to his chest. He raised the clear protective visor of his blue helmet and wiped the sweat from his face.

As Mike started to rise he heard a soft *tap tap* behind him, and froze.

He looked back over his shoulder and saw that Fernando had stopped dead-still in the centre of the cleared track. He was tapping the tin magazine of his AK-47 with a finger to get their attention. The barrel of Fernando's rifle was now pointed towards the bush to Mike's left. The old man was sniffing the air, his broad nose wrinkling in distaste.

Carlos and Mike did the same. Mike smelled its pungent, musky, dirty-washing odour, then heard the telltale crack of splitting wood as it ripped a branch from a tree.

'*Elefante*,' Fernando whispered.

Fernando began to move forward, but Mike placed a firm hand on his iron-muscled calf as he drew alongside him. Mike pointed across to the ground in front of Carlos, indicating the mine the other man had just unearthed. Fernando nodded and stood his ground.

They could all hear the beast clearly now, snapping off branches from a tree somewhere in the bush, maybe forty or fifty metres away. Mike held his breath and craned his neck for a glimpse. It sounded to him like there was only one.

The local newspapers and television news had carried a story the week before about how the South African National Parks Board was relocating elephants across the border from Kruger, to build up the numbers of big game on the Mozambique side of the peace park. But the relocation, according to the media, was happening a fair way north of where the deminers were working.

Perhaps the one they could hear now had strayed across the border on his own, Mike mused, or maybe he was a local boy, a survivor of twenty years of poaching and war. If the latter were true, he would know man only as an enemy.

The stillness of the moment was shattered by the crack of a heavy-calibre rifle shot, followed immediately by a tormented trumpet blast of pain. All three men dropped instinctively to the dirt, but Fernando recovered first, his old instincts guiding his movements. He stood and strode three paces so he was in front of Mike, and brought his AK-47 up to his shoulder.

The big-bore rifle thundered again, close by, and Fernando was punched backwards over the top of Mike. Both men sprawled in the dust. Mike lifted the

Mozambican off his leg and stared into the horror that was Fernando's face. The bullet had entered his right eye and blown away the back of his skull. His mouth was wide open and his remaining eye stared fixedly, lifelessly at the sky.

'Carlos, the sat-phone!' Mike hissed urgently as he leaned across Fernando's body and grabbed the guide's fallen Kalashnikov from the dust.

Carlos nodded, understanding that Mike wanted him to get back to the Nissan, but then he hesitated. From in front of them came another pain-crazed trumpet blast from the wounded elephant. The earth pounded like a rolling quake beneath them and they heard branches breaking. The bull was coming their way.

Mike fumbled with the unfamiliar safety catch on the Russian assault rifle and, still crouched, fired a burst of three rounds on full automatic towards the direction the rifle shot had come from. He aimed low, guessing correctly that the automatic rifle would pull high as he fired the burst. The rifle butt thudded into his shoulder. The acrid smell of cordite burned his nostrils. His heart raced and he suddenly felt like throwing up.

'*Scheisse*,' Karl Hess whispered to himself.

The elephant was wounded, but not fatally; Hess's client, the bloody Russian, was cursing aloud, too loud, and now he had spotted a black ranger about seventy metres away. The ranger had been crouching but he started to stand. Hess didn't think the man had spotted him yet, or else he wouldn't have risked standing, but now the figure in his telescopic sight was raising an AK-47 to his shoulder. The blacks, goddamn them, had excellent eyesight, and Hess knew he would be spotted in a couple of seconds. The other two members of his party, his African servant Klaus and a local Mozambican tracker, crouched behind a tree, watching the hunter intently.

Hess breathed in, watching the crosshairs of the sight rise slightly above the man's wide ebony forehead, then let out half a breath. As the aiming point fell slowly back into place, down over the frizzy grey hair and into the centre of the ranger's forehead, Hess squeezed the trigger. The action was as natural to him as breathing. Hess registered no emotion as the rifle thudded into his shoulder. The black man's face disappeared in a spray of blood.

Killing was Karl Hess's profession and he was very good at it.

Some professional hunters he knew tried to romanticise their job. These men claimed they respected the animals they hunted and felt a kinship with them. They even tried to convince others that what they were doing was all part of the delicate balance of conservation. Rubbish, thought Hess. He had about as much respect for the elephant his client had almost killed as he did for the black man he had just wasted.

The client. *Scheisse*. In truth, he didn't mind the Russian and had even grown to like him a little in the past few days. He could feel some 'kinship' with the man, even although they had fought on opposing ideological sides in different battles of the Cold War. Respect him? No – he had yet to meet a client worthy of his respect, but he did quite like him. Now he just wanted the man to shut up. He raised a finger to his lips, although it was unnecessary now, as the Russian had stopped his whining when he heard the report of Hess's rifle.

'Get down,' Hess said.

The Russian obstinately remained standing, staring in the direction where Hess had just fired. Hess shook his head in frustration, but continued peering through the mopani trees. He couldn't understand what the man in the tatty ranger's uniform was doing there. Poaching, perhaps?

'The elephant?' the Russian whispered in English, the only language they had in common.

Hess shook his head again, raising a finger to his lips to motion the Russian to silence. The elephant was the least of their worries now. He would call the helicopter when he was ready and they would follow it from the air until it tired or died.

Both Hess and the Russian heard the metallic rasp of an AK-47 being cocked. They had been around that weapon for too many years to mistake it for anything else.

Pop-pop-pop. That was the thing Hess always found faintly amusing about the Kalashnikov: its rattling report, similar to a coffee percolator, belied its gruesome efficiency as a weapon. Leaves shredded around him and he felt a whoosh of displaced air past his legs. The shooter was firing blind, on full automatic, but he was firing low, which was dangerous.

Hess dived for the dusty earth and rolled towards the thickest tree he could see. The idea was to get out of sight of the enemy and, when you were ready to fire back at him, to do so from a place of cover, as far away as possible from where he had last seen you. Hess did not panic, for he never panicked in battle, but he did swear quietly again when he heard the Russian cry out in pain in his own language.

To his credit, the Russian did not scream or moan after that first yelp, and this, despite the man's stupidity at not seeking cover when Hess had originally instructed him to, helped stop the man's stocks from falling any lower. Hess leopard-crawled to the Russian, keeping his rifle out of the dust in the crooks of his outstretched arms.

Major Vassily Orlov was wounded, in the leg, and it hurt like the devil. Orlov was no longer a major in the *Spetsnaz*, the Russian Army's elite special forces, but he still liked people to address him by his former rank. It lent an air of legitimacy, he thought, to his business dealings, and reminded those who traded with him that he was not some Moscow street punk or a common pimp.

He was wounded, but he had no intention of dying in the wilds of Mozambique. Orlov had too much money to die like some ragged third-world rebel from a wound inflicted by a rifle manufactured in his own country. He had paid the Namibian, Hess, a small fortune to get him here, but, as Hess knew, he would forfeit the substantial amount still owing if he failed to get Orlov his trophy, or if the Russian died in the process. One thing Orlov had learned in his new career as a businessman was that one could always trust in the power of money. Ideologies, regimes, politicians all came and went, but no one turned his back on cash.

Orlov's new safari trousers were ruined. They were olive green, with detachable lower leg sections that zipped off to leave knee-length shorts. Above them he wore his old *Spetsnaz* camouflaged smock. He acknowledged Hess's concerns about being seen in military attire in the African bush, but countered them by stating the obvious – that there would be trouble if they were seen, whatever they were wearing. Like many old soldiers, Orlov was faintly superstitious and he had worn this same smock on every operation he had been involved in. He regarded it as his good luck talisman.

Judging by the wound, it was probably a ricochet that had hit him in the lower leg. The bullet had glanced off a rock, perhaps, and ploughed into his right calf. Orlov gingerly touched the skin around the entry wound, a neat round hole ringed with dark burnt flesh. He winced as he touched his shinbone. The bullet had hit the bone and, its force nearly spent, had tumbled to rest higher up the calf, near the knee. He knew he was in shock and that the pain would soon come in earnest.

He pressed down on the entry wound, using his palm to staunch the oozing blood. The wound was a bad one because the bullet was still inside him, but Orlov doubted it was life threatening.

He had been shot once before, in Afghanistan, by a sniper, but that was in the upper arm and the bullet had passed cleanly through. His men had caught the sniper later – he was little more than a boy, maybe fourteen or fifteen, with a wispy moustache and beginnings of a beard. Orlov's men had wounded him in a short firefight and managed to capture him – the Mujahideen would never surrender of their own accord. They dragged the wounded teenager into the village square by his long, filthy hair. Orlov shot him in the head in front of his wailing family and the rest of the village.

He sat with his back to a tree, legs spread wide and his rifle resting on his good leg. The gunfire had stopped now and he wondered about the elephant. The animal had been every bit as magnificent as Hess had described it. Orlov had hunted ever since he could remember. His father had taught him to follow tracks, both in snow and on bare ground. They had started with deer and, eventually, graduated to bear. Later in life Orlov had several opportunities to indulge in the ultimate hunt, man against man, in the service of his country.

In Afghanistan, in addition to his military duties, he had begun his business career, starting with hashish and graduating to heroin. He would never indulge in the drugs himself, although some of his men and even his fellow officers had. The vast profits to be made, and the growing lack of confidence he had in his country's rulers as a result of the war, had turned him from soldier to entrepreneur. Now his business interests reached far and wide, across Europe, Asia, the Americas and Africa. Orlov was an importer and exporter – drugs, cars, women, girls, boys, art, animals, weapons, diamonds were all commodities that had passed profitably through his hands. He wanted for nothing in terms of material goods and women, but what he missed was the thrill, the danger and the rewards of his days as a soldier.

An interest in diamonds had brought him to Africa and he had indulged his passion for hunting at the same time. He soon tired, however, of a succession of professional guides who treated him either as a dolt or a cash cow. He had been offered paltry trophies – drugged cats or ancient animals on their last legs. During a trip to Miami in Florida, however, a Cuban businessman, another former army officer and a fellow shooter now living as an exile in the United States, had recommended someone to him. A special hunter who knew what discerning clients wanted and how to circumvent certain regulations, if that was what was needed to satisfy his customers. Ironically, the Cuban believed he may have even fought against the man, who had served as an officer in the South African Defence Force, in Angola.

Orlov was redecorating his dacha in the countryside outside of St Petersburg and wanted an African big-game theme. He could have bought the trophies he had in mind, but he would never be satisfied with other men's prizes. He had arranged a meeting with Hess during his very next business trip to South Africa and, from the outset, had been impressed with the man. Orlov thought the hunter was a cold individual, who would stop at nothing to get what he wanted. Perfect.

Hess knelt before Orlov now, not the slightest

emotion clouding his face as he ran his fingers along the Russian's wounded leg. 'It has hit the bone – it may be fractured,' he said brusquely. 'Exit wound?'

'*Nyet*,' Orlov replied.

Hess drew a hunting knife from a pouch on his belt and quickly sliced open the bloodstained detachable lower half of the trouser leg. Next he took Orlov's rifle from his lap and ripped the combat field dressing from the wooden stock, where he had taped it prior to their setting off from his lodge across the border. Hess carried an identical dressing taped to his own rifle, but, as in combat, he used the casualty's dressing to treat him. He tore open the waterproof packet with his teeth, unfolded the big sterile pad, and pressed it over the wound. He wrapped the long bandage tapes from the dressing around Orlov's calf and tied it off.

From the bush where his shots had fallen, Mike Williams heard a man cry out in pain, but in a language he couldn't place. Not English, not Portuguese, not Afrikaans. It didn't matter.

The elephant burst from the bush onto the open track, not thirty metres from where Carlos and Mike crouched, near the fallen Fernando. It was definitely a bull – Mike could tell from the shape of its oversized, rounded, knobbly head. Females, he had learned, have angular, sharply defined foreheads. This one stood as tall as a house and as wide as a battle tank. His legs looked like the scarred grey trunks of the leadwood. The yellowed ivory tusks, each the length of a grown man, curved inwards until they almost met.

Enraged, rather than scared by the sound of the gunfire, the elephant turned and faced the diminutive figures. Mike had learned that normally when an elephant wants to scare an intruder away it flaps its ears out wide and raises its trunk in the air to make itself look as big and as scary as possible. When an elephant means business and is about to charge, it puts its ears back and tucks its trunk in down between its tusks. Which is what the old bull did now.

Mike swivelled and pointed the AK-47 at the elephant, which began its charge. Puffs of dust exploded from the track with each mighty footfall. Mike looked again at Carlos and saw he was still ahead of him, to the right, and out of his line of sight. He pulled the butt of the rifle hard into his shoulder, took a breath and sighted along the barrel, aiming at the massive skull. He doubted the head shots would kill the bull, but hoped they would slow the animal down before it reached Carlos.

He squeezed the trigger. There was one shot, which raised a tiny puff of grey dust on the mighty skull, then the firing pin clicked on an empty chamber.

'Fuck! Run, Carlos!'

Carlos looked at Mike and smiled. He was silhouetted black against the oncoming cloud of elephant dust as he turned to face the beast. Ahead of him, on the edge of the track, was the landmine he had uncovered but had not had time to disarm. His armoured vest lay in the dirt beside him, where he had placed it just moments before.

He pressed his arms against his sides, as if bracing himself, clenched both fists and fell forward, onto the mine, so that his stomach struck the pressure plate.

The explosion sent up a cloud of dust to more than match the elephant's wake and set Mike's ears ringing. Carlos was thrown back into the air, almost upright again, as though he had just belly-flopped onto a trampoline. He fell once more and landed on his side.

The elephant stopped dead – his charge had not yet gained enough momentum to carry him forward onto Carlos's writhing body. He shook his mighty head, flapped his big ears like ragged flags, and turned and fled into the bush. As he swung around, Mike saw the puckered red and white hole in his side. He assumed the wound had been made by the same weapon that killed Fernando. Fresh blood formed a black stripe down the animal's dusty grey flank.

Mike stood and ran back up the track to the Nissan, bending at the waist to make himself a smaller target, in case the marksman was still watching. There was nothing he could do for Carlos without a first aid kit. As he ran he snapped the magazine from the AK-47 and confirmed that he was indeed out of ammunition.

At last he made it to the Nissan and fired up the engine. The 4WD bounced and juddered along the narrow track, as he floored the accelerator. The sides of the vehicle brushed against the white tape marking the cleared corridor and eventually a strand caught on the front bumper. The tape snapped as a stake was pulled out of the ground and Mike prayed the wheels wouldn't set off another mine. He stopped the truck as close as he dared to Carlos.

The mine had been designed to blow off a foot or a hand, not to kill. When a man falls on his belly on a landmine and it tears him open and shreds his vital organs, however, that man is going to die.

But the mine hadn't killed Carlos outright. He bit into his lower lip to keep himself steady and die like a man. When he opened his mouth to speak, Mike saw the bright blood well from the teeth marks in his lip.

'Don't touch me, Michael,' he warned between ragged breaths.

Mike could smell the blood and the stench from Carlos's perforated bowel and he knew the man was right about the danger, but still he tore frantically at the field dressing. He opened the big white pad and placed it on Carlos's abdomen. The dressing barely covered the ragged hole. The pumping blood soaked Mike's arms to his elbows. The dying man's intestines were visible and Mike had to swallow hard to keep from vomiting.

'Shut up, Carlos, you'll be OK. We'll get you to Isabella.' Mike remembered being taught to reassure the patient during his army first aid training. He thought it sounded as ridiculous in real life as it had in the classroom. 'Carlos, for God's sake, hang on, mate,' he cried.

He cradled the African's head in his lap and grasped his right hand, holding tight. Carlos's whole body shuddered and Mike looked skywards. He leaned back, slumped against the front wheel of the

29

four-wheel drive, utterly exhausted and soaked with the blood of his dead friend.

Mike sat there for what seemed like a long time, but it was really only a couple of minutes, maybe less. He was stirred from his stupor by the sound of the heavy rifle booming again somewhere in the distance. The noise was farther away than before. It was followed a few seconds later by the *pop-pop-pop* of a burst of fire from another AK-47. He realised there were now two weapons in the area, and men who were not afraid to kill.

The adrenaline that had coursed through him just a few moments before was now seeping away, leaving his limbs heavy and tired. Mike folded the rear seat of the Nissan forward, dragged Carlos and Fernando into the vehicle as quickly as he could, then hauled himself behind the steering wheel. His hands were covered in blood and when he wiped the sweat from his forehead it left a sticky smear. He started the Nissan and reversed up the track, trying not to look at the dead men as he navigated his way back to the main road. Once there he turned right, following the railway line south towards Maputo, nearly five hundred kilometres away.

Some of the flies that had already started to settle on the bodies now hovered around him. Mike felt a clutch of them sucking the blood and sweat from his forehead and pointlessly slapped at them as he drove. After a few kilometres he pulled over, wiped his face clean as best as he could, and fumbled for the cigarettes in the top pocket of his bloodstained camouflage shirt. He lit one with shaking hands.

The flies could still smell death on him. So could he, as he drove on into the blinding heat of the day.

Orlov opened his mouth to speak, but he was stopped short by another gunshot, quickly followed by a muffled explosion from the same direction as the earlier shots from the AK-47.

'The elephant,' Hess said. 'Must have hit a landmine. The tracks in this part of the country are littered with them.'

'Go and get it for me. Finish it off,' Orlov said. Despite his pain, the Russian forced a thin smile under his grey-flecked bushy black moustache. 'Or you can kiss the rest of your damned money goodbye.'

Hess nodded. If the Russian died and he couldn't get the rest of his money, at least he would have the ivory. The cost of the helicopter had already been covered by the advance payment, so he would not be out of pocket. He stood and motioned to his servant, a tall African man in smart olive drab fatigues who hovered nearby. 'Klaus, tell that little Mozambican monkey to start earning his money as a tracker and find the elephant for us. He can walk in front of us in case there are any more mines, but don't tell him that.' Klaus, whose smooth, broad ebony face marked him as a member of Namibia's Ovambo tribe, had been Hess's tracker and gun bearer for many years.

Klaus's allegiance to Hess dated back to his role as a trusted subordinate during the war of liberation in South West Africa. His unflinching loyalty to the white man had paid off over the years, but while he

31

was wealthy by black African standards, he could never show his face among his own tribe again if he wanted to live to enjoy his wealth. Klaus passed on the orders to the wiry Mozambican tracker. Next, he laid down his AK-47, unstrapped two short axes from side loops on the rucksack he wore and gave one to the tracker. The bright, razor-sharp edge of the axe glittered in the sunlight as the tracker held it close to his eye for a momentary inspection.

While Klaus shrugged back into his rucksack, Hess undid the Velcro fastening of a black pouch on his belt and extracted a compact black GPS unit which fitted neatly in the palm of his hand. He pointed the device towards the sky, switched it on and waited for the receiver to pinpoint their position. When the latitude and longitude flashed up a couple of minutes later, Hess pushed the button labelled 'mark' and scrolled through the alpha-numeric display until the letter O for 'Orlov' appeared, naming the spot after his wounded client, and entering it in the GPS unit's memory.

'Don't go anywhere,' Hess said humourlessly. 'I'll call in the helicopter once we've finished off the elephant. If we can't find it, we'll get it from the air.'

Orlov nodded and tightened his grip on his rifle.

Hess and Klaus set off, with the middle-aged Mozambican tracker, dressed in tattered cut-off denim jeans and a torn brown T-shirt, leading the way. The tracker paused every dozen or so steps to sniff the air, listen, and check the earth and trees around them for fresh signs of the elephant.

The tracker was leading them away from the

direction in which they had heard the explosion and the last of the firing. Hess was aware of not having addressed the problem of potential witnesses, but the elephant had to be his first priority. The tracker held up a hand and all three of them dropped to a crouch. The Mozambican had kept them downwind, and the elephant, now thoroughly disoriented, had wandered into a natural clearing. Perfect, thought Hess, and raised his rifle.

It had been many years since old Skukuza had heard the terrible sound of thunder this close, but he recognised it as the sound of death. The louder noise, the explosion, had thoroughly confused him, though, and he blinked and rubbed his eyes with the tip of his trunk to clear the dirt that had been thrown up by the blast. He shook his big, knobbly head to try to free himself of the pain and looked for another target to vent his rage on. But there was nothing around him and his world was slowly turning a foggy grey.

Hess was behind and to the left of the huge beast. He instinctively aimed for a spot level with the elephant's left eye, behind the ear, just forward of the vertical line where its front left leg joined the fat grey body. The hunter smiled as he pulled the trigger, knowing the heavy lead bullet would find the elephant's brain. The rifle boomed and the elephant turned towards them and took a few last valiant steps. Hess stood his ground. The beast sagged forward, onto his front knees, and then toppled sideways, raising an immense cloud of dust, as his back legs gave way. Hess motioned the two Africans forward. There was no way he was going to leave his footprints close to the carcass.

Klaus stepped into the clearing and fired a four-round burst from his AK-47 into the animal's belly to make sure it was dead. Then he knelt and picked up the spent bullet casings from the dust. He waved for the tracker to join him. Hess left them to the work of removing the tusks, confident that Klaus would ensure the long, curved ivory was not damaged.

Hess strode back through the bush, quickly but carefully retracing his steps to avoid any stray mines in the area. As he walked he lifted the walkie-talkie that hung from a strap at his side and spoke into the mouthpiece.

'Eagle, this is Leopard,' he repeated twice into the radio. Their call signs, Eagle for the helicopter and Leopard for the ground party, had been Orlov's idea. Since the Russian was paying the bills, Hess indulged his unnecessary romanticism.

The pilot, Jan Viljoen, a former South African Air Force lieutenant, finally acknowledged the call. Hess took out his GPS and read off the coordinates for the pick-up spot, where Orlov lay wounded.

'You'll need to lower the winch when you get there, I have one man down and the bush is too thick for you to land, over,' Hess said. Off to his left, some distance away, he heard the sound of a vehicle engine starting. His unseen adversary was getting away, but Hess was relaxed. I didn't see his face, so I know he didn't see mine, he told himself confidently.

'*Ja*, got it,' Viljoen replied. He had been circling twenty kilometres away out of sight and earshot of the hunt after dropping Hess and the Russian off in the bush. He was near the border of the Kruger park, staying low and following a herd of buffalo that had strayed across the newly unfenced border into Mozambique. Now, thanks to him, the buffalo were stampeding back to the comparative safety of the South African national park. 'Watch out for the lions, now, boys,' he said aloud to himself.

Viljoen felt a pang of regret for the elephant. He had enough love for the bush to know that what they had done was very wrong. However, he, like his former brother-in-arms Karl Hess, was now a soldier of fortune, a mercenary, and money always claimed his first allegiance. His second love was flying, and the Bell 412EP they were letting him play with was a delight.

He dipped the nose and watched the airspeed needle climb as the russet-brown bush whizzed past a scant sixty feet beneath him. He had removed the two front doors from their hinges before take-off to give him better visibility for the close-in work of infiltrating and extracting the team, and the modification also made for a cooler, more exhilarating flight. Viljoen, alone in the machine now, glanced across his shoulder and confirmed that the first aid kit was clipped to the bulkhead where it should be. Hess had a man down, although he didn't say who, and the old bastard had sounded as calm as you please, as though he was asking Viljoen to pick up some more beer on his way. He wondered who was injured as he punched the coordinates for the pick-up point into his own GPS and set a course for the rendezvous point.

He tested the winch by flicking the appropriate switch and watching the yellow jungle penetrator drop a foot or so on its cable. The device, developed by the Americans in Vietnam, was about the size and shape of a small bomb, suspended by its blunt end from a winch cable. Its pointed nose and weight allowed it to fall easily through branches and leaves, avoiding entanglement. Once on the ground, the men who needed to be picked up unfolded the long sides of the 'bomb', which then became seats that two men at a time could straddle.

Orlov's skin was paler than when Hess had left him, but the Russian was still conscious. Hess checked his client's pulse. It was strong, which was good, but he seemed to be in a lot more pain. Hess began to lift the blood-soaked pad of the field dressing and Orlov screamed.

Hess was worried. Orlov was ex–special forces and had hardly made a noise when he was shot. Why was he in such pain now? The Russian was biting down on his lower lip and forcing himself to regain his composure. Hess reached out again and lifted the pad. Orlov shuddered and Hess noticed a thin tear escape from the hardened soldier's tight-shut eyes.

'It is bad, the pain?' Hess asked.

Orlov took a deep breath before answering. 'Worse than it should be.'

Again, Hess lifted the dressing. He shut his ears to the Russian's yelp and shook his head as he inspected the lower leg. It was swollen to nearly twice its normal diameter, the skin stretched taut as a drum. Hess assumed the wound was bleeding internally.

'You will be lucky to keep this leg,' he said matter-of-factly.

Above him he heard the low thump of the helicopter's four blades. Hess shrugged off his rucksack and rummaged inside it. He stood, holding a Day-Glo orange marker panel about three feet long by one foot wide. He held the vinyl panel above his head with two hands, his arms outstretched, and made a high clapping motion.

Hovering above the point fixed in his GPS, Jan Viljoen noticed the flicker of orange below him and slewed the big helicopter to his right for a better view. Below him, he saw Hess. He stabbed the winch switch and the jungle penetrator sailed downwards, whining as the cable unwound freely.

Hess stepped back and waited until the blunt yellow cone of the penetrator thudded into the dust and leaves at his feet. He stuffed the marker panel into the half-open front of his bush shirt and shrugged on his rucksack. Before he tended to Orlov he walked a few paces to the point where he had fired at the ranger and, after a few seconds of looking, found the spent brass cartridge case from the bullet. He slipped it into his top pocket.

'Come on, come on, you bastard,' Viljoen muttered as he fought to keep the helicopter hovering in one place. A stiff breeze had picked up and it was rocking in the thermal up-drafts of hot air rising from the heated earth.

Hess grabbed Orlov under the armpits without ceremony or care for his wound and hoisted him onto one of the splayed legs of the jungle penetrator. He unfolded the opposite side and took his own seat, facing the Russian. He gave Viljoen an unsmiling thumbs-up, and wrapped his long, muscular arms around Orlov's neck. With the casualty now obviously secure, Viljoen flicked the winch switch and the pair rose slowly through the mopani leaves, locked in their lovers' embrace.

Ideally, there would have been a crewman on board to operate the winch from a second set of controls in the cargo compartment of the chopper, and to pull in anyone who needed to be winched aboard once they were level with the cargo doors. The doors weren't a problem, as Viljoen had removed these as well as the crew doors, but Hess had to start a pendulum motion in order to get a leg onto the left skid so that he could then pull the injured Orlov inside. Hess made the tricky manoeuvre look easy, despite Orlov's reluctance to ease his grip on the hunter to allow him to do his work. Eventually, Hess had Orlov seated on a canvas webbing troop seat. He fastened a seatbelt around the Russian's waist, in case he passed out and slumped to the floor or, worse, out the door.

Hess grabbed the back of the co-pilot's seat and peered out the plexiglass windows of the front cockpit. He pointed Viljoen in the direction of the elephant and noted that the pilot had been sweating, presumably with the effort of keeping the machine in one spot for so long. Hess had an infantryman's resentment of aviators and their world of comparative luxury, but now, as on several occasions in his life, he thanked the good Lord for flying machines.

Viljoen was about to earn his pay all over again.

'You are not to touch down, understood?' Hess barked in the pilot's ear as he brought the 412EP down towards the elephant carcass. Viljoen acknowledged the order with a curt nod – there wasn't enough room in the tiny natural clearing to touch down even if he had wanted to.

The two men, Klaus and the tracker, stood on top of the carcass, their faces streaked a dirty grey where the dust being kicked up by the rotors was sticking to rivulets of sweat. Viljoen eased the big machine down through the buffeting turbulence until the front tip of his left skid was nearly touching the top of the elephant's protruding backbone, at the point where it met the skull. The two men on the beast's back crouched and stepped back, holding their hands to their eyes in a vain attempt to keep the stinging dust at bay.

Hess put a foot on the skid then nimbly stepped onto the huge, grey, wrinkled back. He reached down and grabbed the Mozambican tracker by the neck of his tattered T-shirt. Unable to speak the man's language, he simply pointed at the two great shafts of ivory and then to the inside of the helicopter. Klaus had seen and felt his master's wrath before and was already hefting an end of one of the tusks.

Viljoen sweated some more as he waged a continuous battle to keep the aircraft trimmed level as weight was alternately placed on and off the helicopter. Hess climbed back aboard the hovering helicopter to drag on one end of the first tusk, then pounced off again, like a leopard leaving a branch, to chivvy the two other men from the back of the elephant. It needed all three of them to lift each huge curved tusk and to wriggle them, centimetre by difficult centimetre, in through the open sides of the helicopter and along the non-slip floor of the cargo compartment. Hess guessed the tusks weighed between sixty-five and seventy kilograms each, worth every American dollar of the fortune he would exact from the Russian.

Hess pushed on the bloodied end of the second tusk, marvelling at its huge diameter – probably more than fifty centimetres. It was the biggest elephant he had ever shot and no doubt one of the biggest left in southern Africa, if not the whole continent. He climbed aboard again and shifted the huge shaft of ivory next to its mate. In doing so he bumped against Orlov's injured leg. The Russian's scream of pain was lost in the roar of the turbine engines overhead. Klaus followed Hess into the chopper and held out a hand for the tracker, who very nearly slipped from the skid as the helicopter, now heavily laden with its full cargo of men and ivory, climbed away from the desecrated body below.

Hess turned to the Russian and saw that his head was now slumped on his chest. He checked his pulse. The man was still alive, but had passed out with the pain of his wound. Hess spat out of the open door, into the slipstream, then squeezed his way into the co-pilot's seat.

'Give me your map!' he yelled into Viljoen's ear.

2

'Fuck,' Mike said aloud as he rounded a bend and saw the red warning triangles on the road ahead. In the distance he could make out two men in grey shirts. He recognised the uniform – PRMs, Republic of Mozambique Police. One of them was armed with the ubiquitous AK-47, the other had a holstered pistol, probably a Russian Makarov, he thought.

He'd come to accept roadblocks as a fact of life in Africa – police, customs, quarantine, tsetse-fly control points – anything the officials could think of to slow traffic and raise revenue. Mostly he got through with a smile and the flash of his driver's licence or vehicle insurance certificate. Occasionally, he'd needed to smooth his way through with a packet of cigarettes, a few crumpled notes or a ballpoint pen or other trinket. He had no tarpaulin or sheet to cover the bodies and they were plain to see, along with the settling cloud of flies, as soon as he pulled up near the policemen.

Mike had called his headquarters in Maputo on the sat-phone as soon as he thought he was far enough from whoever had shot Fernando and caused Carlos's death. He'd waited on hold for a frustrating few minutes and was eventually put through to Jake, his American boss.

'Carlos is dead, Jake, and so is Fernando,' Mike said, pausing to drag on a cigarette to steady his nerves.

'Carlos? Dead? Who's Fernando?'

'Never mind, just get me some backup, Jake, and call the cops.' Mike ran through what had happened and it sounded incredible even to him in the telling, though he had just lived through it.

'Wait there,' Jake said.

'For Christ's sake, Jake, there are men with guns here and I've got two dead men in my vehicle. Get someone out and I'll meet you on the road.'

Carlos had once asked Mike what exactly it was he didn't like about the retired US Marine Corps lieutenant colonel who was their supervisor.

'It's hard to put a finger on it,' Mike had replied. 'Jake doesn't drink alcohol. Call me a politically incorrect old dinosaur, but I don't trust military people who don't drink, unless they're reformed alcoholics. He doesn't mix. He thinks the job's more important than people.' However, right then Mike had never wanted to see anybody so badly in his life – except maybe Isabella. But the police met him first.

Mike was tired and angry, and needed alcohol and sleep. He decided he was happy to wait in police custody for the two hours it would probably take for the other vehicle from headquarters to reach the road-block. As he pulled up at the roadblock, the policeman with the pistol spoke rapidly in Portuguese.

'*Fala ingles?*' Mike asked, and pointed to the blue and white UN roundel on his uniform sleeve.

The PRM shrugged and motioned to his colleague, who ambled slowly over, making a show of checking the Nissan's headlights and tyres on the way. When he was alongside the driver's window Mike asked him the same question, if he spoke English.

'A little. What you carry in back?' he asked.

'Two dead bodies,' Mike said.

The policeman's eyes widened in shock as he glanced in the back.

The first PRM unholstered his pistol and pointed it at Mike's head as he dragged him from the four-wheel drive. While the man with the rifle covered their prisoner, the other searched and then hand-cuffed him. Despite Mike's protests, the policeman confiscated his satellite phone.

Mike considered demanding that they call the Australian consul general in Maputo if the treatment got any rougher. He was an army officer serving the country under the auspices of the UN. However, he stayed as calm as he could. Better to wait a while for Jake and do the explaining then, rather than risk a fight with the cops.

The policemen bundled him into a stifling-hot tin shed by the side of the road. The ground was stained with bird droppings from roosting doves and the place smelled of urine. The English-speaking PRM, the one with the rifle, stood guard outside and checked on his prisoner every quarter of an hour. On one inspection he held a scratched plastic litre-bottle of warm water to Mike's lips and, on the next, lit a cigarette for him and placed it between his lips. Mike had half expected a beating, so the water and smoke were a pleasant surprise.

Sitting there waiting for Jake gave him time to think. He thought about Carlos, about Isabella and about himself. Carlos had saved his life. Again and again Mike saw him fall slowly to his death. He screwed his eyes tightly shut to rid himself of the image and tried to focus on Isabella. He had to get word to her back at Mapai somehow. He dreaded the coming days of inevitable debriefings, investigations and interviews, and wondered when and how he would contact her.

He had decided, that morning over breakfast, to leave the army when his tour in Mozambique finished in a few weeks. Nothing that happened after breakfast had changed his mind. Mike had been to several former war zones in nearly twenty years' service with the Australian Army, but he had never, until today, fired a weapon in anger. He had seen dead bodies before, but never had someone die in front of him or in his arms. His enemy or enemies had not shown themselves, which left him with a feeling of impotent rage after the firefight. He had held them off, though, and now he was starting to feel the guilt of the survivor who has seen his friends die at the hands of others.

What he wanted most of all now as he squatted in the rank-smelling, stifling makeshift cell was to see his woman. He wanted to tell her he loved her and that he had decided to give up his job to be with her. He couldn't extend his tour in Africa once his time was up and he doubted Isabella would give up her work at the hospital to come to Australia as an army wife. In truth, despite the death and suffering he had seen in Africa, he didn't want to leave either.

'Jesus H. Christ, Williams, you're a mess,' Jake said, when he arrived at the roadblock a couple of hours later and pushed his way into the shed.

Mike squinted as he was led out into the bright sunshine and bundled into the blissful cool of Jake's air-conditioned Patrol. A senior PRM in a starched grey shirt was on hand to placate the local cop, who at first seemed reluctant to hand over his white desperado. Jake gestured to a cold box in the luggage area of the four-wheel drive and Mike opened the lid. Inside were half a dozen Manica beers, covered in ice, along with a bottle of Perrier, which Mike took to be Jake's.

'I could kiss you.'

'Go easy, Williams, you've got a lot of explaining to do,' Jake said in his Southern drawl.

Mike explained. Over and over again, all the rest of that day and all day Saturday and Sunday. He told his story to Jake, the Mozambican police, the Mozambican army, the Australian consul general in Maputo, the head of Army Engineers at Victoria Barracks in Sydney via telephone, and in person to the Australian military attaché from South Africa.

The military attaché was a lieutenant colonel who

had flown in from Pretoria on the Sunday, and Mike sensed the man was pissed off that he had to give up his golf or tennis or bridge, or whatever it was military attachés did on their weekends.

'When's your tour here up?' the grey-haired colonel asked him. He was an infantryman, five or six years older than Mike. Too young for Vietnam, too old for the conflicts the engineer officer had been to. He stared hard at Mike, his cold blue eyes focused on a point in the middle of Mike's forehead.

They were in Mike's office, on the upper level of a two-storey converted warehouse on the Avenida da Angola, in a light industrial area in downtown Maputo. It was Sunday, so the street outside was free of the usual honking traffic.

'One month of work, plus I've got about a month's leave owing,' Mike said.

The lieutenant colonel said nothing, just kept staring at Mike's forehead.

'Sir,' Mike added.

The office building was a rabbit warren of glass-partitioned offices, each with its own air-conditioner. Mike's air-conditioner was broken, again, and the office was like a sauna beneath the iron-clad roof. He glanced over at Carlos's desk. It was clear and neat, in contrast to the stacks of paper that littered his. The glass wall behind where Carlos had once sat was covered with the UN mine-awareness posters he had diligently pinned up. Mike remembered Carlos posing for a photo with a group of laughing children in a village school, holding up one of those posters; the picture was on the cork noticeboard. Mike stared at Carlos's beaming face.

46

'You're a problem, Williams,' the lieutenant colonel said, with a finality that suggested Mike should not challenge his omnipotence. He flicked open the buff-coloured personnel folder in front of him, and took a pair of reading glasses from his pocket. Mike shifted his gaze again, and looked past the other man, out the window over the roof of the neighbouring building.

'Namibia, Rwanda, now Mozambique.' He shook his head slowly as he read. 'You love this shithole of a continent, don't you?'

Mike could tell the other man didn't share his feelings, so he said nothing.

'Well, it's caught up with you now, hasn't it? Take the rest of your time here as leave and go back to Australia as soon as the investigations are complete. I'll fix it up with your superiors here and at LHQ. That's my advice and I suggest you take it.'

'I quit,' Mike said.

The lieutenant colonel looked up, startled. 'I beg your pardon, Major?'

'I quit, sir.'

'Don't play smart with me, Williams. What do you mean, you quit?'

'My twenty's up and I'm not signing on for the last five,' he explained. He knew what the lieutenant colonel was thinking. Most people who stay for the long haul in the army put in twenty-five years because the pension benefits are markedly better than for twenty, but Mike had better things in mind for the coming five years.

'Look, I know you've had a rough time, but think it over,' he said.

The man's mood was conciliatory now; probably, Mike guessed, because he could see more paperwork looming on his desk if Mike wanted to resign his commission immediately.

'Don't worry, sir. I'll take the leave offer and sort things out once I'm back in Australia,' Mike explained.

'What'll you do then, after the army?' he asked. The question that every soldier asks himself. 'Security guard?' His tone was mocking.

'I'm coming back here, to Africa.' He was coming back to Isabella and where they went from there didn't matter, as long as they were together.

'You're fucking crazy,' the lieutenant colonel said, shaking his head and closing Mike's folder.

'Yes, sir.'

Crazy? Maybe I am crazy, Mike thought to himself.

Crazy in love with Isabella? For sure. He realised after his conversation with the military attaché just how much he was in love with her, although he had yet to tell Isabella outright that he would leave his job for her. As he packed the last of the uniforms into his green canvas kitbag in the bedroom of the flat in Maputo, he gazed at a framed picture of the two of them on the beach at Inhambane. She wore a white one-piece swimsuit that accentuated her breasts and was pouting theatrically at the warrant officer behind the camera, looking as sexy as hell, as always.

Was he crazy for being in love with Africa? Definitely. That's what the lieutenant colonel had guessed, and he was dead right. Crazy for joining the army in the first place? Maybe, maybe not. He had seen a sizeable chunk of the world outside Australia and, until a couple of days before, had never been shot at or had to shoot at anybody. Who knows, he told himself, maybe he had even done some good and saved a few lives and limbs by clearing up some of the nasty buried legacies of other people's wars.

Mike had joined the army when he was nineteen. In his own words, he had been an unemployed, long-haired layabout. He grew up with no father, just a mother and a sister, in an outer western suburb of Sydney. There were a couple of run-ins with the cops – under-age drinking for him, and shoplifting for his sister – but nothing too serious. Her convic-tion was never recorded and she was a lawyer now. They still laughed about that one when they got together every couple of years.

The only male influence of any note in his early life was an uncle who had served as a conscript infantry soldier in Vietnam. Stan was a motor mechanic and he would let young Michael hang around his workshop during school holidays.

'You're a fool,' was all Stan said when Mike showed him his enlistment papers. Mike thought that was a bit unfair, since he was largely to blame.

But the army and recruit Michael Williams hit it off immediately. Now it was nearly all over he thought back to the exciting, raucous days of his youth. He was surrounded by a bunch of other nine-teen and twenty year olds whose prime enthusiasms were cars, drinking and girls. And you could even smoke indoors in those days. These had always seemed to Mike to have been the best days of his life, but for the first time in a long while he had a reason to look forward instead of back.

After recruit training, Mike was posted – a funny but appropriate military term for bundling people off like packages and sending them to their next address – to the Royal Australian Engineers. An army careers adviser summed up his future employment prospects succinctly and accurately: 'You'll be building things and blowing things up. You'll love it.'

By the time he was twenty-five he had, despite a couple of brushes with authority, reached the rank of corporal and was posted as an instructor at the School of Military Engineering at Holsworthy, in south-western Sydney. At the time, Holsworthy was a booming barracks town with all of the problems that inevitably entails. Too many young men, too few pubs and too many lonely, neglected wives – like his.

Thinking about what he planned to say to Isabella forced Mike to remember his first marriage. He had just returned from three weeks of jungle training at Canungra, in Queensland, and had a pocketful of cash and way too much testosterone. He met Janice at a Friday night disco at a club in Liverpool, the closest major town to the barracks. They dated a few times, and before he knew it, a girl he hardly knew was pregnant with his child.

They were married in a registry office, a week after she broke the news. Janice was attractive, a local girl who worked as a hairdresser, but he realised now they were never, in any way, soul mates. He'd proposed because he believed it was the right thing to do, and because he didn't want their child to grow up in the same sort of household that he had. Also, Janice would not hear of an abortion and the idea had left Mike cold as well. He had assumed they would grow to love each other in time. He was wrong.

In truth, he thought as he stuffed his army boots into the kitbag, he had loved the army more then than he could ever have loved Janice. Despite barely scraping through school, in the military environment he'd discovered that he had the capacity to learn and, what's more, that he loved learning. He had spent long nights studying for his Higher School Certificate, the senior qualification he had missed by leaving school too early, and weeks away from the dilapidated fibre-cement 'married quarter', as their house was termed in military parlance, on various army courses.

Janice miscarried while he was on the Mine Warfare Instructors' Course. Mike went out and got drunk. He was sad for her and himself and for the little baby. He knew that he had been using his work to stay away from home, but as each day passed he had found himself growing more and more attached to the idea of fatherhood. If I had worked harder on getting to know my wife, he told himself now, things might have turned out differently and maybe we would have tried for another child.

But, as often happens in the closed community of an army base there was another man, a former friend of his, Bill Rogerson, who liked Janice more than he ever would. His love for her was not unrequited. Mike had come home early from the end of his drivers' course and found Janice and Bill on the corduroy-covered army-issue sofa. They hadn't made it to the bedroom.

'Christ!' Bill had yelped.

'Not quite, but I'm a fucking angel compared to you two,' Mike replied. He'd strode across the living room, one fist raised. Bill had rolled to the floor, stumbling as he tried to pull up his trousers and evade the blow he'd expected from Mike. Looking back on it now, Mike could even smile. He hadn't laughed at the time, though. He had started to say something to Janice, but the words wouldn't come.

'What? What is it, Mike? What do you want me to say, what do you want to tell me?' She had been calm. Neither ashamed nor accusatory, she smoothed down her skirt and buttoned her blouse.

Mike hadn't known what he wanted to say back then, and couldn't have put his feelings into words now. That was the problem with his first marriage. Not enough words and, even at the end, not enough passion to sustain the righteous indignation he had felt on first seeing Janice and Bill making love.

'Don't hate me, Mike,' Janice had said as Bill, crimson-faced, had shuffled around Mike and out the front door.

'I don't hate you, Janice,' he had said, standing still in the middle of the room, unsure of where he should be.

'You don't love me, either, do you?'

Mike was hungover and crashing on the living room carpet at a friend's place when the Military

Police found him the following afternoon. Word had already spread of his cuckolding, in the way it always does in the army, and it certainly wasn't the first time this sort of thing had happened.

His commanding officer, a major, was not unsympathetic. He was on his second marriage and Mike imagined the man's first had ended in similar circumstances to his own.

'Look, you're doing a good job as an instructor here,' he said.

Mike had sensed there was a 'but' about to come.

'But you've fucked up. Absent without leave won't look good on your record,' the major said sternly.

'I'm going to get a divorce, sir,' Mike had said, hoping that would be the end of his troubles.

'I think it might be best if you took further action. I'm going to suggest that you apply for a transfer.'

Mike had almost started to protest. He felt like he was being punished for Bill and Janice's deceit; he had known he deserved a kick in the backside, but not a transfer. He held his tongue and heard the major out.

'Word's just come down from Land Headquarters that we're sending an engineer squadron oversees, to Namibia, as part of a United Nations peacekeeping force,' he said, looking up from his desk while Mike stood, at ease, in front of him.

'Where's Namibia, sir?' Mike asked.

'Africa. Used to sort of belong to South Africa. They had a war there – the black people won. You may have seen something about it in the newspapers,' he said with a smile.

'Yes, sir,' Mike lied.

'There'll be a scramble for places. First unit deployment overseas since Vietnam. We're sending 17th Construction Squadron – 'the Bears' – and they're looking to fill some gaps. I can get you transferred next week if you want it.'

Mike hadn't needed to think about it. Africa sounded OK. If he'd stayed he would have had to move back into barracks and continue working with a man who was fucking his soon-to-be ex-wife. Hard choice.

'Count me in, boss. There's nothing left for me here.'

In Namibia, during the short periods of leave they received, he explored as much of the country as he could: unearthly red sand dunes in the Namib Desert that looked like the surface of another planet; the barren desert shores and icy waters of the Skeleton Coast; the wildlife paradise of Etosha National Park.

Namibia, he knew, was where his addiction started.

He'd been mesmerised by the sight of herds of zebra and gemsbok grazing on golden dry grass on the edge of the huge Etosha saltpan. Small families of giraffe, their heads breathing the sweet air above the talcum-powder dust of the saltpan, swayed regally into the blazing red sunset. The white dust coated everything, even the elephant, which looked like lumbering ghosts. The lions he remembered from Namibia were huge, muscled beasts, capable of bringing down a young elephant.

The Royal Australian Engineers had worked hard in the dry heat, building roads and clinics, clearing landmines and the other debris of war, and generally trying to help the country get back on its feet. At night they drank cold German-style beer, a legacy of the country's brief period of European colonial rule, under a desert sky ablaze with stars.

Many of the white South Africans they met during the country's transition to independence resented the presence of foreign soldiers in their former colony. Some hated the United Nations for interfering in what they saw as their sovereign affairs. Many in their army who Mike met were conscripts, doing mandatory national service after leaving school. One young man assigned temporarily to the Australian unit as a guide, Rian de Witt, became a friend.

Rian did not want to be in Namibia, or 'South West Africa' as he still called it. He had deferred his military obligation by studying zoology at the University of Witwatersrand in Johannesburg, but now the system had caught up with him. He was not happy about it.

Mike had wanted to learn more about Africa and its wildlife. Rian was a willing teacher. At night, after work and over a beer at their base at Rundu, near the Angolan border, Rian opened the Australian's eyes to the Africa beyond the minefields and carnage of man's wars.

'I grew up in the desert, in our Kalahari Gemsbok National Park, on the Botswana border. My dad's a National Parks ranger,' Rian had explained.

Mike found it surprising that a tall, blond, blue-eyed Afrikaner would talk for ages with what seemed like a mixture of love and awe for the original inhabitants of his harsh homeland. 'The San people – we whites still wrongly call them "the Bushmen of the Kalahari" – they can teach you more about game and land management than any university. In parts of the desert they're still free to live as they have for thousands of years. Just them and the wildlife. I could live like that for the rest of my life.'

'I'd give it a year or two,' Mike had joked.

'*Ja*, but there's no cold boxes or fridges out there, we probably wouldn't last a week,' Rian had laughed as he fetched two more beers. Mike had watched the last glowing ember of the sun fall behind the trees and wondered what it really would be like to live in Africa. The seed had been planted.

The South African Defence Force had cultivated the San in South West Africa, now Namibia, as allies in its fight against the South West African People's Organisation, the nationalists fighting under Sam Nujoma. The South Africans were capitalising on interracial animosity, which predated the arrival of the white man. Because he could speak the local language, Rian acted as a go-between and translator for the Australians when they encountered San communities in their seemingly endless work of rebuilding.

'One day,' Rian said as he crushed his empty can, 'I want to be able to travel the length of Africa, then tell the rest of the world about what we have here.'

'What's stopping you?' Mike had asked naively.

'My passport. No one wants us, not here, not anywhere in Africa. But it will change eventually. We can't go on as we do in South Africa.'

'I hope you're right,' Mike said. It was 1989 and the

end of white rule in South Africa appeared a forlorn hope, certainly in their lifetime.

'Maybe you'll come back one day and we can go exploring together, hey?'

'Maybe.'

The chance of another posting to Africa had seemed to Mike as unlikely as Australia ever going to war again, and he had set himself to making the best he could of life in a peacetime army.

Back in Australia, he found himself going out less at weekends and cutting down on booze and the pursuit of a future wife. He had, he reflected, learned his lesson well, and besides, all his old cronies were by then getting married and having children. He'd earned a reputation for spending more time indoors with his books than with those few boys who were still single. Inspired by Rian, with whom he kept in touch by mail, he had started a degree course of his own, in zoology, through Sydney's Macquarie University.

A few years later he treated himself to a field trip, returning to Namibia, where he met up with Rian, who, once his compulsory military service had ended, had become a South African National Parks ranger, as his father had been. They had revisited all the old places, Etosha, Sesriem and the Skeleton Coast, and detoured way off the beaten track in the arid wastes of Kaokoveldt, where they tracked a herd of the elusive desert elephants, ancient survivors of their inhospitable environment and man's wars. By now Rian was married to a woman named Susie, and they had a three-year-old son, Jan, who came along on the trip and gurgled at the elephants.

'Rian's talked about you and his days here in Namibia often, you know,' Susie confided to Mike as her husband and son shared a canvas bucket shower behind a tree near their bush campsite.

'This was where I fell in love with Africa,' Mike replied. Susie was a raven-haired schoolteacher, with dark, sparkling eyes and an infectious smile. Mike had yet to encounter a child as placid and cheerful as little Jan. He envied her and Rian their happiness – still did – and they had envied him his country. By then, the writing was on the wall for their South Africa, white South Africa, and no one was sure whether the change to majority rule would be peaceful or a bloodbath.

'Sometimes we talk about moving to Australia, but we haven't the money.'

'Rian could never leave the bush, surely?' To Mike, Australia seemed safe, bland, even boring, compared with Africa.

'You're right. But he's restless. He wants to travel, to see more of Africa, and whatever happens here I guess it would still be hard to leave, even if we did have the cash.'

'Another thing we have in common – restlessness,' Mike said.

'Ach, you should be marrying, settling down, having children. You're past thirty, surely it's time for you to re-marry?'

Mike smiled at her typically South African candour. 'You don't have a sister, do you?'

'Hey, no flirting, you sneaky Aussie bastard,' Rian called, towelling his hair dry.

'Truth is, I think I may have stopped looking,' Mike said to Susie as Rian carried Jan into the family tent.

'Then you should do all the women of South Africa a favour and lock yourself in a monastery. Don't advertise what's not for sale!'

'I'm not quite ready to go that far, but with my job I move around every couple of years, and the money's nothing to write home about. Not much to offer a girl.'

'Don't sell yourself short. In the meantime I'll keep an eye out for you, and you're always welcome in our home.'

'Thanks, Suze, but I've no idea when I'll get back to Africa.'

In 1994, again as part of a multinational United Nations force, Australia sent a medical detachment, an infantry company and a few other specialists into a tiny eastern African country that few Australians would have been able to locate on a map. The country was Rwanda and Mike, newly promoted to sergeant, knew he should have followed that tried-and-true adage that all soldiers swear by: never volunteer for anything. The first thing he had seen as he walked down the ramp of the Hercules transport aircraft at Kigali airport was a dog trotting along the runway carrying a human head in its mouth. Things got worse after that.

In the absence of any mines to clear or ammunition to dispose of, the army engineers, like the doctors, nurses and infantrymen they worked alongside, set to the grim business of cleaning out the hospital at Kigali which the Australian contingent was tasked with reopening. Now the UN badge on one of the shirts in his kitbag caught Mike's eye and he remembered the criticism that had been levelled against the organisation – that it had gone in too late, despite ample warning of the bloodbath that ensued.

The hospital, that place of mercy and healing, had been used by one tribe as a place to slaughter another tribe. Standing outside the gutted building, chain-smoking to try to remove the stench of death in his nostrils, Mike and a couple of other Australians had listened to a French missionary describe what had happened.

'These were people, *oui*, people like you and me, *comprenez*, understand? They herded their former friends and neighbours and workmates, employees and employers, into lines at gunpoint and marched them to the hospital.' The grey-haired priest cast his eyes to the sky, then blinked a couple of times before continuing.

'They did not want to waste the bullets, understand? They used machetes. The victims were made to kneel over a toilet bowl where they were decapitated or had their throats slit. The theory was that the blood could be flushed away.'

The theory didn't hold up, as Mike and the other soldiers discovered. Every toilet in the hospital was choked with blood and flesh and hair and Christ alone knew what else. It was their job to clean them out.

He recalled how the missionary had anticipated their questions before they had a chance to ask them.

'You are asking yourself why the people waiting in

the lines for extermination didn't run, charge their armed guards or do anything else to escape the slaughter, *non?*'

Mike had nodded.

'The answer is simple. A witness, a boy who hid over there in the bushes, explained it to me. The killers hacked off the feet of those waiting in the lines so they couldn't run. Some bled to death where they lay, others were dragged into the toilet blocks where they were finished off.'

Mike recalled that up until then his Africa had been one of sweeping plains, magnificent wildlife and, what they called in the army, low-intensity conflict. In Namibia, the black population had overthrown the white population. There had been killings and atrocities on both sides – that happened in any war – but what he had seen in Rwanda was genocide. One race wiping out another race.

Once the hospital was up and running again, they were kept busy with a host of other projects. The Australians built or repaired orphanages and churches, scraped away more dried blood and tried to restore some order to a shattered country. Who, he had wondered, would ever really want to return to it? It had the smell of a slaughterhouse mixed with that of a freshly burnt-down building. Woodsmoke from thousands of campfires hung over the refugee camps and the towns like a suffocating funeral shroud.

When Mike got home to Australia he realised yet again that he didn't have a home, except for the army. He had started to wonder if he had got it all wrong. After eight years of part-time study he had finally finished his degree, interrupted by sojourns to various war zones, which had never ceased to impress his tutors. But of what use, he asked himself time and again, was a degree in zoology to a soldier?

Rian had left his job-for-life in the National Parks Service, resigned to the fact that he would no longer be entitled to the best posts and pay because of the colour of his skin. However, he had transferred his knowledge of the African bush to his country's fastest growing industry – tourism.

He began by running tours from South Africa into Zimbabwe and Namibia in a second-hand Volkswagen Kombi. After a couple of years he sank the money he had so far saved into two old ex-army Bedford trucks. Like a dozen or more other entrepreneurs with the same idea, he planned to offer overland tours for foreign backpackers, travelling from Cape Town or Jo'burg to as far afield as Nairobi or, civil wars in intervening counties permitting, Cairo.

Mike had visited South Africa on holiday and Rian had proudly showed off his tour vehicles.

'Jesus, mate, you couldn't pay me enough to ride to Nairobi in the back of one of these heaps,' Mike had chided him.

'You may laugh, man, but the English, Germans, Danes, you Aussies, and Kiwis are happy to pay for the privilege of riding in Nelson and Susie,' he said, giving Nelson, who was named after Mandela, an affectionate pat on its bright yellow bonnet. Susie de Witt had mixed feelings about having a stubby, rusting, smoke-belching ex-army truck named in her honour, but accepted the compliment graciously and dutifully christened her with a bottle of Stellenbosch sparkling wine over her bullbar.

Rian could only spend a few days with Mike because he had other work to do. As well as running his own business he occasionally instructed safari-guide courses and, on the spur of the moment, he invited Mike to come along as a student.

'There's been a cancellation,' he explained.

'What, you want me to spend my holiday being ordered about the bush by a South African?' Mike laughed.

'You might learn something. There'll be no favouritism.'

'You mean you won't shoot if I get charged by a lion?'

'It'll be good for you,' Rian said, his tone suddenly less flippant.

Rian was right, and Mike knew it from the first day of the course. Rian taught his students tracking, bird and plant identification, and new and fascinating information about Africa's big game that Mike had never found in any textbook. They also learned how to safely shepherd city-bred tourists through some of the most dangerous country in the world.

After the course, on the drive back to his home, Rian had seemed relieved to again be able to talk to Mike as a close friend.

'You did well. I mean it. A lot of these kids are trying to become guides because they see it as a way of getting rich, which it isn't, or as a fast ticket out of the townships. You're doing it because you love the bush and you love the wildlife. I can't teach them that,' he said.

'But what good is it going to do me?' Mike had asked.

'That's your problem, my friend. But there is work here for good guides and work further north, in Botswana, Zambia and Tanzania. You'll find South African–trained guides in all those countries, and not all of them are South Africans.'

It was a tempting thought. A life in the African bush, impressing rich foreign tourists, some of them no doubt female and attractive, sounded appealing to Mike. He had shelved the idea as a nice dream, however, and promised Rian he would one day return to Africa.

Six months later he was back, once more at the expense of the Australian taxpayer. Mike had known about Operation Coracle, his army's contribution to the mine-clearing effort in Mozambique, for several years, and had made no secret of his ambitions to be part of it.

His army career had progressed steadily, if not meteorically, and he had made the jump from warrant officer to the commissioned ranks, as a captain, by virtue of his years of experience. He was promoted to major after ticking the boxes in a series of boring desk jobs and, after much persistence, finally landed what had seemed like his dream posting – Mozambique.

Now the dream had turned into a nightmare, with the deaths of Carlos and Fernando, but he knew things would be OK if he could wake up next to Isabella every day for the rest of his life.

Mike looked around his Maputo flat once more

to make sure he hadn't forgotten anything. He took the framed picture of Isabella and him at the beach from the wall and placed it on top of the clothes in his kitbag.

3

T he next morning, Monday, Mike headed back
to the UN offices on Avenida da Angola, all his
senses as usual assaulted by daily life in
Maputo. African women in bright blouses and tight
skirts on their way to work gingerly stepped around
piles of rotting garbage. Blue-black exhaust smoke
belched from cars that wouldn't be allowed on the
road in a western country, and pedestrians dodged
speeding *chapas*, small vans converted to taxis, driven
by apparently suicidal young men with booming car
radios turned up as far as the volume dial would go.
The sun was already strong, but any relief from the
heat offered by shady trees on the sidewalk was countered by the stench of stale urine at the base of their
trunks. The stormwater drain by the side of the road
smelled of untreated sewage.

Mike pushed open the heavy wooden door that led
to the UN offices and waved hello to the *guardo*, the
security guard employed by the construction company that owned the building. He pushed a button

and the electric door lock buzzed, allowing Mike to enter.

He nodded good morning to one of the Finns working on the ground floor. The man was seated at his desk behind a glass partition and looked to Mike like a hairy blond fish in a bowl. He headed upstairs to the mezzanine level, where he and most of the other UN officers worked.

Jake's office had a sign, 'Chief Technical Adviser', stuck to the glass partition. Mike walked in without knocking. Now that he had made the decision to leave the army he wanted to sever his ties to it, and the world of mine clearance, as quickly as possible.

'Goodbye, Jake. I'm leaving the army. It's been nice knowing you.'

'Not so fast, you've still got some explaining to do,' Jake said. 'You can't just ride off into the sunset like that.'

'What do you mean?'

'We haven't seen the end of this . . . incident. The higher-ups want to know what you and Carlos were doing digging around in the dirt in the first place. You're a technical adviser, not a mine clearer.'

Mike bridled at the comment, but he had no real quarrel with Jake. 'You wanted us to find a place to take a bunch of glorified tourists, including the press. Carlos spotted a mine virtually on the cleared path. If he hadn't got his hands dirty and lifted it you would have ended up with a dead dignitary – or worse, a dead reporter – on your hands.'

'And now I'm short one technical adviser,' Jake said.

'He had a name. Carlos. And no, you're short two technical advisers. I told you, I'm taking my leave and I'm getting out of the army as soon as I get back to Australia.'

'Then what?'

'I'm planning on coming back.'

'I'll get you a job as a civilian contractor,' Jake offered, his tone conciliatory now.

'Thanks, but no thanks. Anyway, what I do will depend on someone else.'

'Who?'

'A woman.'

'Ah, I see. Been holding out on us, have you? Local girl?'

Mike shrugged.

'Anyway,' Jake continued, 'you're going nowhere just yet. You've got to go back to the scene of the crime, and it's not me, or the UN, that says so. It's the cops. There's some South African detective in town who wants to find out what happened to the elephant.'

'The elephant? For fuck's sake, why?'

'He is, or was, a South African elephant. Something of a national treasure, or so I'm led to believe. One of the big tuskers of the Kruger park and there are some seriously pissed people over the border,' Jake said, consulting a fax flimsy on his desk.

'What's that got to do with me?' Mike asked, annoyed. He wanted to get to the hospital in Maputo where Isabella worked. He had missed the chance to see her at Mapai at the weekend, even though they had only been a few dozen kilometres apart, but there was no phone at the clinic and no way for him to get a message to her, despite several calls to her hospital. He had called her home, a small apartment in the nicer part of town, that morning, but there was no answer. He assumed she was on her way to work.

'You hit that elephant with a round from an AK-47, unless my recollection of your statement is incorrect,' Jake said.

'That round probably ricocheted off his skull, Jake. I might as well have been spitting at him for the harm it did him. And anyway, he was trying to kill me.'

'I know, I know. Take it easy. And I've already heard from your colonel that you're bailing out. Anyway, you're not leaving the country until you come and tell your story to the South African Police.'

'I've got more important things to do first, Jake. I'll call you later.'

He turned and walked out of Jake's office and down the stairs. Outside, he hailed a battered Peugeot cab in the street and told the driver he wanted to go to the hospital.

His first meeting with Isabella, not long after he arrived in Mozambique, was far from romantic. It was due to an ingrown toenail. He was a little embarrassed about the injury, but it was giving him hell and had flared up badly in the African heat.

Before he had left Australia, a warrant officer who had just completed a tour with the mine-clearing detachment had given him some good advice about health care in Mozambique: 'Don't get sick.' But Mike couldn't put off dealing with his problem any longer.

It was too tricky for the UN team's own medic and not serious enough to warrant shipping him across the border to a nice clean hospital in South Africa.

Like most of Maputo, the hospital was built by the Portuguese during their colonial rule and it looked like it had gone to pot in the twenty-five years or so since they had left. Jake's assistant had made an appointment for Mike to see a doctor, apparently Portuguese and allegedly competent. When he arrived at the hospital he had mentioned the name to a bored-looking woman picking her nose behind a cigarette-burned laminate counter. She pointed down a corridor of yellowed linoleum where a fluorescent light buzzed and flickered on and off.

Half-a-dozen African patients were sitting on a collection of battered kitchen chairs and cheap vinyl-covered lounges oozing foam stuffing from knife wounds. Two of the patients, a heavily pregnant woman and a painfully thin man with a blood-soaked bandage on his arm, had eyed him coldly. As he set off down the corridor into the guttering light, the soles of his boots stuck to the cracked tiles every now and then. The place smelled like it had last been cleaned with bleach diluted with urine and spew. He had thought, briefly, of Kigali hospital in Rwanda, then forced the image from his head.

At last, he had found a door with a handwritten cardboard nameplate stuck to it. He knocked, and an African woman in a fraying blue nurse's uniform opened the door. She seemed to be expecting him, which he took as a positive sign. She told him that Dr Nunes – she pronounced it *Noon-ez* – would see him shortly. He pictured an overweight, drink-ravaged, ageing Latin quack, debauched by a life of exile in a former colony, not game to show himself in his homeland ever again.

There was just enough room for a wheeled examination bed, covered in a sheet which, like the nurse, was crisp but a little tatty, a small metal writing desk and a hard chair made of welded steel tubing. On the wall was a poster with Portuguese writing which featured two attractive Africans, one male and one female, and a pink condom with a smiley face. He hoped they would all be very happy together. There was a kidney-shaped dish on the table covered with a white cloth and he didn't particularly want to know what was in it. The floor tiles were cleaner here than in the corridor, but he noted a tiny pile of pellet-like droppings in one corner. Fortunately there was a window and outside he could hear birds singing. He waited fifteen minutes and was contemplating chickening out when the door scraped open again.

She was, quite simply, beautiful. Her skin was the colour of dark honey, her brown eyes sparkling as she smiled her first greeting. Her tight white T-shirt and shortish denim skirt accentuated her lithe figure. Her hair was cut in a bob, and she had a pair of wraparound sunglasses with amber-coloured lenses perched on the top of her head.

'Is hot, no?' She had smiled, fanning herself with a clipboard. 'Major, eh? Big man, no? I am Dr Nunes. Sorry to keep you.'

Mike had coughed, his throat suddenly dry. Here was the most attractive woman he'd so far seen in

71

Mozambique making small talk with him and he couldn't even speak.

'Sore toe, no? Not sore throat as well!' she laughed.

He had thought she must have known the effect she had on men, particularly expatriate men far from home.

She was younger than he was – in her early thirties, he guessed. There was no wedding band on her finger and for a moment he feared she might be a nun, a member of some modern order that allowed its sisters to shave their legs and wear designer sunglasses. No way, he had told himself. God could be unfair, but not that cruel.

'What are you doing here? In Mozambique, I mean.'

He coughed again. 'Clearing mines.'

'Ah, good for you. I treat too many landmine victims and it makes me hate soldiers.'

'Hey, we're *clearing* landmines, not laying them,' he said defensively.

'You are an army engineer, no?'

'Yes.'

'Then you were trained to lay these things as well as clear them, no?'

'Yes. But I never have.'

'Good for you. The work you do is worthwhile, but I think it will never be finished,' she said. As she spoke she prodded Mike's painfully swollen big toe with various implements that looked to him like they had been designed and manufactured during the Spanish Inquisition.

She bit her lower lip as she concentrated. 'Big,

strong man like you does not need anaesthetic, I think. Better we save it for the injured little children, no?' Mike realised, as he winced in pain, that her question was rhetorical.

'Not even a bullet to bite on?' he gasped.

She shook her head.

His adventure in pain finally over, he had found he was still tongue-tied as she bandaged his throbbing toe, but he was saved by a bird.

As Isabella had finished tying the bandage, a grey bird, about the size of a seagull, but with a large, fanned crest, landed on the windowsill and gave a whining call from the other side of the ragged fly-screen. *Kway-kway*, it mourned.

'What do you want, bird? I see him every day, you know, and always he talks to me like this,' Isabella said to both Mike and the bird as she removed her latex gloves with a snap.

'He's telling you to go away,' he said.

'What do you mean, go away? He is the one who should go away.'

'It's a grey lourie – a male. He is called the "go-away" bird because of his call. Listen.' They both stayed silent and the bird gave his call again.

'It sounds like something else to me,' she said, as the lourie took off, perhaps unnerved by their sudden interest in him. 'Like those lizards, the one's that say "fuck you",' she added, utterly deadpan. She had watched his face for a reaction. He had laughed aloud.

She then asked him how he knew about the bird and, when he explained, tested him by pointing out a few more at random from the window. He stood, and to see the birds, all of which he identified correctly, he had to stand so close to her that they were almost touching. He smelled the perspiration on her body and the shampoo on her hair. For a second he felt like he needed to sit down, and he didn't think it was the loss of blood from his wound.

'I've been here in Africa for nearly a year and, do you know, I know no birds and I have not seen any animals at all. Not even an elephant. Have you seen an elephant, Major?' she asked.

They had moved away from the window and he was now lacing his boot. She sat on the edge of the cheap steel desk, her legs swinging like a little girl's as she filled out some details on her clipboard.

'I've seen plenty of elephants, and lion and leopard and buffalo, you name it.'

'Here in Mozambique?'

'No, in the bush here all you see are snakes and landmines.'

She laughed. 'So you have been on the safari?'

'I'm a trained safari guide.'

'Tell me how an Australian soldier becomes a safari guide.'

'Over dinner. It's a long story,' he had said, as he stood to leave, testing the weight on his bad foot. Instinctively, he reached in his top pocket and drew out his cigarettes and Zippo lighter.

'Those things will kill you, you know,' she said, changing the subject.

'Not as quickly as a landmine,' he replied. He feared he had been too forward in inviting her to dinner, and had blown his chances.

She smiled and said, 'May I?' She reached for the packet of cigarettes in his hand. Soft, clean fingers had brushed his as she took one from the pack. 'Come, I walk with you outside.'

As they stood in the strong morning sunshine she raised the cigarette to her lips and leaned towards him. He lit both their cigarettes.

She reclined against the grubby white concrete of the building, cocked her head to one side and said, 'You ask me out to dinner, but how do you know I'm not married?'

'You're here. This isn't a country you bring a husband or a wife to. This is a place for people who are married to their jobs. And besides, you're not wearing a ring.'

'I would not wear a ring during a surgical procedure anyway. Are you married to your job, Major Mike?'

'I suppose I am, but I'd file for a divorce today if I got a better offer. What about dinner?'

'That is the best offer I have had all day.' She gave a little laugh as she exhaled and added, 'In fact, it is the only offer I have had today.'

She must have gone home for the afternoon siesta, he realised, because when he arrived back at the hospital that evening she had changed. She wore a pale blue sleeveless summer dress with a short hemline that showed off her legs. Her leather sandals slapped on the linoleum floor as she walked out into the reception area of the hospital to meet him. A pink tropical flower behind her ear softened her short hairdo. A gold bangle worn high above her elbow complemented her olive skin perfectly and he was almost drunk at the sight of her.

'I'm sorry, I don't even know your first name,' Mike had said as he led her out of the decaying hospital to where he had parked the Nissan.

'Isabella. I was wondering when you would ask.' She laughed. She pronounced her name with the accent on the *bell*. He opened the door for her and offered his hand to help her up. She declined and he had to force himself to turn away as she slid up into the seat, revealing a stretch of golden thigh. They had made small talk during the short drive about the state of Maputo's roads, as he dodged potholes, motorcycles, *chapas* and vendors selling everything from live chickens to bootlaces.

They ate lobster on the verandah of the Costa do Sol hotel, watching the bobbing lights of small fishing boats and their reflections waver like shimmering silver ribbons out on the dark Indian Ocean. He told her how he came to be a qualified safari guide, and of his travels for work and pleasure in Africa. He had brought along an old field guide on the birds of southern Africa and told Isabella she could keep it for as long as she wanted.

She seemed genuinely pleased by the gesture and looked up the page with a picture of the grey lourie. 'Our bird,' she said, finishing her glass of vinho verde. They laughed and he filled her glass again.

'Tell me your story, Isabella. I find it hard to believe you're not married.'

'I prefer women,' she said.

He had coughed, choking on his wine and had to wipe his mouth with his serviette.

'No,' she giggled, reaching out to pat his hand reassuringly. 'I am joking. Are you OK?'

He had nodded and taken another sip of wine while she continued. 'I come from a good Catholic family, from Lisbon. I go to good school and to university, but my parents, they don't like my taste in men. I met a man while I was at university. He was a poet and we lived together. I used my allowance to support him, but my parents, they threaten to cut me off unless we break up.'

'And did you?' he asked, as she paused to take a long sip of wine and stub out her cigarette.

'I told them we were going to get married. He had asked me, but I had been putting it off. I loved him very much and I knew then for sure that I wanted to spend all my days with this man. Then, one day when I was working as an intern at a hospital in Lisbon I see him in the corridor. "What is wrong?" I ask him.'

She looked out at the ocean and took another sip of wine. He sat in silence, letting her finish in her own time. She blinked her eyes twice, took a breath, and said, ' "Cancer," he says to me. We got married and I watched him die. I was with him at the end.'

'I'm so sorry, Isabella.'

'Is not your fault. In Lisbon there was too much to remind me of him. All my friends, they are so sorry for me. And my family, I hate them because I think they are secretly pleased he is gone. So, I disappoint them all and pack up and come to Mozambique. Now is your turn.'

He told her about Janice and the baby and how he had given up on the thought of marrying again, which, he realised as he looked deep into her dark eyes, was a lie.

'I am sorry about your marriage and your baby. You are alone, like me, but I think you like it here in Mozambique, no?'

'I like it here, yes. How can you tell?'

'I see it in your eyes.'

He had stared hard into her dark eyes, watching the dance of the reflected flickering candlelight. He could have stayed like that, transfixed, forever. But it was late, and the waiter was hovering nearby.

They called it a night and she had given him a little peck on the cheek when he dropped her outside her apartment block. He offered to walk her up, but she declined.

'Can I see you again?' he had asked her as she turned to walk up the path to her building.

'Of course, next time you have another ingrown toenail you know where to find me.'

'I'm serious.'

'I know you are. You are too serious, and I am joking.'

He saw her again whenever he could, and she seemed as excited as he was at each new meeting. They went to the beach together at weekends, to dinner in the evenings and to a cocktail party at the American high commission that Jake had invited him to. All the men had stared at her and all their wives did too, but for different reasons.

A month after their first meeting he was in Jake's office looking at a map of southern Mozambique and discussing a new area into which they were about to send a mine-clearing team when there was a knock at the door. It was MacDonald, the team's big, red-faced Scottish quartermaster and transport officer, who complained that one of the Nissans needed a new rear window, and that the Maputo dealership had none in stock.

'How long will it take them to get one in?' Jake asked.

'Near enough two weeks,' MacDonald replied, acknowledging Mike's presence with a nod.

'Without a window it'll get stolen again the first time we park it on a public street,' Mike said. The vehicle in question had already been stolen once, although the South African Police had recovered it in Komatipoort, just across the border. The thieves had re-sprayed the vehicle a metallic blue, which everyone thought was much nicer than the original white.

'I'd head across the border to South Africa and pick up a window over there, only I'm supposed to go north tomorrow for a spot of leave, boss,' MacDonald added in a half-pleading tone.

The germ of a sweet idea crossed Mike's mind and he said, 'I'll go. But give me the weekend as well.'

Jake knew he was up to something; however, he had little choice but to accede as everyone else was out in the field or, like MacDonald, off on leave.

MacDonald signed the Nissan over to Mike and he drove immediately to the hospital. He had to wait for Isabella to finish operating on a young girl who had lost a hand by trying to pick up a mine. Isabella looked tired and gaunt when she finally stepped out into the reception area where he had been waiting.

'Poor thing. She will be lucky to escape gangrene once she's back home in her village,' she said absently.

'Sometimes I think we've got the easy job. We rarely have to see the results of a landmine detonation. You've saved a life today,' Mike said.

'Sometimes I just want to scream. Sometimes I just want to run away from this place.'

'Isabella, I've got to go to South Africa for the week-end. Come with me, and I'll show you all the animals you've ever dreamed of,' he said.

She cocked her head and bit her lip as she stared at him for a few long seconds. He guessed she was wondering where a weekend away would lead their relationship.

'Where will we stay?' she finally asked.

'We'll camp. In the Kruger National Park. There's no better game viewing in Africa.'

'Two tents,' she said.

'Two tents,' he repeated.

They left the next day and sped out of Maputo along the new South African–constructed tollway that links Johannesburg with the beaches of Mozambique. Isabella was wearing khaki bush shorts, rafter sandals and a pink tank top with a black bikini top showing beneath it as a bra. She looked cool and sexy, and Mike realised he had fallen for her completely. He had no idea how the weekend would unfold, but neither, he thought, did she, despite her insistence on separate tents.

The border post was packed with the poor of Mozambique queuing for the chance to serve as cheap labour in the comparative El Dorado of South

Africa. The process was hot, tedious and officious, but they had smiled and tried to ease their snail-like progress through customs and immigration on both sides of the border by being friendly to the bored civil servants who, eventually, stamped their passports with an almighty *thud-thud*.

As always, Mike felt the stress fall off him as they drove through the border gate into South Africa. For a short time at least, he would not be worrying about landmines, the enormity of the job at hand and the risks faced by the men he tasked every day. As a bonus there was a beautiful woman in the car with him this time.

MacDonald had given him the address of a parts place in Nelspruit, the first major town on the South African side, a little over a hundred kilometres past the border. They travelled fast on a road designed for Mercedes and BMWs. Finally, they pulled off the motorway into the hot provincial city and found the auto parts place.

After Mike had signed for the rear window and had it fitted they drove around until they found a supermarket. Together they pushed a shopping trolley up and down the aisles, learning more and more about each other as they stocked up for the weekend.

'Bran. You must have bran in your cereal,' she said.

'I don't like bran.'

'Is good for you.'

'That's why I don't like it. How about sugar?'

And so it went on. Mike loved it. Thinking back on it he felt like they were already married. He found himself not minding that prospect at all. They bought huge fillet steaks and a thick, dark coil of *boervoers* sausage, as well as beers, ice and red wine.

'We can buy food inside the park, but it's getting late and we have to be inside the national park and booked into one of the rest camps by no later than six o'clock,' he told her.

With the sun sinking fast behind them they back-tracked down the N4 tollway and raced for the sleepy highway town of Malelane, which they had passed through earlier that day. Mike's back was sticking to the vinyl seat and Isabella fanned her face with a magazine as they sped through hot, flat country, flanked by sugarcane fields. At Malelane they turned off to the left, following a sign to the Kruger park decorated with the South African National Parks Board's symbol, a kudu's head.

Just short of the entrance to the park they crossed the Crocodile River, which forms Kruger's southern border. Mike stopped on the bridge and coaxed Isabella from the Nissan to the side railing. From below them came a loud honking and bellowing.

'What is it?' she asked, a little nervously.

'Hippo. There, look, he's leaving the water.' The great beast, judging it was now cool enough to leave the water, was wading ponderously up the sandy bank, preparing for a night's feeding.

It was about five by the time Mike had paid their entrance fee to the young woman in khaki at the gate office.

'What do we do now?' Isabella asked as a green-uniformed ranger lifted the boom gate and saluted smartly as they drove through. Isabella returned his salute with a solemn look and he smiled back at her, white teeth splitting his broad black face.

'We look for animals. Roll down your window.'

'But you said there were lions here. If I open my window I will get eaten,' she said, turning big eyes on Mike, and he could see she had some genuine concerns about her safety.

'This is probably the safest place to view game in Africa. All the camps are surrounded by electric fences. The animals are wild, but most of them are used to the sight and sound of vehicles. As long as you keep your head and arms inside, you'll be fine.'

'How far are we from Mozambique again?' she asked.

'Not far, twenty or thirty kilometres. Kruger runs up and down the border between South Africa and Mozambique. The park's about four hundred kilometres from top to bottom and about seventy kilometres at its widest.'

Mike was forced to remember his safari guide training as Isabella's questions started coming in rapid succession.

'What tree is that? Look, is that a monkey? Is that a deer? Where are the elephants?'

He answered her as best he could as he drove along a sealed road for a while before turning off onto a dirt road that followed a snaking path up into an area of mountain bushveldt which dominated the park's south-western corner. They stopped to watch a herd of kudu, large buck which stand nearly as high as a man at the shoulder. Mike leaned into the back of the four-wheel drive and freed two cans of Lion lager from the cold box, popped the ring-pulls and handed one to Isabella. He drank his as greedily as he devoured the sight of the afternoon sunlight playing on Isabella's golden arms.

The big kudu bull, with his long spiralled horns, returned Isabella's stare for a full minute or more before trotting off into the bush. His females followed him, one taking fright and jumping high into the air.

They drove on a little further until Isabella cried, 'Stop!'

There, just off to the left of the road, no more than six or seven metres from the vehicle, was a big male white rhinocerous. Mike killed the engine, and Isabella looked worried. 'It's OK,' he whispered. 'He's half blind, but his hearing is excellent. He'll take off if he's worried.'

The rhino raised his massive head from the grass he had been grazing on and sniffed the air. His big ears rotated like antennae and he squinted through tiny myopic eyes in the general direction of their vehicle. After a moment he returned to his tasty grass shoots. Isabella was rapt. She rested her chin on her hands on the windowsill and stared at the prehistoric beast. 'He is beautiful. Just beautiful,' she whispered.

'We'll stay at Malelane Camp. It's just inside the park, near the gate where we entered. It's small and quiet, and it overlooks the river,' he said.

When they arrived it was nearly dark. Apart from a grassy lawn for tents and caravans there were ablution and cooking huts, and a few accommodation chalets, known as *rondavels* in Afrikaans. There appeared to be only one other couple staying and they were in one of the *rondavels*.

Mike stopped the Nissan near the fence at the far end of the camping ground, away from the huts and under the spreading boughs of a big, shady marula tree. Four small grey vervet monkeys with black faces darted from the tree in alarm. He knew they'd be back in search of any food left lying out. He quickly began unloading their cooking gear and food. He felt a gentle hand on his shoulder and turned around. Isabella stood quietly and left her hand resting on his shoulder for a second more.

'Thank you,' she said, and gave a little smile as she self-consciously removed her hand.

'What for?'

'For getting me out of Maputo, for the rhino, for the unhealthy meal you are going to cook me. Sometimes I think I am dying in that hospital. I feel it eating away at me every day and sometimes I think . . . I don't know, that I will die there too if I don't get out.'

He wanted to reach out and crush her in his arms then and there, and tell her everything would be fine and that he would take her anywhere in the world she wanted to go. 'Forget about it. Let's get the fire started,' he said instead.

Although they had become good friends, Isabella had not opened herself up to him like that before. He wondered if they had left it too late to make the leap to intimacy, whether they would always be nothing more than good friends. He knew she still thought about her dead husband. He busied himself making a fire and opening a bottle of wine.

They followed their beers with cheap red wine drunk out of the plastic mugs from her Thermos flask. The steak was good, and dessert was a tin of peaches doused in tinned sweetened cream.

'What are you thinking about?' he had asked her, marvelling at the way the reflection of the glowing coals turned her skin to pure gold as she stared into the dying embers.

'What?'

'Your thoughts. What's on your mind?'

'Juan,' she whispered.

It took him a second. 'Ah, your husband?'

'Yes.'

She said nothing more for a time and he left it at that. 'I guess we should get ready for bed,' he said. She raised an eyebrow. 'Set up our tents, I mean,' he explained.

Isabella didn't need any help to erect the small two-person dome tent she'd brought with her. Mike climbed the small ladder welded onto the back of the Nissan to the roof carrier above.

'Where are you sleeping?' she asked.

'Up here.' From his kitbag on the roof carrier he took out a large green mosquito net with a metal hoop at the top end to give it shape. He tied the net to a low branch of the marula tree and unfolded it around him. On the roof of the vehicle, tied down with rope, was the rolled-up foam mattress and canvas bedroll he always took out bush with him. The mattress was a little smaller than a normal double one and just thick enough to protect his bones from the ground or, in this case, the aluminium slats of the roof carrier.

'Is it safe up there?' she asked.

'You couldn't be safer,' he said, grinning in the dark.

'Now, I think you are being cheeky, no?'

'Goodnight, Isabella,' he said as he shook the unzipped sleeping bag over his body and fluffed up his cheap, lumpy pillow.

'Goodnight, Mike,' she said, her words followed by the sound of a long zipper being fastened. And, after a few seconds, 'And thank you, again.'

He lay on his back, one arm crooked behind his head and smoked his last cigarette of the day as he gazed at the stars peeking through the leaves of the marula tree. No other campers had shown up and the couple in the *rondavel* had long since retired.

Later, he found he couldn't sleep. The night was warm and a pair of bats squeaked noisily away, their calls sounding like a rusty gate swinging in the wind. Every now and then he caught the *swish-swish* of nylon on nylon. Isabella was tossing on the floor of her little tent. Eventually he dozed off, succumbing to the effects of the wine and the beer.

The lion woke him. He checked his watch and saw it was a little before midnight. He lay still and listened intently. He heard it again – the low, almost painful moan of a big male lion calling to his lionesses.

'Mike . . . *Mike*!' Isabella called. 'What is that?'

He smiled. 'What do you think?' he called down to her.

He was answered with the long buzz of her zipper opening. Bare feet padded across the grass and the four-wheel drive began to rock as she negotiated the ladder. His heart started to beat faster, and it wasn't because of the lion. The cat was probably more than a kilometre away.

The mosquito net rustled and jerked and then she was beside him, lying rigid on her back. In the starlight he could see she wore a long white T-shirt and her legs seemed to stretch forever into the night.

'I could not sleep,' she said, as the lion groaned again in the distance.

'Me neither.' He rose on one elbow, reached his other arm out across her, and rested his hand on her belly.

'I was not worried by the lion, you see, just . . .'

He placed a finger on her lips. In a moment, he replaced his finger with his lips. She stiffened, hesitating for a second, and then she opened her mouth to meet his. She reached around his neck, drawing him closer.

They made love that night. Urgent, hard and fast at first, like starving people sating their hunger. Later they kissed, caressed and explored each other beneath the stars. The vehicle rocked and squeaked beneath them again, but there was no one about to mind and they were, to all intents and purposes, alone under an African sky.

'This is right, no?' she asked, as they shared a cigarette beneath the mosquito net later.

'This is as right as it gets.'

4

The cab stopped outside the hospital. 'Quanto?' Mike asked the driver as he pulled out his wallet.

The fare was outrageously high. No doubt, Mike thought, the driver had thought he was a tourist, thanks to the kitbag he was lugging. Normally he would have bargained the driver down, but he was in too much of a hurry to see Isabella and tell her he was leaving the army. He hadn't quite worked out what he was going to do with his life, or what he was going to tell her. He'd just have to wing it. He peeled off a few grimy meticas notes, climbed out of the cramped, dusty little cab and retrieved his bag from the boot.

He and Isabella had made love like newlyweds for the rest of that bliss-filled weekend in the Kruger park and afterwards at every opportunity their inconvenient jobs allowed. That wasn't often enough for him, as he regularly travelled north, to Maxixe, on the coast, to meet with the warrant officer who made up the other half of the Australian mine-clearing contingent in Mozambique. Isabella occasionally travelled to remote clinics, such as the one at Mapai, where she had spent the weekend. Mike hoped to find her back at work now and, despite the weight of his kitbag, bounded up the cracked concrete stairs into the dingy hospital.

He walked past reception and the usual collection of walking wounded down the yellowed corridor to Isabella's surgery. Patience, the nurse whom he had met on his first visit who looked after Isabella's schedule, intercepted him before he knocked on the door.

'*Bom dia*, Major, how are you?' Patience asked with a smile. Africans are the beneficiaries of some unusual names. The nurse shared hers with a virtue that was not one of Mike's strong points.

'Where's Dr Nunes?' he asked, not bothering to return her greeting. He knew it was rude of him, as Africans like to take their time in coming to the point of a conversation, starting with a ritual round of pleasant greetings.

Patience recoiled. 'Ah, but she is not back from Mapai yet.'

'Why?'

'There was a bus accident. Some men from the ambulance, they say it was very bad. Very many people hurt. I think Dr Isabella has had to operate at that place. Maybe we will see her tomorrow.'

Shit, he said to himself. 'Thanks, Patience.' It was clear she had no idea when Isabella would be back.

He weighed his options. He could go back to his flat for a day or two while he waited for Isabella to return, or he could swallow his pride and go back to

Jake and cadge a lift to Mapai. He had no wish to revisit the scene of Carlos's death, but he had no other way to get north, short of buying a ticket on one of the ridiculously crowded local buses and risk ending up as another of Isabella's patients.

He borrowed a pen and paper from Patience and scrawled a quick note to Isabella, explaining he was on his way to Mapai and hoped to catch her before she returned to Maputo, or maybe on the road in between. Patience promised to deliver it to her the moment she saw her. Hot, sweaty and angry, he stormed outside and hailed another cab.

Dr Isabella Nunes was so tired she felt like crying. She had arrived at the small clinic at around nine on Thursday night, an hour later than planned, thanks to a punctured tyre. Father Patrick – she found it odd calling a man five years younger than herself 'Father' – had greeted her warmly as usual. Patrick was a good-looking, lanky, red-haired Irish boy of twenty-six and she marvelled at his commitment, isolated in the bush, half a world away from his homeland. She, too, was far from home, but against the odds she had found someone special in this sad, torn country.

'How are things, Father?' she asked.

'Oh, you know, Isabella, same as always – never enough medicine, generator on the blink, water pump broken again. Bloody Africa, excuse my French.'

The mission had been built by Portuguese priests

in the early part of the twentieth century and expanded over the years with donations from around the world. Father Patrick lived in an old two-bedroom cottage made of stone daubed with a mixture of mud and cattle dung which had set to the consistency of concrete and then been reinforced with countless coats of whitewash over the decades. The cottage, like the neighbouring one where the nuns lived, was topped by a steep-gabled thatched roof. Across a dusty square were the schoolhouse, which catered for seventy children of all ages from infants through to high school, and the clinic itself, where Isabella worked during her visits. Both these newer structures had whitewashed breeze-block walls to waist height, topped by flyscreen mesh the rest of the way up to their new corrugated tin roofs. The clinic had the added protection of metal louvres over the flyscreen mesh, which could be closed to keep out dust during high winds. When she visited, Isabella slept in Father Patrick's spare bedroom.

He led her to the cottage, carrying her backpack for her. Once inside, he placed her pack in her room and led her back to the small kitchen. He pulled two bottles of Dois M beer out of the paraffin refrigerator and opened them with a Swiss Army knife. 'I'm probably blaspheming, but you won't find any Irish whisky here. I detest the stuff,' he said as he passed her a bottle. 'Cheers.'

As often happened, Father Patrick was using Isabella's visit as a chance for him to slip away to Maputo for a couple of days. He had a meeting planned with his bishop and also needed to stock up on food and supplies for the mission. He would leave Friday, around lunchtime, and be back the same time on Sunday. With Isabella at the clinic, along with two African nuns who had trained as nurses, he felt sure the mission was in good hands in his absence. Isabella had no fears for her safety, as the mission had a nightwatchman armed with an old shotgun and, besides, Father Patrick and the sisters were well liked and respected in the local community.

Isabella was sleeping soundly on her first night at the mission, thanks to the effects of the long journey and two more of the priest's cold beers, but woke with a start to the sound of thumping on her bedroom door. She looked at the luminous dial of the man's diving watch she wore, and saw it was nearly one o'clock in the morning. '*Quem e?*' she called out, annoyed and confused at the disturbance. 'Who is there?' she repeated in English.

'Isabella, it's me,' Father Patrick said. 'Come quick, there's been a terrible accident. A bus and a lorry have had a head-on. The bus was full of passengers.'

Isabella fumbled for the flashlight on her bedside table and awkwardly slid into her knee-length khaki skirt and matching long-sleeved shirt. She always dressed more demurely when travelling to these remote rural towns than she would have in Maputo which, by comparison, was cosmopolitan and relaxed.

Father Patrick had been woken by the screams of a woman passenger who had run into the mission from the nearby main road. Her son, a toddler of three, was dead in her arms. He had been flung from her lap when the two vehicles collided, and his neck was broken when he slammed into the back of the seat in front of him. There was nothing Patrick could do for the child or the mother, but a stream of walking wounded were heading for the clinic building, its big red cross on the shiny tin roof clearly visible in the moonlight.

After waking Isabella, Patrick roused the gardeners and the two nuns and set off for the scene of the accident. He left one nun to cope with the injured that had already arrived.

'Fetch stretchers from the clinic,' he yelled to the gardeners, who stumbled from their housing compound, blankets wrapped around their shoulders. The young priest was a teacher, not a doctor, but had studied first aid to an advanced level. He prayed Isabella would not be far behind him.

Isabella stepped into her sandals and ran out into the night. She paused briefly, hopping on one leg, to pull the strap of one up over her ankle. In her other hand she clutched the small zip-up canvas holdall that contained her medical supplies and operating instruments.

The crash site was like a scene from a disaster movie. Blood dripped from the windows of the bus where people, alive and dead, were being dragged out without care for their injuries, pain or dignity. Isabella beckoned to the African nun, who was still wearing a dressing gown, to join her. Quickly but calmly, Isabella assessed each patient in turn and gave her instructions to the nun.

'Lacerations to the face and arms – broken glass most likely, he can wait for cleaning and dressing.

Broken arm, he can walk. Shattered kneecap – get the gardeners to carry him. Give him a shot of morphine, Sister, then quickly dress yourself,' she added kindly to the nun. 'I'll see you back at the clinic.'

The dead, the two drivers and the passengers sitting closest to the front of the bus, were horribly mutilated and most were trapped in the wreckage of the vehicles. Of more concern to Isabella were the two people who lay at her feet, a man in his forties and a young girl, probably no more than seventeen. Isabella called Patrick over to her.

'These two, Father, they are the most serious. The others I can bandage or stitch up, but these both have serious internal bleeding from where they were thrown into the seats in front of them. If we do not get them to a hospital, they will die.'

The priest nodded. 'Right. Do you want me to take them, or do you want to get back to Maputo yourself?'

Isabella knew there was nothing she could do for the seriously injured people between Mapai and Maputo. Her only hope would be to get them to theatre as quickly as possible, and Patrick could drive as fast as she, if not faster. If she left, the two nuns would be swamped with the forty or more other injured people from the bus and, besides, there were other patients who would have been waiting for weeks to see her at the clinic. 'No, you go, Patrick,' she said finally.

'You're sure you'll be OK?' he asked. The question was a stupid one, she thought, but she was too tired to rebuke him.

'Go. The sisters and I will be fine. But please, find my assistant at the hospital – you know her, yes? Tell her that this accident has put my schedule back at least a day, so I probably won't be back in Maputo until Monday or Tuesday. It is important, as someone may be looking for me.' She had no way of knowing if Mike Williams had got her message and would be able to meet her here, at the clinic, over the weekend, or if he would be waiting for her to return to the capital.

The priest jogged back to the mission and returned shortly with their battered old Land Rover, a gift from a parish in England whose hearts were bigger than their bank accounts. Isabella supervised the lifting of the critical patients into the back of the four-wheel drive and wondered silently if there was any chance they would survive the agonising trip.

'Good luck, and God bless,' Father Patrick said with a wave. Despite his best efforts, the priestly words never seemed to gel with the image of a young, freckle-faced man in a T-shirt and shorts, Isabella thought. Suddenly she felt very alone.

Her exhaustion was starting to show, while the tin roof of the clinic pinged and squeaked as it expanded with the warmth of the morning sun. She found it hard to focus her eyes and twice now she had dropped the forceps she was using to pull chips of glass from a teenage boy's arm.

For nine hours she had been suturing, bandaging, plastering and comforting. The nuns had worked tirelessly at her side and had even found time to make her a sandwich and coffee sometime in the early hours. Isabella had lost count of the total number of people she had treated after the first thirty. Most were minor injuries, thankfully, and the majority of the patients had been released.

News of the accident spread, somehow, to the town of Mapai a few kilometres up the road and enterprising minibus taxi drivers had been running a regular shuttle service all morning, picking up those who were able to travel. Isabella was left with just nine patients, those with broken limbs, head wounds or other injuries that needed monitoring over the next day or so. That meant all the clinic's beds were full.

A steady stream of general patients, those she had actually come to the mission to treat, had been arriving in ones and twos all morning, and been turned away by the sisters. It broke Isabella's heart to see them turn and walk back to the main road, especially the very old and the very young, clutched to anxious mothers' breasts. All had been told the doctor would see them the very next day, at the same time, and word had soon passed back through the town.

Isabella stepped out of the clinic building into the bright mid-morning sunlight and had to shield her eyes from the glare with her hand. As her eyes adjusted to the brightness, she reached in the pocket of her dark-stained skirt for her cigarettes and lit one with a small gold lighter. She wondered again if Mike had got her message. She desperately needed to talk to him. She wanted him to hold her, right now. His muscled arms encircling her always made her feel safe, wanted, loved.

Looking around her at the mission compound she knew she would make the right decision when next they spoke. His time in Mozambique was drawing to a close and he would soon be returning to Australia. They had avoided discussing their future in any great detail. She didn't think of their time together as a fling, but she had been as reluctant as he to broach the subject of a more lasting commitment.

Isabella was pretty sure Mike loved her as much as she loved him. Their careers, though, were poles apart and, very soon, they would be living worlds apart. She had been in Mozambique for two years and, despite the sadness, the death, the poverty and the frustrating bureaucracy, she loved Africa. She knew Mike loved this crazy continent as well, but she doubted he was ready to leave the army. Isabella had a guaranteed tenure at the hospital for as long as she wanted it, but what would he do if he stayed in Africa? If he became a safari guide – something he had trained for – she worried she would see even less of him than she did now.

I am making the right decision, she told herself. When they finally met again she would tell him how she had always wanted to visit Australia, maybe even work there. It was a white lie – she had never wanted to visit Australia as she thought the country sounded too boring for her liking. Of course, it would not be a subtle hint, but if he wanted her to come stay with him, she would leave Mozambique, for good. If he asked her to marry him, she would say yes immediately. She loved him. She was sure of it, more sure than she had been of anything since Juan's death.

The life of a soldier's wife was not one Isabella would ever have contemplated, but now, she realised, she would do anything to be with Mike forever. The Australian government, she had read, was advertising for nurses in places as far afield as Zimbabwe and South Africa. Apparently the country also had a shortage of doctors willing to work in rural areas. She was sure she could find work, perhaps assisting Aboriginal people. She would make the overture and, if Mike was truly serious about them being together, she would sacrifice all for him.

Despite her tiredness, she smiled as she stubbed out her cigarette. They would be going soon, too, if she had her way. The only thing more appealing to her than being with her man was the prospect of creating a new life, or two.

She started to turn back inside the clinic to her patients but a low thumping noise, the beat of an engine, made her look up.

5

Mike had to suffer a smug look from Jake and a stony silence on the five-hour drive north back over the shocking road.

'You're lucky you showed up when you did,' Jake said as they drove. 'The South Africans probably would have got the PRMs to issue a warrant for your arrest.'

Jake was lucky, Mike felt like telling him, that he had shown up. The American would have had egg all over his face trying to explain to the South African cops why their star witness, and his subordinate, had gone AWOL. The two men were even, for the time being, but Mike noticed there were no beers in the cold box this time.

'I suppose you'll want a lift back to the airport when we're finished?' Jake said.

'With any luck I'll be making my own way back. Just drop me at Mapai when we finish in the bush.' Mike had no idea if Jake now knew all about Isabella and him, and he had no wish to explain their relationship

100

or why he was travelling halfway across Mozambique in search of her.

As they turned off the main road and juddered their way along the corrugated dirt track that led towards the spot where Carlos had died, Mike's mouth became dry and he found he was swallowing repeatedly. He liberated a Coke from Jake's cold box.

There were two vehicles waiting for them at the head of the pathway, a white South African Police Land Rover and a tan-coloured South African National Parks Land Cruiser pick-up truck, a *bakkie*, as they are called in Afrikaans.

Four men – two African, two white – were comparing notes on a sheaf of papers spread across the bonnets of their respective vehicles. They all looked up as the UN vehicle pulled to a halt, showering them in a cloud of fine dust. None of them seemed to mind. These were all tough guys by the look of them, Mike thought. Introductions were made and the pecking order for the rest of the stifling afternoon established.

'Milton Tambo, officer in charge of poaching investigations,' the short man in National Parks khaki introduced himself.

Mike thought he looked like a Xhosa, a member of the ruling tribe of South Africa.

'This is Gareth Hornby,' Tambo said, introducing a much taller and younger dark-haired man with tanned arms and legs protruding from an olive drab bush uniform, the type worn by rangers in the field.

Hornby rested a large-bore bolt-action hunting rifle on his left shoulder, holding the barrel with his left hand as he shook hands with Mike. 'Ranger,' he said.

'Captain Fanie Theron, Animal Protection Unit, and this is my driver, Sergeant Ndlovhu.' Theron pronounced his first name as *funny*.

He looked like any other detective Mike had seen in any other police force around the world. He reckoned the cop was about his age, late thirties, with big arms, thick neck, beer belly and a red-veined drinker's nose. Mike liked him at first sight. His 'driver' was a big-boned, bald Zulu, aged somewhere between twenty-five and fifty-five.

'Good afternoon,' Sergeant Ndlovhu said.

Tambo led off, asserting his authority from the outset. 'It's good of you to join us, Major Williams. As the only eyewitness to this terrible chain of events, we very much wanted to meet you.'

Major Williams. Mike wasn't in uniform. He'd dressed in tan chinos, hiking boots and a navy polo shirt for his failed rendezvous with Isabella. He wondered what it would be like to be a civilian again after nearly twenty years in the military. The sun stung his bare arms and sweat beaded his forehead.

'No trouble,' Mike lied. He had no wish to be there in the bush again. He looked at his watch and wondered whether Isabella was still at the clinic and if he would ever get there.

'Shall we, Gareth?' Tambo said, indicating to Hornby to take the lead as the group headed up the track.

'There are still mines out there, past the end of the tape,' Mike said to Hornby.

Jake interrupted. 'Sven and his team have been here all weekend, under the watchful eye of the Mozambican police and Captain Theron, clearing mines without disturbing a crime scene. Not an easy task, I assure you,' he explained for the benefit of everyone. The men carried on walking, National Parks leading, with the police duo content to bring up the rear.

A crater the size of a large washing bowl showed where Carlos had died. Everyone stopped, silent for a moment. The line of white tape had been repaired where Mike had broken through it with the Nissan, and the cleared path now extended much farther into the bush. 'This is the place,' Mike said.

Beyond the crater, Tambo pointed out the distinctive oval-shaped tracks of the elephant, showing where it had stopped short of the blast that killed Carlos. 'And you,' said Theron in his heavily accented English, causing Mike to turn back towards him, 'were about here, crouching, when you fired the AK at the elephant, *ja*?' He knelt in the same spot where Mike had been, raising two arms in pantomime of a man firing a rifle. 'Bang-click, eh!' He smiled.

Despite himself, Mike smiled too. Theron had a way of relaxing people and lightening the mood around him. One of his interview techniques, Mike guessed.

'Yes, how can you tell?' Mike asked.

Theron raised his considerable bulk and brushed the dust from the knees of his faded jeans. He was in mufti, wearing hiking boots, jeans, and a polo shirt souvenir of the 1999 Rugby World Cup. On his leather belt was a Glock nine-millimetre automatic pistol in a clip-on holster. Sergeant Ndlovhu wore a blue police field uniform with matching peaked cap and an automatic pistol in a flapped canvas holster.

Theron, who missed little, noticed Mike looking at his shirt. 'You Aussies won this one,' he said, stabbing the World Cup emblem on his chest, 'but you nearly lost this one, eh?' he added with a chuckle, pointing a finger down the track. 'We found the spent casing from the AK round you fired – the Mozambicans missed it.' He shook his head in disgust. 'We dug the lead out of the elephant's skull. From the entry wound in the skull I could tell you must have been down low. You didn't expect to kill him with a front-on head shot from one of those popguns, did you?'

Mike shrugged, but Theron had centre stage now and seemed reluctant to take a bow.

'They would have taught you how to bring down an elephant at your field guide school, would they not?' he asked Mike, as he fished a hand-rolled cigarette from a small leather pouch on his belt and lit it with a match.

Mike remained silent, impressed and a little scared by how much the South African Police seemed to know about him. Jake shot Mike a questioning look, which Theron also noticed.

'Sorry, Major Williams, maybe Colonel Carlisle didn't know you were a registered field guide, a safari guide, in South Africa?'

'No, I did not,' Jake confirmed, staring at Mike.

'We have computers in South Africa, too, Major. You would be surprised what we have in South Africa.'

'Am I being charged with something here?' Mike asked.

'No, don't worry. I don't think you were indulging in some freelance hunting – the death of the ranger, and your poor comrade, and the fact that you probably knew you couldn't kill it with the shot you took, make that obvious,' the South African said. 'It's just that we,' he gestured to include the National Parks officers as well, 'don't like people taking shots at our national treasures, like Skukuza, for whatever reason.'

'The bull was trying to kill me, and besides, I think it had already taken a serious hit from the same rifle that killed Fernando,' Mike said in his defence.

'Correct on all counts, Major.' Theron smiled as he exhaled tobacco smoke.

'What's a Skukuza?' Jake asked.

Milton Tambo spoke, obviously keen not to be left out. 'Skukuza means "he who sweeps clean". It was a name given by African people to the first game warden in the Kruger park, Colonel James Stevenson-Hamilton, for his efforts at wiping out poaching in the park. Skukuza is the name of the park's headquarters and largest rest camp and it was also given to this elephant, because of the way his long tusks and trunk used to drag in the dirt, sweeping aside sticks and leaves.'

Mike had seen an exhibition on Kruger's so-called 'magnificent seven' elephants during a visit to the elephant museum in the park's Letaba Camp. The seven, and presumably Skukuza was one of them, were big beasts aged in their sixties who had survived years of threats from poachers and other big bulls and were easily identified by their enormous ivory. The lesson ended, the group continued walking along the track.

After thirty metres or so, Hornby turned right and led them off the track into the dense mopani bush, following a path that had also been cleared of mines and taped. He hefted the rifle from his shoulder, cocked the bolt and fired a shot into the air. Jake gave a start, then looked around to make sure no one had seen him jump. Mike smiled at Jake and brushed irritating little mopani flies from his eyes and ears.

The air filled with the thump and swoosh of beating wings and they looked up to see at least a dozen white-backed vultures rising reluctantly into the air. Hornby chambered another round and fired into the air again, sending a further half-dozen of the scavengers aloft. The wind direction changed perceptibly and now Mike could smell old Skukuza. He would sweep no more.

The elephant lay in a small clearing, on his side, and Mike could not equate the ragged, stinking lump of meat with the mighty beast that had so very nearly taken his life. He looked smaller than Mike remembered him, as if the poachers and the hyenas and the vultures had stolen more than his tusks and his innards. There was a large hole in his now bloated belly where hyenas had taken the shortest route to his huge organs, and dried blood crusted around the two ragged holes where his giant tusks had been.

Oblivious of the stench, Theron climbed up onto the carcass, near Skukuza's shoulder, using the beast's protruding backbone as a foothold. He leaned across the massive cranium and put his finger inside a small hole in the centre of the forehead.

'This is the major's shot. Right between the eyes,' Theron said, for the benefit of the rest of the group. He shifted on one knee and pointed next to a puckered black hole above the point where the left front leg joined the body. 'This is the entry wound of the shot that killed him.'

'Can you tell the calibre of the weapon?' Jake asked.

'If we were in South Africa we'd carry out an autopsy. But by the time we found a qualified vet in this country, there would be nothing left of this old chap but bone. No, I can't tell you exactly what calibre, but I can tell you what I think – this was the work of a white man. Maybe two.'

'On what do you base that supposition?' Tambo, the senior National Parks man, asked. His tone betrayed a hint of annoyance that a government official of the new South Africa should be making presumptions based on race.

'This is a large-calibre weapon, Mr Tambo, a hunting rifle. These weapons are out of the economic reach of most poachers from this part of the world. He, or they, had helpers, of course, foot soldiers to cut out the ivory and carry it away, armed with AK-47s. Major Williams claims he heard a Kalashnikov firing. Isn't that right, Major?'

'Yes,' Mike confirmed.

'Your *African* poacher,' by which it was plain to Mike that Theron meant a black poacher, 'kills by pouring twenty or thirty rounds from his AK-47 into the animal's guts, not by a single, well-aimed shot like this one, which is too risky. A *hunter*, as opposed to a poacher, will try to bring an animal down with one shot. Major Williams tells us he heard one shot before the elephant charged. The Kalashnikov Major Williams heard later was probably the hunter's helpers putting a few rounds into the elephant's belly as they approached him, wanting to make sure he was dead before they started on the ivory. Those bullets are probably in some hyena's belly by now. The Mozambican police dug the slug that killed the ranger out of a tree, but they haven't got a result yet. Even if they do identify it, it will be a long time before they get around to telling us what type of weapon it was.'

'What about tracks?' Mike asked.

'That is our nice little puzzle, which we were discussing when you arrived. See if you come to the same conclusions we did. Sergeant Ndlovhu will explain,' said Theron, nodding to the black policeman who now stepped forward to address the group.

'We found two sets of footprints only. One was a man wearing cheap *veldtskoen*,' he said, referring to the lightweight, ankle-high suede leather boots favoured by many men of the bush in this part of the world. 'The other was wearing sandals made from old car tyres. We think this was the tracker – somebody local who knew the area well enough to avoid the minefields. I backtracked these two men's spoor into the bush for a while, but then was advised to stop because of the landmines. The tracks finish here, where they climbed up on the elephant to cut the ivory. You can see the scuff mark, here, and another mark where one man slipped on some blood. But the spoor stops here. They did not walk back into the bush.'

Puzzling, all right, thought Mike. He peered down at the spoor – a tracker's term for the footprints of man or beast – the sergeant had been referring to, but they were hard to read. 'I'm no tracker, Sergeant, but these look older than a couple of days to me.' The tracks were little more than faint indentations. There had been no rain to wash them away and Mike wondered why the spoor was so nearly obliterated.

'Ah, yes. But there has been much wind here, I think,' the sergeant said, smiling again.

Mike didn't recall it being windy on the day Carlos died. Like today, the stillness and heat were oppressive. He wiped a hand through his hair, and it came away damp with sweat.

'Let us see, Major, how good your powers of deduction are,' Theron said, sliding down the elephant's back on his bottom. He dusted off his jeans as he walked towards the group, lighting another cigarette in the process.

Mike thought for a moment then asked a couple more questions. The sergeant confirmed that there was only one set of tracks for each of the two men he identified – that is, they arrived at the carcass, chopped out the ivory and then vanished.

'Those tusks must have weighed hundreds of kilos,' Mike said, thinking out loud. 'Drag marks?' he said to the sergeant.

Ndlovhu shook his head.

'Was the ivory stacked somewhere for any length of time?'

The sergeant pointed to the top of the carcass, where Theron had been standing a few minutes before. 'There are a couple of patches of dried blood and some scratches on his hide where the tips of the tusks were dragged. They pulled the tusks up onto his back and stood up there for a while.'

Odd, Mike thought, but then he remembered what the sergeant had said about the tracks. Much wind. He looked up into the afternoon sky, shielding his eyes against the sun, which was now heading for the horizon.

'Helicopter,' Mike said.

Theron nodded. 'The question, of course, is who were they and where did they fly to?'

There was a blood-red smudged fingerprint on Jan Viljoen's aerial navigation chart on the spot next to the town of Mapai, which was accompanied on the map by a small cross in a circle, indicating a hospital or clinic in or near the town. Viljoen was using the main dirt road and the parallel railway line that led to Maputo as a navigational aid, and saw the red cross on the tin-roofed building before his passengers did. He swivelled in his seat. 'Hess!' he yelled.

The Namibian crouched in the cargo compartment now with his blood-soaked fingers pressed against the Russian's neck once again, checking his pulse. The man who was paying all their bills had turned a ghostly white.

Having got the hunter's attention, Viljoen pointed down at the building. Hess nodded, then leaned close to the pilot's ear. 'Do you have a tarpaulin or some other cover for the helicopter?' he shouted.

'*Ja*, there's a small one to cover the windscreen to keep dew and frost off overnight. It's under the troopseats,' Viljoen yelled.

Hess rummaged under the seat, between the unconscious Russian's legs, and found the folded square of green canvas. He steadied himself against the padded bulkhead and tossed the canvas to Klaus, then he leaned closer to the African and said, 'Cover the ivory as best as you can. Stay here and guard it, but keep your weapon out of sight.'

Hess unzipped Orlov's Russian camouflage smock and, with difficulty, removed it from the unconscious man. He stuffed the jacket under the seat. He wanted to arouse as little suspicion as possible.

From the clinic doorway Isabella could see the helicopter now, coming in low and fast over the trees like a gigantic dragonfly. What I could have done with that ten hours ago, she thought.

The machine slowed and reared up on its tail as it approached the square between the mission buildings. Isabella held up her forearm to her face as the stinging dust struck her and the wash from the rotor snatched the cigarette from her fingers. The fools would be spraying the patients with grit. She had left the louvres on the clinic windows open as there was not a breath of wind that morning.

As the helicopter touched down, the rotors began to slow and the dust storm abated. Isabella angrily

111

started to stride across to the chopper. This was a clinic, damn it, not an airport, she would tell them. She was checked by the sight of a tall blond man – unusually handsome, was her first thought – lifting an older, heavier man with a moustache down from one of the helicopter's seats. The older man, both men in fact, were covered in blood. Isabella forgot her anger, doubled over to clear the spinning rotor blades, and ran to the helicopter to help them.

'Gosh, ma'am, are we all glad to see you,' the tall blond man called above the noise of the dying engine, his accent a thick American drawl. Hess had noted Isabella's olive complexion and guessed that she was a 'Porc', South African slang for Portuguese.

'What has happened?' she asked in English. The two gardeners, who had been resting in the shade of the clinic, came rushing out with a stretcher.

'Hunting accident, ma'am. My friend here, he accidentally shot himself in the leg. Sounds stupid, I know, but it happens. It's his calf. He might have a fractured shinbone. He sure is in some pain.' Hess hoped that by appearing as guileless as possible he would throw the woman off-balance and avoid too many probing questions. They lifted Orlov onto the stretcher, and Isabella checked his pupils and pulse as she and Hess trotted alongside the litter.

'Why didn't you fly him to Maputo? There isn't even a doctor here normally,' she said, annoyance at the men's stupidity hardening her voice. Boys with guns, when would they ever learn?

'Well, that was our plan, but then we passed over-head and saw your red cross, and decided to chance it.

112

My buddy here, he didn't look too good and I didn't know if he'd last much longer,' Hess said, a little too rapidly.

'Well you were probably right about that,' Isabella said, pushing open the swinging screen door of the clinic with her back. There was something odd about what the man had just said, but she didn't have the time to stop and analyse it. The gardeners carried the unconscious Orlov past the row of beds in the main room of the clinic and then into the small treatment room at the end of the building. There they placed the stretcher on a surgical bed and stepped back. Isabella thanked them and said they could go. 'And it would be better if you left us now, too, Mr . . . ?'

'Schultz, George Schultz, ma'am. But, I sure would like to be here when my buddy comes to. He'll be very confused.' Hess wanted to be there to urge Orlov to silence when he regained consciousness. If the man started babbling in Russian, it would be one more oddity he would have to explain away.

Isabella hurriedly washed her hands at the sink in the corner of the treatment room and pulled on two fresh pairs of rubber gloves. With the prevalence of AIDS in southern Africa she always double-gloved, just to be sure. 'Yes, well, Mr Schultz, I understand your concern for your friend, but unless you give us room to work, your friend may *never* come to. Please wait outside now, OK? You can sit on the step there.'

Hess nodded. It was clear the woman knew what she was doing and a black woman was scrubbing her hands in the sink, preparing to help the female doctor. Hess had to hope Orlov stayed quiet until he

113

could get to him first. The doctor was filling a syringe from a small glass bottle, presumably an anaesthetic. His main problem now would be getting Orlov away from the clinic before the woman began to ask too many difficult questions.

'Well, if you're sure I can't be of assistance, Doctor, I'll just wait outside,' he said in his thick phoney accent.

Isabella cut away the bloodstained field dressing and surveyed the wound. 'It's a mess,' she said in Portuguese to the nun. 'Compartment syndrome – the blood is trapped in the leg. We'll have to cut him. Shit . . . Sorry, Sister.'

Sergeant Jose Mpofu shook his head and licked the tip of his pencil. He began writing in his ponderous hand in the police-issue notebook. This would be a long report. A lot of paperwork, he sighed.

Every now and then there was the screech and clang of twisted metal being wrenched as the two mechanics struggled and sweated at the work of levering apart the prime mover and the bus. The bodies of the two drivers, or what was left of them, were still enmeshed in the glass and steel and plastic of their vehicles, and it would probably be nightfall before they were freed.

Already the sun was low on the horizon. The sergeant didn't have a watch, but he guessed the time to be close to five. He had hoped to get to the mission clinic just up the road before dark to interview the last of the surviving passengers, but his orders were to stay at the scene of the accident until the remaining bodies, those of the drivers, were retrieved. He didn't want to be too late home. There had been a basket of live chickens tied with the other luggage on the roof of the bus but, sadly, it appeared the four chickens had suffered broken necks as a result of the accident. As their owner had not come forward to claim them (probably because he or she was now dead), Sergeant Mpofu had decided to take the bodies of the birds into protective custody. His wife would be pleased, for once.

The sun was setting by the time Isabella again emerged from the clinic. She was tired and she stank, and she was looking forward to a bath.

The tall blond American – Mr Schultz, she recalled after a moment's thought – was walking towards her across the square. He had been talking to his African friend, who stood by the helicopter along with the machine's Caucasian pilot, whom Isabella had still not met. The man was sitting in the open cargo door of the helicopter smoking a cigarette. Isabella wondered why they weren't all crowding her for news.

She studied the American as she lit a cigarette of her own. She guessed him to be in his mid to late forties, but his muscled arms and broad shoulders showed he exercised regularly and there did not seem to be a gram of fat on his big frame. There was something not quite right about him, though. Something cold, maybe something false. It is in the eyes, she thought, as he approached. She looked into them and saw no emotion, no concern, even as he mouthed the words.

'How's my buddy, Doctor? We've been worried sick about him. Is he gonna pull through?'

'Yes. It was difficult. It was the artery, but I have repaired that now. He lost a lot of blood. You must let him rest here tonight, at least. If you move him now and the wound reopens, he may bleed to death.'

Hess frowned. This was not what he wanted to hear. He had hoped to be on his way at dusk, and to cross the border in darkness. The longer they stayed at the mission, the greater the risk of their being discovered for what they were.

'You're sure, Doc? Only, I've been thinking about what you said earlier today. Maybe we should fly him to Maputo tonight. No offence, but maybe he'd be better off in a bigger hospital now?'

'None taken, Mr Schultz,' Isabella said. 'But, no, the best thing for your friend now is to rest. If you wish, you can send your helicopter to Maputo to the hospital and pick up some more blood, plasma and dressings for us and then you can move him when he regains consciousness tomorrow.'

Hess did not want the helicopter out of his sight. It was their only means of escape.

'I'm taking our friend now, Doctor,' Hess said, stepping around Isabella as he started for the clinic.

Isabella reached out and grabbed the man's upper arm. Anger flared in her eyes. 'I saved his life, Mr Schultz, but you might kill him if you move him now!'

Hess checked his pace. He took a deep breath and

116

forced himself to stay calm and not drop his disguised accent. 'He can't stay here. He needs to get to a proper hospital. We're leaving.'

'And if he starts to bleed again? If he needs a transfusion in the aircraft, can you or your colleagues do that?'

Hess frowned. He had started intravenous drips on combat casualties in his time, but he knew nothing about blood transfusions.

'The other factor to consider is that I have precious little blood here, certainly none that I would let you take away if you left now. If your friend does need a transfusion, I may have to take the blood straight from you or one of your men.'

He looked into her eyes. The woman was not exaggerating. 'OK, Doc,' he said, forcing a smile. 'You win. We'll stay the night. We'll leave in the morning, if our friend is well enough to move, and I'll bring you back some more supplies tomorrow after we've dropped him at Maputo,' he lied. 'That's the least we can do.'

'Very well, Mr Schultz. Now, I need to get some details. Your friend's name, nationality, passport number. All your details as well. I'm sure you'll appreciate this continent's love of paperwork, and it is even worse for us poor doctors.' Now it was Isabella's turn to lie. This was a non-government clinic, dispensing health care to anyone who needed it. There were no records to be kept or papers to fill out – that was one of the reasons she liked working there. However, she wondered what reaction her questions would provoke from the American.

'Sure. Happy to help, ma'am. But if you don't mind me saying, you look as if you're about to fall asleep on your feet. I'm sure we'll have time for all this in the morning and I want to make sure my boys,' he jerked a thumb towards Klaus, Viljoen and the Mozambican tracker, 'are squared away with some chow and a bed before it's too dark.'

Isabella nodded, concerned by his blatant evasiveness. 'Tomorrow will be fine. I will tell the mission cooks to put on some extra food for you and your men. It will not be a gourmet feast, but it will be filling.'

'We've got rations on board the chopper, ma'am. Don't bother, please.'

'No, it is no trouble at all,' she said. 'Come to the house over there around seven. OK? Now, if you'll excuse me, I must go and freshen up.' Before she headed for the cottage, though, she went in search of Joseph, the nightwatchman.

'So, what were you hunting?' Isabella asked later, as she ladled goat's meat stew into four enamelled bowls. The nuns were eating by themselves, as they usually did, leaving Isabella with the American, his African assistant and the helicopter pilot.

Hess had introduced Klaus and Viljoen under false names and told Isabella that the fourth member of their party, the Mozambican tracker, had hitched a lift to Mapai to visit relatives. In truth, Hess had paid the man his promised sum and told him to disappear. The man was no longer of any use to him.

He had tried to leave Klaus at the helicopter, to

guard the ivory, while the rest of them ate, but the doctor had been insistent that the African join them for dinner and reassured him that no one would approach the aircraft. He realised that if he had pushed the point he would probably arouse her curiosity.

'Buffalo. At least, we were trying to hunt buffalo,' Hess lied, then tasted the stew. It was bland and oily, but Hess didn't care. To a soldier, food was nothing more than fuel for the body.

'Surely you don't need a helicopter to shoot buffalo?' she asked, smiling.

'Well, our friend, Mr Jankowski,' Hess had described Orlov as a wealthy Polish immigrant businessman who now lived in the United States, 'is not short of cash. We've been staying on the coast, near Beira, doing some diving as well, and the chopper makes it easy for us to get around and do everything in a short period of time.'

'Looks like you were rushing things a little too much,' she chided.

Hess laughed, but secretly bridled at the woman's insolence. He would dearly have loved to teach her a lesson in respect. 'You've been most kind, but Frank here,' he said pointing to Viljoen with a fork, 'gets kinda nervous if he's away from his chopper for too long, and Luke,' Hess nodded to Klaus, 'has offered to help him check the rotor blades. In fact, we all need to turn in. It's been a big day.'

Isabella nodded. Clearly her questioning was making the men nervous and they had stayed with her the bare minimum amount of time. She hoped Joseph had had time to follow her instructions. 'You're sure we can't fix you a bed in the storeroom?'

'No, but thanks again, Doctor. We'll sleep in the helicopter. It won't be the first time.'

'Very well, gentlemen. Goodnight.'

Soon after the men departed, Isabella answered a soft knock on the back door of Father Patrick's cottage. Joseph, the nightwatchman, dressed in green overalls with his aged shotgun slung over one shoulder, greeted her in Portuguese.

'Ivory, Doctor,' the nightwatchman said. He had followed her directions, and sneaked through the bush around the mission station and come in behind the nuns' cottage, where he could approach the parked helicopter unseen while the hunters were dining with Isabella. With the cargo doors removed, there was nothing stopping him from examining the interior of the machine. Joseph had smelled elephant as soon as he stuck his balaclava-clad head into the strange machine. Under a green tarpaulin were two of the biggest tusks he had ever seen in his life. Although he didn't tell the doctor how he knew, he had a good idea how much money tusks such as these would fetch.

Isabella took a deep breath when he told her the amount, knowing the end value of the ivory, wherever it was destined for, would be many times the sum a Mozambican poacher could expect to earn. She debated the merits of sending Joseph into Mapai immediately to fetch the police. However, she didn't know if the police station would be manned at that hour and, besides, she would feel safer if she had an armed guard of her own at the mission during the night.

'Tomorrow, Joseph, first thing you go to Mapai. Fetch the police. Tell them what you have seen. I will keep these men here until the police arrive. Understand?'

Joseph nodded.

Sergeant Mpofu was up early. His belly gurgled pleasingly every now and then. The unclaimed chickens would never be claimed now.

The sun was coming up in front of him as he cycled up the long dirt driveway to the mission. He wanted to get this business at the mission over with as quickly as possible. Some of the other officers from the station were taking a trip into Maputo later in the day and the sergeant did not want to miss his lift. It should have been his day off, but the bus accident had ruined all their rosters and he still had to interview the surviving passengers. The cocking handle of the AK-47 slung across his back dug painfully into his kidneys every time his old cycle hit a bump, and there were many bumps on this road.

Isabella was awake early as well and had just finished repeating her instructions to Joseph for the third time, when she saw the portly police sergeant cycling up to the mission clinic. Relief flooded through her, calming her jumpy nerves. Joseph was loyal and hardworking, but she doubted he would be able to convey the seriousness of the situation to the police on his own.

Karl Hess had slept on the cargo floor of the helicopter in his sleeping bag, sandwiched between the plundered ivory and Viljoen. Klaus sat on the ground with his back resting uncomfortably against one of the upright supports of the helicopter skids. His AK-47 rested on his lap, but was hidden by the coarse woollen blanket draped across his knees.

Hess checked his watch. Six o'clock. With luck they would be across the border and safely ensconced at the lodge before nine.

'*Baas!*' Klaus hissed.

Hess looked up and swore when he saw the policeman. He sat up, unzipped his sleeping bag and then reached into the rucksack he had been using as a pillow. Using his back as a shield to the fast approaching policeman, he pulled out a Glock automatic pistol and thrust it into the waistband of the trousers he had slept in. He swung his long legs out of the chopper, at the same time digging Viljoen in the ribs with an elbow. 'Wake up. Be ready to start this thing in ten minutes, or on my signal.'

Viljoen rubbed his eyes and started to protest, but then held his tongue when he saw the uniformed man dismounting from his bicycle a scant fifty metres away. Hess strode across the square and arrived at the policeman's side at the exact same moment as Isabella.

Sergeant Mpofu recognised the doctor. How could he not? He fancied himself a ladies' man and, though he did not remember his former colonial masters with anything other than hatred and contempt, he knew a beautiful woman when he saw one, and acted accordingly.

'Good morning, Doctor, and how are you this fine day?' he asked, smiling, in Portuguese.

Isabella flashed him her warmest smile and replied, in her native tongue, 'Sergeant, say nothing and do nothing to alarm this man. He is a criminal and he and his men are armed.'

The smile fell from the sergeant's face for a second until he regained his composure.

'Good morning, officer. Schultz is my name. Do you speak English?' Hess butted in, delivering his lines in his thick American drawl.

The sergeant looked at Isabella. He had no idea what the tall white man had just said.

Isabella filled the awkward silence that followed. 'I'm sorry, Mr Schultz, the sergeant speaks no English. Perhaps I can translate for you both?'

Hess nodded warily, and launched into his story about a hunting accident. To Isabella, he asked, 'How is our friend doing? I'm getting really worried about him and I think we should move him to Maputo as quickly as possible.'

'A moment, please. Allow me to translate for the sergeant,' Isabella said, desperate to buy time and not let the American bully her. To the policeman, she said, 'He thinks I'm translating for him. There is ivory in the helicopter. They are poachers and one of them has been shot. He is in the clinic. You must arrest them now!'

Sergeant Mpofu was overwhelmed by the information the woman had just told him. If it was true, the arrest would be the highlight of his career. Promotion and a posting to Maputo. Alternatively, he wondered how much the ivory would be worth on the black market, his mind exploring all possible avenues. First, he decided, he needed to inspect the helicopter to verify the woman's claims. 'Tell him I want to have a look at the helicopter,' he said to the doctor.

'No! He will be suspicious. Why don't you just arrest him now?' she replied testily, still in Portuguese.

Hess did not like the look on the woman's face as she spoke to the policeman, who was himself starting to look agitated. While the pair babbled away in their foreign tongue, Hess slowly reached around his back and felt for the Glock in his waistband.

Mpofu was not going to be dictated to by a woman, attractive or otherwise, and he pointed towards the helicopter, indicating to the white man that he should accompany him. As he did so, he began to unsling his assault rifle.

As fast as a striking cobra, Hess pulled the pistol from his waistband and rammed the short barrel into the policeman's temple. 'Tell him to lay down his rifle, slowly,' he hissed at Isabella, all trace of his American accent now gone. 'I'll trust you to at least get that sentence correct.'

She did as he asked, then added, in English, 'You won't get away!'

'Wanna bet?' he said with a smile, slipping back into the phoney drawl.

The tense silence was shattered by the boom of a shotgun. Isabella felt the whip of pellets slicing through the air, uncomfortably close to her shoulder. She spun around and saw Joseph, the nightwatchman, standing at the corner of the clinic. He had circled around the vignette unfolding in the square and timed his shot perfectly.

Hess flinched as a few lead pellets ripped through the fabric of his shirt and into his upper right arm. Although the wound was not serious, the force of the hit was enough to make him drop his pistol in the dust.

Joseph raised the ancient double-barrelled shotgun to his shoulder again and started walking towards the people in the courtyard.

'Joseph, look out!' Isabella cried, too late.

Klaus was on his feet now, the blanket falling to the ground as he raised his own weapon. He fired the AK-47 twice and the accurate hammer blows of the bullets punched Joseph backwards. Blood welled from the twin holes in his chest as he lay motionless in the dust.

Isabella dropped to her knees and reached for Hess's fallen pistol, but the hunter, still on his feet, kicked her hard in the stomach and she doubled up in agony. Hess heard the whine of turbine engines starting behind him, and knew he would live to fight again. The African policeman had instinctively dropped to the ground as the gunfire began, his rifle still awkwardly slung over his back. Now he writhed in the dust as he reached up over his shoulder for the barrel. Hess stooped, the movement almost leisurely, and retrieved his pistol. He raised it, took a step towards the struggling policeman, and shot him between the eyes.

'Enough killing! Stop it, damn you! Go. Just go,' Isabella cried between painful gasping breaths.

Klaus was at Hess's side now, awaiting orders. 'Kill

the other patients, Klaus. Oh, and them, too.' Hess pointed languidly with his pistol to the two nuns who were running across the square, heedless of their own safety. 'Take whatever valuables and drugs you can find. Make it look like a robbery.'

Tears started to well in Isabella's eyes as she thought about Mike. Where was he? She wanted him here, by her side, so badly. She raised herself up onto her knees and looked up into the pitiless blue eyes of the man standing above her. She hawked from the back of her throat with all her might and then spat, full into his face.

Jan Viljoen busied himself checking the dials and gauges of his instrument panel. The engines were coming up to full power as he glanced across at the square. From the clinic building he heard the sound of rifle fire, above the engine's roar. In the square he saw Hess standing over the kneeling form of the pretty female doctor. The Namibian had his arm out-stretched, his pistol centimetres from the woman's face.

Viljoen screwed his eyes tight, knowing what would happen next and not wanting to be a part of it. He flinched as he heard the single shot.

Theron and Sergeant Ndlovhu had to go to Mapai to pay a call on the local police commander there. Mike told them he needed to get to the town and Jake raised no objections when the policemen offered a lift. Theron wanted Mike to talk through his story once more. Mike and Jake shook hands, the briefest of farewells passing between them. The National Parks officers took copious photos of the now deceased national treasure and also left for Maputo.

As he walked to the police vehicle, Mike noticed a wide brown leather strap lying in the back of the National Parks *bakkie*.

'It will take us a good two or three hours to reach Mapai. We'll be lucky to make it by nightfall. Take the back seat and have a rest, Tobias,' Theron said to Sergeant Ndlovhu.

The detective climbed in behind the wheel of the Land Rover and opened the passenger door from the inside for Mike. As the vehicle moved off, Mike rolled down the window and lit a cigarette. It was good to clear the stench of rotting flesh from his nostrils.

'Did that collar in the back of the Parks truck come off the elephant?' he asked Theron.

'*Ja*. Those Parks *okes* are pretty embarrassed about it,' he said, using the common Afrikaans slang term for 'men'. 'That was a radio collar on the old boy. They monitor their locations regularly and he shouldn't have been allowed to get that far across the border.'

'Surely they do, though? There's no fence now to stop them from crossing into Mozambique and I thought that was the general idea, to let the animals go back to migrating across international borders.'

'Not for a special elephant like old Skukuza – they wouldn't let those tusks wander into Mozambique. The National Parks Board has helicopters and when they noticed him getting too close to the border they would have used their chopper to shepherd him back to safety.'

'So what happened this time?'

Theron took a long drag on his cigarette and swerved to miss a pothole. He did not answer straightaway and Mike had the feeling he was weighing up whether to confide in him or not.

'Sabotage. But keep that to yourself, eh?' he said, jabbing his cigarette in Mike's direction to emphasise his point. 'Their helicopter was down for two days before this hit, and it took them that long to work out it was no accident.'

'What makes you think there were two whites involved?' Mike asked.

'More, maybe, if you include their helicopter pilot. This was a hunting trip, not a bunch of ragtag Mozambican poachers. A big, expensive, illegal hunting trip. There are African helicopter pilots in Africa, and black professional hunters, but these are two areas where affirmative action has yet to make serious inroads,' he said with a wink.

'Go on,' Mike urged him.

'OK. You get a helicopter, you charter it, maybe even buy it – I don't know for sure. Your helicopter pilot tells you how you can sabotage the National Parks helicopter and you buy someone to do that for you. You take your helicopter and you use it to drive one of the biggest elephants left in Africa across the border, away from where he is protected by men with guns, into a godforsaken part of one of the world's poorest countries, where you know you won't find any police or rangers for hundreds of kilometres. You shoot your elephant, or try and shoot it, but you stumble on to some people who shouldn't be there – you,' he said, nodding to Mike. 'One of them points a rifle at you so you kill him. You don't want any witnesses. You kill your elephant, your blacks cut out the ivory and you hover over the dead elephant while they load in the ivory. Then they climb aboard.'

'Sounds expensive,' Mike said.

'It is. More than even those tusks are worth. Assuming you could find a buyer.'

'Why not shoot the elephant from the helicopter and be done with it?' Mike asked. He lurched forward and grabbed the dashboard as Theron geared down suddenly and swerved to miss a fallen branch that had partially blocked the road.

'This comes back to my theory, that this is a hunt. For a trophy – a bloody big trophy, man. It's not about money, it's about men on foot tracking big game – with some help from a helicopter, of course. Have you ever hunted, Major?'

'Call me Mike. No. I've seen enough killing in my time.'

Theron nodded. 'Me too. But I used to hunt when I was a boy, with my father. Small buck, impala mostly, but there was nothing like that thrill. Primitive, you know.'

'Why *two* white men, plus maybe the helicopter pilot?'

'The professional hunter and his rich client. In this case, the very rich client.'

'American?' Mike guessed.

'Maybe. Or German, or Italian.'

'But you've got your suspicions about the hunter. You think you know who he is?'

'Ah, now that would be wrong of me to accuse a

man without any proof. Let us just say that we know of a few hunters who have bent the rules from time to time, yes?'

Bending the rules. Letting a client shoot a couple more buffalo or kudu than their permit allowed them was one thing, but to chase a protected animal out of a national park across an international border, kill it and murder a Mozambican ranger in the process was not bending the rules – that was obliterating them. Mike wondered briefly what sort of man would pay so much for the pleasure of killing one creature, but gave up. He had stopped really trying to fathom mankind after Rwanda. They left the theories there and filled the rest of the bumpy road trip with the stories of their lives.

'I also was in the army. I was in Angola, but I had enough after that. Mind you, I've seen more than my share of action in the police since then.'

Theron explained that his love of wildlife and the bush had led him to the Animal Protection Unit. The unit was high profile, and specialised in infiltrating and busting poaching and smuggling rings.

'Must be pretty nerve-racking, working under cover,' Mike suggested.

'Sometimes. We pose as sellers or buyers of wildlife. On one trip I went to the Netherlands. We were targeting a ring that was smuggling reptiles from South Africa to Europe. I was supposed to be a snake collector and I hate the goddamned things! I actually had to hold a rock python and pretend I was in love with it. Man, I nearly shit myself!' His whole body shook as he laughed out loud. 'So, why am I taking you to Mapai, to a clinic in this godforsaken part of the country?' he asked.

Mike told him about Isabella.

'Sounds like you're serious about her?' Theron ventured.

'It's looking that way.'

'Good for you, man,' he said. 'I'm married. Three teenage daughters. You can't beat a family – they'll lock you up if you do!' He laughed again.

From Isabella's description of the clinic Mike knew that it was part of a mission station, run by a Catholic priest, a kilometre before Mapai on the road they were travelling. He checked the map and gave Theron the directions, telling him to look out for a right turn.

'Jesus, what a mess,' Theron said, pointing to the side of the road.

An ancient bus was interlocked with the prime mover of a long-distance lorry. The trailer was nowhere to be seen. The two vehicles were meshed as one, obviously having hit head on at some considerable speed. Most of the bus's windows had either shattered on impact, or been smashed so that survivors could be extracted. The faded blue sides were now painted dark brown with streaks of dried blood.

'Isabella was held up here because of this bus accident.' Mike wondered if by tomorrow he would be describing Isabella as his fiancée.

As they neared the town, the bush was thinning out, felled for building and cooking fires by the residents of the unseen settlement ahead of them. When they crested a small rise, Mike looked across to his left and saw the setting sun was the colour of blood.

131

6

'Theron needs to speak to you.'

The policeman's name reverberated around Mike's head as he drove through the gates of the Punda Maria rest camp in the north of Kruger National Park and stopped the yellow overland truck in the camping ground.

Jane Muir leaned into the front cab of the truck from her seat behind him. 'Are you OK?' she asked, placing a hand on his forearm. 'You look a little pale, and you've been very quiet since you took that call. Do you want to talk?'

Sarah, the journalist, gave the pair a brief glance, then opened her door on the passenger side of the cab and climbed out.

'Sure. Later. We've got to get dinner on soon, though. I have got to go to the bathroom. Back in five,' he said. Mike walked across to the thatch-roofed ablution block. Inside, he stopped at one of the sinks and turned on the cold tap. He splashed water on his face and stared at his reflection. Long hair, stubbled cheeks flanking his goatee beard, face a little fuller. His old friends from the army wouldn't recognise him now.

He was desperate to know what Theron had found out – why he wanted to meet him after nearly a year had gone by. At the same time, he dreaded the meeting.

Punda Maria was higher, altitude-wise, than any other camp in the Kruger park, cooler and wetter than the bushveldt and grasslands to the south. As night encroached, the temperature dropped and he felt goosebumps on his bare arms. A chill coursed through his body as he recalled the drive to Mapai with Fanie Theron.

They were met by a policeman at the gate to the mission. A nervy, jumpy policeman who kept his right hand on the pistol grip of his rifle. Sergeant Ndlovhu tried a few words of Tswana, the common African patois that originated in the gold and diamond mines of southern Africa.

'He understands,' the sergeant said to Theron and Mike. 'Worked in Jo'burg for a few years. He says people have been killed here, including a policeman.'

'In the bus accident?' Mike asked.

The sergeant and his Mozambican counterpart exchanged a few words. Ndlovhu looked at Theron, then at Mike. 'No. Something else.'

Mike's heart beat faster. 'What does that mean?'

'He says we should go up there, to the mission buildings. His superior is there. He speaks English.'

133

'Thank him, Tobias, and let's go have a look,' Theron said.

Mike had known Isabella was dead as soon as they were stopped by the policeman at the mission gate. He knew it before they saw the bullet holes in the buildings, the bloodstained floor of the clinic, and the patch of sand in the mission square where Isabella had died.

They spoke to the PRM in charge of the investigation and the look on the officer's face confirmed Mike's fears as soon as they asked about the fate of the female doctor who had worked at the mission.

'You identify body?' the policeman asked Mike.

Hands clenched in rage and swallowing hard to keep from throwing up, Mike had wanted to hit someone. There was obviously not much scope for sympathy and condolences from someone for whom English was his third language.

The bodies had been taken to a butcher's shop in Mapai, the only place with a coldroom big enough to store them all. There was no morgue like the ones Mike had seen on television cop shows. No shiny white tiles, no body laid respectfully on a polished steel table, no crisp white sheet lowered just enough for a grieving relative to give a little nod from the other side of a window in an air-conditioned viewing room. Just Isabella, his Isabella, laid out on a trestle table in a refrigerated shipping container with a hole in the centre of her forehead. No smooth pale skin for him to lay a hand on, no white cheek to kiss farewell and complete the mourning process, just a mask of dried, flaking blood. He choked, staggered from the room and vomited in the street.

'Come with me, Mike,' Theron said, wrapping a meaty arm around Mike's shoulders.

Theron took him to the local police station, found a telephone and called the Portuguese embassy in Maputo, something the local police hadn't got around to doing.

'Spend the night here with us, Mike. We'll drop you back at Maputo tomorrow. There's nothing more we can do here.'

Numb and in shock, Mike accepted. 'Thanks, Fanie,' he said.

'I want to go back to the mission, see what else I can pick up,' Theron said, not minding they were both on a first-name basis. As well as sympathy for him, he felt a kind of kinship with the Australian soldier.

'I'll come with you,' Mike said.

'No. Tobias will stay here with you. You'll gain nothing by going back there, and I've got official police business. You'll do me a favour by staying out of the way.' His words sounded dismissive, but his eyes were kind.

'Come, I think you need a drink,' Sergeant Ndlovhu said.

They went to a *shebeen*, an African bar. Concrete floor, loud music and cheap booze. The sergeant stayed by Mike's side through long periods of silent staring, until the tears finally welled up from deep within him. Theron was there too, later in the night, when Mike wanted to get into a fight, and by his side when he was sick in the gutter. In the early hours of the morning the two policemen half carried him up the street to his cheap hotel.

'Sleep now. She is gone, but that does not mean you will ever forget her,' Ndlovhu said as they stared down at the unconscious form on the bed.

They left Mapai early, Theron driving. Breakfast was *pao* in the truck, plus a beer from the cold box for Mike to help ease the pain in his head.

'OK, tell me what you found at the mission yesterday,' he said.

'Those Mozambican clowns didn't want me there, man, I tell you. Said it was a robbery, simple as that. I told them what I had been doing, what had happened to you, Mike, but they couldn't see a connection,' he said, pausing to take a long pull from a can of Coke. Sergeant Ndlovhu snored in the back seat while his captain drove.

'Could you see a connection?' Mike asked. His head hurt, but his mind and heart were moving on from sorrow in another, more dangerous direction. Revenge.

'Well,' Theron said, weighing up how much he should tell the other man, 'there were some things that didn't add up.'

'Like?'

'Like the weapons used. The local boys found a lot of brass from an AK – in the clinic and near where they . . . where they shot the nuns.'

Mike could tell Theron was trying to spare his feelings, but he also sensed the detective needed to get his theory out in the open, to talk it through with someone. 'But not near where Isabella was shot?'

'No, not near her. Look, I understand if you don't want to talk about this . . .'

'It's OK. I want to know as much about the bastards who did this as you do. Probably more.'

'She wasn't shot with a Kalashnikov, Mike,' the policeman said.

'What then?' Mike asked. All he could remember was the ruined face, once so beautiful.

'I went back . . . to see her again. I checked the wound. It was a pistol shot, up close.'

'An execution?' Mike asked, closing his eyes at the thought.

'I've seen that type of wound before. Anyway, so I'm asking myself, who would rob that place, a church-run clinic? It doesn't make sense. I spoke to the priest – he was in a bad way. But he said they had hardly any drugs, no money. The injured bus passengers – they were the people killed in the clinic – had nothing but the clothes they were wearing. It doesn't make sense.' He shook his head.

'People kill for a lot less on this continent,' Mike said, playing devil's advocate.

'Ja, I know that, but people kill over here for another reason. To cover their tracks. You cross a border, you do something you shouldn't, meet some-one you shouldn't. You don't want any witnesses. Besides, there was more I saw there, before those local boys got rid of me.'

'What?'

'Two things. One, dust and sand in the clinic, and –'

'Have you ever seen a Mozambican hospital?' Mike

137

interrupted, remembering the less than sanitary conditions Isabella had worked in.

'This was a new building. The rest of it, the treatment room, the priest's house, were spotless. It looked like a big wind had blown dust in through the flywire windows, all over the bodies in the clinic. A big wind . . . you remember?'

Mike recalled the elephant's carcass, the wind-blown tracks. Had a helicopter landed at the mission station? 'Why would they have flown there?'

Theron swallowed hard. 'Mike, the other thing I found there, in the treatment room, was lying in the top of a dustbin. The local police wouldn't have recognised it, or known what to do about it. Besides, they hustled me out before I had a chance to tell them what I'd found.'

'What was it?'

'A field dressing. You know what a field dressing is?'

'I know,' Mike said, remembering the green-wrapped shell dressings they practised with in the army during first aid lessons. He had never had to use one for real until Carlos threw himself on the landmine.

'There was one in the dustbin. Lot of blood on it. It was a South African Defence Force dressing. I could tell by the written instructions printed on the back. There was only one and the priest told me that he didn't keep any ex-military first aid stuff at the clinic.'

'So one of the poachers was wounded,' Mike said, and the realisation of what that meant hit him like a fist square in the middle of his face. He felt as though he was going to throw up again. He wound down the

138

window, but the oven-hot African air did nothing to revive him.

'Don't blame yourself, Mike. You did the right thing and so did the doctor,' he said.

Theron's words could do nothing to calm the rising tide of anger, hurt and sorrow that threatened to blow Mike's mind and soul into a million pieces. He realised he had wounded one of the poachers with his wild burst of firing from Fernando's rifle. They had flown to the nearest clinic. Isabella had treated the injured man, and then they had killed her and everyone at the mission.

'I killed her,' Mike said softly.

Theron protested. 'It was someone else, Mike. A criminal pulled the trigger, not you. I won't stop until I've found these bastards. Believe me.'

Mike knew there was nothing more he could do or tell the police, and nothing more that Fanie Theron was allowed to do in Mozambique. He withdrew into himself for the rest of the trip.

They stopped at the Portuguese embassy at Maputo and an officious bureaucrat in a white suit told them that Dr Nunes's parents had been informed of the tragedy and were on their way to Maputo to collect her remains. Mike had no idea if Isabella had ever told her parents he existed, and he had no wish to make his introductions in these circumstances. Fanie offered him a lift to Johannesburg, and he accepted.

Theron dropped Mike at Rian and Susie's place the next day.

'If you ever need to get hold of me, these people

will know where I am,' Mike told Theron. 'Thank you, again, for everything.'

Theron wrote Rian's name and address in his notebook, then shook hands with Mike, holding his hand longer than custom dictated. 'Policemen aren't in the business of making promises, but I promise you we will find these men. As soon as I have a new lead I'll be in touch. Don't blame yourself, Mike.'

In the backyard of their fashionable Sandton home, the de Witts' three kids laughed and shrieked as they played in their swimming pool. Theron was going home to his family. Mike was going home to nothing.

Theron's words had sounded hollow. Mike doubted the police would find the murderers and, even if they did, no one would be able to identify them by sight. Mike prayed that somehow, somewhere, he would find them first.

Mike had flown back to Australia and completed the formalities of ending twenty years' service with the army. Funnily enough, he didn't find it an emotional experience. There were no old friends to farewell him, no party, no presentation. He signed the official forms at Victoria Barracks in Sydney, and handed in his pack, his webbing, uniforms, identity card – the chattels that had defined who he was for half his life.

He walked out through the big sandstone gates into noisy, exhaust-choked Oxford Street. He was alone and adrift, but in a sense he had been this way for many years, until Isabella, so it didn't feel too strange. There was nothing left for him in Australia – no job and no prospects.

A bell chimed as he opened the door of the travel agency, the first one he had come to after leaving the barracks.

'Good morning, how can I help you?' the woman behind the desk asked.

'I'd like a ticket to South Africa. One way. Leaving as soon as possible.'

He needed a new home, money and a job. Rian provided all of these. When Mike arrived back in Jo'burg, Rian was in trouble. He had just lost one of the regular drivers of his overland trucks – Piet, a white South African. Mike remembered him as a friendly, confident young man. Piet had evidently worked his charm on a female English passenger on a previous trip and he was now off to England to marry her, in a hurry. He had apparently broken Rian's cardinal rule that all drivers had to swear to obey, on pain of death and or dismissal.

'Rule number one: no sex with the tourists,' Rian said.

Piet was going to be a father in a few months, so even if Rian had decided to bend the cardinal rule and let him stay on in his job, the young man wouldn't have been able to take advantage of his reprieve.

'I'd do the next trip myself, except Susie would kill me,' Rian explained.

Rian, too, was going to become a father, yet again. Susie was heavily pregnant with their fourth child and was due to give birth the week after Mike's arrival. Rian's problem was that he had a group of twelve tourists arriving from all points of the globe in two days' time and, with Piet's sudden departure, no one to drive them on their overland adventure.

'My relief driver is on holidays in Zambia, and there's no way I can go. It'll be easy, Mike. It's a short trip. Jo'burg, Kruger, cross the border into Zimbabwe at Beitbridge, Bulawayo, Vic Falls, down the Caprivi Strip into Namibia, Etosha, then finish in Cape Town. You know the way, you're a qualified guide and you can drive a truck. What are you waiting for?'

'I'll give it a go,' Mike said.

Susie went into early labour the very next day, shortening Rian's briefing to Mike on the trip and Susie (the overland truck) to all of ten minutes. 'You'll find everything and get sorted as you go,' he said with a wave as he sped off to the hospital. All the camping sites along the route had been booked, which was one less thing for Mike to worry about, and he had a list of names and flight times for the arriving tourists. That was it.

He was straight from the army, still with a crewcut and a soldier's high expectations of planning and preparation for any endeavour. His first load of passengers was a shock to him and he supposed they felt the same way. He hadn't mixed with young people for quite some time, and those who he did meet were usually fresh out of recruit training with haircuts like his and no body jewellery. This lot were pierced and tattooed, tie-dyed and dreadlocked. He pretty soon worked out that he was not what they were expecting. Other overland tour trucks he saw on that first trip all seemed to be driven by tanned young men with long hair, sideburns, assorted bracelets and, at the very least, an earring. Mike had none of these.

He managed to collect them all from the airport, but that was where things stopped going to plan. The old Bedford overland truck broke down on the way to Kruger, on the first day. The clutch fluid pipe sprang a leak and they had to wait four hours in Witbank while a backyard mechanic made a new pipe. That's the good thing about African mechanics, he learned – if they don't have a part in stock they'll make one. The bad thing about tourists was, no matter how young, hip and laid-back they pretended to be, when it came to unexpected delays they tended to get mad with their tour guide.

When they finally made it into the national park, just on closing time, his passengers were surprised to learn that he had no idea where anything was and the tents, kitchen utensils and gas bottles all had to be searched for. Around the campfire, after a makeshift dinner of potatoes, tomatoes and bananas, he came clean and explained he was not the African Crocodile Dundee they had been led to believe would be guiding them through the dark continent. A couple of the Brits seethed and he later overheard them mumbling something about the amount of money they'd paid to be stuck with a learner driver, but most of the crew could see the position he was in and pitched in to help him find his way.

'Overlanding is like that,' he said as he recounted the story to his second load of passengers. 'It's about people working through their problems and learning to pull together as a team. In some ways what we're

143

doing is like any other organised tour – me, the tour guide driving a bunch of tourists around in a bus. I'm expected to know where we're going, what we're going to be doing next, how much things cost, exchange rates, international dialling codes, and everything you ever wanted to know about the country we're currently in and its people and wildlife. But, in other ways, it's much more than that. Here, everyone's expected to pitch in and help with the day-to-day running of the trip. There are meals to prepare and cook, dishes to wash, shopping to be done, and problems to solve. If someone's not pulling their weight, it's up to the group to pull them into line.'

The people on the first tour had helped pull him into line. None of them knew the tragedies he had endured, but he thought they had guessed he needed some sorting out. The sheer volume of work that had to be done getting three meals a day on the table for a big group, as well as taking them on game drives and sightseeing expeditions, left him little time to dwell on his personal situation. In the end, tourists and guide parted as friends. The passengers had worked well as a team and Mike found he had learned a lot about people twenty years younger than himself.

He found they were not like him in so many ways. They didn't drink a lot of alcohol, but they did smoke dope, something he hadn't done since he had joined the army. He liked music – they liked a strange thumping sound. They liked long hair and flared trousers – he had been very glad to turn his back on both decades ago. The men didn't shave – he had short hair and scraped his face religiously every day.

Soon they found some common ground, however, as any group of people thrust together always does, and they learned from each other. They started rolling their sleeping bags and zipping up their little canvas bell tents after he caught a mopani snake – a harmless, pencil-thin little thing – that had slithered into one of the girl's tents and nearly given her a heart attack. He learned to like Pearl Jam and discovered that a couple of tokes of Malawi Gold can ease a tension headache and give you a new perspective on world politics.

Susie broke down two more times on that first trip and he later told Rian he could find another driver if he didn't find Mike another truck. Rian was chuffed with his new baby son and did not fancy going back on the road again himself. He assigned Susie to Dave, a diesel mechanic from Sheffield in England, who was his other regular driver. Dave loved mucking around with cantankerous engines, so it was a match made in heaven. On Mike's second trip, and every one thereafter, he put his faith in Nelson Mandela, and the truck did not let him down.

In the months that followed, Nelson and Mike took scores of young Britons, Australians, Canadians, New Zealanders, Americans, Danes, Swedes, Germans and Swiss tourists to some of the most beautiful places on earth. In those days the longest trips they did were from the Cape to Uganda. Rian had taken his trucks all the way to Cairo when he first started the business, but the perennial wars in the Sudan and Ethiopia were hotting up again, and the fighting in the Democratic Republic of Congo meant it was just about impossible to reach Egypt anymore. Still, they were epic trips, taking in places like Victoria Falls, the Zambezi Valley, the Masai Mara and Serengeti in Kenya and Tanzania, Zanzibar and the Virunga Mountains, where Mike had seen the mountain gorillas on the Rwandan side many years before.

The new job was changing his life, and he hoped it was for the better. He let his hair grow long and was soon sporting a goatee beard. Except for the odd strand of long grey hair and some wrinkles, there was now not too much difference in appearance between him and the other guys driving scores of overland trucks up and down the African continent.

The army had given him an AIDS test when he left, and he had passed with a clean bill of health, despite his futile attempts to save Carlos's life. He was a single, healthy, heterosexual male, but he found it easy to stick to Rian's golden rule of tour-guiding despite the occasional offer. The groups were technically aimed at the eighteen to thirty-five age bracket, although some people a little closer to his age slipped through the net, and they were usually women. Single women. At the end of each trip they always had a party, a big night with plenty of booze and sometimes, depending on the crew, plenty of dope. It was here that most of those offers arose. Some of the women were very attractive and it was not only always the older ones who wanted more than a group T-shirt as a souvenir of their trip.

But Mike still found himself thinking of Isabella and none of the women he met on those early tours could compete with the memory of her. The daily routine of driving and organising meals and tours, crossing borders and changing money kept him busy. At nights, in his tent or just under a mosquito net looking up at the stars, he still thought of her and the life they might have had.

7

M ike didn't know if it was the typically chilly
Punda Maria air or the shock of Theron's
message that caused his shivering. He had
retired to bed early, avoiding Sarah's questions about
his conversation with Rian.

Mike knew from the moment he met her that
Sarah Thatcher would be trouble. From the outset, his
latest tour had started to shape up as his most difficult. For the first time he had a non-paying passenger
on board – a journalist on a junket – Sarah Thatcher.
He feared she would not fit in with the rest of the
group. He thought she did not like him, and he knew
she did not really want to be riding around southern
Africa in the back of a bright yellow ex-army truck.

As usual, the day before the tour started the
tourists had arrived on their various flights, mostly
from London, and assembled at the Holiday Inn at
Jo'burg airport. He had stopped by their rooms, introduced himself, checked each of them off his manifest,
and then given them all a basic briefing over crisps

and Guinness in the hotel's imitation Irish pub that night.

'You all know the route and the itinerary from your brochures – from Jo'burg to the Kruger National Park, then north through Zimbabwe to Hwange National Park and Victoria Falls. We'll transit through Zambia and back into the other side of Zimbabwe at Lake Kariba for a trip on a houseboat, then head back into Zambia to South Luangwa National Park. After that we'll cross into Mozambique and then follow the coast south until we cross back into South Africa from Maputo,' he explained.

'We'll get to know each other better during the trip. That, I promise you. The only thing I've got to add to that,' he said, winding up, 'is you've all got to remember that this is Africa and things don't always go according to plan, so stay flexible, stay happy and we'll all have a great time.'

Sarah had sat slightly apart from the group, jotting in her reporter's notebook, which made Mike feel uneasy. He didn't know how she wanted to play this game, so he'd let her introduce herself and explain what she was doing in her own time. A couple of the other passengers eyed her suspiciously as well.

The next day they boarded Nelson and set off for Kruger.

'Ooh, look. Two rhinos. Fantastic. Aren't they gorgeous?' cooed Linda, one of the English girls.

She was a redhead, attractive and slim. Too young for Mike and not his type. No one seemed to be his type these days, he reflected. That was the problem. Maybe it was being back in the Kruger National Park again. Maybe it was the light. Maybe it was the rhinos. Maybe it was the attractive girl. All of it made him think of Isabella.

'That's a young one, walking behind the bigger one. That must be its mother,' said Nigel the New Zealander. Nigel was already annoying Mike, and it was only the first day of the trip. He was a know-it-all who didn't know very much.

'They're a mating pair. Mummy and daddy,' Mike said.

'How can you tell?' Nigel asked.

'The smaller one's walking behind the larger one. They're white rhinos and white rhino cows always make their calves walk in front of them, where they can see them. The smaller one's a female.'

'They look dark grey to me. Maybe they're *black* rhinos,' Nigel said, challenging the guide yet again.

Mike sighed inwardly. There was one on every trip. 'The terms "white" or "black" don't refer to their colouring. The term "white" is a contraction of an Afrikaans word, for wide, referring to its wide mouth, which it uses for grazing. The *black* rhino has a narrow mouth, with a prehensile lip. After the name "white rhino" caught on, people just started calling the other species black, for convenience.' Mike refocused his binoculars so he didn't have to look at Nigel as he spoke. He had to give the boy room to back down with grace.

'Got a degree in this stuff or something?' Nigel asked sarcastically.

150

'Yes,' Mike said, and Kylie, a plump Aussie girl with glasses, giggled. Mike liked Kylie already.

'Time to make camp,' Mike said, and turned Nelson's key. The truck started first go, with a belch of black diesel smoke and a noisy rattle.

They had entered the park via the Malelane gate, but they weren't going to stay at Malelane Camp, where Mike had taken Isabella, where they had made love for the first time. He didn't want to stir up any more old memories than he had to and, besides, he thought his charges were in need of a swimming pool and a shop where they could buy cold beer and carved wooden elephants. Mike thought of Isabella again, though, as he put the truck in gear and his tourists babbled away in the back.

It was nearly five o'clock when they coasted through the wooden gates of Pretoriuskop Camp, about sixty kilometres further north into the national park. The rhino sighting had delayed them. Mike pulled into the car park outside the thatch-roofed reception building.

'OK, everyone. Toilets are over there, shop's that way. I'm going to check in and we'll drive down to the camping ground after that. Stretch your legs and don't get lost.' He sort of hoped Nigel would get lost and bump into a lion, but the electric fence around the camp meant the odds were in Nigel's favour, not his.

Mike walked down a paved path edged by manicured lawns to the reception building. The young man behind the desk gave him a big smile.

'My friend, good to see you again,' he said, extending his hand. They shook, three times, in the African way, first shaking their right hands in the usual European manner, then lifting them to clasp and shake with the thumbs interlocked, then once more in the European way.

'Lloyd, how's it? Campsite for eleven, please. It's already paid for and booked under the company name.' Mike handed him the National Parks booking slip and they exchanged small talk about the weather. Once Lloyd had placed a receipt in Mike's park entry permit he went outside and rounded the crew up from around the car park for the short trip across to the camping ground.

Kylie and Linda were the last aboard, having stopped to place a green-headed pin on a large map of the Kruger park on a board outside the tourist information office next to reception. The map was for game sightings, and tourists placed coloured pins corresponding to different animals at spots on the map where they had been seen. The green pin was for the rhinos they had just been watching.

'Pretoriuskop is the oldest camp in the park,' Mike said over his shoulder to the group as they drove through the camp. 'It dates back to the '20s.'

They passed rows of circular tan-coloured *rondavels*, each hut topped with a pointed thatched roof. The buildings faced onto grassy lawns shaded by mature trees. The *rondavels* ranged in size from simple two-bed affairs, with communal shower and toilet blocks, to larger, fully self-contained structures with toilets and kitchens.

They drove past the small service station and another circle of *rondavels*. The first *braai* fires of the evening were flickering brightly in the fading light and the smell of woodsmoke filled the air.

'Look, reindeer,' Kylie said, pointing out a herd of a dozen fawn-coloured antelope grazing on the lawn between the huts, seemingly oblivious to the humans who sipped drinks and watched them from shaded verandahs.

'Impala,' Mike said, gently correcting her. 'There are about a hundred thousand in the park and they're the most common antelope you'll see.'

A few people waved at them as they negotiated their way along the camp's winding internal roads. 'Most of the people who come here are white South Africans. Altogether nearly a million people, including foreigners, visit Kruger each year,' Mike said, continuing his tour guide's spiel.

The camping area was only about a third full so he had a good choice of sites. Night was falling and Mike quickly set about the business of setting up camp. The first set-up was always the slowest, as he had to give a demonstration of how to erect the two-person green canvas dome tents the tourists would sleep in.

That first night, as usual, Mike cooked the meal pretty much solo. He always prepared something simple at the start of the trip – boiled potatoes, coleslaw and a green salad he'd made the day before and stored in Nelson's portable refrigerator, and a *braai* of steaks and sausages. He found that looking after the first meal on his own always taught him about the group. It showed up the helpers – those who would eagerly volunteer to assist; the loafers – who would gladly sit back and watch others work;

and the leaders – those who organised the washing-up at the end, a chore he deliberately left undone.

At last they were sitting around the campfire on fold-out canvas and aluminium camp stools, stomachs full and tongues loosened a little by beer and wine over dinner. A million stars blazed above them and burning embers swirled up from the settling fire to join the light show. Mike felt everyone was suitably mellow for the business of formal introductions. He invited Sarah, who was seated next to him, to begin.

'I'm Sarah Thatcher. I'm twenty-nine, I'm from Highgate in London. I'm a journalist and I don't really know what I'm doing here. In fact, I don't even know if I want to be here,' she said.

'Why don't you want to be here, Sarah?' Mike said, breaking the cold silence that followed her opening salvo.

'God, this is painful. You sound like a psychiatrist,' she said melodramatically.

'Missing your regular appointment, eh?' Nigel piped in from the shadows. Someone chuckled.

Mike ignored him and said nothing, waiting for her to continue. Cicadas chirped in the bush and somewhere nearby a bullfrog croaked, but they were all waiting to hear more from Sarah. From her accent she sounded upper class, or at least from a moneyed family. He knew why she was there, but he wanted her to let everyone else know.

'I'm a journalist. I work for a travel magazine in London, *Outdoor Adventurer*,' she made the title sound faintly distasteful as if she herself would never be caught outdoors, or adventuring. 'Everyone else on the magazine has been abroad with work, to Bali, to Chile, to Nepal, to India. This is the first trip I was ever offered, so, naturally, I couldn't say no . . .'

'Naturally,' a female voice echoed mockingly from the other side of the fire, but Mike couldn't be sure who it was.

'Carry on, Sarah,' Mike said, after the ripple of laughter died down. He could see in her lively blue eyes, which shone in the reflected glow of the fire's embers, that she was getting her hackles up and didn't like to be mocked.

'Well, I wanted to go to Africa. No problems there, but, well, not quite in this way,' she said, not seeming to notice the open-mouthed faces around the campfire. 'You see, when the editor said "Africa" I thought I would be staying on a private game reserve. I didn't expect to be with a crowd of backpackers in the back of an old military vehicle.'

Mike wondered how the rest of the group, who had paid to be there, would react. He kept his mouth shut.

'So you're here for *free*?' came an incredulous English male voice.

'And what, we're not good enough for you?' said a girl with an accent from the East End of London.

'Would I pay to do this? No,' Sarah replied matter-of-factly. 'But it's my job, and I should tell you I'll be writing an article about this *adventure*, and taking photographs. I may want to interview some of you for my story.'

'Pig's arse,' said Nigel. 'You're not putting my photo in some yuppie wanker travel magazine.'

'OK, OK. That's enough,' Mike said, holding up his

hands. 'Sarah was invited along by the travel company that books our tours to do a story on a typical over-land trip for her magazine. It may not be everybody's cup of tea, but a trip like this is as good as you make it. You get out of it what you put into it.'

'All I've got so far out of this trip is clichés,' Sarah said, loud enough for everyone to hear.

'I'm sorry, Sarah,' Mike said with feeling. 'My boss gave me photocopies of some of your old stories to read. Perhaps that's where I've picked them up from.'

She eyed him coldly.

In fact, her stories read quite well, he thought. They'd been about canyoning, parachuting and ski-ing at various spots in the United Kingdom, and each 'adventure' had probably ended with dinner and drinks at a luxurious country hotel. Still, she obvi-ously wasn't as prissy as she first appeared, and her outdoor adventuring had not done her figure any harm.

In fact, although she was acting like a bitch, he thought she was very attractive. She had bobbed blonde hair, natural as far as he could tell, those icy-blue eyes, and a longish but aquiline nose, which didn't make her look any less arrogant than she was trying to be. Her skin was fair and unblemished. Her clothes were safari-chic, straight from the expensive camping stores around Covent Garden, Mike guessed. She wore a grey sleeveless button-up shirt which showed off her lithe arms, and khaki trousers with too many pockets and detachable legs. Her Hi-Tech hiking boots, like the rest of her outfit, looked like they'd never been worn before. She continued to glower at him across the campfire. He wondered if he would still have a job once Rian received the December edition of *Outdoor Adventurer*.

Mike had an old soldier's distrust of the media and he doubted Rian's wisdom in inviting a reporter on one of their overland trips. They were not at the top end of the market by any means, and even on the best planned and managed trips they still had problems from time to time.

'Let's move along,' he said.

Most of Rian's bookings came via a UK-based chain of travel agencies, but that didn't mean that only English people travelled on the trucks. The agencies advertised in the many free magazines published in London catering for Australian, New Zealand and South African backpackers living in the United Kingdom, as well as glossy magazines aimed at young men and women. The company also advertised itself in *Outdoor Adventurer*, another reason why Sarah was with them.

The introductions continued. Kylie was an Australian nurse enjoying London and working at Guy's. Linda, the redhead, worked in a pub in Nottingham, and wanted to see the world and be a dancer.

Sam, an American studying at Cambridge, tried to compensate for his intellect and geeky study choice of physics with high-street hip clothes – baggy shorts with a drop waist that showed off his boxers, a Mambo shirt and a necklace made of steel ballbearings. He also used the word 'dude' way too much for Mike's liking, but he had organised the washing-up party after dinner and had pitched in to do his share of the post-dinner chores.

Melanie, or 'Mel' as she preferred, was the child of Jamaican immigrants from London's East End. To an antipodean like Mike, the cockney accent didn't gel with the smooth ebony skin and the corn-row hairdo. She had a nice smile and no airs and graces. Mel had also been a good helper during the cooking.

Next there were the lads. George the Geordie from Newcastle in the north of England, a ginger-haired lorry driver, and his rotund, pasty-faced sidekick Terry, who was from London originally, but worked as a plumber in the same town as his friend. There was a growing pile of empty Castle beer cans at their feet.

George and Terry, as Mike could have predicted, were inclined to loaf, and Linda had been keener to share a beer with the two boys than take part in the cooking chores earlier in the evening. Sam, however, had ensured that the two Englishmen helped out with drying, and Linda had felt obliged to help Mike stack the plates and cutlery back in the storage boxes as a result.

Nigel, the Kiwi, told the group he worked for the tax office back home. Mike wondered if he had any friends at all. Nigel had sat on a stool and read his book until the food was served up.

Apart from Sarah and one of the other women, Jane, none of them was older than twenty-two. Biologically speaking, Mike realised he was old enough to be the father of most of them. For the next few weeks, he mused, he would be their guardian, tour guide, drinking buddy, bodyguard and chauffeur.

The circle of introductions was nearly complete, save for the two women sitting to Mike's left. Both were good looking, with strawberry blonde hair, pale eyes, high cheekbones and wide, sensual mouths. They could have passed for sisters, he thought, except for the tiny wrinkles that showed around Jane's eyes when she smiled.

'Hi, I'm Jane, from Bristol. I'm an estate agent,' she said, with a saleswoman's smile and a rolling West Country accent. 'My age is my business, but Julie and I are both really excited about this trip, even though we're a little bit nervous about lions and tigers. Hopefully Mike will get us through in one piece,' she finished with a laugh.

'Give over, Mum. Don't be daft. There's no tigers in Africa,' said the younger Muir. 'I'm Julie. And, yes, she is my mum. I'm eighteen so you can work out for yourself how old she is. I'm studying journalism at college,' she said, directing the last remark towards Sarah Thatcher, who didn't seem to acknowledge her presence.

Jane wore a loose black singlet top printed with gold elephant motifs that looked like it had come from Thailand or some other Asian holiday spot, and a short stone-coloured skirt that showed off her toned, crossed legs. Julie sported a pink tank top and grey cargo shorts.

Julie turned back to Mike and said, 'I've got to do a travel story as part of my assessment this year, so maybe *I* could write something on the trip as well, if that's OK with you, Mike.'

'Fine by me,' he said.

The introductions were over and conversations started between small knots of people around the fire as embryonic friendships were formed. Sarah was the first to head for her tent. Mike had assigned her to share Linda's tent.

'Why can't I have a tent of my own? The truck's not full, so I'm sure you have spares,' she said as she left.

'You could, but you'd have to set it up and pull it down by yourself each day,' he replied.

'Well, that's fine by me,' she said stubbornly.

'Hang on, it's not fine by me!' Linda chimed in. 'I'm not putting up my own bloody tent every day. You can muck in and help like the rest of us. Just don't snore.'

Sarah strode off to the little tent in silence.

Mike had organised the ten travellers in five two-person tents and he, as usual, would sleep on a fold-out mattress on the floor in the back of Nelson. He liked to be in the truck at night, to make sure it and the valuables and backpacks locked in the rear storage locker were not left unattended.

Most of the group were still recovering from their flights, so the first-night party wound up around ten.

'Don't forget, everyone,' Mike said as they folded their stools and headed for their tents, 'you've got to take your anti-malarial medication, either daily or weekly, depending on the brand you're using. Keep your tents zipped tight as well.'

'Yes, Mum,' a male voice chimed in from somewhere in the shadows.

160

8

Mike crouched by the remains of the previous night's fire and felt the residual warmth of its embers grow as he blew steadily into the white coals. The end of a half-charred stick finally glowed red and he used it to light his morning cigarette. It was a good time of the day, chilly and half dark, with the top of the new sun just peeking above the ridge to the east.

He heard a click and a mechanical whirr behind him, then a woman's voice said, 'Did you learn that from a movie? *Crocodile Dundee*, maybe?'

He turned and saw Sarah Thatcher, her blonde hair tousled by sleep, an expensive camera hanging from a broad strap around her neck. She wore a blue Polartec fleece, to ward off the morning's chill.

'I left my lighter in the truck,' he said. 'Shouldn't you ask before you point that thing at someone?'

'I get better pictures this way. You're not going to order me to stop doing my job are you, *Major* Williams?' she asked.

'How did you know I used to be in the army?' he asked, surprised that she knew of his background. He deliberately gave away as little as possible when he introduced himself to the travellers. In particular, he never dwelt on his military background.

'I dig. It's my job. In fact, all it took was a call to your boss in Johannesburg. He was fulsome in his praise. Described you as something of a hero. Said you'd tangled with some elephant poachers in Mozambique.'

'Rian's prone to exaggeration,' he replied. He made a mental note to punch his friend and employer next time he saw him.

'There was also a small story in one of the South African newspapers, the *Citizen*, last year. I found it on the net. What can you tell me about your time in Mozambique?'

'Nothing,' he said.

'Top secret?'

'Personal.' Mike took the cigarette from his mouth and blew hard on the stick he had used to light it until he got a flame. He lit the big gas cooker ring sitting on the ground. Then he placed a large kettle of water on the blue flames and stood, staring at the rising sun rather than the reporter behind him.

'I'm sorry,' she said, and she seemed to mean it. 'Your friend told me about your girlfriend and . . .'

'Jesus Christ. What else did he tell you? Criminal convictions? Bloody shoe size?'

'Look, I'm sorry,' she said again. 'It's just that if I give you, the tour leader, a little colour, if you've got an interesting background, it can make my story better and a lot more favourable to your company.'

'So my past is "colour". Is this blackmail now?' he asked.

'Maybe I just want to know a bit more about the man in whose hands I'm placing my life for the next few weeks. These overland trips can be quite dangerous, from what I've heard,' she said.

'You'd be in more danger driving to work on the M25 than you will be on this trip. I'll tell you about overlanding, the itinerary, the wildlife we see, African culture, but that's it. Got it?'

'Not yet.'

'Are you married?' he asked her.

She looked startled by the question, but quickly composed herself. 'What's that got to do with anything?'

'How old were you when you first had sex?'

'I beg your pardon!'

'What's your bra cup size. About a C, I'd say. Am I right?'

She took a step towards him, hands on her hips, her face reddening. 'How dare you!' she hissed.

Mike held up his hands, palms out, in submission. 'Sorry. I really am. But how do you like batting off a few personal questions at five in the morning? Look, we've got off to a rough start,' he said, pausing to drag on his cigarette. The nicotine was calming him now. 'I'll do whatever it takes to give you a good story, but please, leave my personal life out of it. That's all I'm asking.'

He thought she wanted to smile. The corners of her mouth started to curl up ever so slightly, but she forced them back into a frown.

'I take your point. But I do expect full cooperation from you. This story can make or break your outfit and I'm sure your boss wouldn't be very happy if you cocked it up for him.'

He shook his head and stubbed out the butt of his smoke with his white-water rafter's sandal. 'You don't give up, do you?'

'Never.' She smiled and he had to force himself to turn away.

Mike left Sarah, and roused the others from their tents and pointed them towards the tea and coffee. The plan was to go for an early-morning game drive and then have a big, greasy cooked brunch when they got back. If he could get them moving in time, they could be out of the gate of Pretoriuskop Camp by five-thirty, when the gates first opened, and back by about eleven.

'Bit early, isn't it?' asked a bleary-eyed Mel.

'Ah, so that's what a sunrise looks like,' said Terry, the Englishman, who looked even bulkier than usual with a sweatshirt and fleece stretched over his stomach. 'That'll do me for the next fifty years, thanks. Can I go back to bed now?'

They rolled out the gate ten minutes behind schedule.

'The idea of an early start is to get out of the rest camp first so we can catch a sighting of the predators – the big cats – when they're still on the move in the early hours. We might see a leopard slinking across the road or a pride of lions returning from a night's hunting. The animals in Kruger are used to the sight and sound of cars, but even the most patient will push off once they're cornered by eight or nine vehicles full of tourists,' Mike explained as they drove.

Most of the group had come to Africa to experience the continent's unique wildlife, so the game drives were an important part of his job. Luck was a big factor in game viewing, but he had also found that good eyesight and a little local knowledge of where animals hid and what they did at different times of the day increased the odds of spotting something interesting.

The art of leading a successful game drive, Rian had taught him, was to lower the viewers' expectations and to keep them interested in the bush around them, even when there was apparently nothing to see. A good guide needed to know about birds – there are about five hundred species in southern Africa – trees and other plants and their uses, and insects, as well as the better-known larger mammals.

'If you take a twig from that tree over there, and rub it on a rock, you get a bristly, fibrous end which you can use as a toothbrush. If you burn the wood of that tree, the leadwood,' he said, pointing to a big specimen on the other side of the road, 'you can use the fine ash as tooth powder. There are hundreds of other plants with special uses, like the sickle bush, whose leaves ease the pain of toothache when you chew them.'

'Fascinating,' said Kylie, the nurse. 'I'd like to learn more about the medicinal uses of different plants.'

'Where are the lions? It's been nearly an hour already,' Nigel complained.

Mike scanned the long dry grass for the flick of an

ear or the twitch of a tail. His eyes roved from right to left, an old army trick which he found made it easier to spot movement. Because westerners read from left to right they automatically tend to scan their surroundings in the same direction. Looking from right to left takes more effort and forces the watcher to slow down, to concentrate more. He made himself peer through the dry vegetation and long grass, rather than simply stare at the bush. He scanned the leafy branches of the larger trees in the hope of catching a camouflaged leopard lying up there.

Old Nelson was well laid out for game viewing. Rian had fitted a large box-like cab on the stripped-down chassis of the ex-military Bedford. He had furnished the cabin with all the comforts he could find and afford. The travellers sat on old airline seats, which Rian had picked up at a South African Airways auction. The seats reclined and still had the little tray tables in their backs. He had the seats re-upholstered in a green, water-resistant rip-stop canvas, which was better suited to the dust and rain that inevitably found its way into the cab. The cab had a flat tin roof, which was also covered in canvas to cut down the sun's heat, and big open windows on the side. The windows could be closed with roll-down flaps of soft clear plastic, which gave some protection from the rain. On the inside front wall of the cab was a painted map of Africa, showing the various routes the expeditions took. Much of the remaining space on the walls was covered with stickers from various destinations and faded, peeling paper labels from beer bottles from the length and breadth of the continent. There were a couple of bookshelves stacked with dog-eared paperback novels, battered Lonely Planet guides and field guides to the birds and mammals of Africa. A car radio-cassette player was fitted to the front bulkhead, and speakers were mounted in the front and back of the passenger cab.

The truck was not full on this trip – there were seats for another three passengers – so there was room for the group to spread out in the cab. There was no discussion or vote about it, but Mike noticed no one had invited Sarah to sit next to them. She sat quietly at the far end of the driver's cab from him, staring out through her window, occasionally snapping a photograph or two.

Mike was quite comfortable up front, but he knew the passengers in the back would be feeling the cold, with the wind rushing in through the big open windows as they cruised eastwards into the rising sun, up the main tar road from Pretoriuskop.

'There, on the left. Zebra. About five or six of them,' he called back into the main cab.

'Where?' asked Mel. 'I can't see anything.'

'He's making it up,' George said.

'OK, I see them now,' said Sam. 'Your eyesight must be very good.'

'It's just what you're used to. You'll find it'll take you a couple of days to differentiate shapes and movement in the bush,' Mike said. 'All your senses come alive in Africa. Not just your sight, but your hearing gets better the longer you spend out here. Soon you'll be smelling elephants a mile off.'

They headed for Skukuza, the main camp in the

park, which would be their first rest stop that morning. Mike thought briefly of Skukuza the elephant, the grand old man of the Kruger park who had been destroyed, along with so much of Mike's life, just a year before. He remembered the vultures and the stench of the elephant's rotting flesh, and the ragged holes where his mighty tusks had been. Mike was sure there was a picture of him in the elephant museum at Letaba Camp, further north in the park, and he wanted to stop by if the chance arose. He had avoided the museum on previous trips, but now felt he was ready to pay his last respects to the animal's memory and close the book on another little piece of that terrible time. Later that year, he told himself, he would visit Portugal. In December, when the summer rainy season is in full flight in southern Africa, there were no tours booked and Rian expected his drivers to take leave.

The weather would be cold in Portugal, but he wouldn't be looking for the sun or a beach holiday. He would find Isabella's grave, maybe even look for her parents. He knew that he had to make his peace with her ghost once and for all, or she would never leave his dreams. There was another way to put her memory to rest, but he could not see how that could ever happen. Flowers on a grave were one thing, but every now and then he still fantasised about what he would say to the man who killed her, just before he sent him to hell.

'Do you think you'll ever go home?' Sarah asked.

'Sorry?' Mike had been lost in his thoughts.

'Will you ever leave Africa, and go home? Off the record, if you like.'

168

'Off the record?' Mike had paid enough attention to media training from army public relations officers over the years to know that phrase meant absolutely nothing. 'I don't know where home is.'

'Australia. Big, empty country, lots of beer and kangaroos.'

'You know about my background. People sometimes say the army's a home, but it's not. It's just a job. A job that feeds you and clothes you, but it's not a home. I've lived all over Australia, all over a lot of the world. Here's as good a place as any.'

'Wherever I lay my hat? That sort of thing?' she asked.

'Wherever I park my truck. Yeah. I don't know. Sometimes I think I'd like to buy a place over here, if I could get the money together. Maybe a small game farm. Do you want some more info on the company, or on our itinerary in Zimbabwe and Zambia?' he added, trying to change the subject.

'No. Are you running away from something?'

He took a deep breath and tried to concentrate on the road ahead. The last thing he wanted was to lose his cool and run into an impala. 'Look, I lost a girlfriend, a mate and a job in Africa. I've seen famine, I've seen massacres, I've seen little kids dissected by landmines here, but I'm still in Africa. Wouldn't you say I'm a textbook case of confronting one's fears rather than running from them?'

Sarah's cheeks reddened. 'Sorry. Put that way, I see your point.'

'Forget it. But let's just keep this about the trip, OK?'

Mike turned the truck to the right, following a sign to the Transport Dam. The small earthen-walled dam was a watering point for the horse-drawn transport wagons that used to take people and goods from South Africa across to Mozambique in the old days.

'This is a pretty spot,' he said to Sarah as they trundled along the corrugated dirt side road. 'It's got water all year round and good birdlife.'

When they arrived at the dam, a couple of kilometres down the road, an African fish eagle, with its distinctive snowy-white head atop a dark body, was keeping watch on the water's surface. The bird whined a mournful melodic call. A moment later it was joined by another. Mike pointed them out to the crew in the back of the truck, who dutifully raised an assortment of binoculars and cameras, large and small.

'Fish eagles mate for life,' he said as he stared at the beautiful big birds through his binoculars.

'Unusual,' said Sarah.

'You didn't answer me this morning,' he said.

'Which of your inane questions was that? The one about the bra size?'

He lowered his binoculars and noticed that she was smiling.

'The one about marriage. Are you?'

'Married to my job, yes,' she said.

'And you reckon I'm one for clichés,' he replied, shaking his head.

'Touché. But it's tough to get on in journalism and I certainly don't want to stay at *Outdoor Adventurer* for the term of my natural life.'

She made the title sound about as interesting as *Modern Shopfitting*, or *Plasterer's Monthly*. Mike had met people on his travels who would have given their right arm to be sent around the world to write about adventure holidays.

'Marriage would tie me down, kill off my career before it's really had a chance to start,' she said.

'Rather be exposing corruption and bringing down governments?'

'It'd beat driving a tour bus full of teenage hippies,' she replied. Sarah raised her binoculars to the birds again and Mike resumed his sweep of the dam shore. He sensed they would never fully recover from the bad start they had got off to, and that it was going to be a very, very long four weeks.

There was nothing else to see at the dam, except for a pair of yellow-billed hornbills that hopped comically on the ground around the truck, hoping that crumbs or other rubbish would fall like manna from heaven.

'Make sure you don't feed the birds, or any of the animals we see in the park. They get dependent on humans and eventually become a pest. Some of the bigger ones, like baboons and hyenas, eventually get too bold and have to be shot by rangers,' Mike said. He started the engine and glanced in the wing mirror. Nigel was crumbling potato chips and sprinkling them from the window. The hornbills were jostling and pecking each other to get to the crumbs and squawking with delight. Mike shook his head and despaired at the confrontation that he knew had to come.

They drove back up the dirt road to where it met the main tar road. 'How's the left?' he asked Sarah.

She stuck her head out the window, and screamed, 'My God!'

'What is it?' he asked, leaning over.

'Lions. Two of them,' she said breathlessly. 'They're – they're . . .'

'Screwing!' Linda called delightedly from the back.

Mike felt the truck lurch as all the passengers in the rear compartment shifted to one side and craned out for a better view. The click and whirr of insta-matic cameras sounded as soon as their initial surprise had worn off. He cut the engine so as not to disturb the big cats any more than necessary.

They were in the middle of the road. The big black-maned male chomped down on the rippling muscles on the back of the lioness's neck to steady her, then entered her repeatedly and furiously. After about a minute he sat back on his haunches then flopped lazily onto one side, temporarily exhausted. The lioness, restless and unsatisfied, stood and flicked her tail disdainfully in his face. She turned her big head to give the humans an equally contemptuous glance.

'They'll be doing that about every ten minutes for a twenty-four-hour session,' Mike said, keeping an eye on his passengers now. A couple were leaning a little too far out the windows to get better shots. The last thing he needed was for a backpacker to wind up as part of a feline ménage à trois.

'Sounds like my kind of man,' Jane Muir said from the seat behind Mike.

'Do they mate for life?' Kylie asked.

172

'No. There'll be a couple of males with a pride. The males take over a pride when they reach their prime, and kick the existing males out. Then, once they get too old, at between twelve and fifteen, they get kicked out themselves by a couple of new guys. The female initiates sexual contact and the male only stays close for the twenty-four hours or so that they're mating.'

'Now that's *my* kind of man,' said Julie, not to be outdone by her mother.

There was a chorus of laughter from the back and both lions looked up sharply. It wasn't the noise that had disturbed their post-coital relaxation, though, it was the sight of movement. Mike looked back again to see that Terry, one of the English boys, was now standing on a windowsill. All Mike could see were Terry's pudgy white legs in the window. He was hanging onto the roof, and his head and shoulders were sticking out above the top of the rear cab. Mike realised that the lions, while used to the uniform silhouettes of vehicles and even large trucks, had noticed the movement of Terry's head and pointing arm. They fixed cold yellow eyes on the unfamiliar form.

'Get inside, Terry,' Mike called.

He started the truck's engine again, then turned back to look inside the cab. Nigel was reaching theatrically for one of Terry's legs. Mel giggled as Nigel grabbed hard on the Englishman's right calf. Terry yelped and kicked his leg out in a reflex motion.

'Stop!' Mike knew what was going to happen next and there was nothing he could do to prevent it.

Terry lost his grip on the smooth roof of the cab and pitched forward, out of the truck. His arms windmilled as he fell and landed heavily on his side.

Linda screamed.

'Get him in, get him in!' Sam yelled.

Mike rammed the gearstick into reverse and heaved down as hard as he could on the steering wheel, spinning it to the left. He let the clutch out savagely and the Bedford leapt back violently. There were wild screams from the back as the passengers slammed into each other when the truck started to move.

Mike managed to get the vehicle between Terry and the lions, but the animals were not going to be so easily fooled.

'They're coming around the front now!' Sarah yelled from the passenger's seat.

The maned lion growled, deep and menacing, showing yellowed fangs each as long as an adult's finger.

Mike knew what that meant. 'He's going to charge!' he shouted. He climbed into the back of the cab, knocking Nigel aside as he elbowed his way to a window. 'Terry, here! Give me your hand.'

The lion and lioness moved as one, a tawny blur as they rounded the truck and charged towards Terry.

Terry screamed, a high-pitched wail of primal terror.

'Hold on!' Mike yelled as he clasped the Englishmen's hands in his own. He leaned back into the cab, dragging Terry up the metal side. 'Give me a hand, for Christ's sake!' Terry was overweight and

Mike feared his slippery palms might slide out of his grasp.

Sam and George each grabbed hold of Terry, under the big man's armpits.

The male lion ended his charge with a leap, his huge paws outstretched, hooked claws extended. Mike felt the tug on Terry's body and saw the unbelieving fear in his wide eyes. 'Pull!' Mike bellowed.

The lion hit the side of the truck with his shoulder and the whole vehicle rocked. His jaws closed and locked around the thick sole of Terry's hiking boot.

'Oh God, he's got me!'

Mike, Sam and George all leaned back as one and, just when they feared they might lose Terry, they crashed back in the cab in a heap, the writhing, screaming Englishman on top of them.

Mike recovered first. 'Are you hurt?'

'Oh Jesus. Fucking hell.' Terry was almost weeping. He pushed himself further away from the open window, back against Sam. 'It's not going to climb in and get me, is it?'

Mike shook his head. 'Relax, Terry. You're safe now. The lion only noticed you the first time because you put your bloody head up above the truck's roofline. All he can see now is the silhouette of the vehicle, not what's inside. They've got lousy depth perception. He's lost sight of you and he's confused now. Are you OK?'

Kylie knelt by Terry and inspected his foot. 'You're fine, Terry. He didn't break the skin at all.'

Sam sat up. 'Dude! He took your boot.'

Mike could hardly believe he had almost lost a passenger. It was the most serious incident he had witnessed since starting work as an overland tour guide. 'Terry, are you all right?' he asked again.

The big man nodded, the colour slowly returning to his cheeks. He glowered at Nigel.

'OK, everyone back to their seats. Kylie, would you mind sitting with Terry for a moment?'

'No problem, Mike,' she said. 'Pass us some water, please, Mel.'

Outside, the lion held Terry's boot down with one paw while he tore at the suede upper with his fangs. When Mike put the truck into gear and they started to move forward, the beast gave a deep roar so loud the metal sides of the cab reverberated.

The lioness, unfazed by the noise and commotion, sidled up to her mate and tugged at his shaggy black mane with her teeth. 'Good girl,' Mike whispered to her.

The lion dropped the mangled boot and, with a last backward glance at the truck, reluctantly followed his mate. They walked into long yellow grass and the old man prepared to do his duty again.

Nigel was leaning out the rear window, snapping pictures of the retreating lions with his tiny camera. Mike ran a hand through his hair and then down his face, trying to steady his nerves. Sarah climbed back into her seat next to him. Mike noticed the camera in her hand and recalled the whirr of its motor drive and the searing light of the flash during the rescue. He realised, with dread, that she probably had the whole episode on film.

He pulled the vehicle over once they were well and truly out of sight of the lions, switched off the engine and turned back to face the passengers in the cab.

'Now listen up, everyone. You too, Nigel,' he said. 'I think you can all see now why we don't lean out the windows.' A couple of the group managed a chuckle, though most of them were in a mild state of shock at the near disaster they had just witnessed. 'And why it's important not to screw around in the back of the truck. Not too much, anyway.' He deliberately did not look at Nigel or Terry as he delivered his sermon. He hoped they had both got the message. He was pretty sure Terry had.

'Terry, there's a doctor at Skukuza. We can get you checked out there,' Mike added.

'No, it's OK,' Terry said sheepishly. 'I'm not hurt at all . . . although I near shat myself.' More of the group laughed now. 'But it wasn't your fault, Mike, and I don't want you having to report this, if that's all right.'

Mike appreciated the gesture. Nigel remained silent at the back of the truck. 'Thanks, Terry. Let's put it behind us, then, OK?' He returned to his seat and started the engine again.

As soon as they moved off, Sarah dropped her camera in the open bag on the floor near her seat and pulled out her spiral-bound reporter's notebook. She then left her seat and climbed into the back cab.

Behind him, Mike could hear her interviewing Terry.

'What was it like? . . . What did you feel when you were on the road? . . . Did you think you were going to die?'

Mike eyed the expensive camera on the floor. He looked back over his shoulder once more, just to make sure she wasn't looking his way and that no one else could see him as he quickly reached across.

After the morning's excitement, Mike decided to cut the game drive short. The crew had already seen two of the big five – lion and rhino – in their first two days in Africa, and almost seen one of their number eaten. He wanted to lower their expectations, not raise them. At this rate he'd have to feed Nigel to a leopard at the end of the first week just to keep the rest of the passengers interested. Not an unattractive proposition, he thought, as they drove through the imposing thatch-topped gate into Skukuza Camp.

Skukuza was more like a town than a rest camp. Hundreds of National Parks staff and their families lived there, and it was the park's administrative and operational headquarters. Big and noisy and crowded – Mike hated the place.

As he drove down the paved road he pointed out the main reception complex to their left. The building was laid out in a horseshoe shape and included a post office, a bank, a bookings office and a car rental agency. Chattering maids in bright printed uniform pinafores and matching headscarves moved in and out of rows of round, thatch-roofed *rondavels*, gardeners watered and tended immaculate lawns, and sand-coloured National Parks vehicles whizzed past.

They came to a T-junction and Mike swung Nelson off to the left, to a parking area reserved for trucks and buses.

'OK, the main shop and restaurant are off to the

right, the big thatched building over there, and there are toilets and a picnic area just past it. Stretch your legs with a walk along the riverside, if you like. You might see some elephant grazing there.'

He told the passengers to take an hour and a half. In the shop they could buy postcards and stamps, safari clothes, carved wooden animals and other tacky curios, books and maps, food and camping gadgets.

'I don't suppose there's anywhere I can get some film developed, is there?' Sarah asked.

'There's a photo-processing place in the shop,' Mike said. 'But the quality is rubbish, so I've been told,' he added quickly.

He suggested the group have brunch in the restaurant or cafeteria, or at least get some snacks for the ride back to Pretoriuskop, which was just under fifty kilometres away. After the morning's dramas he was tempted to start the day properly, with a beer, but he was the only one allowed to drive the truck.

Terry and George set off for some food and most of the others headed for the souvenir shop. Mike ambled along behind the group and lit a cigarette as he walked. It had been quite a morning and he needed something to settle him down. He sat on the dark log fence that separated the paved car park from the picnic ground and enjoyed his smoke in peace. There was still a slight tremor in his hands, he noticed inspecting the cigarette, as he thought about how close they had come to disaster.

It was a busy day in Skukuza, like any other in the bustling camp, and the car park was full. Many of the spots were taken up by game- viewing vehicles, open-sided four-wheel drives fitted with three or four rows of seats behind the driver and topped with a canvas sunshade. The game viewers ranged from old ex-army Land Rovers, converted to their new role, to brand-new purpose-built Nissan Safaris. The game viewers and their drivers were waiting for coach-loads of well-heeled foreign tourists, who were ushered by their guides out of their climate-controlled coaches into the open vehicles. There were also private cars and rental cars driven by local South African tourists and independent travellers from around the world.

By the time they returned to Pretoriuskop it was mid-day. The truck was quiet, and the mood was not helped by the fact that they saw virtually no game on the drive back, save for a small herd of impala and a leopard tortoise. The morning had been cool and overcast, but the sky was now a cloudless blue and the temperature was nudging thirty-five degrees Centigrade.

Sarah sat in icy silence next to Mike all the way from Skukuza. He guessed what was going through her mind, but she didn't say a single word during the return drive. She flicked through her notebook occasionally, checked her camera often, and stared fixedly through the windscreen.

As they climbed down from the truck at the site, Mike said, 'There's a swimming pool on the other side of the camp. It's a nice day for a dip and we could all use a little cooling off.'

There were a few murmurs of thanks and appreciation, but not enough for his liking. Tension was mounting and, in this heat, he knew it wouldn't be long before it erupted. Most of the group began drifting off to their tents to change, but Terry, George and Linda were standing in a huddle. Every now and then they pointed in the direction of Nigel's tent. Mike climbed into the truck to change into his swimming trunks, but only got as far as unzipping his kitbag when he heard angry voices.

'You stupid Kiwi prick. I'm going to fucking do you! Right fucking now!' It was Terry.

Mike jogged across to the tents and saw that all eyes were on the Englishman, who was standing outside Nigel's tent. George stood behind Terry, who was red-faced with rage.

'Come out, you fucking coward,' Terry shouted.

Nigel emerged from his tent defiant. 'What, can't take a joke, eh? Typical bloody pom. Just chill out, will you.'

As much as Mike wanted to hang back and let nature take its course, he found himself leaping guyropes and striding across the little clearing at the centre of the tents. Sam, too, was on an interception course for the two men.

'You could have killed me!' Terry screamed. He lashed out with his right fist and landed a blow on Nigel's jaw. Nigel lurched back, raising his arms to shield his face.

'Get him, Terry,' said Linda.

'Enough,' Mike said. 'Cool it. The rest of you back off.' He stepped between Terry and Nigel and held up an open palm to the Englishman's fist. Nigel jabbed around Mike with his left, catching Terry in the stomach.

'Gutless bastard,' Terry gasped, but he held his punches.

'I said *enough*!' Mike repeated, rounding on the dark-haired New Zealander.

'This isn't the way, guys. Just leave it be,' Sam said. He was at Mike's back.

Good kid, Mike thought. He chided himself for being surprised that the American boy had the guts to step in and break up a fight.

'Nigel,' Mike said, 'apologise to Terry.' The way he said it let Nigel know it was an order, not a request. Mike guessed that he would back down, for he believed Nigel was a coward.

'All right,' Nigel said, after a moment's pause. 'I'm sorry I grabbed you. It was just meant to be a joke, OK?'

Terry did not look convinced, and shook his head.

'Terry,' Mike said, turning to him and speaking softly, so only he and Sam could hear, 'you shouldn't have been leaning outside the truck and Nigel shouldn't have been messing around. Let's call it quits, OK? Help me out on this one.'

Terry hesitated a moment, then nodded his head.

'Thanks,' Mike said, and clapped him on the shoulder. 'Nigel, shake,' he ordered. Nigel obeyed.

'OK,' Mike said, turning to the assembled audience. 'Pool time. I'll pick up some munchies and some beers for lunch on the way.'

'Now you're talking,' said Mel.

'Well done, Mike,' said Jane Muir, smiling. He smiled back.

The rest of the crew got changed and drifted off to

182

the pool, but Jane Muir hung back. She had changed into a one-piece black bathing suit with a plunging neckline. Around her waist she wore a wraparound skirt with the same elephant motif as her singlet top.

'Can I help you with the shopping?' she asked.

'Thanks. Nice skirt, by the way. Where'd you get it, Thailand?' Mike asked.

'Thanks for noticing. Laos, actually. Julie and I were there last year.'

She was standing close to him now and he could smell her perfume – a faint musky smell that jump-started several of his nerve endings.

'Do you travel together often?' he asked, as they walked across the lawns between the *rondavels*, towards the camp shop.

'We've been on a few trips. Greece and Turkey, as well as Thailand. It's not as odd as it seems, you know. We genuinely get on, unlike most mothers and daughters. She hasn't accused me of cramping her style yet.'

'What about the other way around?' he asked.

Jane laughed. 'I could show her a thing or two. Still a few years left in this old girl. We have a laugh, but I do like to look out for her. She's all I've got.'

She was an attractive woman – vivacious and friendly as well. Mike found it was a nice change talking to someone who wasn't half his age.

The camp shop was a cool haven stocked with souvenirs, books and food staples. Mike put three six-packs of Lion beer and half-a-dozen packets of crisps into the plastic shopping basket as they walked up and down the aisles.

'What do you think?' asked Jane from the next aisle.

Mike looked up from the magazine rack and saw she had tried on a pair of black wraparound sunglasses. The triangular tag bounced on her turned-up nose.

'Very stylish,' he said.

'Not sexy?' she replied, smiling.

'The tag doesn't do it for me.' He believed this woman was flirting with him. He smiled back at her.

'Well, I'll just have to snip the tag off then, won't I,' she said, and winked at him when she removed the glasses. 'I'll take them,' she said to the woman working behind the counter.

They walked to the pool in a companionable silence, no more flirting for the time being, although every now and then Jane's hand seemed to brush his as she swung her shopping bag. She spotted a blue-headed lizard basking on the side of a fig tree and, when she pointed it out to him, she laid a hand on his forearm. Mike remembered Rian's golden rule and decided it was probably the golden rule for a very good reason. But then, he told himself, all rules were made to be broken.

They arrived at the pool to find the rest of the crew sitting in the shade or sunbathing. As usual, Mike noticed cliques were already developing. The Pretoriuskop pool was his favourite in the park. It was built on the site of a natural spring-fed waterhole and incorporated a large granite rock that was half in and half out of the water.

Nigel was by himself, basking on the top of the

rock like a lizard. Terry and George had stopped by the shop on their way and were already into a couple of beers. They sat in the shallow end sipping Castles from the can and throwing their soccer ball to each other. An old Afrikaner couple watched them with ill-concealed loathing. In other circumstances Mike would have told the boys to tone it down a bit, including their language, which was a bit crude at times, but for the moment he was just glad none of the passengers were hitting each other.

Jane left him and walked over to Julie, who was lying on her belly on a towel on the grass. Mike left the beers and the chips with Sam and wandered over to Sarah, who was sitting on her own on a green park bench under a big, shady marula tree. She was reading a glossy South African travel magazine he'd seen on sale in the camp shop. She looked up when she saw him approaching, but there was no welcoming smile.

He couldn't quite read her face. It was a mixture of suspicion, the usual disdain, and puzzlement. 'How's things?' he asked.

'You weren't happy about me taking pictures this morning, were you?' she said.

'It was a tense situation. Terry was at risk. Taking snapshots didn't help the rescue effort.'

'It would be very embarrassing, wouldn't it, if my magazine published pictures of one of your tourists falling out of the truck and nearly being eaten by a lion?'

'It would be more embarrassing if the lion had actually got him and not his shoe,' Mike said.

'But it would reflect badly on you. You might lose your job, your licence or accreditation, or whatever qualification you have. That's what worried you, wasn't it?'

'You've seen our brochures. We tell our customers we'll get them close to Africa's wildlife,' he replied.

She didn't smile. 'I had the roll of film in my camera developed at Skukuza this morning while the others were buying their naff souvenirs. Do you know what I saw when I got that roll of film back from the photo shop?'

'No,' he lied.

'I wonder if you do. Nothing. Nothing is what I saw. It seems the entire film was blank. I was quite terse with the man behind the counter, you know.'

He could picture her being quite terse. 'I can imagine.'

'He suggested maybe I had given him an unexposed roll by mistake, instead of an exposed roll.'

'Possible,' Mike said.

'Impossible,' she said, staring into his eyes.

Fortunately he was wearing sunglasses. 'Not much of a story without pictures, I suppose,' he said. Her eyes were cold, as he'd noticed before, but they were also captivating.

'I had pictures on that roll of you dragging Terry back into that truck, not to mention some very nice pictures of the mating lions. Pictures can be used selectively, and can tell a story in any number of ways. A cock-up can be made to look like an act of bravery,' she said.

'But we'll never know now, will we, how you would have used those pictures.'

'No. And I'll never know just what went wrong with my camera today. But if I find out, I'll be sure and let you know.'

'Thanks,' he said, turning to leave.

'And Mike,' she called. He turned. 'If it turns out someone tampered with my camera, I'd make sure their employer was informed. Ham-fisted attempts at censorship would probably add a nice angle to my story, in fact. Pictures or no pictures.'

Mike nodded and walked back to where the rest of the party had descended on the chips like a flock of vultures. The film canister in his left breast pocket felt like a lead weight around his neck.

9

Mike drove the overland truck north from Pretoriuskop to Satara Camp, where the group stopped for lunch. Storm clouds were gathering in the hills around Pretoriuskop and he was glad they packed when they did. The canvas tents used on the tours were strong and durable, but not as waterproof as the cheaper, lighter, nylon version. The last thing any of the touchy tourists needed now was a night in damp sleeping bags.

On the drive north he spotted a trio of cheetah crossing the road as they neared the Paul Kruger Tablets, a couple of plaques commemorating the founding of the park, stuck on to an enormous boulder. The mother cheetah and her two grown cubs scooted past the vehicle warily. One of the cubs was a little curious and stayed for a few moments in the long grass after he had crossed the road, crouched low and giving the truck a good once over before his mother gave a little squeak and he bounded off to join her.

From Satara they continued north to Letaba, a beautiful camp teeming with bird and animal life of its own and richly entwined in thick, dark green tropical plants and trees. Bushbuck, small antelope with delicate features and milk-chocolate coats painted with chalky stripes, wandered among the huts, and elephant drank or browsed in the riverbed below the camp.

While the rest of the group adjourned to cold drinks and hot pies at the restaurant overlooking the broad Letaba River, Mike wandered over to the Elephant Hall, a museum where park visitors could learn virtually everything there was to know about the mighty pachyderms.

The museum was air-conditioned, cool and inviting. A young brunette woman in a sleeveless National Parks uniform seated at the reception desk smiled at Mike as he entered. Around the wall were pictures of Kruger's original magnificent seven, the biggest tuskers in South Africa – probably in all of Africa – along with their actual tusks. There were also displays on poaching and anti-poaching, including an information panel on Fanie Theron's Animal Protection Unit, and photographs of the significant bulls still alive in the park today plus a few that were recently deceased. Mike finally found Skukuza's picture, the second last near the exit door.

The elephant was not as Mike remembered him, with his ears back, trunk down, bleeding and bellowing. Instead, his photo showed him grazing contentedly at a waterhole at the foot of the Lebombo Hills, which follow the Mozambican border. Mike

189

wondered if the poachers who killed him had stood in this exact same spot and chosen the old bull because of the information thoughtfully provided by the well-meaning architects of the Elephant Hall.

'Skukuza can often be seen in the area around the Grootvlei waterhole, in the north-east of the park,' read the information panel below his picture. And perhaps this further gem of information had sealed his fate: 'Most elephants favour one tusk over the other – this is sometimes referred to as the "working tusk" and is usually significantly shorter than the other as it has been worn down over a number of years. Skukuza is one of a small percentage of "ambidextrous" elephants who use both tusks. This accounts for the fact that both of his magnificent tusks are of equal length and diameter.'

Below the original information panel, which had yellowed with time, was a new laminated sign printed on white paper. It read: 'Sadly, Skukuza was killed by poachers, believed to be from Mozambique. His tusks were stolen and have yet to be recovered.' There was nothing about the Mozambican ranger who was killed as well, and Mike was angry that the National Parks officials seemed too keen to blame the elephant's death on some dirt-poor villager from a neighbouring country. If Fanie's theory was right, Skukuza was killed by a highly organised gang, possibly from this very country.

Mike remembered the dust and the overpowering smell of the bull elephant as he thundered down the track towards him and Carlos. He felt the recoil of the AK-47 in his shoulder again and he recalled the blind panic as the firing pin clicked on the nothingness of the empty chamber. He remembered Carlos turning to him and then falling onto the uncovered landmine. Mike reached out to the picture and touched the spot on the elephant's big knobbly forehead where he had seen his bullet strike. He closed his eyes and let the memories wash over him.

When he opened them and turned for the door, Mike saw Sarah standing there. She looked at him for a long moment and seemed about to say something, then thought better of it. She turned and wandered off to look at an information display with a cross-section of an elephant's foot.

Mike walked out into the lengthening afternoon shadows and put his sunglasses on. He was grateful she hadn't spoken.

They continued their journey the following day, on the good tar road that ran the length of the park, through kilometre after kilometre of shoulder-high bush. Big fires had swept through this part of the park in recent months, and nature was busily re-establishing the endless mopani forests. Here and there big bull elephants stuck incongruously up out of the juvenile trees, silhouetted black against the red-gold dawn sky.

North of Mopani Camp, Mike stopped the truck beside a large man-made boulder with a plaque fixed to it.

'What's this, then?' George asked from the back of the truck.

'The Tropic of Capricorn,' Mike said.

A couple of the tourists dutifully took photos and Kylie tried to explain to Linda where the Tropic of Capricorn passed through Queensland in Australia. Mike stared out to the east, towards Mozambique, and remembered a morning of death and the end of a dream that took place on the same arbitrary line drawn on a map.

'Can you see anything out there?' Sarah asked.

'Nothing. Nothing at all,' he said, as he put the truck into gear.

They stopped that night at Shingwedzi Camp, on the river of the same name, in the far north of the Kruger park. Mike parked the truck under an umbrella thorn tree, close to the swimming pool at the far end of the camping ground; he then spent a hot, frustrating hour banging in tent pegs, and bending a few in the process, into hard-baked earth. The name 'Shingwedzi' means 'place of ironstone'. The name was a good one, he thought, as he wiped the sweat from his face and swung the hammer again.

The overlanders compensated for their lack of success in finding a leopard with early drinks around the camp's swimming pool, where Mike gratefully sluiced off his midday sweat. Dinner that night was a hearty *braai* of steak and sausages, foil-wrapped baked potatoes and salads. Mike found he was getting on well with everyone, except for Nigel and Sarah, who both gave him a wide berth. But then, they gave everyone a wide berth.

When the two outsiders retreated to their tents, the mood of the group always relaxed noticeably. They were seated around a blazing campfire, nursing drinks and laughing. A spotted hyena loped past the camping ground's electrified fence looking for bones and food scraps, but Mike discouraged any of the group from feeding the animal.

He had already finished off a six-pack of Lion lagers and was sipping cheap South African brandy from a plastic coffee cup when Mel pulled out a joint. Mike passed on the marijuana as he was experiencing enough of a buzz from the alcohol, but noticed Jane, who was sitting next to him, never missed the opportunity for a toke when it came her way. A couple of times, when Jane leaned over to pass the joint to Terry, she let her leg rub against Mike's or laid a hand on his knee to steady herself.

Julie had elbowed Sarah out of the front cab for a couple of hours that morning and, true to her request on the first night, had interviewed Mike about his job for the travel feature she had to write for her studies. Like her mother, she was friendly and outgoing. She asked straightforward questions about his experiences driving an overland truck, the countries he'd seen and the ups and downs of the job. Another trait she had apparently inherited from her mother was a tendency to touch people to emphasise things when she spoke. He had thought Jane had been flirting with him, but now wondered whether both mother and daughter were simply very extroverted people.

'Tell us about your first time. Your first sexual experience,' said Jane.

Mike coughed as his brandy went down the wrong way. There were laughs all around the fire.

The conversation was getting more and more outrageous as the night wore on and Jane had just upped the ante.

'Boy or girl?' asked Linda with mock seriousness. Everybody laughed.

The stories tumbled out of embarrassed, drunk and stoned mouths. Back seat of a car, village green, high school dance, sand dune.

'Where's Sarah?' asked Linda, draining another glass of South African white wine.

'The virgin?' said Mel.

'Bitchy,' replied Julie.

'What about our Nigel?' asked George aloud.

'Baa-ah,' said Terry, doing a credible sheep impersonation.

'What about you, Jane? You started this,' said Terry, lighting yet another joint.

Jane swirled her wine in her plastic cup and looked up at the stars, then across to Julie. 'Julie's dad,' she said softly, and there was silence around the fire. 'I was sixteen, he was seventeen. He was lead guitarist in a covers band and I used to sneak into the night-clubs around Bristol to watch him play.'

'Tell the rest, Mum,' Julie said earnestly, laying a hand on her mother's knee.

'Well . . . When I found out I was pregnant I thought he'd run, but he surprised me. Said he wanted to spend the rest of his life with me. I was going to be in terrible trouble with my folks – and I was, in the end – so we decided to elope. I packed my bag and waited for him to come fetch me in the middle of the night. We lived in a small village then, way out in the countryside. It was winter. The roads were icy. He rode a motorbike.'

Mike could see Jane's hands gripping the cup tightly and she looked up into the star-filled sky again.

'He'd been gigging that night and when he didn't show up I thought he'd changed his mind and done a runner.'

'But he hadn't,' said Julie.

'No. He hit a patch of black ice and ran into a parked lorry. Not a mile from our house. Julie never met her dad.'

There was silence around the fire now. Some of them looked up at the stars, others gazed into the flames.

'It's OK, you know,' Julie said to no one in particular. 'From Mum I've only got good memories of my father.'

'How about a refill, Mike, before everyone gets too maudlin,' Jane said. 'And you can tell us about your first love,' she added, trying to sound brighter.

'It was so long ago I can't remember,' he lied. He looked at Jane and she just smiled back at him.

The numbers around the fire slowly dwindled.

'So, was there ever a true love in your life?' Jane asked again, quietly. The other stayers, Linda, Terry and George, were engaged in their own conversation, about football, on the other side of the fire.

'One. But I don't want to talk about it, if that's all right,' he said.

'Strong silent type, eh? Typical Aussie,' Jane said, tipping the last of the half-bottle of brandy into their mugs. She put a hand on his thigh to steady herself as she poured, and, despite his inebriation, he was acutely aware of the warmth of her hand, the smell of her perfume.

He just nodded, and they both laughed. He knew he had drunk too much, but he opened them both another can of beer once they finished their brandy.

The paraffin lantern hanging off the back of the truck started to gutter at one in the morning and Mike didn't bother refilling it. He realised he might set fire to himself if he tried, given the state he was in.

'I think we'd better call it a night,' he said to Jane. The others had just left them.

'It's a night,' she said, giggling.

Even drunk, Mike was a light sleeper. The rocking of the truck, slight as it was, woke him immediately. He was lying on the floor, in the aisle between the seats near the back. He fumbled under the rolled-up fleece he used as a pillow for his mini torch.

He could see a slight form standing in the aisle, silhouetted against the starlight outside. The figure crept closer, but he didn't switch on the torch. He doubted it was a thief, as the South African national parks are all but crime-free. He could see the swell of her hips now, her shapely legs. His heart rate went into overdrive.

'Hi, it's only me,' Jane whispered. 'Did I wake you? Sorry. I felt like some company.'

She padded the length of the cab in white socks now coated with the camping ground's gritty sand.

Her feet made tiny scratching sounds on the tin floor of the cab. She was wearing a long, baggy T-shirt and shorts.

'Mind if I sit down?'

He ran a hand through his long hair, which was hanging loose, brushing it off his eyes. 'Sure – I mean, no, I don't mind at all,' he said, moving as far across the narrow aisle as he could to make room for her.

'It was all that talk about first loves and all,' she whispered as she slid her back down the rear wall of the cab and landed with a soft thud on her backside on his sleeping mat. She pulled her knees up to her chin and wrapped her arms around her legs. 'I know I started it, but it gets me down, when I think about the past and what might have been. Do you ever feel that way?'

'Yes.'

'You don't give much away, do you?' she asked, turning to stare hard into his eyes. Her lips stayed slightly parted and he could smell the alcohol on her breath and sweet marijuana smoke in her hair.

'No.'

'Tell me if you want me to leave now.'

'I'm not sure, Jane. We've both had a bit to drink.'

She moved a finger to his lips. 'Shush. I know, but I'm not feeling drunk now, are you?'

He knew what she had gone through, losing her boyfriend, and his heart hurt for her. He thought of Isabella and of the rule about sleeping with passengers. He was about to protest, but his body betrayed him.

Jane leaned closer, moved her finger from his lips

and traced a line from his mouth, slowly down over his chest and belly. Lower. She smiled and placed her lips on his, her hand tracing him now, through his shorts.

Mike reached a hand behind her head, his fingers tingling at the feel of silky female hair for the first time in too long, and drew her to him. He pressed his lips hard against hers. She opened her mouth and he felt her hot tongue probing his mouth.

They lowered themselves to the warm sleeping bag. Jane broke from the kiss for a brief moment to lift his T-shirt over his head. He slid his hands up under hers and felt warm skin, soft breasts and nipples that stiffened instantly to his touch. She pulled her shirt up and he shifted his mouth to her breast. She moaned low as he bit down on the protruding nipple.

'Yes,' she said. 'Please.'

She fumbled with his shorts and giggled as hers finally came unstuck from her feet, toes pointed high in the air. She was naked underneath and the dull gold of her pubic hair was caught in a moonbeam through the window. When he touched her she was wet already. She arched her back and ground her pubis into his hand as his finger circled her hard little clitoris. He saw she was biting her lower lip and she was breathing heavily. After a moment she shifted her body. Awkwardly, for it was cramped between the seats, she rose to her knees and turned her back to him.

Mike reached out for her, but she knew what she was doing. She spread her legs and placed her knees on the floor of the truck on either side of his chest, opening herself to him. He shut his eyes in a moment of ecstasy as he felt her hot mouth close around him.

When they were both near to orgasm she turned again on her knees. He grabbed her forearms and pulled her to him, thrusting his tongue into her mouth as they kissed again.

She broke the kiss. 'I can taste myself,' she purred.

She lowered herself onto him and he guided her with his hands on her hips as she slid rhythmically up and down.

He drank in the sight, the feel and the taste of her and she moved, faster and faster, above him, eyes closed and head back. Her pelvic muscles squeezed and twitched involuntarily and, as she gripped his shoulders hard with her hands, he came too, for the first time in a long time.

Mike woke up alone and hungover. He lit a cigarette before getting out of his sleeping bag. Even through the smoke he could still taste her. He ran a hand through his hair and closed his eyes. 'Shit,' he mouthed.

They had done it again and Jane had fallen asleep in his arms. God, she had felt good. Like a miracle balm to soothe his pains. In the cool dawn, he told himself she had been good for him. But now he felt guilty. Stupid, he knew, because Isabella had been gone for a year now and at some point he had to move on.

They met over coffee. There was no early morning drive planned, just a leisurely transit to Punda Maria Camp in the bushy north of the park, where they would spend one more night before crossing into Zimbabwe. She smiled at him as she accepted the cup. No one else was with them. A couple of the crew were showering, the others still sleeping. Sarah had gone for a power-walk around the inside of the perimeter fence.

'Do you want to say it, or should I?' Jane asked, both hands wrapped around the steaming mug.

She was wearing a fleece and jeans. Her fair hair was tousled, her eyes red, although she still managed to look sexy, he thought. But there were complications. She had a daughter and lived in England. He imagined there had been other holiday romances, and that was all they were. 'Say what?' he asked.

'About last night . . .' She laughed. Forced, too loud.

He smiled back at her. 'What should I say? Thanks? I'm out of practice at this sort of thing.'

'Didn't seem that way last night.'

He laughed. 'I like you, Jane, and yes, it was great. It's a sackable offence for me, by the way.'

'We didn't do anything illegal – at least, not this time.'

She was being good about it, which made him smile again. 'That reminds me, I'm expecting a call from my boss today, once we get back into mobile range around Punda Maria Camp. I'll try not to sound too guilty,' he said.

'Seriously, though, I'm not looking for anything . . . deeper at the moment. You're right, we both had too much too drink. I was lonely. You said you know how that is.'

'I do.'

'Maybe we should leave things as they were for the time being.'

She was right, but part of him immediately felt disappointed by her words. 'I agree completely,' he said quickly, and wondered if he saw in her eyes the same brief flash of mixed emotion he'd felt.

'Here comes the nosy reporter again,' she said gesturing to Sarah, who was walking furiously, arms pumping.

10

Vassily Orlov pulled the butt of the rifle into his shoulder and laid his right eye against the black rubber eyepiece of the starlight scope. Through the green tinge of the night sight, which amplified the ambient light from the moon and stars above, he made out the outline of the leopard.

This was not hunting, Orlov thought. Hess had had his man hang a haunch of impala meat from a tree branch to lure the big, sleek cat to its certain death. No, this was no more than a mildly enjoyable way to zero the sights on his favourite rifle, in case they had been knocked out of alignment during the flight from Moscow via London.

The night sight was American, state-of-the-art. It magnified the target in the crosshairs, like a normal telescopic sight, while also allowing him to see in the dark. It was much better than anything the Russian Army had developed. Orlov remembered the night vision devices they had used in Afghanistan – cumbersome things that weighed a tonne and only worked intermittently.

Orlov aimed for the beast's heart. The hide would make a fine rug for the bedroom of his dacha. The huge elephant tusks, their rough ends now capped in solid gold, took pride of place above the enormous fireplace in his banquet room. On this trip he would be collecting the trophies denied him by his wound twelve months before. The leopard would be the first, followed by a black-maned lion, a bull buffalo with magnificent curled horns and, most exciting of all, the head of a black rhinocerous. Orlov knew the last of Africa's big five would be the hardest to bag, and that it could not be done legally in the wild.

Hess had risen to the challenge and organised a safari guaranteed to sate his prize client's lust for adrenaline and danger. He knew the trophies were almost incidental to Orlov and wondered how close to death the Russian would come this year.

They were on Hess's private hunting reserve near Messina. Orlov, Hess and his servant, Klaus, lay in the thick bush that flanked the small river running through the reserve. Frogs croaked at the edge of the still water and mosquitoes buzzed noisily around the trio's ears. The hunter knelt in the long dry grass next to his client, while a metre behind them Klaus watched out for other, unseen game in the night, his trusty AK-47 resting on one knee.

Hess wondered how the Russian would fare on this, his first night back in the African bush since the near disaster in Mozambique a year before. Tonight would be a test for his client, and a chance for Hess to gauge whether the old soldier was ready for the rigours they faced. Tomorrow they planned to leave for Zimbabwe, by road, in the rented four-by-four. In Zimbabwe, where National Parks rangers followed a shoot-to-kill policy against poachers, the danger would be real enough, and Orlov would get his adrenaline fix.

The leopard had climbed the pale green fever tree and it crept silently along the exposed branch towards the suspended meat. After every silent, padded pace it stopped and slowly looked left and right. Its ears twitched, straining for any sound that might alert it to a possible trap.

While the Russian squinted into the night sight and slowly traversed his rifle to keep the crosshairs centred on the cat's heart, Hess turned to Klaus and gave a little nod. On cue, the big African dropped his rifle, letting it clatter noisily on a fallen tree branch in the grass.

The leopard stopped and turned wide yellow eyes towards the sound for a split second. Its muscled body seemed to spin in midair as it turned and bounded back along the branch to the trunk of the fever tree. Orlov did not turn towards the sound behind him or utter a word. As the leopard stretched its front paws to grasp the thick trunk, the Russian fired. The leopard was still moving and the bullet missed the heart, but burned a deep furrow along the cat's lower rib cage. The creature called in pain, its eerie, rasping call piercing the silence that followed the gunshot.

'It's wounded,' Hess said calmly in his ear.

Orlov did not acknowledge the blindingly obvious comment. Instead, he kept the sights focused on the leopard. The cat half-slid, half-ran down the tree and headed straight towards the trio of men crouched in the grass. The fever tree was no more than forty metres away and the leopard, its heart and lungs untouched, rapidly gained the speed it needed for its lethal charge. Orlov worked the bolt action of his hunting rifle, chambering another round.

He heard Hess rise to his feet beside him and, from the corner of his eye, saw the Namibian raise his rifle to his shoulder. Behind him, he heard the oafish African cock the mechanism of his retrieved assault rifle. 'Still! Both of you. It's mine,' he said in English, their common language.

Hess smiled and lowered the rifle slightly so he could get a better view. The leopard was a mere ten metres away from them when Orlov fired again. The bullet entered the dappled fur of the cat's breast and penetrated the heart. With each of its remaining bounds the life force pumped from the animal until it fell, on its knees, not two metres from the Russian's feet. Orlov stood and watched its death throes. He chambered another round and turned to face Hess and his manservant.

A smile played across his lips as he said, 'Perhaps, when you two have tired of your games, we can start the hunt.'

Hess smiled as well and clapped the Russian on the shoulder. Klaus grinned sheepishly in the dark behind them and resumed his vigil. 'Come, now we drink. Klaus, bring the leopard.'

*

Orlov stood with his back to the roaring leadwood fire in the dining room of Hess's lodge. The night was unseasonably chilly, exacerbated by the ride back in the open-topped Land Rover, and Orlov rubbed the ache in his right leg, recalling as he did the wild excitement of his last trip to Africa.

'Still giving you trouble, Vassily?' Hess said as he handed the Russian a heavy square glass tumbler containing golden liquid and ice.

'Ah, Johnnie Walker Blue Label. Good of you to remember we don't all drink vodka,' Orlov said as the warming liquor coursed down his throat. 'My leg only troubles me in the cold, which means quite often, in Russia. But don't let it concern you. I am in the peak of physical condition, for a man of my age and wealth.'

Orlov surveyed the masculine domain around him. Magnificent trophies lined the walls – the horned heads of sable and roan antelope, gemsbok and kudu, a pair of tusks almost as big as the ones that adorned his own fireplace, as well as buffalo and rhino heads. A huge maned head glared up at him from the rug on the floor and genuine leopard skin–covered pillows dotted the deep upholstered leather lounge beside him.

Hess took a seat in a wing-backed leather armchair and unfolded a map on the heavy dark wood coffee table between him and the lounge. 'Please, have a seat, Major,' he said, remembering the Russian's fondness for his defunct rank. 'I thought we could review the itinerary now.'

'Yes. But first, tell me the latest news. You said the

police had been making inquiries,' Orlov said. He drained his glass then refilled it from the decanter Hess had placed on the table.

'Routine inquiries only. A fishing expedition, as the English would say,' Hess said with a dismissive wave.

'Yes, but have they had any bites?' Orlov asked, taking another sip of whisky.

'They guessed we had used a helicopter. The lack of tracks leading from the elephant would have made that obvious anyway. It would have taken them a long time, but the police did try and interview as many helicopter pilots as they could in South Africa –'

'And did they find our pilot?' Orlov interrupted.

'Yes. Viljoen called me as soon as the police had spoken to him. He told me he gave nothing away, but he said he wanted to talk to me urgently. I met him and he was rattled. The business at the mission, it seems, had unsettled him.'

Orlov nodded. He had been recovering from the anaesthetic when the gunfight had erupted at the mission clinic, but Hess had made sure he was fully aware of all that had happened as soon as he had pulled through. 'Regrettable, to be sure. But there was no alternative. You acted in the correct manner and I would have done nothing differently.'

Hess acknowledged the praise with a curt nod. 'The pilot was a risk. Unfortunately, he met with an accident. I believe it was reported as an armed robbery of his house, that went bad.'

Orlov smiled. 'This is a violent country you live in, Karl. These things happen, eh?'

'As far as I know there is nothing to link us to

Viljoen,' Hess said, studying the map to indicate the subject was closed as far as he was concerned. 'As you know,' he continued, 'this safari will take us out of South Africa, away from our police, into some of the wilder parts of the continent.'

Orlov leaned closer to the coffee table so he could follow the route of Hess's slender finger. I bet he has his pick of the women, Orlov thought as the tall, fair-haired Teuton began reciting the itinerary.

'From Messina we will cross into Zimbabwe at Beitbridge. I'll allow you to sleep late tomorrow – we will have plenty of time to reach our first stop, at Bulawayo. You may need your sleep after your dessert.'

'Let us hope so,' Orlov replied with a smile of antic-ipation. 'But back to the safari, please.'

Hess had been appraising the Russian since he met him at Johannesburg airport. There was a little more grey in the neatly trimmed moustache and wavy hair. Orlov had always had a heavy build, he could see, but unlike many rich men he had not succumbed to obesity. The cold, he had said, affected his leg wound, but Hess had not detected any sign of a limp. Anyway, Hess told himself, it would become warmer and warmer the farther north they moved from the Limpopo. Most important of all, Orlov had not lost his nerve after the previous year's fiasco. That was what Hess's prearranged stunt with Klaus had been designed to test during the leopard hunt. He contin-ued with the itinerary.

'From Bulawayo we move on to Victoria Falls. Your first visit, yes?' Orlov nodded. 'I have allowed time for you to visit the falls. The town itself is disgusting – a seething mass of low-budget tourists and blacks trying to sell them drugs or steal from them, but I have arranged suitable rooms for us.' Orlov again nodded his assent and Hess continued.

'On the way to the falls we will take a side trip to a hunting lodge here,' he said, moving his finger to a spot south of the well-known destination, 'on the northern border of Wankie National Park.' Hess, like most whites in southern Africa old enough to remember Zimbabwe as Rhodesia, used the former name of the park now known as Hwange.

'There you will be able to bag a sable, the most attractive of all the African antelope.' Hess gestured to the wall behind him, where his own sable trophy was hung. Glass eyes stared mournfully from the beautiful black and white head. Massive ringed horns curved back away from above the eyes until they almost touched the wall behind.

'From Victoria Falls we will take the road south of the Zambezi towards Kariba, here, where the dam wall forms Lake Kariba. There are a number of excellent safari areas south of the lake and I propose to set up camp in two of these, here and here. This should be suitable for you to take lion and buffalo. All the trophies taken in Zimbabwe will be mounted by reputable taxidermists in the nearest major town – I have already forewarned them. They will arrange shipment, legitimately, to Moscow for you.'

Hess paused to take a sip from his own drink, a gin and tonic. 'Now, for the most difficult, and riskiest part of the trip.' The detour Hess had planned for this hunting trip would take them across another border, and across the line that separates legal, sustainable hunting, from common poaching. This, Hess knew, was what Orlov craved most, and what made this whole arrangement, which ordinarily would have seemed preposterous, such a lucrative business venture.

'We will cross the border at Kariba. We actually drive along the dam wall to enter Zambia and there we will base ourselves in the town of Siavonga for the next part of our expedition.'

Hess was a cautious man. That was how he survived wars and the not inconsiderable dangers of his chosen peacetime profession. He did not want to alarm his wealthy client, but he could not be sure Viljoen had not mentioned his name to the police, even though they had not sought him out. If the police were watching him, there was the possibility, however remote, that they may have been able to plant a listening device in the lodge.

'From Siavonga we will travel to the safari area by small boat, where our Zambian guide will assist us to track our . . . quarry.'

Orlov knew enough about the methods of law enforcement officers in the west to know that Hess was being deliberately obscure in his description of this element of the safari. He was not unduly concerned, and thought the Namibian's obvious caution was only prudent.

He looked more closely at the map when Hess mentioned the words 'safari area'. The hunter was pointing clearly to a location not on the Zambian side of Lake Kariba, but on the opposite, Zimbabwean shore. It was not a safari area, a place where hunting was legal and controlled. When Hess lifted his long, tapered finger, Orlov read the black print on the shaded area: 'Matusadona National Park'. Orlov knew from his research through press clippings and the internet that the remote, spectacularly beautiful Matusadona was the last preserve of the endangered black rhino in the Zambezi valley. Poachers had decimated the once thriving population of the prehistoric animals in the 1970s and '80s. When Orlov had e-mailed the confirmation of his travel arrangements to Hess he had mentioned that he was keen to 'see' the remaining members of the big five that he had missed on his last trip to Africa. In particular, he specifically wanted to 'see' a black rhino.

Hess had replied via the internet that it would be difficult to see such a rare animal, but that he could arrange it for a premium price. As was their usual practice, the actual price of the tailored safari Hess had put together for Orlov was ten times the figure he quoted in his final e-mail. If either man's computer system was being hacked by police or other agencies, the prices quoted for the safari would not arouse suspicion.

'Next we will move down the river to the Lower Zambezi National Park in Zambia, opposite Mana Pools National Park on the Zimbabwean side. You said in your e-mail that you would arrange shipment of this final trophy from Maputo. Is that still correct?'

'Yes,' Orlov replied. He had told Hess he would give him an address in the Mozambican capital where the special trophy should be delivered. There, they would be collected by a mid-ranking official from the Russian embassy. The man, who had been in Orlov's pay for many years, had proved an asset worth far more than the comparatively paltry amounts deposited every six months into a Swiss bank account. Orlov had already used the man to arrange illegal diamond shipments out of Angola and South Africa via the diplomatic pouch from Maputo. This next shipment would be much bigger, but the diplomatic immunity of the container would not be impinged upon, no matter what size the 'pouch'.

'Good. I propose moving our prize by boat down the Zambezi, and have made the appropriate arrangements,' Hess said. A telephone call from a satellite phone would provide the time and latitude and longitude for the pick-up. The boat, piloted by the same Mozambican tracker who had accompanied them on the previous year's safari, would speed downriver into Lake Cahora Bassa, in Mozambique. There the trophy would be sealed in a watertight container and then welded inside a 200-litre fuel drum filled with water, prior to being moved by road to Maputo.

'And your contingency plan, should we encounter problems again?' Orlov asked, draining his whisky.

Hess bridled at the inference that he had somehow been responsible for the close call they had experienced on the last trip. But he kept such petty emotions in check and instead said, 'I have arranged for a helicopter to be on standby, at Livingstone, on the Zambian side of Victoria Falls. The pilot will travel there independently of us and charter a local machine. He will stay with it, twenty-four hours a day, until I tell him he is no longer needed.

'In the event of a problem, the pilot will fly us to the Zambian capital, Lusaka. We both have open-ended first-class air tickets out of the country.'

Hess felt comforted by the knowledge that emergency evacuation was only a radio call away. The pilot he had chosen was ex-military, like the late Viljoen, but seemed to be made of stronger stuff than his predecessor.

'Finally,' Hess said, 'I propose we end our trip with a visit to the South Luangwa National Park in Zambia for a few days' relaxation at the luxury private lodge I mentioned in my e-mail. By the time we finish there, your special trophy should have arrived in Maputo. Afterwards, I will drop you at Lusaka, where you will catch a flight to London and then connect to Moscow, while I will return here via Namibia. Klaus will return the hired four-by-four to Jo'burg.'

'It is good, Karl. I am impressed, as usual, by your thoroughness and attention to detail. Now, you said something about dessert?' Orlov said, raising an eyebrow.

'Of course, Vassily. I don't think you will be disappointed. You can take it in the privacy of the guest wing. There is everything there you will need, I believe,' said Hess. He stood and walked to a small white intercom box fixed to the wall near the light switch. Hess pushed a button and said, 'Klaus, bring in our guest.'

Hess returned to his armchair and crossed his long legs. He settled back into the soft leather and raised

213

his drink to his thin lips. He watched the Russian over the rim of his glass and held back a smile at the man's anticipation. The brute was nearly salivating, Hess thought.

There was a knock at the door connecting the dining room to the kitchen. 'Come,' said Hess.

Klaus walked in, towering over a petite young black girl dressed in a short red satin evening dress and tottering unsteadily on black patent-leather platform shoes. Her long chocolate-coloured hair was braided and piled high, but the sophisticated style and heavy make-up did nothing to hide her age. Her legs were long and slender, her breasts tiny and barely showing against the flimsy fabric of the dress. Her eyes were wide and nervous, like a startled impala in the moment it senses the presence of a predator.

'She's Swazi. Sixteen, or so her parents claim. Isn't that right, Klaus?' Hess said with a bemused smile.

'Yes *baas*,' the big African said with a leering grin.

'And a virgin, yes?' Orlov asked, unable to hide his eagerness.

The girl turned her face away to hide her embarrassment and fidgeted with her hands, intertwining her long, thin fingers.

'Certified, by a doctor,' Hess said. 'Klaus, show Herr Orlov and his guest to their quarters.'

Orlov nodded his thanks as he stood to leave. 'You have done well, Karl, as always.'

Hess thought this man, this former soldier, pathetic at that moment. 'Enjoy,' he said as he raised his gin and tonic in a mock salute.

11

'Theron needs to speak to you.'

The phone call from Rian on the drive to Punda Maria continued to rattle Mike. He spent the rest of the next day in the camp by himself, as much as he could with ten other people dependent on him. He was particularly conscious of Sarah, who kept watching him with a suspicious look on her face. That was the worst part of the job – the inability to escape from people when he needed to.

He busied himself cleaning the truck's fuel and air filters, checking the tyre pressures, oil and water – anything to give himself time to think. He avoided Jane, feeling even guiltier now that he was faced with the prospect of news about Isabella's killers after so long. He hoped the police had caught someone. He longed to call Theron, to ask him what the meeting was about, but Rian had not given him the policeman's number.

The next morning they drove through their last stretch of Kruger to the Pafuri gate in the very far

215

northern tip of the park. Usually, he felt a little sad to leave the park, with its bounteous game, good roads, spotlessly clean facilities and almost Teutonic efficiency. He knew things would get rougher the farther north they travelled, but today he was in a hurry to leave.

The drive to Messina was long and hot. They wound through the old African homeland of Venda, where the standard of living wasn't as good as in other parts of South Africa. In Venda many people still lived in poverty, in simple huts with mud walls and thatched roofs, although there were signs of new housing projects under construction.

They rolled into the border town of Messina around eleven and Mike dropped his passengers at the Spur restaurant, a fast-food joint with an American wild-west theme, on the outskirts of town.

'My boss called yesterday and asked me to pick up a spare alternator for one of his other trucks. He's got a good deal on a reconditioned one from a guy in Messina,' Mike told them. 'I've got to go pick it up now, but you'll be fine here for a while. Enjoy your lunch. I'll be back soon.'

They bought his story, although he couldn't help but notice Sarah's doubting frown. He wondered if she had been able to hear Rian through the mobile phone.

He had to move fast, as the border post was a good fifteen kilometres from the town itself. He wanted to get back to the crew within about an hour and a half. Any longer and they would start to worry. He had learned as a tour guide that passengers soon became overly dependent on him.

As he neared the border he swung off the road and followed a sign to the South African Police Service post. A uniformed officer in a peaked baseball-style cap and matching blue fatigues waved him through a wire-mesh gate, topped with coils of nasty-looking razor wire.

'Captain Theron, please,' he said to the hot and bored looking female officer behind the charge desk in the main police station. She picked up the phone and spoke Afrikaans into the receiver when her call was answered.

'Down the corridor, up the stairs. First office on the left,' she said, fanning herself with a manila folder.

His rubber sandals squeaked on the polished linoleum floor. At the top of the stairs he knocked loudly on a door with a sign that said 'Investigations'.

'Mike, Mike, come in, please. How have you been? My God, where did all that bloody hair come from, man!' Fanie Theron grabbed his hand and shook it vigorously. 'This is Captain Radebe, the local head of investigations,' he continued.

Mike shook hands with an African man who had a high-and-tight US Marine–style haircut, and wore a white shirt and black trousers. Theron was wearing a white polo shirt and jeans. An air-conditioner hummed noisily and dripped water into an overflowing foam cup on the floor. Mike took a seat in a hard-backed metal chair. On the desk in front of him was a cheap radio-cassette player. Radebe sat behind the desk, Theron sat on it. He took out a cigarette and offered Mike one. He accepted the smoke and a light.

'We're not supposed to smoke in here, but Thomas

and I, we can't do our job without them, eh, Thomas?' Theron said to the other policeman, who just smiled.

'Fanie, it's good to see you again. Is there some news? I've got people waiting for me,' Mike said.

'*Ja*, we know. Jo'burg, Kruger, Zimbabwe, Zambia, Malawi, Mozambique. We got your itinerary from your boss,' the big detective said.

Mike was surprised, as he couldn't see what his full itinerary had to do with anything the police were up to.

'Mike, let me get to the point. I've got a question for you, and, maybe, some news for you about the men who killed your girlfriend.'

Mike nodded.

'First, the question. In your statement regarding the events of last year you said that after you fired the AK at the poachers, after the ranger was shot, that you heard a man call out in a foreign language, but that you couldn't place that language. That's right, isn't it?'

'Yes.'

'Since then, have you been able to recall anything about that voice, that strange language?'

'No,' Mike said. Then added, 'Sometimes I hear it, in dreams, you know? But the words are a jumble.' He didn't want them to think he was a basket case, but it was true that the whole scene, the elephant charge and the gunfire, sometimes featured in his dreams. Isabella also sometimes walked towards him, arms outstretched, beckoning, with blood dripping from the hole in her head, but he didn't mention that to Theron.

'If you heard that language, that accent, again, would you be able to place it?' Theron asked.

Mike got the impression this was very important to him – it must have been for Theron to travel to the border from Pretoria for their meeting.

'I don't know, Fanie. I really don't know.'

'I'm going to play you a tape, and I want you to listen very carefully. It's a tape of a couple of our linguists saying some things in different languages and I want you to tell me if you recognise anything that sounds familiar from that day.'

Mike nodded, and Fanie stabbed with a meaty finger the *play* button on the ghetto blaster.

What followed was a string of short phrases, each of three or four words, repeated, Mike imagined, word for word, in five different languages. The first, he could tell, was German. He recognised none of the words, and none sounded like the cries he had heard in the Mozambican bush.

The next language he wasn't sure about – maybe Italian, or possibly Romanian. Again, he shook his head.

The next string of phrases he recognised as Afrikaans. He'd heard that language enough, and even knew a few words of it. He shook his head again.

Mike looked up as the fourth set of phrases rolled off the tape. The first phrase, whatever the person was saying, meant nothing to him, but there was something about the guttural accent, the rhythm of the words that started the wheels of his mind spinning. In the pause between the first and second phrases he tried to recall the words from his nightmares. He heard them, again, when the voice on the tape resumed speaking.

'Stop! Play that again.'

Theron pressed the *rewind* button and re-cued the tape. He pressed *play*.

'That's it, or almost it. That's the language I heard. Maybe not word for word, but close enough,' Mike said. He was excited, and eager to learn more. 'What's he saying?'

Theron gestured towards the black policeman. 'Captain Radebe can help us there. He spent a bit of time in the old Soviet Union in the good old days.'

Radebe nodded. 'In the good old days, before I was a policeman,' he said with a smile. 'The voice is speaking Russian. The man is saying, "I've been hit, I've been shot, help me".'

'Russian?' Mike replied, surprised, although now that he had heard a few phrases spoken in a row he could identify the language more easily.

'We get a few Russian mafia types snooping around Africa. Usually it's diamonds or weapons. Sometimes they're here for fun. Sometimes for hunting,' Theron said.

'You're chasing a Russian?'

'A foreign national is the subject of our investigations into the death of that elephant last year. I'll need you to add to your statement, now that you can identify the language you heard spoken on that day.'

'What about the deaths of Isabella and the Mozambican ranger, and all those people at the clinic?' Mike snapped.

Theron held up open palms to placate him. 'I'd ask

220

the same question if I were you, too, Mike, but that, unfortunately, is not our jurisdiction. I'm keeping the Mozambican police informed of everything that's happening with our investigation. I wish I could tell you they've made progress on the murder inquiries, but they haven't. They are still treating the deaths at the hospital as a separate incident from the elephant kill and the ranger's death. As far as they're concerned, the hospital deaths were caused by bandits.'

'Bandits don't fly helicopters. So what can you do now?' Mike asked.

'There is a man who is, or, I should say, has just been in South Africa. He is a Russian citizen and he is here on a hunting safari. So far, all the indications are that it is a perfectly legal trip. We've been keeping an eye on him where we can, and we have the means to get closer to him and his guides if the right opportunity presents itself.'

'So why don't you talk to him? Bring him in and question him?'

'It's not that easy, as I'm sure you'll appreciate. The man has done nothing wrong, broken no laws, and he's not even a South African citizen.'

'Then what about the hunter who's leading him around?'

'You're quick, Mike, and we're on the same wavelength. He, the hunter, is also the subject of surveillance and an investigation. He is . . . what's the term in English? He is *known* to us. Known to me, actually.' Theron stubbed out his cigarette and reached for another. Mike declined his offer, intent on learning more.

'You remember my theory, about the helicopter being used in the hunt?' Theron continued. Mike nodded. 'After I left you last year my officers and I interviewed the owners of every helicopter charter company in South Africa and as many freelance helicopter pilots as we could track down.'

'Big job,' Mike said.

'Yes and no. I know a few ex-military pilots. Some of them are in business for themselves and, when business is slow, they will do almost anything for a price.'

'You found the pilot?'

Theron shrugged his shoulders. 'I don't know, and that's the truth. There was a suspicious incident during our investigations. I spoke to one man I knew from my time in the military in the old days, in South West Africa . . . er, sorry, *Namibia*,' he corrected himself and smiled at Radebe.

'Anyway, this *oke* seemed . . . well, he seemed not very relaxed when I started questioning him about charters to Mozambique. He denied ever flying across the border, of course, but I told him to contact me if he heard of anyone else who had been taking on illegal charters. About a week later I got a message that he had telephoned and needed to speak to me urgently. I went around to his house the next day and found him. He was dead. Shot with an assault rifle – an AK-47, most likely – during a robbery of his home.'

'An unfortunate coincidence,' Mike said.

'I don't believe in coincidences like that,' Theron said, shaking his head. 'I interviewed his latest girlfriend – this pilot was a stud of note back in the old days, I can tell you, and he was still doing well for himself. The woman arrived at the house just after me. Fortunately she was not living in the house at the time and had not been there when the killers arrived. She had been with the pilot, Viljoen was his name, for a few weeks. During that time she said he had been gone on a job for a few days and that when he returned she could tell he was a changed man, even in the short time she'd known him. He became moody and started drinking more than before. She said there was something that seemed to be eating him up inside.'

'This is a violent country you live in,' Mike said.

'You don't have to tell us that, we see it every day. But this killing was one for the books. Viljoen had been handcuffed and tortured first – cut several times. One of his ears was missing. At some point the killer raped him as well.'

The killers at the mission station had shown no mercy. Mike shivered inwardly. 'What was the link between the dead pilot and the man you're following now?' he asked.

'I checked Viljoen's telephone address book. There was a card from a hunting lodge in it – the only hunter's name in the book, from what we could see.'

'Where is this man now? Who is he?' Mike asked. The memory of Isabella's body, of Fernando the ranger, and of Carlos dying in his arms made him clench his fists in silent rage.

'Steady, Mike. By rights, I should tell you none of this,' Theron said.

223

'So why are you about to tell me?'

He gave a little laugh. 'Because, you are going where they are going, and where I cannot go.'

'Where?'

'To Zimbabwe. They crossed the border an hour ago, travelling in a white Gauteng-registered Land Cruiser.'

Gauteng is the South African province that encompasses Johannesburg. The province's blue-and-white vehicle registration plates carry the abbreviation 'GP' which, given the city's reputation for crime, is often translated by non-residents as 'Gangster's Paradise'.

Theron continued. 'The vehicle was hired, and not in the name of either the hunter or his client. There's an African driving and two white passengers – the hunter and the client. No offence, Mike, but I didn't come here just to talk to you. I've followed these two as far as I can – my jurisdiction ends here. I've alerted the police, my counterparts, on the Zimbabwe side, but they've got problems of their own up there.' Theron paused.

'So you want me to what, follow these men? Spy on them? I couldn't keep up with a Land Cruiser in that old crate of mine even if I wanted to,' Mike said.

Radebe joined the conversation again. 'No, no, of course not, Mr Williams. This man, the Russian, is a foreign national. You're a foreign national, on a valid work visa, I assume. I can't very well order a civilian from another country to spy on a foreign tourist in another country, can I?' he said with a conspiratorial smile.

Mike's work visa was perfectly valid but it was up

for renewal in three months' time. He didn't think Radebe was threatening him, but it was a pretty strong hint.

'But if I were to note anything unusual, anything suspicious, about this South African hunter and his Russian client, it would be my duty, as a resident alien, to report it to the police in South Africa. Is that about the size of it?' Mike asked.

'That would be most commendable of you,' Theron said with a broad smile. 'But Mike,' he added, his tone suddenly serious, 'I don't have to tell you how dangerous these men are, assuming they are the men we're looking for. You would have no protection from the law in this country or any neighbouring country if you took it upon yourself to do anything illegal. All we want you to do is let us know if you see anything unusual on your travels. We know where they are planning to stay in Zimbabwe, but we don't know when they will be at each of these places or for how long. Also, we don't know if they are coming back to South Africa after Zimbabwe or heading somewhere else.'

'How do you know where they will be in Zimbabwe?' Mike asked.

'As you probably know, when you fill out your entry card on your way into Zimbabwe you have to state exactly where you will be staying and for how long. A couple of entry cards came into my possession about half an hour ago. Your timing couldn't be better.'

Theron handed Mike a page from his notebook on which he had listed a string of five-star hotels and luxury game lodges. They were not exactly the sort of places where an overland tour guide would be able to lounge inconspicuously around the bar.

'I'll do what I can. Do these men have names?' Mike asked

'The Russian's name is Vassily Orlov. Interpol keeps a close eye on him. He's a suspected mafia boss – drugs, porn, smuggling, you name it – but he's never been busted for as much as a parking ticket so far. We checked the immigration records for last year. Orlov was registered as a visitor to South Africa at the time of the incident in Mozambique. He returned to Russia a week after Isabella's death. I checked all the airlines flying to Europe on the day he left the country. He flew British Airways and there was a note on the computer booking saying he needed special assistance, that he was using a wheelchair because of an injury.'

Mike took a deep breath. If Orlov was the man they were looking for, then Mike had been responsible for the Russian's injury. He felt the hairs rise on the back of his neck.

Theron continued. 'The professional hunter's a white Namibian, of German descent, living in South Africa.'

Mike took a pen from the desk. Cleverly, Theron had not written either of the names on the notepaper, just the hotel addresses. 'What's his name?' Mike asked.

'Hess. Karl Hess. As I said, I know him from the old days.'

Mike sensed Theron did not want to reminisce about his time in the former South African protectorate

226

while he was sitting in the room with a Russian-trained former ANC cadre.

'Be careful of him in particular, Mike. Let's just say he can be a very dangerous man.'

Theron gave Mike the licence-plate number for the Land Cruiser Hess and Orlov were using, and passed a flimsy piece of fax paper across to him. 'That's Orlov. It's a copy of his passport photo, and you know what they say about passport photos.'

'If you look like your passport photo you're too sick to be travelling,' Mike said, studying the grainy image. 'What about Hess?'

'I don't have a photograph on me, but you can't miss him. One-ninety centimetres, athletic build, tanned, short blond hair, blue eyes. Hitler's wet dream.'

After Mike finished writing an addendum to his original statement, he said his goodbyes to Radebe and Theron.

At the front door of the police station, Theron shook Mike's hand and said, 'Remember, we just want information on where they're heading, what they're up to. Nothing more. Don't do anything foolish.'

'Goodbye, Fanie,' Mike said.

He sat in the cab of the truck and stared hard at the grainy photo of the Russian. If Theron's assumptions were true, then this man's greed had caused the deaths of many innocent people.

He thought of the tourists waiting for him back at the restaurant in Messina. His first duty, he knew, must be to them; their safety was his paramount concern. He weighed his options. He could quit, cancel

227

the tour and take them back to Jo'burg, but by the time he sorted all that out the hunters would nearly be leaving Zimbabwe. On the other hand, the overland truck provided him with a perfect cover – no one would expect to be tailed by a tour vehicle.

He thought of Isabella's body laid out in the butcher's coldroom, of Fernando and Carlos.

Mike knew what he should do, and what he had to do. They were not the same thing. He had a new priority on this trip. It was time to do something foolish.

12

Mike drove back to Messina town and parked the truck outside a gun store he'd noticed on the way to the border. From the locked box behind the seat he took out his wallet, which contained cash and his South African gun licence. Rian had insisted Mike get a permit when he first came to stay with him, even though, despite Rian's repeated advice, he had never felt the need to buy a gun for his own protection.

Things were different now, though. Mike had heard the dead man's click once in his life. He never wanted to hear that sound again.

'*Goeiemiddag*,' the overweight Afrikaner man behind the counter greeted Mike as he walked into the shop.

'Sorry, I only speak English. I'm looking for a pistol. Automatic. Nothing fancy,' Mike said, pulling the licence out of his pocket and dropping it on the glass-topped counter. He looked around and found he was surrounded by weapons – knives, coshes, pistols and

229

rifles. On the counter to one side of him was a long, thin sword whose sheath looked like an ordinary walking stick.

'Sure,' said the man, who seemed a bit miffed at Mike's straightforward approach.

Mike didn't care. He didn't have time to gossip.

'Is there a type you are familiar with?' the man asked.

Mike had only been trained on one type of pistol in the army. 'Browning, nine millimetre.'

'You are English?'

'No.'

'But ex-military if you know that pistol.'

'I haven't got much time. Have you got one?'

The dealer nodded and reached under the cabinet. 'It's in good condition.' He drew back the slide mechanism on top of the pistol to show Mike the chamber was empty, then handed it to him. The weight of the black hunk of metal in his hand was oddly comforting. Mike looked down the short barrel, at the floor.

'I'll take it, plus a box of ammo,' he said. He paid in cash.

'Let's hope you only ever need it on the practice range,' the shopkeeper said as Mike turned to leave.

'Let's hope,' he replied.

Mike had to squint against the glare of the sun as he opened the door and stepped from its cool air-conditioned interior into the baking heat of the main street.

'Fuck!'

In front of him was an overland driver's worst nightmare. A cloud of black smoke blurted from

Nelson's exhaust pipe and Mike heard the unmistakable rattle of the big diesel engine coming to life. He looked up into the cab and saw a young black man behind the wheel, quickly glancing behind him to check the traffic in the main street. Mike started running as the yellow truck reversed ponderously into the street.

What he saw next confused and alarmed him even more. From across the road, Sarah Thatcher left a telephone booth and sprinted out towards the truck. Mike had left her with the others, a couple of kilometres away at the Spur restaurant. What was she doing across the road? He could see that she would reach the truck first and was suddenly afraid for her safety. The thief had Nelson in first gear now and was pulling away. Sarah was beside the truck, though, her legs pumping and arms outstretched.

She grabbed the handrail next to the passenger cab door, where Mike normally fitted the fold-out steps. Without the steps, however, it was a metre and a half from the ground up to the bottom of the doorway. She got both hands on the railing as Mike closed on the back of the truck and for a few seconds she was dragged along, her feet alternately dragging and skipping on the hot bitumen of the road. Finally, she lifted her body weight, her slim arms straining with the effort, and got her knees onto the door sill, then she disappeared inside the cab.

Mike's heart was pounding with the effort of running and he was breathing harder than he had in months. Sitting in a truck driving for weeks on end had done nothing to improve his fitness level. There was a fold-down tailgate on the back of the truck where he stored firewood and the spare gas bottle. He just about had his hand on the chain supporting the tailgate when the thief knocked Nelson into second and the truck opened the gap a few more centimetres. Mike looked left and right as he ran, but there wasn't a policeman in sight. The mobile phone was in the locked box behind the seat. On board were cash, cards and all the belongings of the ten people in his charge.

He briefly thought of his new pistol, which he still clutched, incongruously, in a plastic shopping bag. By the time he got it out and loaded it, the truck would be long out of range. Besides, Sarah was on board. He dismissed the idea. 'Shit!' he swore again as he started to slow his pace. He would have to call the police from a shop.

As he started to veer off the roadway the truck lurched to a sudden halt, not twenty metres away. A mix of adrenaline and rage pumped power to Mike's legs and he sprinted to the now stationary vehicle. He grabbed the handrail and was about to hoist himself up when he heard Sarah scream.

Think, he ordered himself. Mike let go of the handrail and crouched by the side of the idling truck. He fumbled in the plastic bag and took out the pistol. He thumbed the magazine release and the empty magazine slid out of the hand grip into his left hand. As he opened the box of bullets, the truck started to move again. Mike clenched the plastic bag containing the bullets between his teeth, thrust the empty pistol into the waistband of his shorts, grabbed the handrail and hoisted himself up into the rear compartment of the truck.

In the driver's cab, Sarah was on her knees on the passenger seat scratching and clawing at the face of the driver. The man took his left hand from the gearstick and swung his arm around in a savage backhand. Sarah reeled from the blow to her cheek and slumped back in her seat, stunned. The driver looked to his left and right, probably checking for police. They were just outside the main shopping district now and he swung the steering wheel around to the left, pulling over on the edge of the road.

As Mike dashed up the inside of the rear cabin the man grabbed a handful of Sarah's blonde hair and wrenched her towards him. His right hand moved to his trouser pocket. With a click and flash of sunlight on steel the flick-knife was suddenly at her throat.

'Quiet, or you die, bitch,' he hissed into Sarah's face. Still she struggled and reached for the hand holding the knife. The point touched the pale skin of her neck now. Feeling it, she lowered her hands.

Mike leaned into the driver's cab through the connecting window from the rear compartment, catching them both by surprise, and rammed the squat muzzle of the Browning into the man's temple.

'Drop the fucking knife,' Mike said.

'Christ,' said Sarah. 'Where have you been?'

He looked at her, annoyed at her question. 'Drop it or you're dead!' he said, louder this time. He pulled the hammer back with his thumb and the click seemed to echo in the confines of the cab. The man's glance shifted from Sarah to Mike. Slowly, he lowered his arm and let the knife drop to the floor beside him.

'Now open the door,' Mike ordered.

As the young man opened the door, Mike clapped the butt of the pistol down hard on his temple and shoved him out. He fell, landing heavily on his side with a yelp of pain.

'Go!' Mike yelled at him as he staggered, then broke into a run.

Mike climbed through into the front cab and dropped the pistol on the driver's seat. 'Sarah, how are you? Did he hurt you?'

'Thank you,' she said softly, as she gingerly fingered the darkening welt on the side of her face. Her fingers moved to the point on her neck where the blade had rested.

'No, it's me who should be thanking you,' he said. 'You saved the truck, all of our stuff. Without you he would have got away and –'

'He would have killed me,' she said, even quieter than before. The realisation was beginning to hit home and Mike could see her hands starting to shake. The tremors spread up her arms, and she hugged herself to try to steady her nerves.

'It's OK,' he said gently. He reached out for her and wrapped an arm around her shoulders. He felt her go limp against his body and the sweet smell of her hair filled his nostrils. 'It's all right now.' They sat like that, together, for a few brief seconds. She had goaded him from their first meeting and he had done nothing to earn her friendship, but she had just shown extraordinary courage and had risked her life to save what – a handful of replaceable possessions? She was not the molly-coddled, spoiled brat he had her pegged as after all.

The tender moment melted suddenly in a searing white flash of anger. Sarah sat bolt upright, breaking away from Mike's embrace. She shifted her bottom on the seat to put more distance between them and turned icy-blue eyes on Mike. 'Just what the fuck have you been playing at today?'

He felt anger start to colour his reply, until he realised that he was guilty of every charge she was probably going to level at him. He had lied to his passengers. He had agreed to help the police and, by doing so, might even expose them to risk. He had also broken his own cardinal rule of never leaving the truck unattended. 'It's a long story,' he said.

'Spit it out. Give it to me. You owe me that much.'

She was probably right, but first he had some questions. 'Were you following me?'

She frowned. 'Of course I bloody well followed you. I took a cab and tailed you to the police and back into town. Now I see you've bought a gun,' she said, looking at the weapon, which he had moved from the seat to the dashboard. 'And just what do you need that for?'

Mike stuffed the pistol back into his shorts, out of sight of any passer-by.

'I think we've just seen what I need it for, haven't we?' he replied.

'Bullshit. Give me a cigarette,' she ordered, running a hand through her golden hair.

He took two out of the pack in his shirt pocket and

235

handed her one. She accepted the smoke and the light from his Zippo without thanks, then inhaled deeply and blew the smoke straight up, so that it hung like mist at the top of the cab.

'Are you in trouble with the police?'

'No.'

'Then what were you doing there? Buying an *alternator*?'

He smiled at that one, and he thought he saw her eyes soften and the slightest trace of a smile play across her pale lips.

'No,' he said again. 'Look, I don't know about you, but I could use a drink.' He climbed past her into the rear cabin, and opened the clasp on the refrigerator they used for storing drinks on the road. He took out two cans of Windhoek Lager and offered her one. She nodded and he passed her the chilled beer. She climbed out of the driver's cabin and took an airline seat across the aisle from Mike.

'Well?' she asked.

'I told you, it's a long story,' he said.

'I've got time,' she said, sipping her beer. She looked into his eyes. 'Tell me something, would you have used that pistol? Would you have shot that man if he hadn't dropped the knife?'

Mike pulled the pistol out of his waistband, thumbed the hammer, pointed it to the roof and pulled the trigger. Sarah winced at the click. 'No bullets,' he said.

She shook her head and gave a little laugh. 'No, but if it *had* been loaded, would you have shot him? Would you have killed him?'

236

He returned her gaze, and thought of Isabella and the countless times he'd replayed those terrible few days over and over in his mind, wondering if there was anything he could have done to save her life. 'Yes.'

'Tell me what this is all about, Mike,' she said, and for the first time her tone was not accusatory, not angry, not indignant.

'Off the record?' he asked.

She hesitated a moment, then said, 'OK. Off the record.'

He checked his watch. He reckoned he had about half an hour before the rest of the crew started to panic.

'It started in Mozambique, about a year ago.'

13

'OK, I'll keep quiet about your deal with the police, but on one condition,' Sarah said as Mike stopped the truck outside the Spur restaurant in Messina, where the rest of the passengers had long since finished their lunch.

'What's the catch?' he replied, dreading but guessing the answer.

'You keep me informed of any information you pick up about the poachers. And I want to be in on any snooping you do. You'll need help and I've been trained to get information about people without them necessarily knowing about it.'

'Sure,' he said. He didn't expect to be breaking into hotel rooms or sneaking about with a camera, rather just keeping an ear to the ground as they travelled, so he didn't see any harm in Sarah knowing what he was up to. She thought she was on to the story of a lifetime – an investigative exposé of poaching and smuggling that would propel her out of the pages of *Outdoor Adventurer* and onto the front page of *The Times* or *The Guardian*.

'Jeez, Sarah, what have you done to your eye? And where have you two been?' Kylie, the Australian nurse, asked when they got out of the truck.

'I went for a look around town and this guy tried to mug me,' Sarah said, and was greeted with a chorus of gasps and 'no-way's from the assembled crew. 'But Mike was on his way back from the garage and saw it happening. He saved me.'

Mike could see the cheeky glint in her eyes, but everyone else turned and gave him approving nods.

'That's not quite true. Sarah had fought the guy off, I just chased him away,' Mike said modestly. As they climbed back into the truck, Sarah sitting next to Mike in her usual position, she smiled and winked at him. There was a bond between them now, of shared conspiracy and white lies. She thought she had conned him into letting her join a grand adventure. He hoped to give her nothing worth writing about.

The border crossing between Messina and Beitbridge, on the Zimbabwe side, was uneventful. This was the first crossing for the passengers and Mike shepherded them through the intricacies of African customs and immigration form-filling.

After the barcoded stamps in their passports were scanned and bleeped by officials on the South African side, they drove to Zimbabwe across the broad, mostly sandy Limpopo River on a bridge lined with razor wire and high steel fences. The former British colony of Rhodesia is less prosperous than its southern neighbour and, consequently, slower to adopt new technology. Mike thought it would be a long time before computers and barcode readers replaced the deafening thud of the rubber stamp at Zimbabwean border posts.

The different nationalities of the passengers on board the truck presented its own problems. 'Everyone needs a visa, but the rates are different. The poms will have to pay more than the Aussies,' he said as they parked outside the whitewashed customs and immigration office.

'That's not fair,' Linda said.

'Few things in life are.'

The hot, sticky, slow process involved a lot of queuing and called for even more patience than the previous border crossing. From the South African side, scores of Zimbabwean ex-pat workers were crossing the border in cars and vans loaded down with household furniture, pots and pans and bicycles – anything they could sell or take home to their families.

'Does it always take this long?' Julie asked. She fanned her face with her Zimbabwean entry permit.

'This has been quick, believe me,' Mike said. The border formalities for both countries had so far taken them a little more than an hour.

Once through the formalities on the Zimbabwean side they passed a long row of ramshackle stalls selling carved wooden African animals. Giraffes, some as tall as a man, dominated the menagerie. Interspersed among them were carved buffalos and rhinos, still huge at about a third the size of the real thing.

Mike took the left fork in the road onto the A6, towards Bulawayo. The countryside was hot and flat – dry red dirt and low scrubby bush – tough country in which only goats seemed to thrive, and they were doing a good job of denuding what vegetation was left. He honked the horn as they overtook a donkey-drawn cart made of rough planks on top of the rear axle and wheels of a scrapped motor car. The skinny young boy on the reins waved at the truck and lashed the back of his two donkeys with a wicked-looking whip.

'Tough life here if you're a donkey,' Sarah said, shaking her head.

'Tough life if you're a human,' Mike said. 'People are doing it hard here, no doubt about it. A lot of the other overland companies have stopped driving through Zimbabwe because of all the bad press about violence, farm invasions, fuel shortages and various other economic and political problems. But I still love the place.'

'Good for you, but are we safe here?' Sarah asked.

'The political violence, intimidation and oppression is real, but it's also carefully targeted against opponents of the government and minorities. The average Zimbabwean, black, white or coloured, is friendly and welcoming to tourists. I've never encountered any aggro on my previous trips.'

The countryside started to change as they drove north, moving from the arid, flat low veldt into rolling hills with more trees and prominent granite koppies. They passed game reserves surrounded by high electric fences, cattle and sheep ranches, and the one-street one-horse country towns of Mazunga, Makado and West Nicholson. A big open-cast mine at a place called Colleen Bawn was well advanced in the job of dismantling a hill.

241

Mike knew that Orlov and Hess had a good lead on them and that the men appeared to have no plan to stop on the way to Bulawayo. There were so few cars on the road, thanks to the intermittent fuel shortages and recent price hikes, that Mike was sure he would have noticed their hired South African vehicle easily if they had stopped for some reason.

'We'll stop here for the night,' Mike said to Sarah, as they entered the outskirts of Bulawayo. 'This place reminds me of a large Australian country town. Our streets are the same – wide enough to turn a bullock cart – and you often see the same jacaranda trees.'

They stayed in a tranquil walled campsite with manicured green lawns, at the back of a sprawling single-storey house in leafy Hillside, Bulawayo's nicest suburb. The next morning Sarah pestered Mike to go and look for Orlov and Hess, who, according to their immigration entry declaration, were staying at the Bulawayo Holiday Inn. Sarah had spotted the conspicuous mini sky-scraper that was the hotel.

'I don't think they'll have got up to much between here and the border,' Mike said to Sarah outside the TM supermarket in Hillside as they unloaded bags of groceries from a shopping trolley into the storage boxes under the cab of the truck.

Mike reached in his pocket for a crumpled Zimbabwean five-hundred-dollar bill and tipped the uniformed security guard, who had been hanging around the vehicle expectantly. The man touched the peak of his cap and smiled, even though the note was barely enough to buy a drink.

'You should have gone with the rest of the crew to the Matopos,' Mike said to Sarah.

The other passengers had opted for an early morning safari in open-top vehicles to the nearby national park. The Matopos, he had explained on the trip up, was a collection of granite hills topped by impressive stacks of boulders precariously balanced by nature. Cecil Rhodes, the founder of Rhodesia, was buried there and the caves and outcrops in the hills were alive with bushman paintings of hunting scenes and wild animals.

'What did you do with the gun, by the way?' Sarah asked as they drove back to the campsite from the supermarket.

'I sealed it in plastic and stowed it in a tin of grease in the tool box at the back.'

'Hard to get to in an emergency,' she said.

'Hard for the cops or customs officers to find when we cross a border,' he replied. Mike had no wish to declare the pistol and wondered what he would do when they entered a national park. By law, he knew he should surrender the weapon when they entered a national park in South Africa or Zimbabwe and that, in the latter country, rangers have the authority to shoot on sight any armed person they come across in a park. 'Anyway, I'm not planning on using it,' he said.

They struck their tents and packed up after the rest of the passengers returned from the game drive. The others were excited about having spotted some rhino, but Sarah and Mike were both looking for different game from now on.

'If you want a real story, take a look over there,'

Mike said to Sarah as they drove out of the Bulawayo city limits on the road to Victoria Falls. On their left, in what once had been an open field, half-a-dozen bare-chested black men sweated in the midday sun, swinging picks down into the rocky bare earth.

'What are they digging?' she asked, shielding her eyes from the glare as Mike geared down, slowing the truck a little.

'Graves. That's the new cemetery. The old one's full, thanks to AIDS.' He pointed out row upon row of fresh graves, topped by nothing more than mounds of rocky red soil.

'But where are all the headstones, the flowers?'

'The funeral industry's the only one that's growing in Zimbabwe these days, but no one can keep pace with the growth. You'll see as we travel some more, there are roadside undertakers selling coffins springing up everywhere. In Harare it's getting hard to find your way around town because the undertakers are stealing the metal road signs to melt them down to make coffin handles.'

'Amazing.'

'More than amazing. It's a nightmare. It's almost like living in the time of the black plague, in Europe, in the Middle Ages.'

'You talk like it's personal.'

He thought of Carlos, choosing a quick death instead of the alternative. 'It is.'

The scenery on the drive from Bulawayo to Hwange National Park turned to rolling tree-covered hills as they passed through forestry estates. Road signs warned drivers to keep watch for antelope and elephant, which moved freely through this part of the country.

They stopped for fuel at a restaurant and service station called the Halfway House, midway between Bulawayo and Victoria Falls. As the attendant topped up the tank and Mike's passengers bought ice creams and Cokes, a brand-new white Toyota Land Cruiser flashed by without stopping.

Sarah trotted down the service station driveway, Coke in hand, and raised her free hand to shield the sun from her eyes as she watched the fast disappearing white speck. 'Did you see that?' she said breathlessly, as she strode back towards Mike. 'Jo'burg plates. That's got to be them.'

'Could be,' Mike said. He felt his chest tighten. He wasn't sure whether it was fear or anticipation, but he knew that he would have to confront those men somehow, somewhere. What he would do when he met them and if he was able to link them to Isabella's death, he wasn't sure. His mind turned to the can of grease in the tool box.

'I like to think of Hwange as the grandmother of all African national parks,' Mike said to Sarah as they walked along a sandy track from the camp ground to a complex of old buildings housing the park's offices, restaurant, shop and bar.

'Why as a granny?' Sarah asked.

'A bit decrepit, old-fashioned, but worth making the effort to visit. This place doesn't have the same concentration of game as Kruger, but it can surprise you. I've driven for days and seen nothing but elephant and trees, then come across three leopard in the space of half an hour.'

'Where are we, by the way? I haven't looked at the map today.'

'We're in the north-western corner of Zimbabwe. Hwange's western boundary is the Botswana border. Up north it's about a hundred kilometres from the top of the park to Victoria Falls and the Zambezi. Zambia's on the other side of the river.'

Mike thought the park's facilities, accommodation, roads and shower blocks all resembled a grandmother's house. Clean, where the broom can reach, lovingly cared for as far as a tight budget will allow, but looking a little tatty and outdated. There was a musty air about the camps and their official buildings, like an open-air museum of the late 1960s and early '70s. The camp reception areas were decorated with fading black-and-white photos of strapping white men with sideburns, shorts and long socks watching on while their trusty black foot soldiers hog-tied captured rhino. The once-glossy public relations photos of the various camps showed ruddy-faced men and women with big hair lounging outside newly whitewashed lodges. In the car spaces were big cars with even bigger tailfins. The clock seemed to have stopped around the mid 1970s, when war took hold of the country and the poachers moved in virtually unchecked.

Still, the park and its wildlife had survived – just. Mike had seen rhino there but they were few and heavily guarded. Unlike most of Kruger, Hwange was not fenced. Animals, particularly the park's tens of thousands of elephants, were free to migrate to and from neighbouring Botswana, and also into the hunting concessions which bordered parts of the park.

Mike knew it was in one of these private hunting concessions that Vassily Orlov would start his international killing spree. He had driven past the lodges before, or rather, past the turn-offs to the lodges. They were very private concerns and there was no chance of him lumbering ten or twenty kilometres up a private road in a bright yellow truck on the pretext of asking for directions.

'Why can't we go and visit the hunting lodge where Hess and Orlov are staying? We could say we wanted some information about a hunting trip,' Sarah asked.

Mike was more than a little disconcerted that Sarah was apparently able to read his mind. He shook his head in reply to her question. Sarah and Mike took a seat at an outdoor table on the lawn in front of the Waterbuck Arms, the pub and restaurant at Hwange's main rest camp. Mike had finished driving for the day, the dome tents were up in the camping ground, everyone had had lunch and it was time for his first beer. The waiter, dressed in a loud African-print shirt which reminded Mike of a 1970s cushion cover, set a dew-coated green bottle of Zambezi Lager and a white-frosted beer glass down in front of him. Sarah was sticking to Coke, in a glass with a slice of lemon.

'You should go on a game drive this afternoon. Everyone else is,' Mike said, then sipped the deliciously chilled beer.

247

'Don't try to get rid of me. Let's go find this lodge,' she said doggedly.

'The lodge is on the northern border of the park. That's over a hundred and fifty kilometres from here and, besides, we can't take the truck through the middle of the park.' Because of its weight, the Bedford attracted a ridiculously high entrance fee in Zimbabwe's national parks if they wanted to use the park's internal roads. Rian wouldn't spring for the fees, so game viewing was courtesy of a fleet of obsolete ex–Rhodesian army Land Rovers and converted Japanese pick-ups driven by enterprising African locals, some of whom were ex-rangers.

'So we'll have to wait until Victoria Falls,' Sarah said. She looked disappointed.

Mike nodded. He savoured both the beer and the thought of revenge.

'This place has a life and a noise of its own,' Mike said to Sarah as they crested a hill and caught sight of the town of Victoria Falls.

Clouds of mist made the Zambezi look like a bushfire from a distance.

'You can buy every kind of high here, from dope to bungee jumping, white-water rafting, parachuting, microlighting, joy-flighting, even elephant rides.'

In his mind, Mike mulled over an action plan for the two and a half days they would spend in the town. For the passengers the plot was simple: two days of free time for action and a half day to recover from the hangover that always followed the second night. Among the many Generation X–rated attractions the place offered were dance clubs and all-night bars.

Mike reckoned they were now a day ahead of the hunters. Theron had copied the addresses of their accommodation down from their entry cards, but there were no dates. If hunting was the purpose of their trip, Mike guessed they would stay at least a couple of nights in the lodge listed on the card. It wouldn't be too hard to find out from the hotel in Victoria Falls when they were due to arrive – probably in the next day or two, sometime during his group's stay.

The air was hot and sticky as the overlander rolled into the business district, down the hill towards the falls themselves and their home for the night, the Municipal Campground.

'The place we're staying at is about as appealing as it sounds,' Mike said to Sarah. 'A patch of dirt set in the middle of the turf of a couple of hundred petty criminals.'

'Look,' he said, addressing the rest of the crew as they pulled to a halt inside the camping ground, 'Victoria Falls is a fun town, especially when you've been on the road for a while, but keep your wits about you. If you buy dope, don't tell me about it, and don't get sold garden herbs. Remember, we're crossing a border in a couple of days and I don't want to get busted for smuggling dagga, OK? Also, keep your valuables locked in the back of the truck. It's free time while we're here, and I'd like to get out for a look around as well, so if anyone wants to volunteer to watch the truck for a couple of hours in the next two days, that'd be great. Any questions?'

'Where's the party?' Linda asked.

'Three, two, one, bungee!' yelled a tall dreadlocked New Zealander.

George screamed as he reluctantly tumbled forward in a week-kneed approximation of a swan dive from the bridge one hundred and ten metres above the churning, rock-strewn Zambezi River. Somewhere below, in a chasm downriver, Mel, Linda, Kylie, Sam, Jane and Julie were hurtling down a raging river in an inflatable boat.

Sarah sidled up to Mike, who was staring out over the iron railing of the road and rail bridge that linked Zimbabwe with Zambia.

'You don't go in for this adrenaline-junkie stuff?' she asked.

'I've had enough thrills in my life,' he said.

'What, driving a truck full of spotty backpackers around Africa?'

'You'd be surprised.'

'Is that it, the Victoria Falls Hotel?' she asked, pointing across to the sprawling two-storey building on the other side of the chasm.

'That's it. The grand old lady of the falls. *The* place to stay here,' Mike replied. Now part of an international hotel chain, the opulent colonial relic was certainly one of the most expensive places to stay in the area.

'What are we waiting for?' she asked.

'We need a plan, in case they're there. Let's talk.'

Sarah insisted on showering and changing first, and by the end of the long walk up the hill from the border crossing to the camping ground Mike needed a cold shower as well. As Sarah headed for the ladies with her shower bag and towel he wandered over to Nigel, who was sitting on a fold-out chair, reading a book under Nelson's roll-out canvas awning.

'How's it?' Mike asked him.

'You're starting to sound like a local,' Nigel said without a trace of humour.

'All quiet on the western front?'

'I'm glad to have a bit of time by myself. Some of these people are getting on my nerves.'

Mike bit his tongue. 'Fine. Not interested in throwing yourself off a bridge or seeing the bottom of the Zambezi?'

'You wish,' he said, and smiled. 'So, is she going to do you over in that story of hers?' Nigel asked, gesturing with a flick of his head to Sarah, who had just disappeared into the shower block.

'We've got a good working relationship going now,' Mike said.

'What does that mean? Are you screwing her as well?'

'What are you talking about?'

'You know. I saw her, Jane, go into the truck that night. I heard you as well. I'd have thought there were rules against that sort of thing.' Nigel shook his head as he spoke.

'I'm going for a shower, Nigel.'

*

251

Sarah and Mike emerged from opposite ends of the men's and women's shower block at the same time.

'Je-sus,' he said, and gave a low whistle.

'If that's your idea of a compliment, you need to work on your vocabulary,' she said.

'No, I mean, yes, it is, but . . .' He thought she looked extraordinarily beautiful, and that was the problem. He'd left her as just another backpacker with uncombed hair, sweat-stained T-shirt and baggy shorts and rafter sandals. She stood there now with blonde hair blow-dried and brushed, and make-up that accentuated her high cheekbones and enhanced her large blue eyes, and soft, full-painted lips.

Her unisex traveller's outfit had been exchanged for a low-cut little black dress with spaghetti string shoulder straps that showed off her cleavage and smooth legs. Her only jewellery was a thin gold necklace and a single gold bangle. On her feet were a pair of black dress sandals with just enough heel to pass for evening wear. Her toenails were painted silver and, for the first time, he noticed a little silver ring with a heart on the second toe of her right foot, which he thought looked very sexy. She also carried her expensive Canon camera in its case, slung over her bare shoulder.

'Don't you think you're just a tad overdressed?' he ventured, and immediately regretted it.

'Bloody hell. It's a five-star hotel, not some dosshouse,' she countered, her cheeks turning pink through the make-up. 'How am I supposed to get talking to an organised crime boss, who's probably a millionaire, if I'm dressed like a nineteen-year-old hippie?'

Sarah had expressed a willingness to try to engage the Russian if they saw him. Mike was sure she would have no trouble attracting the man's eye.

'I suppose you're right,' he said reluctantly. He had changed into lightweight khaki trousers and his cleanest polo shirt, the closest he ever got to formal wear in Africa.

'You'll be the one who sticks out, not me. Let's go,' Sarah said.

14

As they walked into the elegant, cool reception foyer of the Victoria Falls Hotel, Mike saw a large sign on a noticeboard which read 'Welcome, Mr and Mrs Harold Carter and guests. Congratulations on your wedding day.' The board also gave the location of the function room where the Carters were having their reception.

'Looks like you're not going to be overdressed after all,' Mike said to Sarah.

'Told you.'

A shriek behind them heralded the arrival of the newly wed Mrs Carter, an attractive but painfully thin redhead in her early thirties in an ivory mini dress. It sounded like she had just been goosed by one of the wedding party.

A tall young man with pale skin, lank brown hair and a diamond stud earring pushed past Sarah and Mike and strode across the polished floor to a reception desk framed by a portal of antique red mahogany. When he spoke, it was with the plummy, languid drawl of the English upper class.

'Mr and Mrs Carter have arrived,' he announced with a pompous flourish of his right hand to the young white woman at reception.

About twenty chattering men and women now filled the foyer. They sounded to Mike like a herd of braying zebra. Sarah's little black dress, which had stood out like a mink coat in the camping ground, was just one of many in the foyer. From the noise and laughter around them, Mike suspected the wedding party had probably kicked off the day with too much champagne and not enough orange juice.

'Very good, sir. James will take you through to the Bulawayo Room for cocktails. James?' The woman behind the desk beckoned to a young African bellboy, decked out in a long-sleeved red mess jacket, cropped at the waist, and black trousers. Mike felt hot just looking at him.

Once the revellers had been led away to their function room, Sarah and Mike approached the receptionist.

'Good day, can I help you?' she asked. She took in Sarah's dress and then added, 'The wedding reception is through those doors, madam, across the courtyard and to the left.'

'No, we're not actually here for the wedding,' Sarah said. 'We're looking for a friend of ours – two, in fact. They're booked in to stay here, but I've lost the fax they sent me with the date that they were due to arrive. Stupid of me, I know.'

'No problem, madam. The names, please?'

'Mr Orlov and Mr Hess,' Sarah said.

Mike looked around the foyer.

'One moment, please, madam.' The woman smiled and tapped on a keyboard beneath the reception counter. She consulted a computer screen then looked up and said, 'Yes, you've got the right day. They are booked in to arrive today but . . .' she checked the screen again, 'but no, they haven't arrived yet.'

'Thanks, we might wait on the terrace. Oh, and please don't tell them I was asking about them. I'd hate them to think I was careless enough to forget when they were arriving,' Sarah said with a conspiratorial wink.

'Not a problem, madam.'

Mike needed a smoke, but, as was his habit, he had left his lighter in the dashboard of the truck again. He walked over to the concierge at the door and asked the man for a light. The concierge produced a Zippo and lit the cigarette with a flourish. As Mike thanked him he looked outside through the glass door and saw a new, but dusty, Toyota Land Cruiser with blue and white South African plates pull up. The concierge dispatched two bellboys to meet the vehicle.

Two white men stepped from the vehicle and stretched their cramped limbs. Mike knew it was them. Orlov was a little shorter than Mike had expected, but the moustache and wavy hair gave him away immediately. Hess was as tall and good looking as Theron had described him. He looked like he had just stepped out of the frame of a Hitler Youth recruiting poster, although Mike reckoned he must have been a few years older than himself.

Mike stared hard at the pair. On the balance of

probabilities, these were the men who had killed the woman he loved. Their nonchalant arrogance mocked him, enraged him. What right did they have to walk as free men in public? He wanted to punch the smile from Hess's face, to see the Russian on his knees begging for mercy.

He turned and strode quickly across the polished floor. Sarah was looking at him with an annoyed frown. He took her by the crook of the arm and felt her flinch at the overly familiar gesture. 'Let's get out of the foyer. They're here.'

'Where?' she asked, craning her head to see past Mike's shoulder. She shrugged her arm from his grasp.

They moved near the doorway which led from reception to the hotel's inner tree-lined courtyard and the terrace bar and restaurant beyond. Sarah sauntered over to one end of the foyer, to a display of tourist brochures advertising elephant-back safaris and various other activities around Victoria Falls. Mike followed her and also pretended to browse.

'Karl, I need a drink, to celebrate our day's work,' the Russian said loudly in heavily accented English. From his expansive manner and flushed face, Mike guessed Orlov had already started his celebrations during the road trip from the hunting lodge where they had stayed.

'Yes, Vassily,' the tall blond man said patiently. 'Of course, but I would like to shower and change first. I will join you in twenty minutes.' He turned to a tall African man in khaki trousers and short-sleeved shirt who had followed him into the foyer.

Mike looked the man up and down. An Ovambo, he thought. Also from Namibia. Despite the heat, the man looked as cool and impassive as an ebony statue.

'Klaus, have the vehicle cleaned and ensure security keeps a close eye on it. I will come with you to deliver the trophies tomorrow. Pick me up at eight in the morning.'

'Yes *baas*,' Klaus said with a nod and left the foyer. Hess moved to the reception desk with the angular grace of a giraffe, tall and aloof from the lesser creatures around him.

'Very well, Karl, I will see you in the bar,' Orlov said, leaving the other man to see to the formalities of checking in.

'The Russian's half cut already,' Sarah whispered. 'This is going to be easier than I thought.'

'You're sure you want to go through with this?' Mike asked. Her proposed approach had sounded risky, even foolhardy. But his military training had taught him that sometimes the boldest plans had the best chance of success.

'Definitely,' she said.

She led the way, following Orlov out into the late afternoon sunshine. The pathway from reception bisected the manicured lawns of the hotel's inner courtyard. Nearly a century old, the hotel was only two storeys high. The white-painted walls gleamed like pale gold with the reflected rays of the descending sun.

Once across the courtyard they entered the building again and passed between a restaurant on their right and the Bulawayo Room on the left. In the function

258

room the wedding guests were snatching drinks and canapés from silver platters with the tenacity of yellow-billed kites attacking roadkill. Young men in dinner suits, no doubt chafing in the afternoon heat, and pretty young women in short dresses stood and chattered amongst the chintzy, over-stuffed sofas, antique side tables and potted palms.

Sarah's dressy sandals tapped on the gleaming wooden parquetry floor as she and Mike followed Orlov out onto the terrace. The Russian sat down at a shady table in the covered section. His uninterrupted view took in Batoka Gorge and the Victoria Falls Bridge, stretching between Zimbabwe on one side and Zambia on the other. It was the same bridge where Mike and Sarah had stood watching George make his bungee jump earlier in the day. From where they now stood, while they waited for their table, Mike could see yet another daredevil parting with a large chunk of her travelling budget. Thankfully the diners on the terrace couldn't hear the screams from the bridge.

They chose a table three away from the Russian and settled into deep wicker armchairs. Mike pretended to study the cocktail menu and ordered a beer when the waiter appeared. Sarah ordered a mineral water with a slice of lemon.

'Put your cigarette out,' she ordered him.

'Why?' he asked. 'You smoke, it shouldn't bother you.'

'Just do it, OK?'

Reluctantly, he stubbed it out.

'Here goes,' she whispered. Sarah stood and started

walking towards Orlov, who had just taken delivery of a double scotch on the rocks in a heavy tumbler.

He was dressed in khaki trousers and a grey long-sleeved shirt. The trousers were dirtied at the knees and pocked here and there with little holes and scratches, as though he had been in thorn thickets. His boots were heavy brown leather, and looked almost military. His hair was dry but plastered back and unkempt. There were sweat stains on the armpits of his shirt, but other than that, it appeared to be clean.

Despite his concern for Sarah, Mike couldn't help but let his eyes linger on her shapely backside, accentuated as it was by the slow rise and fall of the thin material of her short dress as she sashayed across to Orlov's table. Her legs were long and tanned. In the slender fingers of her right hand was an unlit cigarette. He hoped she was having the same effect on Orlov as she was on him.

'Excuse me, do you have a light?' she said to Orlov, in a low, husky voice.

'Pardon me?' Orlov said in his heavily accented English.

'A light, for my cigarette,' she said, leaning closer to him, holding out her cigarette.

Mike imagined the great white hunter was a little taken aback by the perfumed beauty who hovered above him.

'Of course, of course,' he said, reaching into the top pocket of his shirt for a gold lighter. He lit her cigarette and she straightened her lithe body so the first puff of smoke didn't go into the Russian's face.

Mike sipped his beer and strained to hear their conversation.

'You look like you've been in the wars,' she said, placing her left hand on her hip.

'Excuse me?' he asked, puzzled by the idiom.

'In the bush, you look like you've been out exploring,' she said with a girlish laugh.

'Oh, of course. No, I have been hunting,' he replied, leaning back in his chair so he could appraise her better.

'I love hunting,' she cooed.

'Really? I think we are, how do the English say, a "dangerous species",' he said.

Sarah giggled again. '*Endangered* species, you mean. But, yes, I suppose we are also dangerous as well!'

Now Orlov laughed. 'I see your joke. A play on words. Endangered and dangerous, that is us, no?'

'That is us, yes,' she said.

'And what does a beautiful young woman hunt?' Orlov asked, raising his tumbler to his lips and downing the remains of his scotch.

'Foxes, mostly. I love the hunt. I love the baying of the hounds, the chase, the excitement. I even love . . .'

'The kill?'

She smiled a slow, wicked grin and drew heavily on her cigarette. She blew the smoke out slowly towards the Russian and said, 'Especially the kill.'

'Can I buy you a drink, Miss . . .'

'Grey, Sarah Grey. Yes, please. Gin and tonic, and please, call me Sarah, Mr . . . ?'

'Vassily Orlov.' The Russian beckoned a waiter over.

261

Orlov stood and pulled out a chair for Sarah. She eased herself down with catlike grace and crossed one leg over the other, doing nothing to stop the hem of her short dress sliding further up her thigh. Mike watched Orlov. He reluctantly lifted his gaze from her legs as she replied to his question.

'And your . . . companion? Will he be joining us?' he said.

'Yes, I suppose so. He's not my companion, by the way. He's my driver, my *safari* guide, actually.' She beckoned with an imperious wiggle of her finger for Mike to join them, and he walked over, self-consciously, drink in hand.

'You are hunting here, also? But not, I think, dressed like this?'

Sarah gave her girlish chortle again and said, 'No, sadly. Though I wish I *were* hunting here. I'm on a photographic safari.' She held up the camera slung over her shoulder. 'As for my clothes, Mr Orlov, a hunter dresses to match his or her environment, don't you agree?'

A lascivious smile crossed Orlov's face as he caught her meaning. 'I wish you well in your hunting this evening, Sarah, and please, call me Vassily. And this is . . . ?' he asked, turning to Mike.

'Mr Wilson. Michael, this is Mr Orlov. Say hello to Mr Orlov, Michael, there's a good boy.'

'Good afternoon, Mr Orlov,' Mike said, biting his tongue.

'Please, it is all informal here, yes, Sarah?' Orlov asked.

Sarah nodded.

'Call me Vassily, please. A drink, Michael?'

Orlov's face was redder now and Mike could tell he was a man in the mood for celebration. He asked for a beer and Orlov placed the orders with the hovering waiter, who scooted off.

'So, Sarah, do you shoot, as well as ride?' Orlov asked, turning away from Mike.

'Since I was eleven years old. Daddy insisted on it. Mummy was horrified, but then older men always seem to know what's best,' she said, leaning back in her chair. 'Shotguns, mostly. We shoot pheasant and grouse, occasionally stags on the estate,' she said languidly.

'*Your* estate?'

'One day,' she said, and winked theatrically at him.

The waiter brought the drinks and laid them with slow, deliberate care in front of them, halting the conversation temporarily. When, at last, the waiter departed, Orlov was eager to pick up where he had left off.

'And why are you not hunting in Africa?'

'Not enough time, really. I'm here for a wedding – friends from England – and some photography, of course. Then it's back to work in a couple of days' time.'

'And what do you do?'

'Photographer. Fashion magazines, mostly, but I'm doing a book of female nudes at the moment,' she said deadpan.

Orlov took a long drink from his tumbler and Mike thought he was about to choke on an ice cube. 'How interesting,' he said.

Mike reflected that the pig was almost drooling now as he stared at Sarah's cleavage.

'But tell me, Vassily, what are you hunting? Have you had luck today?' she asked, leaning forward in eager anticipation of his answer while at the same time allowing him a better view of her breasts.

'Today has been most excellent for me. Today I bagged a sable antelope with the most magnificent horns you will ever see. A perfect shot, if I do say so myself. A clean kill.'

Sarah gave a little shudder. 'How exciting. I'd love to see the trophy.'

'I wish you could, but it is on its way to the taxidermist. He will ship it back to Russia for me.'

'I'd love to visit Russia one day.'

'Well, my dear, if you do I would be most glad to show you my collection of trophies. I think you would be impressed.'

'I'm sure of it,' she said coquettishly from across the rim of her glass. 'What next?'

'Ah, next are two of the famous big five. Lion and buffalo. We are going to a safari area south of the Zambezi. Near Chizarira.'

'What about leopard?' Sarah asked.

'Already in the bag, as they say. I took a beautiful male at my professional hunter's lodge, down in South Africa, just the other day.'

'How wonderful. And rhino?' she asked.

Orlov seemed to mull over his answer. 'The most difficult and expensive of the big five, I fear.'

'What about elephant? And please, let me get the next round of drinks.' She was matching him sip for sip, and made a circular motion with her hand over the table to let the waiter know it was the same again all around.

'No, I will pay. I insist. Yes, elephant I bagged last year. Such a bull you would not believe,' he said proudly.

'Gosh. But it must have been dangerous,' she said in well-acted awe.

'What is life without danger, Sarah? Yes, it was dangerous, but in the end it was worth it,' he said, as he took his fresh drink off the table.

'In the end?' she probed.

'There were . . . complications. Even the best-planned safaris can sometimes, what is the phrase – come unstuck?'

'Where were you hunting elephant? Here in Zimbabwe?' Mike asked. It was the first time he had joined the conversation and he noticed Orlov was surprised by the question.

Orlov turned and fixed Mike with steel-grey eyes. The short breath he took, as if he were about to say something else, and the split-second pause before he finally said, 'South Africa,' told Mike what he needed to know. Orlov was lying.

Mike gripped his glass so hard he thought it might shatter in his hands.

'That's only four of the big five, Vassily. You can't go home without a rhino,' Sarah interjected from the other side of the table.

Orlov turned back to Sarah and said, 'You are right, of course, but these days it is an expensive business to hunt rhino. They are few and far between and it is hard to find someone who is willing to part with one.'

'But where would you hunt a rhino?' she asked.

'On a private game reserve. Some owners will let you shoot one, usually an old bull past his prime.'

'Personally, I can't see what satisfaction a hunter would get out of shooting an old half-tame white rhino. They're practically blind and most of the ones on private reserves have been hand reared,' Mike chimed in.

He knew it was foolish to goad Orlov, in case he dismissed them or, worse, became suspicious, but he couldn't help himself. This man had been involved in Isabella's death – he was sure of it – and he wanted to see him squirm.

'Perhaps you've never tracked a rhino before,' Orlov replied.

'I've walked to within ten metres of a white rhino before it even knew I was there. Where's the skill in taking a shot from ten metres? Shooting a white rhino's like shooting a cow. I don't know how anyone could even consider it a worthy trophy,' Mike said.

'Clearly, Mr Wilson, you've never stalked a black rhino. They are much more aggressive than the white and will often charge. A fitting challenge for any hunter, I assure you.'

Orlov's face was flushed red now and it was plain to Mike it wasn't just from alcohol.

'I didn't think you'd find anyone in southern Africa who'd let you shoot a black rhino,' Mike said.

'I haven't . . . I mean, of course not. Who began this talk about shooting black rhinos, anyway?' Orlov was flustered and he laughed, a little too loudly, trying to dismiss the current line of conversation.

'Well,' said Sarah, 'I hope you do get your rhino, Vassily. Black, white or pink, I'm sure it will be a hunt worth remembering.'

'Thank you,' he said to her, studiously ignoring Mike after his overt impertinence.

Mike wondered if it was Orlov who had shot Isabella. He fantasised briefly about stalking him through the bush and putting a bullet through his head with his new pistol.

'Please excuse me, Sarah,' Orlov said, shifting his chair back from the table. 'It was a long journey today and I must answer the call of nature. I will be back in a few minutes.'

'Of course, Vassily,' she said sweetly.

'"Of course, *Vassily*." You're laying it on a bit thick, aren't you?' Mike caustically said to Sarah after Orlov had left them.

'Shut up. You nearly blew it with all that talk about white and black rhinos,' she hissed back as she fished for another cigarette.

'But we know what he's after now,' he replied.

'Yes. It was pretty obvious, wasn't it?' she conceded. She lowered her voice. 'Where can he find a black rhino around here? I thought there were hardly any left at all.'

'You're right. There're bugger-all left. South Africa and Namibia have quite a few in their national parks, but they'd be hard to get at there. They're well guarded and they're naturally a lot shyer than the white rhinos. Also, unlike the whites, they do a lot of their moving and feeding at night. Orlov's problem is that he'll need to move the head or the horn, or whatever they're after, pretty quickly. That would be another problem in South Africa or Namibia, getting the trophy out of the country.'

'How would they have moved the elephant tusks last year?' she asked.

He pondered the question for a moment. 'From Mozambique, I suppose. They herded the elephant over the border by helicopter to shoot it and my guess is they would have moved the ivory from there as well. I imagine it's a lot easier to bribe a customs or port official in Mozambique, given the poverty over there.'

Orlov was on his way back to them, but was intercepted by the tall blond man, Hess. Sarah whispered quickly to Mike, 'Orlov's suspicious of you. Take it easy, OK?'

'I know,' he agreed. 'Give me my marching orders soon after they join us. Try and find out where they're headed and what their timetable is.'

'Where are you going?' she asked. 'Your leaving me with them wasn't part of the plan.'

'To do a little reconnaissance. I think it's time I took the fight to the enemy. Keep flirting with them – you're doing fine,' he said.

'What are you going to do?'

'I'm going to find out what Mr Orlov and Mr Hess pack when they're travelling. I'll meet you outside in about half an hour. You've got my mobile phone number, haven't you?' Mike had given the passengers on the truck an information sheet with all sorts of dos and don'ts on it, and the list also included the truck's mobile phone number for emergencies, in case they got lost or were separated from the vehicle.

Sarah checked in her camera case for the contact sheet and nodded when she found it. 'I keep it in here because my camera's always with me.'

'Call me if there's trouble,' he whispered as the two men approached them.

'Sarah, please allow me to introduce Mr Karl Hess, professional hunter. He's from Namibia originally. Sarah is one of the small minority of attractive young people who shares our passion, Karl.' Orlov was beaming; the tension of a few minutes ago seemed to have vanished.

'Charmed, madam,' Hess said, taking Sarah's hand in his.

For a minute Mike thought the oily bastard was going to kiss it. His skin glowed from scrubbing and he wore a cologne the scent of which stuck to the back of Mike's lower teeth. He was dressed in a black silk shirt and tan chinos.

'It's miss, actually,' Sarah said in her phoney, horsy upper-class accent. 'But do call me Sarah and I shall call you Karl.'

Hess nodded, but Mike sensed her false charms were wasted on him. Hess turned to Mike next with a pale-eyed gaze that reminded him of a Mozambican spitting cobra he'd once seen in the Pretoria zoo.

'And this is Mr . . .' Orlov began.

'Wilson,' Mike said quickly, refreshing his memory. He was pleased he could remember his false name, even if Orlov couldn't. Hess and Mike shook hands.

269

The hunter's skin was cool and dry, like a snake's. Mike somehow sensed that it was more likely to have been Hess rather than Orlov who had pulled the trigger on Isabella. He would have been as unmoved by her beauty and innocence as he was by the stunning blonde in the evening dress he had just been introduced to, Mike thought.

As Hess and Orlov took their seats, Sarah said, 'Michael, didn't you say you had to have something seen to on the vehicle this afternoon? I've already kept you too long as it is.'

'Of course,' Mike replied deferentially. 'Good afternoon, everyone. I hope you enjoy the rest of your safari,' he said to Orlov as he stood and turned to leave.

Mike made it look like an afterthought, but he was watching Hess closely as he said to Orlov, 'Oh, and I hope you get your rhino one day.'

Mike saw the alarm flash in Hess's blue eyes. The Russian's cheeks coloured. Mike walked away and Sarah picked up the conversation.

'Now, Mr Hess. Karl? How would someone like me go about getting a permit to shoot a lion and a leopard? I need a new rug for my living room and a new coat for the English winter! Fur is back in this season, you know.'

Mike was relieved to hear both men laugh as he strode quickly back inside, through the hotel and across the courtyard.

15

'Excuse me,' Mike said to the same young woman at reception whom he and Sarah had spoken to earlier, 'I need to have some things delivered to Mr Hess and Mr Orlov later today. Can you give me their room numbers, please?'

'Of course, sir,' she said, and tapped the keys on her computer. 'Mr Hess is in 202 and Mr Orlov is in 203.'

'Thank you,' he said.

'Pleasure,' she replied.

He retraced his steps back across the courtyard. Instead of continuing on through the open doors to the terrace, where he could see Sarah was still holding court, he took a left and headed up a broad staircase. A gold-lettered sign pointed him in the right direction down a long, carpeted corridor and he found the rooms a few seconds later. At the far end of the hall a rotund woman was pushing a housekeeping trolley from room to room as she finished cleaning and making up each one. Her back was to Mike. Ahead of him he saw a door with an illuminated 'fire exit' sign

271

above it. He opened the door and stepped into the stairwell.

Inside the musty enclave he quickly undressed, down to his underpants. Mike wrapped his trousers, shoes and mobile phone in his shirt and loosely tied the arms, to stop the bundle falling apart. He left the clothes in the stairwell and, checking the maid was not in sight, slipped out into the corridor. Placing both hands in front of his crotch in a gesture of pained modesty, he headed down the hallway. Finally, he came to a room with an open door and heard the woman whistling inside.

He coughed loudly. 'Ah, excuse me,' he said into the room. The portly maid appeared at the door and placed a hand over her mouth. 'Sorry. Look, I seem to have locked myself out. Could you please let me into room 202?'

The woman fought back a chuckle and said, 'Yes, sir. Come, let's go. This happens all the time, you know,' she said with another laugh.

'Really?'

The maid let him into Hess's room and Mike smelled the man's cloying, vaguely effeminate cologne as soon as he stepped inside. After looking back out the door to check the maid had returned to the room she was cleaning, he propped a Bible from a bedside table against the doorframe to stop the door from locking, and then rushed across the corridor to the fire escape to retrieve his clothes. Quickly he dressed, clipping the mobile phone to his belt, then set about exploring the room.

Fortunately, Hess was a light traveller. There was a

canvas holdall on the bed and a suit bag hanging in the wardrobe. Mike imagined Hess kept his fresh clothes, for dinner and socialising, in the suit bag. In the holdall were detailed topographical maps of Hwange National Park and its surrounds, and of the Zambezi valley, from Victoria Falls down as far as Lake Cahora Bassa, in Mozambique. That was interesting, and Mike wondered if they were planning on driving down into Mozambique when they had got whatever they were after in Zimbabwe. There was also a map of South Luangwa National Park in Zambia. Theron had said nothing about the men crossing into Zambia, so that was interesting as well.

Mike opened the map for the area covering Chizarira down to Kariba. There was nothing written in pencil or ink on the chart to indicate where they were going or what they were up to. Mike hadn't expected there to be. Hess was ex-army, and one of the first things they teach you in army navigation classes is not to write notes or route marks on maps, in case they fall into enemy hands.

Also in the holdall was a Glock pistol in a leather shoulder holster. Mike wondered, if Hess were ever arrested and this weapon examined, could a forensics expert identify it as the weapon that killed Isabella? Were there even forensics experts in Mozambique?

He continued rummaging but found nothing of use. A packet of chewing gum, a mini torch, a hunting knife, underclothes, bush shorts and shirts, and a leather-bound organiser with diary and notebook. He checked the diary, but there was nothing incriminating noted down for the next few days. Mike was about to give up when his hand touched something solid, about the size and weight of a mobile phone. It was a portable GPS unit, similar to the one he had used to plot the locations of minefields in Mozambique and, while this model was a couple of years older, the buttons were all basically the same.

Mike turned the device on and punched the *menu* button, scrolling through the options until he came to one that said 'landmarks'. These would be pre-set points on the earth's surface that Hess had entered. Some would be for destinations he had previously visited – by pushing the *mark* button he could record his exact location at that time and give it a name. Others, Mike hoped, would be points he had set for this present trip by taking their latitude and longitude from a detailed map, such as the ones he carried in his bag. Mike hit the *enter* button and then scrolled through a long list of landmarks.

Predictably, there were landmarks named 'home', which he guessed was Hess's hunting lodge, and 'joburg', which had probably been entered by a sales assistant in a camping store when he bought the gadget. Others would have been landmarks on walking or driving safaris, used as an aid to get to or back from a particular spot. These had names such as 'caves', 'koppie1' and 'mount'. When the alphabetically organised list came to the letter O there was an entry entitled just that – 'O'. The entry intrigued Mike, even more so when he read the latitude and longitude of that landmark.

The line of latitude was the Tropic of Capricorn. Because of what had happened to him on that imaginary line its coordinates would stay in his mind forever. He felt his pulse quicken. He pulled the personal organiser from the holdall and unzipped the leather cover. Mike used a pen from the elasticised holder to scrawl the longitude co-ordinate for point 'O' on a blank page.

Mike quickly scrolled through the remaining land-marks. Only one other caught his eye, a point called 'Tashinga'. Tashinga, he knew, was the main camp of Matusadona National Park, a wild reserve on the southern shore of Lake Kariba, in the far north of Zimbabwe. Hess and Orlov would pass the land entrance to Matusadona on their way to Kariba and would be only a short boat ride away from Tashinga, on the lake's shore, once they reached the town.

There was no hunting allowed in the park – not that that would have stopped them – and, as far as Mike knew, nothing out of the ordinary worth hunt-ing there. All the rhino and most of the big elephant had probably been poached decades ago. He tore the sheet of paper with the coordinates for point 'O' from the notebook and stuffed the sheet in his shirt pocket.

Mike started to leave, then had a thought. He took the pistol from the holdall and unholstered it, then thumbed the magazine release catch, and the mag slid silently into the palm of his left hand. It was full of snub copper-nosed bullets and he laid it down on the bedspread. He slid back the cocking slide of the pistol and, as he expected, there was another bullet in the chamber. Although it wasn't the safest way to trans-port a firearm, it meant Hess could cram an extra round into the pistol, on top of the thirteen in the full magazine. He laid the pistol on the bed, picked up the magazine again and thumbed the top bullet out into his palm, then replaced the bullet in the magazine, but not as the makers intended. He replaced the magazine, wiped the pistol on the bedspread to remove his fingerprints, and placed it back in the holster. Then he rearranged the contents of the holdall to how they first appeared and zipped it closed.

The phone on his belt beeped loudly four times.

'Shit,' he said aloud as he snatched the phone. The illuminated screen read 'One message'. Someone must have called him, he realised, when his clothes were bundled in the fire escape and the message had only just been transmitted.

He dialled the number to retrieve his messages and, as it was a South African number, it took long, agonising seconds for the call to get through. Finally the litany of recorded options began. He angrily stabbed the numbers to retrieve the new message, then took a deep breath to steady himself when he heard Sarah's voice.

'Mike, Hess is on his way. He says he's left something in his room that he needs! It's . . . it's four fifty-five. You've got about five minutes. Get out! Get out now!'

'Fuck!' He checked his watch. It was a minute to five, and he was surprised he had been in the room such a short time. He opened the door a crack and heard a woman's voice, slurred and overly loud.

'No, no. Really, really, I'm going to be fine. Please, Vass-ly, please don' make a fuss. Karl, Karl, thank you, thank you.'

Mike peeked down the hall and saw that it was Sarah. She had dropped theatrically to one knee in her feigned drunkenness and held on to both Hess and Orlov, with one hand on each man's arm. They bent over her, trying to help her to her feet.

Both men had their backs to Mike and he softly pulled the door to Hess's room closed and darted across the hallway to the emergency exit. Sarah saw him, though, and their eyes locked for a second. She gave an urgent nod to tell him that she was, indeed, sober. He slipped into the fire escape and ran down the stairs. When he got to the first floor he barged through the door and ran along the corridor to the main stairwell, then he took the thickly carpeted stairs four at a time on his way back up to the second floor, where he nearly knocked over an elderly American couple in matching photographic vests and floppy bush hats.

When he got to the hallway he slowed his pace as he approached the two men, who still held Sarah between them. Orlov was working his key card into the lock on the door of his room.

'Gorra be sick now. Sorry. So sorry, Vass-ly,' she cried, breaking free from their arms and pushing into the Russian's suite.

'Excuse me! Mr Orlov, Mr Hess. It's me, Michael, Sarah's guide,' he called from down the corridor. Both men turned. 'Excuse me, did I just see Miss Grey with you?'

'Yes. Er . . . Miss Grey is not well,' Orlov said, clearly embarrassed. 'We brought her here so that she could . . . recover herself.'

'I was on my way out to get the car and a man from

the wedding party stopped me. This is difficult, but, well, I believe he's her boyfriend and . . .'

'Her boyfriend?' Orlov said, a look of shock passing over his face.

'Yes sir,' Mike said, playing the humble servant now. 'He was very anxious to find her. I think, perhaps, if it's all right with you, maybe I should escort her back downstairs to the wedding reception.'

'Yes, yes, of course,' Orlov said quickly. 'Sarah? You can come out now. Your guide will take care of you.' The Russian was keen to extricate himself from such an embarrassing situation as quickly as possible.

Hess eyed Mike coldly and said nothing.

Sarah stumbled from the suite, crashing into the doorframe and rebounding straight into Mike's arms.

'Mike? Zat you, Mike? Take me home, Mike,' she slurred. She had splashed water on her face and done an excellent job of ruining her make-up.

'Thank you, for, for looking after her, Mr Orlov,' Mike said deferentially and, with an arm around Sarah, led her down the corridor.

Orlov looked back at them with a visage of half-drunken confusion. Hess had his serpent's eyes fixed on Mike as he propelled Sarah around the corner and down the stairs. Once on the stairs they broke into a run. Sarah stumbled and Mike reached out and grabbed her hand to steady her. She left her hand in his until they burst out of the ground-floor corridor, back into reception.

The girl at reception gave them a puzzled look as they exploded from the cool interior into the red-gold heat haze of the dying afternoon. They stopped outside to catch their breath and Mike called across to the concierge, 'Can you hail a taxi for us, please?'

'Certainly. Where to, sir?'

A porter struggled into the foyer of the hotel with the last armfuls of tourist bags from outside.

'Municipal Campground,' Mike said, fighting to get his breath back.

The concierge held up his hand to stop a battered Peugeot from pulling away and told the driver their destination.

'Let's go, man!' Mike said to the driver, bundling Sarah in front of him into the cramped back seat.

Sarah threw back her head and laughed out loud. 'Whoa! Yes! We did it!'

Her rush was infectious and Mike laughed too. 'What were you doing up there with Orlov? I nearly shat myself when I got your message.'

'I told him I wanted to fuck him,' she said, wiping a tear of laughter from her eye. The driver looked up at his rear-view mirror.

'Eyes on the road, *shamwari*,' Mike said, using the Shona word for friend. 'You *what*?'

'Hess left the table ten minutes after you'd gone. He said he left his wallet in his room,' she explained, gasping as she brought her breathing under control. 'I knew I'd have to warn you so I told Orlov I had to make an urgent call, to cancel some plans for the evening. He was well confused by now. Anyway, when I called and you didn't answer I thought the only way was to get upstairs before Hess found you.'

'So Orlov all of a sudden got lucky,' Mike said, marvelling at her audacity and quick thinking.

'You should have seen the pig,' she said, shaking her head and letting out another laugh of released nervous tension. 'He nearly lost it there and then. Boy, was I *bad*! Anyway, as we got to the stairs I pretended to start dry-heaving. I asked him his room number and, when he told me, I started running as fast as I could, saying I needed to be sick. We bumped into Hess and I saw you had just made it out of the room in time. Great fun, wasn't it?'

He ignored her last, flippant, remark. 'Hess wasn't looking for his wallet – or if he was, it wasn't in his room.'

'Shit. Do you think he was on to us?' she asked. The cab swung into the gates of the camping ground and stopped. Mike paid the driver, and they climbed out. He was keen to continue their conversation, but away from prying ears.

'I'm not sure. But Hess is a man who travels very light. The only things he didn't have on him of value were his pistol and his GPS. I think he was going back for one or the other, or both.'

'A GPS?' she said, as they walked towards Nelson. Mike could see a few of the gang were gathered around, sitting on camp chairs or lounging in the back of the truck.

'Global Positioning –'

'I know what a GPS is,' she snapped. 'What's so important about his toy?'

'It may give us some leads about where they're really going and what they're planning. I think it also contains some incriminating evidence about where they've been. I took down one of his stored coordinates.' Mike fished the sheet of notepaper out of his top pocket and showed it to her.

'"O"? What does that mean?'

'I want to find out. Once I've checked out the co-ordinates I'll call Theron, the cop who's pulling my string.'

Linda stood up as soon as she saw them approaching. Mike could see that she was dressed for a night out. She had on a lime-green mini dress made of layers of some sort of see-through material.

'Oi, here they are,' she called to the rest of the group. 'Where have you two been? And, more to the point, what have you been up to?'

'High tea at the Victoria Falls Hotel, if you must know. I was taking some more photos for my story,' Sarah added.

'Really know how to have a good time, don't you,' Linda said, then lightened her tone. 'Here, it's George's twenty-first birthday today. Terry just told us. He's in the shower and reckons he didn't want to make a big deal out of it, but Terry wants to wind him up big time.'

Terry chimed in, 'Yeah. He's just being a twat. So I reckon it's party time for George. Linda's found a club up the road. Are you in, Mike?'

Mike had work to do, but he realised his passengers still had to be his first priority. After all, it was his job to look after them. 'Let's do it,' he said, trying to sound enthusiastic. 'Give me ten minutes to sort some stuff out.'

'OK,' Terry said, 'but you've got to be here in ten for the presentation of George's birthday present. I've brought it all the way from England and he hasn't a clue. I told him I wouldn't make a fuss on his birthday. Bollocks to that.'

'Mike,' Sarah said, 'weren't you going to show me that promotional blurb about the company?'

'Oh, right. Yes. I've got it in the cab. Come and take a look now, if you like,' he said, catching on.

Sarah sat beside Mike in the cab and he switched on the interior light, as it was nearly dark outside. He took out the canvas satchel containing his maps from behind the driver's seat. They were an odd assortment, ranging from highly detailed charts prepared by government offices to tourist maps that were little better than those in a junior school atlas. The map of Mozambique wasn't bad and at least it had lines of latitude and longitude on it. Mike unfolded it and checked the margins.

From the first glance he could tell the longitude of the point listed simply as 'O' was somewhere in Mozambique. He found the Tropic of Capricorn and traced his finger across the page, getting a rough approximation of where the coordinates of degrees, minutes and seconds intersected the line of latitude.

'Oh Christ,' he said, meaning it for once. He squeezed the thumb and forefinger of his left hand to his eyes to try to shut out the kaleidoscope of images that the list of numbers on a piece of paper had conjured up.

'Mike, what is it?' Sarah asked.

'It's them.'

'Who's them?'

'This spot. Point "O". It's where the elephant was

282

killed last year. I know this area. It's where I was working.' He opened his eyes and saw little pinpoints of silver light flashing in from the peripheries of his vision. He felt weak and clammy, like he was going to pass out, but the weakness disappeared as quickly as it had taken hold. He clenched his right hand into a fist, balling the map with it.

'Then "O", presumably, is for Orlov,' she said triumphantly.

But this wasn't a game for Mike. 'Yes. That's probably the spot where I shot him. Hess would have had to have given a precise location to the chopper pilot to pick them up.'

Sarah at last saw the quiet anger that was gripping him. 'Mike,' she said softly, 'I know you blame yourself for . . . for what happened afterwards. But you mustn't. You were under fire and you did the only thing you could have. The important thing is that we've got enough evidence now to nail the pair of them.'

'Have we?' He doubted it would be enough for a court. But he was certain, now, that Hess and Orlov were the men he was looking for. And if the police couldn't catch them, then he would.

'What did you make of that?' Hess asked Orlov as the Englishwoman and the Australian man disappeared quickly down the stairs.

'Make of it? Nothing. A drunken whore. A whore of good breeding, for sure, but nothing more,' Orlov replied, though the beads of sweat on his forehead belied his nervousness.

'What about their questions, and that remark about the rhino? What had you been talking about before I arrived?' Hess asked.

Orlov's face coloured with anger and he lowered his voice. 'Listen, my friend, do not be accusing me of having a loose tongue. Remember, it is I who pay the bills and I who stand to lose the most in this venture.'

'Of course, Vassily,' Karl said, rubbing his hand through his blond hair. 'I didn't mean to suggest you had done wrong, but we must be careful.'

'I realise this, of course. We were talking about the big five, and the difficulty of shooting a rhino these days. Harmless banter, nothing more. As for the woman, a man of my standing, my wealth . . . well, let us just say that I never have to try hard to win the ladies.' Orlov forced a laugh.

Hess didn't doubt what Orlov said. He was sure that back in Moscow, where he would be known by reputation, and where he probably wore his wealth like a cheap tart wears her perfume, the Russian would be surrounded by dozens of gold-digging women. But here in the hotel, Orlov looked like just another tourist and, thanks to his early morning hunt, like a bedraggled tourist at that.

'The other thing that concerned me was how quickly she slipped from seductress to drunkard,' Hess said.

'I've seen it happen,' Orlov countered. 'Perhaps she was taking drugs as well. Ecstasy or cocaine, maybe?'

'It's possible,' Hess conceded. Indeed, it was possible that the woman was just an innocent philanderer. However, Hess had not survived more than twenty years in the African bush in war and peace by ignoring his instincts. Those instincts told him their armour had been pierced and their secrets compromised. 'Please wait for me, Vassily, I want to check my room.'

Hess left Orlov in the corridor and worked the key card in the lock of his door. At first glance everything in the room seemed to be as he remembered it. He crossed to the bed and unzipped the holdall. The pistol was still there. The weapon was what he had been coming back to the room to collect, his urge to have the gun on him driven by nothing more than his instincts.

He took the pistol from the holster and pulled the slide partially backwards. Then he checked in the chamber, to confirm the weapon was still loaded, and eased the slide forward again. He replaced the weapon in its holster, shrugged his arms into the shoulder rig and continued his checking.

Hess was about to zip the bag closed again when his eye was drawn to his leather-bound personal organiser. Particular about most things, Hess was obsessive regarding zippers. He had seen comrades who should have known better discover venomous puff adders in their sleeping bags because they were too lazy to zip and roll them. He had heard his hunting clients cry out in alarm when they discovered a scorpion or spider in a tent because they had ignored his exhortations to keep their tents zipped at all times. The shiny brass teeth of the half-open zip on his organiser grinned incongruously at him. He unzipped the casing all the way and flicked through his diary. He was not stupid enough to have left any incriminating information in the pages of the diary, and he next leafed through the notebook.

There, again, was another inconsistency. If Hess tore pages from the notebook he did so slowly and carefully. The last fresh page of the book was preceded by a ragged tear where a page had been hastily torn. There was a pencil in the centre of the organiser, next to the gold pen, and he slipped it from its elastic holder.

Hess switched on a bedside lamp and held the notebook near the light. He tilted the fresh page of the notebook until the light caught the faint indentations on its surface. Quickly he rubbed the pencil across the surface and swore silently when the figures and letters appeared, as if by magic, in white amid the dark rubbings.

'Vassily! Come here, quick,' he called from the room.

He beckoned the Russian in and closed the door. Orlov did not want to believe the evidence he had uncovered, but Hess even turned on the GPS and showed him the coordinates.

'Someone has been in this room. I can only assume it was the man, the Australian, and that the woman was a decoy to keep us distracted,' Hess concluded.

'You kept the coordinates from Mozambique?' Orlov was unable to hide his incredulity.

'I have coordinates in that thing from three years ago,' Hess replied. 'The important thing, Vassily, is not what this man found, but that he knew what he was looking for.'

'But you said you had my position, where I was wounded in Mozambique, listed only under the letter O, yes?'

'That's correct,' Hess said irritably. He knew he had made a mistake, a rare enough occurrence, and he was as angry with himself as he was with the Russian for reminding him again.

'Why would this man attach significance to a co-ordinate with a single letter for identification?' Orlov pondered aloud.

There was only one answer. 'He must have recognised the coordinates as being in Mozambique.'

Orlov nodded, recalling the pain of his wound. How he had wanted to kill the man who did that to him.

'Then they – whoever *they* are – now have proof of where we have been. And they may have worked out where we are going,' Hess said in summation.

'They have no proof,' Orlov countered. 'Delete the coordinates. Karl, I did not get where I am by turning back whenever I met resistance. I came here to hunt, and I mean to complete my hunting. This problem can be resolved, one way or another.'

Hess nodded, fully aware of the path Orlov was heading down. If they were police, then they were not South African Police. Interpol, perhaps? That meant the authorities already had a lead on him and Orlov, though how they had got this far he could not deduce. They had to find out who the couple were, who they were working for and how much they already knew. Orlov would get his hunt, and it would start immediately.

'The man said he was taking her back to the wedding reception downstairs. That much we can check,' Hess said. He strode across the room to his suit bag and selected a lightweight tan sports jacket. He put on the coat in order to conceal the pistol in its holster.

Hess closed the door behind them and they walked briskly down the corridor to the stairs. They crossed the open foyer to the reception desk where a young woman was just saying her farewells to her similarly uniformed colleague.

'See you tomorrow,' the woman said.

'Excuse me, miss,' Hess said to the woman who was coming on duty. 'I'm looking for two friends of mine who are attending the wedding function. Can you tell me where in the hotel it is being held, please?'

The woman checked a diary on the desk in front of her, but the departing receptionist, who was now on the same side of the counter as the two men, stopped and turned. 'Hello. Mr Hess and Mr Orlov, isn't it?'

'That is correct,' Orlov said.

'The reception's in the main banquet room, just down the hallway there on your left. You can't miss it,' she said brightly. It had been a long day and she needed a drink and a long bath to soak her sore feet, but service was the name of the game in the hotel industry and she wanted to go far.

'Thank you, my dear,' Orlov said. 'Come, Karl.'

'Pleasure,' said the girl. 'Your friends did find you, didn't they?'

Orlov and Hess both stopped and turned to face the girl.

'They were waiting for you this afternoon. Quite

288

keen to catch up with you when you arrived,' she continued.

'Yes, they found us all right,' Orlov said, trying to suppress the mix of fear and anger boiling inside him. He fought to keep his voice steady and forced a benign smile. 'Have you seen them just now?'

The woman paused a moment. In the hotel business there was a fine line between being helpful and being indiscreet. She couldn't lie to a guest, though. 'Um, yes, they left a little while ago, in a cab.'

'Ah,' Orlov said with a knowing smile. 'Our Sarah, she likes a drink, I can tell you. Maybe Michael took her back to the hotel where they are staying.'

The woman was relieved that the two men obviously knew what was what. 'Well, she was a bit excited. I don't know about a hotel, but I did overhear the man asking the concierge to hail a cab to take them to the Municipal Campground.'

'Thank you for your help, my dear,' said Orlov, reaching for his wallet. He selected a crisp American ten-dollar bill and palmed it to the woman as he reached to shake her hand.

16

Sarah had managed to convince Mike that Orlov and Hess had no idea what they were up to and, after his fourth tequila slammer, even the memory of Hess's eyes was dimming. Her ebullience was rubbing off on him. She had stayed close by his side all night. Their shared risk-taking earlier in the day at least gave them something to talk about. He found himself not minding her constant presence, and that surprised him a little.

The party went from bad to debauched. They had started drinking at the camping ground and by the time Terry got around to presenting George with his birthday present, an inflatable sex doll, everyone was wasted enough to appreciate Terry's schoolboy antics. The doll, christened Britney by Linda, seemed to be enjoying the party as much as everyone else. George and Terry had snuck their new friend into the night-club, deflated, and re-inflated her once inside.

The club was dark and noisy and smelled of spilled beer, as well as a faint trace of urine and a big dose of sweat. The sound system pumped an eclectic mix of upbeat Shona music and the occasional thump of western techno. None of it made any sense to Mike. He had called Theron from the camping ground. The number he had for him was for a mobile phone and all he got was the detective's voice mail. Mike left a long message outlining what they had and hadn't discovered.

Sarah mouthed something, but Mike couldn't hear her over the music's din. The thumping bass of the techno was like someone tap-dancing on his temples.

'What?' he screamed.

'Next! What are we going to do next?' She had to move close to him so that he could hear.

Mike caught the heady mix of her perfume and perspiration, and tried to concentrate on his answer to her question. 'Not much. We can't contact them here again – not anywhere. They'd be too suspicious, even assuming they bought that Hollywood performance of yours.'

She laughed. 'I thought I was pretty good.'

'You were, you were,' he said. He signalled to a passing waiter and ordered a beer. Sarah nodded and Mike ordered one for her as well. It had, in fact, been a hell of a performance. She had quite probably saved his life, and risked her own in the process. He thought, however, that she still underestimated what these men were capable of.

'We've told the cops all we can at the moment, and that's a lot more than they knew before they sent us on this wild goose chase,' Mike continued. 'From what you got out of Orlov, it's possible we might bump into them again at Kariba. If they want to go to Tashinga they'll probably do it by boat from Kariba.'

'Why?' she asked. 'Can't they drive into the national park?'

'They can, but it's a lousy road and there's no fuel or supplies in the park. They'd have to lug everything in with them. Besides, the best way to see game in that part of the country is by boat, when the animals come down to the lake shore to drink.' He wondered again what it was that had drawn Hess's interest to the remote national park.

Terry and George were posing for a photograph with Britney a couple of tables away. Linda was pointing the camera and a waiter was looking annoyed. Mike's crowd was getting restless and he wondered how long it would be before one or all of them were chucked out of the nightclub. At the next table along, Jane and Julie Muir were deep in conversation with a couple of tall, muscled men.

'The Muirs have got lucky,' Sarah said, following Mike's gaze. 'Those guys don't look like your average tourists.'

'River gods.'

'What?' Sarah yelled, as she moved even closer to hear Mike's answer.

'River gods. That's what the white-water rafting instructors here like to call themselves. They do OK with the tourists, especially the female tourists, if you know what I mean.'

The Muir women had gone rafting earlier in the day and hadn't stopped talking about it, and their instructors, since. Jane was leaning closer to one of them, a hugely muscled African, resting a hand on his thigh as they spoke. The other man had furtively slipped an arm behind Julie's back, encircling her waist without her mother noticing.

'What are you smiling about?' Sarah asked, leaning close again.

'Nothing.'

The rest of the crew were on the dance floor, screaming the words to a retro number from the movie *Grease*, which Mike remembered seeing on first release, before most of them were born. No one in the group was looking at Sarah and him.

'Shit!' Mike said.

'What?'

'That guy. The tall guy over there. Recognise him?' The man was dressed in black from top to toe. Tailored trousers, black silk shirt and, incongruously considering the heat, a long black leather jacket.

It took Sarah a moment, then she said, 'Christ! He was with Hess and Orlov today.'

The man hadn't seen them yet, but he was walking through the crowd towards Mike and Sarah. The ladies and gents toilets were on the far side of the packed room from their table, as was the exit. There was no way they could barge through the heaving dance floor without passing the man or attracting attention to themselves. Mike knew that if they stood and started to move, the rest of their party would call out for them to join their drunken gyrations, focusing all eyes on them.

The man was ten paces from them now, his eyes scanning the room from side to side like the needle on a radar scope. Mike saw him reach instinctively under his left armpit, probably subconsciously reassuring himself his pistol was still there.

Sarah looked at Mike and he saw the earlier bravado drain from her face, along with all colour. 'What are we going to . . . ?'

He reached his right arm out until it was around the back of her neck. Mike felt her recoil reflexively at the embrace, but pulled her forcefully towards him nonetheless. Sam had been sitting at their table earlier and had left his floppy khaki bush hat on his chair. Mike grabbed it with his left hand and pressed it to the back of Sarah's blonde hair, hoping the man had been given a suitably vague description.

Mike leaned back in the deep padded velour of the booth cushions, smelling years of stale body odour and tobacco, and pressed the back of his head into the fuzzy material to hide his ponytail. Sarah shrugged viciously for a brief second, then suddenly seemed to understand what he was trying to do. Mike's mouth was only two or three centimetres from hers. From the corner of his eye he saw Hess's henchman standing to one side, very near to them. He probably wouldn't have noticed if they weren't actually kissing, but Mike didn't want to take the chance.

He pressed his lips hard against Sarah's. Again she recoiled – whether from disgust or simple surprise, he couldn't tell.

Then her lips parted.

Their tongues met and he tasted tobacco and tequila. She relaxed slightly in his embrace and he tightened his arms around her. Her tongue was in his mouth now, her eyes half-closed. The man looked around him again, turned on his heel and strode back to the door, pushing through the throng of dancers. He hadn't seen them, but Mike suddenly didn't want to stop the subterfuge.

Their teeth gnashed for an instant as she broke the kiss. 'Is he gone?' Sarah whispered, for they were close enough now to hear each other and there was a brief lull in the music as the DJ fast-forwarded a skipping CD.

'I think so,' Mike said.

'Good,' she said. She placed her palms on his chest and gently, but decisively, pushed him away.

They both looked around to see who had noticed. No one from their group.

'Sarah, I'm –'

'Leave it,' she interrupted. 'Had to be done. Um . . . good thinking, by the way.'

'Yes, I suppose so.'

The waiter arrived with their beers, giving them both a reprieve from the awkward moment.

Sarah poured her Zambezi into a frosted glass, slowly, as if buying time. Finally, she said, 'Look, nothing happened. It was just part of the act, right? I don't need this . . . *this* right now.'

What didn't Sarah Thatcher need right now? Mike asked himself. Him, he supposed was the answer, and he could understand that. Sort of.

'No problem,' he called over the increasing din as the music returned.

'Good. I'm glad to hear it,' she said, as if that was the end of the matter.

Sarah gazed out at the crowded dance floor to avoid meeting his eyes. Her cheeks were flushed red and her hand was a little unsteady as she raised the beer glass to lips still moist from his. Mike thought of Rian's golden rule again and realised now why it was called that.

'I'd better get back to the truck. Nigel's been there all day. The poor bugger probably needs some sleep,' Mike said, leaning close to Sarah's ear again so she could hear him. Her perfume unsettled him, and he couldn't stay in the club anymore.

'Sure,' she said, nodding her head. 'Good idea. I'll head home with the others.'

'Right,' Mike said. He didn't look back as he threaded his way to the exit. He wondered if she was watching him leave.

He was glad to get outside into the night air, away from the smell of body odour and stale cigarette smoke. It was warm out, but not oppressively hot and humid like the club.

Once he'd taken his fill of clean air, Mike pulled out a cigarette and lit up. It was only a short walk from the club back down the hill to the camping ground, just a couple of blocks. The tequila had left him feeling dehydrated and he wished he'd bought another beer for the road. He resolved to get one from the fridge in the truck, even if it meant conversing with Nigel, assuming he was still awake.

Mike snuck into the camping ground the same way that everyone else obviously did, over a side security fence that had been trampled down by a couple of decades of drunken party animals short-cutting their way back from the nightclubs, not to mention the occasional thief. As he unhitched a rusty barb from his trousers he heard the distinctive whooping of a car alarm. He assumed the fool owner had triggered it by mistake and didn't know how to turn it off. However, when he heard the crash and tinkle of breaking glass he quickened his pace.

The camping ground was nearly empty. There had been another overland truck in during the day, but it had left in the afternoon. The only other vehicle that was still there when the group had left for the nightclub was a new-looking white Toyota double-cab four-wheel drive with a Jo'burg registration.

Mike rounded the shower block and saw the Toyota, its hazard lights flashing and its alarm whooping. This was no false alarm, he realised. The headlights were smashed and the vehicle sagged low to the ground – all four tyres had been slashed. A man emerged from the far side and, even in his alcohol-induced fug, Mike had no trouble recognising him – bald head, black trousers, black leather jacket. There was no mistaking his tall, hulking build, either. The man brought a long arm up over his head and the street lighting glinted on the length of pipe in his hand. The windscreen of the expensive vehicle shattered into a crazed spiderweb of broken glass.

Mike dropped his cigarette and stubbed it out. He briefly considered running to his truck and making for the police station, but dismissed the idea just as quickly. He – they – were on to Sarah and him, but there was nothing to suggest they knew they were travelling in a bright yellow overland truck along with a bunch of tourists. Mike assumed Hess and Orlov now knew Sarah and he were staying in the camping ground, but how they had found out escaped him for the moment. Obviously the man in black thought Mike and Sarah were the owners of the Toyota.

Mike decided to fetch the police, or security, or whoever he could find. He turned and took a step, but the remains of a broken beer bottle crunched loudly as he lowered his foot. He looked over his shoulder and saw the man staring at him. They both started to run.

Mike had a good twenty-metre start on the intruder and, although he supposed they were about the same age, there was not an ounce of fat on the pursuer's long, lean body. He caught Mike a few metres short of the fence, beneath a broken streetlight.

They went down in a tangle of arms and legs, and Mike fell heavily on his right side, grazing his arm and elbow beneath his short-sleeved shirt. He curled into a ball and rolled to the left, quick enough to avoid the full force of the first blow of the pipe. The metal glanced off his left shoulder. No bone cracked, but the pain was enough to make him gasp in shock. The next blow was better aimed, landing just below the left side of his rib cage. The breath shot from his lungs with a painful burst and he lashed out uselessly with his legs.

He rolled onto his right side, gasping for breath, and felt something dig into his ribs. He flexed the fingers of his right hand feeling for the object, hoping to find a weapon of some sort. His attacker straightened above him. The big man transferred the pipe to his left hand and reached into his jacket with his right.

'Make a sound and you die here and now,' the man said in a deep, measured voice. 'Now tell me, who are you? Who is the girl, and who do you work for?'

The man fidgeted for a second, as if he was undoing the clasp on a shoulder holster. Mike reckoned he had less than a second. His fingers closed around the object underneath him. It was a half-brick, heavy and jagged. He flipped his body to the left, using the momentum to add power to his throw. The brick scraped his fingers as it left them and glanced off the man's high ebony forehead with an audible thud.

The man staggered but didn't fall. Instinctively his free hand, the one that had been reaching for his pistol, moved to the painful wound on his head. Mike was on his feet now and he rushed the man, hitting him in the chest with a shoulder. The man flailed with the pipe, but couldn't move his arm high enough to swing down with any real force. Mike hooked the fingers of his left hand and gouged the man's eyes as he raised a knee hard into his groin. It was the assailant's turn to gasp now, but the blow from Mike's knee was not enough to fell him. The man threw his head back and Mike felt his short fingernails scratch harmlessly down his cheek. Before Mike could move his hand away the man had his index finger between his teeth. The pain was excruciating and Mike moved his whole body away to give weight to his bid to free himself from the other man's wildly grinning jaws.

This was the reaction the man was hoping for and

he drove his left fist, with the pipe still clenched in it, up into Mike's solar plexus. Mike doubled over and dropped to his knees. The man's teeth scored the length of Mike's finger as it finally came free. The man jumped back, using the room to deliver a brutal kick up into Mike's jaw, knocking the Australian all the way to the ground.

Blood ran freely from the gash on the man's head and he wiped it from his eye with the back of the hand that held the pipe. Mike was having trouble breathing, his finger and face afire with competing agony. He felt like he was going to throw up and tasted stale tequila rising at the back of his throat.

The man again reached under his jacket for his pistol. This time it came out easily. It was an automatic with a long silencer screwed to the barrel.

'Who are you?' he asked again. He was breathing rapidly, but there was little doubt who had come out of this fight the worse off.

'Fuck off,' Mike managed painfully, wasting the little air he had been able to drag back into his lungs.

The man kicked again, this time finding Mike's stomach. Mike curled into the foetal position. Somewhere in the darkness he heard running footsteps on the road. I'm going to die, he thought to himself. But there was another thought, as well. He knew he had to protect Sarah and the rest of the people in the truck. Even if he died, the others must not be dragged into this mess.

'I've been told to kill you, you know,' the man said matter-of-factly, his rich, deep voice steady again. 'Tell me what I need to know and the girl will go free.'

'There's nothing to tell,' Mike gasped. 'Why the fuck did you smash my truck?'

He gave a satisfied snigger. At least Mike now knew Hess, Orlov and their henchman had nothing to connect Sarah and him to the garish overland truck parked in the shadows.

'Have it your way, then,' the man said. He straightened his arm.

Mike saw his finger take up the slack on the trigger. He realised with a clarity that sliced through his pain that he wasn't ready to die, and that he wouldn't be until Hess and Orlov and whoever had assisted them were locked up or dead – preferably the latter. He had to think of something to stall the man above him. 'It was money,' he rasped.

The man relaxed his arm slightly and looked over the foresight of the pistol. 'What?'

'Money. We get information from contacts, sources, in the top hotels about wealthy male clients. The girl distracts them, gets into their rooms on the promise of sex, then she drugs them and rolls them. Sometimes I do the rooms while she keeps them busy. This time it didn't work, we got busted.'

Mike spoke quickly and hoped the man's command of English was good enough for him to take it all in. The story was flimsy with a dozen holes in it and wouldn't stack up in front of Hess and Orlov, but Mike was hoping it would be enough to stall the enforcer.

The man hesitated and Mike could see him concentrating on the story, weighing it up in his mind. 'Bullshit,' he said, smiling. 'I don't believe you, but if that's the best you can come up with, I'll tell the *baas*. But now you got to die.'

The man straightened his arm again and Mike grabbed a handful of sandy earth. He'd throw it into his eyes, he thought, and maybe the gunman would miss his head. Not much of a plan.

A loud whistle and a dog's bark shattered the quiet. 'Stop, police!' Mike heard a voice shout. 'Drop the gun!'

The man was suddenly trapped in the beam of a flashlight. He turned, one arm raised to shield his eyes from the glare, and fired a shot towards the light. Mike heard more shouting and swearing as he rolled, then crawled as fast he could into a patch of deep shadow. He looked back and saw his attacker was gone. He heard the fallen fence squeak and rattle in protest as the man scrambled over it, and he rose painfully to one knee to get a better view. He was running up the street, past darkened shops, scattering a few drunken late-night revellers from the footpath. He disappeared into the shadows of the first alleyway he came to.

Mike turned sharply as he heard someone approach him. He had his fists out in front of him, ready to strike. It was Nigel, looking red-faced and breathing hard. 'Where the fuck have you been?' Mike spat.

Nigel looked hurt and said, 'Saving your bloody life by the look of it.'

'What do you mean?'

'This character dressed up like Shaft comes up to me an hour ago at the truck and asks me if I've seen an Australian with a ponytail and a pommy chick with blonde hair. This dude looked bad, but he said he was a friend of yours. I told him I hadn't seen anyone like that, but that there was a blonde woman and a man driving that Toyota four-wheel drive over there.' Nigel smiled as he recounted the conversation.

Mike nodded. 'Good work. What happened then?'

'Well, he wandered around the camping ground. Checked the gents, and the ladies, which made me suspicious. He peered into the windows of the four-wheel drive and the next thing I knew, the alarm was going off. He'd broken into it, rooted around for something and then got out a knife and slashed the tyres! I took off and went looking for the security guard. He was outside gasbagging with his mates and the two of us hailed some passing cops.'

'Thanks,' Mike said.

'No problem. Who was that guy, anyway? Why was he after you two?'

'Just some crim,' Mike said, as two Zimbabwean policemen approached them. The security guard was pulling hard on the leash of a barking Alsatian that looked like it wanted to tear a hole in the security fence with its teeth. Mike guessed the security guard's duties didn't extend to pursuit and capture. He supposed the police, too, were happier to stay and take statements rather than pursue an armed man on foot.

The police wanted to know what had gone on and Mike gave them a cobbled-together version of Nigel's good deed and his arrival on the scene. Mike said he had interrupted the man vandalising the truck and had tried to stop him. Mike and Nigel went through

303

the motions of giving descriptions and the police said they should both go to the station and give a statement. Neither of them wanted that. They were saved, however, by the arrival of the hapless owners of the four-wheel drive. Mike felt sorry for the young South African couple – they looked like they could have been honeymooners. However, he was relieved that their presence, and Nigel's quick thinking, had saved the day. Mike left the couple with the police, and he and Nigel retreated to Nelson and their circle of tents. The rest of the crew stumbled into the campsite a few minutes later, minus Jane and Julie Muir.

'Oh my God, what happened?' Sarah asked when she saw the bruises on Mike's face.

Mike told the rest of the crew the semi-made-up story about him and Nigel surprising the car vandal.

'Where are Jane and Julie?' Mike asked when he'd finished the tale.

Mel laughed. 'Don't worry about those two, they're kicking on with the rafting guys. They said they'll catch up with us tomorrow morning if they don't make it back tonight.'

Mike led Sarah around the back of the truck. She had fetched the first aid kit from the truck and insisted she let him treat his cuts. As she swabbed his face with cottonwool soaked in antiseptic, Mike told her the truth. The antiseptic hurt like hell, but he found the sensation of her soft fingers brushing his face was soothing.

'Christ, you were lucky,' she said, when he had finished explaining.

'I don't feel very lucky.'

When she was finished tending his cuts Mike broke away from her. He unlocked the tool locker and switched on a fluorescent light connected to the truck's spare battery. He rummaged in the locker and pulled out the can of grease.

'What are you doing?' she asked.

'Evening the odds a little,' he said, as he fished the plastic-wrapped bundle from the can.

From the other side of the truck Mike heard the sound of beer cans popping and a cork being withdrawn from a wine bottle. There were giggles and squeals again now that the drama was over. The party would go on into the small hours, which was good. Hess, Orlov and their henchman were unlikely to come back to the camping ground with so much activity. Also, Mike reasoned, the criminals couldn't be sure the police weren't patrolling the area in search of the phantom car vandal. Still, he couldn't afford to take any chances now that he and Sarah had been partly compromised.

Sarah watched in fascination as Mike unwrapped the plastic and drew out the pistol and cardboard box of ammunition. He removed the magazine and filled it with squat little bullets.

'You load it like this,' he said, holding the pistol in the light so Sarah could see as he slid the full magazine into the butt and slapped the bottom with the palm of his hand to make sure it was fully seated. 'This is how you cock it,' he explained as he grasped the slide with the thumb and forefinger of his left hand, pulled back and then let it slide forward. 'That chambers – loads – a bullet into the spout. Don't point it at anyone unless you plan on killing him. To fire, just pull the trigger. Got it?'

'Me?' she asked, recoiling as he held the pistol out to her.

'I'm fucked,' he said. His head had started to spin and he felt like throwing up again. He couldn't work out which he needed most, to vomit or sleep. 'I've got to lie down. Wake me in three hours. The party will probably be just about over by then. I'll take the next shift until dawn.'

'Do you think they'll come back?' she asked, as she hesitantly took the pistol. She hefted it experimentally and pointed at a nearby tree.

'I don't know. My guess is that their man will report back with the story I gave him before the cops arrived. They probably won't believe it, but I doubt they'll risk checking on us themselves. I suppose they'll try to put as much distance between us and them as they can, maybe change their itinerary a bit to throw us off.'

'OK. Get some sleep. I'll wake you in three hours,' she said, peering into the darkness beyond the truck.

17

Sarah didn't wake Mike up after he left her with the pistol. He awoke with the sun in his eyes at seven in the morning. He ached all over, from his stinking feet to the tips of every long strand of cigarette-smoke and blood-encrusted hair. Gingerly he felt a bump and a scabbed cut on the back of his head.

'You said it yourself, you were fucked,' Sarah told him when he angrily asked why she had let him sleep in. 'For God's sake, Mike, you'll kill us all if you fall asleep at the wheel.'

There was no hot water in the communal shower block, but at least the cold spray revived him a little. He was still annoyed with Sarah for not waking him, but grateful for the extra sleep. Sarah dozed in the seat beside him as he drove through Zambia and a succession of forgettable farming towns. The continuous whine of the diesel engine and the afternoon heat combined to give him a headache of epic proportions. He pulled a couple more paracetamol from his sweat-stained shirt pocket and washed them down with warm water from the plastic bottle on the dashboard.

Mike glanced over his shoulder into the main cab behind him and thought it looked like the aftermath of a plane crash. Bodies were strewn everywhere – across seats with arms and legs akimbo, on the floor and leaning up against the rear wall of the cab. George was half in and half out of his airline seat with his head hanging back at an unnatural angle. A silvery stream of drool connected his mouth to the floor of the cab. Jane and Julie lay on the floor. Jane still had her party clothes on from the night before and had added sunglasses to protect her bloodshot eyes. She and Julie were the reason they would not reach Kariba that day. Mike was annoyed at the pair of them.

Although their itinerary didn't call for them to leave until mid-morning he had roused everyone reluctantly from their tents as soon as he was up. Mike couldn't tell them it was because he didn't want to risk a return visit by the hunting party. Sarah alone knew why he was so concerned and why he had reverted to army-officer mode.

'But *why* do we have to leave so early?' Linda had asked in a whining tone as she clutched her head.

'Because I *say* so, that's why!' he had barked. She sulked off and a few of the others had given him puzzled stares.

'Where the bloody hell are they?' Mike had asked for the fourth or fifth time as he paced up and down outside the truck in the camping ground. He glanced at his watch and saw it was eleven o'clock. He had wanted to put as much distance between the over-lander and Orlov and Hess as quickly as possible. He knew from the accommodation list Theron had given him, and from Sarah's conversation with Orlov, that they planned on spending time hunting in the safari areas south of the Zambezi before they, too, passed through Kariba. But there was the possibility they would change their plans and come looking for him and Sarah instead.

Finally, a minibus bearing the logo of a white-water rafting company had pulled up with a skid on the gravel road. The sliding door opened and Jane nearly fell in her struggle to get out. Julie supported her mother as she regained her balance.

'Sorry, are we late?' Julie asked apologetically after she and Jane had said their farewells to the strapping rafting guides. 'It was my fault, not Mum's.'

'Sorry. Sorry,' Jane chimed in and then giggled. She looked like she was still drunk, or stoned, or both. It must have been a hell of a party, Mike thought.

'It's OK. Just get in the truck. We've packed your tent and your gear for you,' he had said.

'Ooh, cranky are we?' Jane slurred.

'Yes,' Mike said.

He had felt better once they had cleared customs and immigration on both sides of the river and were at last on the open road. He fished the map from the console between him and Sarah, and the movement roused her from her sleep. They had passed through Livingstone, the older, quieter, shabbier version of Victoria Falls town on the Zambian side, and were heading towards the capital, Lusaka.

Sarah was back in her normal backpacker gear of shorts and tank top. Her hair was tousled and there was still a hint of dark eyeliner under her bloodshot eyes. He thought she looked just as sexy as she had when she was dressed up the previous day.

'Where are we?' she asked, yawning.

'Buggered if I know,' Mike said.

She smiled. 'Seriously,' she said.

'Somewhere in Zambia. There's no way we'll make Kariba, but it's no real drama. I know a place near the next town where we can stay. It's off the main road and not many people go there.'

'Do you think we're being followed?' she asked.

'No. It'd be easy to spot a tail on this road, there's not much traffic. But it's safer from now on for us to avoid the usual haunts. If they work out we're travelling in an overlander they have only to ask one of the other drivers to find out where we'd be likely to stop.'

'What's this place called where we're staying?'

'Jambo Safari Lodge. Jambo means "hello" in Swahili. Zambia is a kind of transition zone between southern and eastern Africa. As you move north and east in Africa the people start speaking Swahili and the prices get more expensive.'

Jambo Safari Lodge was really nothing of the sort. Mike found the dirt road turn-off and followed the signs to what was, in reality, a large-scale commercial farm, growing wheat and maize and supporting a herd of beef cattle. The lodge, such as it was, was ten small but tidy chalets clustered around a well-kept lawn and garden, a camping ground and a block of unisex showers and toilets.

They were met by a woman in a green maid's uniform who directed them to the camping ground. Mike's passengers slowly struggled awake as he parked the truck.

'Curer?' George asked Mike, opening the cool box and selecting an icy can of lager for himself.

Mike was tempted to say something sanctimonious, but he ached all over so he said, 'Yeah, fuck it, why not. Can't make me feel any worse.' He popped the can and took a long guzzle. The cool liquid spread right to his fingertips and the throbbing in his head slowed to a murmur.

'Christ,' Terry said, accepting a beer from George, 'you don't half look like crap, Mike. I hope the other guy looks just as bad.'

'Hardly dented him,' Mike said crushing the empty can. 'Chuck us another one, George, and let's get the tents up.'

They set up camp and, like vampires, the crew started coming to life as the red sun slid lazily towards the horizon. It was a moment of peace, watching the sunset and drinking a cold beer. Sam and Terry had started a fire in a cut-down drum in the middle of the camping ground, and most of the others were grabbing chairs out of the truck and sundowners out of the cool box. Mike took another beer, his towel and toiletry bag, and headed for the showers.

Mike stripped and hung up his towel and clothes on the shower room door. The door lock was broken. He shrugged his shoulders, turned on the water and opened his can of beer. Carefully he shampooed his hair, trying not to aggravate the wound on his scalp, then rinsed and took a long draught from the cold can on the ledge beside him. The near-scalding water soothed the bruises on his side, which had turned a nasty purple during the day, and he found his headache was disappearing nearly as fast as his third beer. He was about to start singing when there was a knock at the wooden door of the small shower room.

'Occupied,' he called out. To his surprise, the door creaked open, and he turned to face the tiled wall. He turned off the water and looked back over his shoulder.

'Not pleased to see me?' Julie Muir asked in a tone of mock disappointment. 'Did you think it would be my mum?' She was wearing a cropped, tight-fitting white top that showed off her pierced belly button, and a purple tie-dyed sarong skirt that barely reached the middle of her smooth tanned thighs.

She undid the knot at the side of her skirt and it fell to the floor. She was naked underneath and she said, 'I just wanted to say how sorry I was for being late today.'

'Julie, I don't think this is a good idea . . .' Mike reached for a towel, but she blocked his reach with her body. 'Julie, put your clothes back on.'

Her young body was lithe and hard, with not an ounce of fat anywhere. Her breasts were high and firm and the nipples strained hard at the stretch fabric of her top.

'I know I've been bad,' she said as she hooked her hands under her top and slid it up over her head. 'You were angry at me and Mum this morning, but you look pretty pleased to see me now,' she said with a giggle.

'You shouldn't be here –' he tried again, but she cut him off.

'Because of you and Mum? Don't worry, she told me. And I told her it was my turn next.'

She stepped into the cubicle with Mike and wrapped her arms around him from behind. He shrugged her arms away.

'Julie, this isn't right!'

There was another sharp rap on the shower room door, followed by a female voice.

'Mike, are you in there?'

'Shit,' he said. It was Sarah.

'Oooh,' Julie moaned theatrically. A wicked smile played across her lips, and Mike glared angrily at her.

'Mike? Are you OK?' Sarah called again.

Julie put a hand to her mouth to stop herself from laughing out loud and then reached up for the door handle.

'No!' Mike said sharply.

'What?' cried Sarah. She gave a hard shove on the door just as Julie turned the handle.

Sarah flew into the tiny room, and bumped into Julie. She bounced off the naked young woman, forcing her into Mike's arms. Julie made no move to cover herself but instead eased her body back against Mike's and reached up behind her to encircle his neck. He grabbed her hands firmly and tried to place them by her side.

'Hi Sarah, want to join us?' Julie asked, then giggled.

'Sarah, I . . . this is . . .' Mike stammered.

'Sorry,' Sarah said, and her cheeks burned scarlet.

She looked at Julie, at Mike and then up at the ceiling. 'It's just that, well, I thought, you know, that you might still be hurt and . . . Oh, God . . .' She didn't finish, but quickly turned and stepped out into the darkness.

'Shit,' Mike said, running a hand through his wet hair.

'Party pooper,' Julie said, turning to push her slim body against his.

'Christ, what a mess. I'm sorry, Julie, we can't do this. I could lose my job.'

'Makes it more fun, doesn't it?' she said smiling broadly. Then she took a step back from him and became more serious. 'You're soft on her, aren't you?'

'Who? Your mum?'

'No, silly. Sarah.'

'No. What makes you think that?'

Julie picked up her skirt and retied it. Mike looked away as she retrieved her top.

'You went to pieces. It was like you'd been caught cheating on your wife.'

'No,' he protested again, but he wasn't so sure.

'Oh, yes. I've seen that look on men's faces before. Believe me!'

'I bet you have,' Mike said, reaching for his towel.

'Cheeky sod. She's got it bad for you, as well,' she added matter-of-factly.

'No way. She's made that quite clear.'

'Sure you don't want to play with me, then?'

He shook his head and smiled. 'Get out before I spank you.'

'Promises, promises,' Julie said as she shut the door behind her.

18

Sarah and Mike had exchanged the bare minimum of words since she had caught him with Julie in the shower room on the previous evening. He had tried to explain that nothing had gone on, but she had ignored him.

'Look, I don't care what did or didn't go on between you two, no matter how sordid or innocent it was, OK?' she had protested.

On the rest of the long, boring drive through Zambia to the border crossing at Siavonga, across the dam wall from Kariba, Sarah had alternately slept, or pretended to sleep, and stared out the window. Mike had divided his attention between her and the road. She was wearing olive green pedal pushers and a red tank top. Her small feet rested on the dashboard with the soles pressed against the windscreen in that peculiar position that only a woman can attain and enjoy. Her calves were smooth and firm. He was annoyed with her that she wasn't talking to him, and with himself for being unable to strike up a conversation.

The temperature and the humidity had climbed steadily as they dropped into the hot, sticky Zambezi valley. It was after two by the time they cleared Zambian customs and immigration and coasted down the hill and on to the top of the massive concrete dam that divided the two countries.

'Awesome,' Kylie said, peering down over the man-made precipice to the Zambezi River far below. On the other side of the wall the waters of Lake Kariba shimmered in the afternoon heat.

'Later on this evening, we'll go for a game drive,' Mike said through the window connecting the driver's compartment to the main cab at the back.

'Where to?' Linda asked.

'Just around the town. Kariba is teeming with wildlife.'

'How come?'

'When they built this monstrosity, in the mid 1960s, the flooding displaced a lot of wildlife and a lot of people as well. Many of the people, and all of the wildlife, couldn't understand just how fast and how high the waters of the Zambezi would rise once they were blocked. The government authorities rescued the villagers who were left stranded by the flood, and hundreds of volunteers came here to rescue the thousands of animals and reptiles that were left clinging to trees and hilltops. The campaign to save the wildlife was known as Operation Noah. Kariba town never grew big enough to completely displace the wildlife that had always lived on the shores of the river, and now the animals just mingle with the people around the lake shore.'

'What sort of animals?' Linda wanted to know.

'Hippos wander up from the lake into gardens in the evening and leopards snatch family pets. I've seen lions on the main road between Kariba and the main north–south highway. There are hyenas scrounging in the municipal rubbish dump every night, and plenty of zebra and antelope species in the hills and valleys along the lake shore.'

The tour group's main reason for visiting Kariba, however, was to indulge in one of the lake's best-known pastimes: houseboating. Kariba houseboats are more like mansion-boats. Huge multi-storeyed aluminium-sided floating gin palaces. Ostensibly a houseboat and its tender vessels are meant to be good platforms for game viewing or fishing, but in Kariba a houseboat holiday was as much about drinking and partying as it was about getting close to nature.

Mike was looking forward to getting out onto the lake. After long, hot, sometimes tense days on the road this was to be his two days of pure R and R. With a skipper to drive the boat and a crew to cook, it was the closest thing Mike ever got to time off during an overland trip. There was also the chance that he would once more cross paths with Hess and Orlov. They were leaving on the houseboat the morning after they arrived at Kariba, but their first night in town would be spent, as usual, under canvas.

After breezing through the laid-back Zimbabwean border formalities, Mike drove uphill from the dam and took a right turn down towards Andorra Harbour.

'Welcome to Kariba, the Zimbabwean Riviera,' Mike said to the crew.

'Looks more like a ghetto to me,' said Nigel, unimpressed.

'Kariba's a frontier town. It's got a Wild-West feel about it, a hangover from the days when the only Europeans who lived in the Zambezi valley were crocodile hunters and the roughnecks who came to build the dam,' Mike explained. 'It's also the closest thing that Zimbabwe has to a seaside. Boating and drinking are the main pastimes here. There are marinas, hotels, camp grounds, even a casino at Caribbea Bay.'

'Hey! Buffalo,' said Sam as he scrambled in his pack for his camera.

The entrance to the camping ground Mike had stopped outside was blocked by four scarred, mean-looking black buffalo bulls. 'Buffalo are known in Africa as "black death". That's the name big-game hunters gave them because of their tendency to charge when wounded or startled,' Mike said. 'Stay in the truck.'

After a few blasts of the horn the old males eventually ambled down the road towards a sign pointing to the Kariba Yacht Club.

Mike smiled and waved at the security guard as they drove in, past a sign welcoming them to the MOTH campsite.

'What's a MOTH?' Terry asked.

'Large flying insect, I expect,' said George.

'It's an acronym,' Mike said. 'It stands for "Men of the Tin Hat Society". The "tin hats" was the nickname for Rhodesia's old soldiers, veterans of the First and Second world wars. The campsite and chalets were set up as a fundraising venture by the society.'

The campsite was well laid out, with electricity

boxes and garden furniture to make life a little more comfy for campers. They were right on the edge of the lake, although thick vegetation on the other side of the camp fence obscured any view of the water. A deep drainage ditch bisected the camping ground and ran into a small inlet of stagnant lake water.

Huge acacias shaded them from the afternoon sun as the group set up camp, but Mike was still sweating freely in the moisture-laden air by the time they finished. He needed a swim and a beer.

'OK,' he said to the crew, who clustered around him in the middle of the circle of green dome tents, 'we leave for the houseboat at ten tomorrow morning. Before that, I'll do a quick run up to the supermarket for any last-minute munchies or necessities that people need. Make sure you put your mozzie repellent on, the bugs are bad here. Also, if you do walk outside the camp, beware of animals.' As if in confirmation a hippo honked from not far away. Everyone laughed – some a little nervously.

'I'm heading for the yacht club. They do a mean steak there and excellent fish and chips. Otherwise, you know where the gas cooker is,' Mike said.

About half of the crew, including Sarah, followed him out through the gates to the right and up a small hill towards the yacht club. The remainder, including Jane Muir, stayed around the camping ground, writing postcards or snoozing in their tents. A few opted for a walk. Nigel was playing solitaire at a picnic table and drinking a Coke.

The yacht club was an asbestos sheet and tin building which Mike thought must have looked slightly less tacky when it was built during the 1960s. 'What it lacks in style it makes up for in location,' he said as they walked through the car park at the rear of the clubhouse.

The long single-storey building was perched on a steep rise overlooking Lake Kariba and the far-off, purple-hued mountain range of Matusadona National Park. An elevated walkway jutted out from the bar to the bridge, a covered patio from where sailing races and sunsets alike could be appreciated. There was an air horn on the bridge, which Mike guessed was sounded to start and stop the races.

Mike bought the first round after paying a nominal day membership fee and distributed lagers, lemonades and Cokes. He smiled at Sarah when he handed her a gin and tonic but she didn't smile back. As he waited for his change he glanced at the memorabilia behind the bar. Rhodesian army beer steins sat comfortably below a portrait of the whites' one-time enemy who now ruled the country. A brass ship's bell was screwed to the wall.

Sam walked into the bar, puffing from the exertion of the short walk in the afternoon heat. He was wearing his floppy bush hat and Mike knew there would be trouble when the thin, darkly tanned man who was sitting at the bar reached out for the cord on the bell's ringer.

'Decided to catch up with you guys after all –' Sam started, but he was cut short by the loud clanging of the bell. 'Hey, what was that? Beer time?'

'Certainly is, and it's your round, my boy!' said the man, with a glint of joy in his blue eyes.

'What do you mean?' Sam asked indignantly.

'Hat, hat, hat, my boy. Against club rules, don't you know? No hats inside!' he said with mock anger. He was thin but muscled, and had the look of a man who had spent his life on the water or in the bush, or both. He wore khaki shorts and a two-tone green and beige bush shirt. On his feet were ankle-length suede boots with no socks. By the amount of grey in his ginger hair Mike judged the man to be in his fifties, although his skin was deeply lined from years in the sun. His tan was mottled with darker spots that Mike guessed might one day turn to skin cancer.

'No, I didn't know,' Sam said, quickly removing his hat.

'Well, you do now. Ignorance of the law is no excuse,' the man said.

'Don't sweat it,' Mike chimed in. 'Will you allow me to cover his debt?' He was the only other customer in the bar, so it was going to be a cheap round anyway.

The older man scratched his chin thoughtfully and paused for a moment before conceding. 'Highly irregular, you understand. I'll accept your kind offer, but just this once. Also, if the boy were to oblige me with a small tot in the next round we might consider this delicate matter closed. Fair enough?'

'Fair enough. Sam, can you take the rest of these drinks outside for me, please? What'll it be, Mr . . . ?'

'Gerald O'Flynn, but call me Flynn, everybody else does. Whisky, straight, plus a Castle chaser, if you please.' They shook hands and Mike introduced himself.

Mike ordered the drinks and asked Flynn what he did for a living.

'This, that and everything in between. Hunter, safari guide, heartbreaker and soldier of fortune,' he said with a smile. 'I came up here to Kariba during the war – our little war – and never left. That would have been around '67, or '68.'

The broken blood vessels in Flynn's nose told Mike a fair amount of the man's time in Kariba had probably been spent right where he was, on a bar stool in the yacht club.

'So what are you doing now? Breaking hearts?'

Flynn laughed and said, 'Maybe this evening. No, I've got a little job in a day or so. On standby, as it were. Couple of chaps coming up from down south who want to go for a walk in the bush.'

Down south, Mike knew, referred to South Africa.

'Where are you taking them?' Mike asked, savouring the first draught of cold liquid from the frosted beer glass. The yacht club was clearly as much about drinking as it was about sailing.

'Across the water, to the Matusadona. I'm qualified to lead walking trips in the park.'

The untamed thick bush of Matusadona National Park rose up from the lake shore to the steep rocky cliffs of a low mountain range. The day was clear and the range was visible as a long, thin purplish smear on the far horizon. One of the girls shrieked as she jumped into the water of the club's green-tinged swimming pool, which was set into a grassy terrace below where Flynn and Mike sat in the bar.

'A few attractive girlies in your push, eh?' Flynn said with a lascivious wink.

'One or two,' Mike said, looking down at Sarah, who had removed her tank top to expose a simple but sexy black bikini.

'Am I right in thinking you're the shepherd of this flock, Mike?'

'For my sins. We're off an overland truck, an old Bedford. I'm the driver, tour guide and father confessor.'

Flynn laughed. 'You'd have to be paying me money to ride through Africa in the back of one of those things. Come to think of it, even when someone did pay me money to ride around in an army Bedford I still didn't like it. Particularly when we hit that land-mine in '72!'

A phone rang behind the bar and the barman, who had been polishing glasses with a tea towel, answered it. 'For you, Mr O'Flynn,' he said. Neither the barman nor Flynn looked surprised. Mike imagined the guide took calls in the bar quite often.

'Karl, good to hear from you, my boy.' Flynn spoke loudly. 'Speak up, I can hardly hear you. You're on a what? A satellite phone? Bloody useless new technology, give me the drums any day, eh.'

Mike's ears pricked up at the mention of the caller's first name and he listened closely, straining to hear the voice on the other end of the phone.

'OK. So you're arriving when, now? What, tomorrow? That doesn't leave me a lot of time to get the boat ready, but we'll make a plan here and get everything organised for you. Just the three of you, still? Good.'

Flynn waved at the bar tender and pantomimed writing. The barman handed him a pen and Flynn turned over a cardboard beer coaster. Mike craned his head to see what the man was writing. He coughed as the beer suddenly slid down his throat the wrong way, and held up a hand to his mouth. Fortunately, Flynn was too busy winding up the conversation to notice the other man's surprise at the words he had just written.

On the beer mat, in a bad but unmistakable hand, were the words: 'Hess, 10am Friday'.

Flynn handed the receiver back to the barman. 'Bloody German,' he said with annoyance. 'That's my weekend stuffed.'

Mike tried to sound nonchalant. 'You've got German tourists coming?'

'No. He's a Namibian, actually. But those Krauts are all the same, eh? Let me buy you a drink.'

'No, please, this one's on me. The last was just my friend's penalty.' Mike ordered two more beers and another whisky from the barman.

'Cheers,' Flynn said. 'Where was I? Ah, yes, Karl Hess. I know him from way back. He served up here with the SAS – the Rhodesian Special Air Service – in the last couple of years of the war. Pretty boy, you know, but he was no softie, and that's for sure.'

The drinks were loosening Flynn's tongue, not that Mike sensed it needed too much to get him talking. The way the bartender studiously returned to polishing his glasses made Mike think the man was grateful there was someone else in the bar for the old hunter to bore.

'What do you mean, "no softie"?' Mike asked.

Flynn scratched the bristly salt-and-pepper stubble on his chin and stared out over the lake, which shimmered like liquid silver in the low afternoon light.

'It was a dirty little war, that's for sure, and we were none of us angels.'

The barman had finished with the glasses and was checking the fridge in preparation for the evening crowd. He walked out through a doorway at the back of the bar, presumably to a storeroom. Flynn waited until he was gone before continuing.

'Karl was only a youngster then, in his twenties. Not in my patrol, but word travelled, you know. I heard a story once, don't know if it's true, that he beheaded a captured gook – that's what we used to call the terrs, the terrorists, before they became known as freedom fighters. Apparently he did it in front of the man's family to make them give up the location of some arms and the whereabouts of the rest of the man's cell. Then, so the story goes, he put the man's head in his pack and took it back to the Special Branch police, who were keen to make positive identification of any terrorists we killed.'

Mike sipped his beer. A man who was capable of an atrocity such as that would have had no qualms about executing Isabella and the other witnesses at the mission clinic. 'No softie at all,' he agreed.

'None of that happened in my push, though. I'll tell you that now. Still, Hess got results and he made it to sergeant before the end. Went back to his own army, down in South West Africa after that, and spent some time with the *koevoets*, a special police anti-terrorist unit, in Angola. Quite a few hard bastards in that little lot too, from what I heard. He's been up here a few times over the years, bringing hunting clients with him. Europeans, mostly.'

'So are these the people you're taking across to Matusadona?' Mike asked.

'Indeed they are,' Flynn said, then drained his whisky in one go. He chased it down with cold beer from a dew-encrusted glass. 'Mother's milk,' he added appreciatively.

'But surely they won't be hunting over there?' Mike said, gesturing across the water.

'Good lord, no. National park over there. No, we're only going for a walk, or a few walks, every day until we find what we want. There's nothing to shoot over there, and he'd take a rifle into the park over my dead body. No, no. The rangers over there don't muck about. It's shoot to kill if they see you with a weapon in the parks up here.'

'So I've heard.' Mike was genuinely puzzled about why Hess and Orlov would have cut short their safari in the legal hunting concessions between Victoria Falls and Kariba to go sightseeing in a national park. 'So what's there that's so special?'

'We're going in search of the rarest and one of the most unpredictable animals in the Zambezi valley,' Flynn said, lowering his voice theatrically.

'What's that?'

'Rhino, my boy. Black rhino. There's half-a-dozen young orphan animals under armed guard over there that the rangers are getting ready to release back into the wild. The word from the Parks staff is that one of the few remaining wild bulls has been sniffing around the wee ones lately and that we'd have a very good chance of seeing him on foot.'

'Where do they keep the orphans?' Mike asked, although he could now guess what Flynn was going to say.

'Tashinga.'

19

'Y ou worry too much, Karl. I have no lion and one undersized buffalo trophy to take home. We should have stuck to the original schedule,' Orlov said as Hess parked the Land Cruiser at the end of the rutted dirt road that led down to the Cutty Sark Marina on the edge of Lake Kariba.

Hess had heard the complaint too many times in the last two days. Orlov was a man used to getting what he wanted, and a man not afraid of the law. That was OK in countries where half the police force was in your pocket, but Hess knew just how diligent the South Africans could be when it came to hunting down poachers. Indeed, many of the men he had served with on *koevoet* operations in South West Africa and Angola were now working for the police on anti-poaching patrols.

'You want the rhino, don't you?' Hess said testily as he fetched his bags out of the back of the vehicle.

'Of course, Karl. You know I do,' Orlov replied. The

argument had gone round and round in this manner a number of times.

'As I have said before, we must assume the police are looking for us. The sooner we get the rhino, the sooner we can get to safety. You can bag a lion or a bigger buffalo any day of the week in South Africa.'

'Very well, Karl,' Orlov said in a resigned tone.

Hess saw Gerald O'Flynn standing on a wooden jetty, hands on hips, supervising the last-minute loading of two long, low aluminium-hulled speedboats.

'Karl, good to see you. My chaps will carry your bags aboard,' Flynn called.

Hess mentally reviewed the plan once again. It was a simple one, the best kind. Flynn would take them across to Tashinga in his boats and they would go through the motions of visiting the *boma* where the orphan rhino were kept. Orlov would take, or pretend to take, rolls of photos of the beasts. Once that was over, Flynn would guide them into the bush on foot in search of the bull rhino that had reportedly been visiting the small herd of orphans.

Diceros bicornis, otherwise known as the black rhino, is normally a solitary animal, and adult males and females are generally only found together when the female comes into oestrus. Hess guessed that one of the orphans must be a female of at least six years old, the age when females reach sexual maturity. It would be she the lone male would be searching for.

They would be accompanied on the treks at all times by an armed park ranger, as was normal practice when walking in most of Zimbabwe's national parks. Once they sighted the animal, or at least

329

sighted fresh spoor, Hess would call off the sight-seeing expedition. They would return to Kariba immediately and cross the border into Zambia as soon as possible. From Siavonga, on the Zambian side of Lake Kariba, they would return the very next night in their own boat, with their rifles, and pick up the spoor they had located during the day.

Hess believed that Orlov underestimated the amount of planning and preparation that had gone into making such a simple plan a reality. Hess had visited Flynn and the park on a reconnaissance trip and sent Klaus across the border to recruit some local help. Klaus had found three supposedly retired poachers in the *shebeens* around the Zambian border town. They, along with Klaus, would provide the muscle to carry the rhino's massive skull out of the bush, as well as additional firepower in case they ran into an anti-poaching patrol.

'Good to see you again, Flynn,' Hess said warmly as he shook his hand and introduced Orlov. In truth, Hess had his reservations about Gerald O'Flynn. The man drank to excess, as was evidenced by his red nose and redder eyes, and had a tendency to talk too much when he was drunk. With the police possibly already on their trail he was worried about Flynn blabbing. However, Hess had limited his participation in the operation to strictly legal activities. They would play the innocent tourists for the duration of their stay with the guide.

Flynn was probably the best bushman available in Kariba. Hess remembered him from the war as not only a good officer, but an honourable and idealistic one. In Hess's book, idealism and honour had no place in war. He doubted whether Flynn would have assisted them at all if he had any inkling of what they were really up to. Indeed, he would probably have immediately reported them to the police.

Hess had told Flynn to choose a boat based on the need for speed rather than comfort, and the old guide had done well. The roar of the twin outboards and the slapping of the aluminium hull made conversation difficult, if not impossible, as they bounced across the small swell out on the lake. Hess appreciated the lack of distractions and enjoyed the feel of the warm sun on his back. There were five of them in the boat – himself, Orlov, Flynn, Klaus and a young African man who would set up and maintain their campsite in the national park for as long as it was needed.

The waters of the vast inland sea seemed to stretch to eternity around them, the empty vista broken only occasionally by another vessel. Orlov pointed at what looked like a barge with a crane jutting out from the top. 'Kapenta rig,' Flynn shouted above the noise of the motors. 'Little fish. The Africans catch 'em by the tonne and dry them. Very tasty!'

Hess pulled on aviator sunglasses to ward off the glare from the lake's surface and cast an idle glance at an ungainly, angular houseboat chugging along on the port side. He smiled as he noticed Orlov unashamedly ogling a trio of women in skimpy bikinis sunbaking on the roof of the craft. They waved at the speeding boat and Orlov waved back.

'Should we take a closer look, Mr Orlov?' Flynn

called out, looking back over his shoulder from his place at the helm and flashing the Russian a wide yellow-toothed grin.

'No,' Hess said, shaking his head to make sure he was understood.

'Karl is the dull boy. All work and no play,' Orlov called back cheerfully.

The journey took a little under an hour. As they neared land they passed an ever-increasing number of dead trees jutting out of the water, their trunks and branches stark and white. Fish eagles and cormorants perched on the branches, their droppings turning the dead branches whiter still. These were all that remained of the forests that once carpeted the hills flanking the floor of the Zambezi valley.

Flynn cut the engines when they were twenty metres or so from a long, narrow grey sandy beach. 'I'd be obliged if you'd keep an eye out for sticks just below the surface,' he said to his passengers as the boat glided noiselessly into shore. They encountered no obstacles and the boat beached with a soft shush. 'It's sandy here, so you shouldn't have any problem with bilharzia. The little snails that carry the bug usually only live in reeds and weed – but take a big jump for terra firma, just in case.'

Tashinga was an attractive camping ground located right on the water's edge. It was also the head-quarters for Matusadona National Park. 'The park office is just up the road a bit. I'll go and pay and fetch our guide. Matthew, set up camp and put the kettle on for the gentlemen, please,' Flynn said to his young African assistant.

'Yes, boss,' the boy said.

'Forget the tea, Flynn, we've got work to do,' Hess said.

Flynn nodded and set off up a dirt road. Matthew carried plastic crates full of camping gear and canvas tent bags to a nearby campsite, which consisted of two simple A-frame shelters set onto concrete slabs. The shelters would make handy storage areas and were also big enough to pitch a tent under, for those visitors who wanted to feel a little more secure.

'The camping ground is unfenced here,' Hess said to Orlov. 'I've seen elephant, buffalo and even lion once, wandering through on their way to drink at the lake.'

Flynn returned twenty minutes later with a Zimbabwean ranger in a dark green field uniform. The man, whom Flynn introduced as Samson, carried an AK-47. The Russian assault rifle was old but well maintained, and its once-black metal parts were burnished bright silver.

Samson led them out of the main camp along a dusty road, past a grass airstrip where a herd of impala grazed peacefully.

'Here is the *boma* where we keep the rhinos,' he said, pointing up a short track to a cluster of rough wooden pens, 'but they are not there now.'

'Where are they?' Orlov asked. 'I thought you kept them locked up all the time?'

'No, they eat for most of the day and then we return them to the *boma* at night-time. Follow me.' He left the dirt road now and turned off into the bush, his eyes scanning the ground for fresh spoor that would lead him to the animals. He picked up the trail after less than a minute and they set off into the thick scrub, pausing every now and then to disentangle themselves from thorn bushes or to negotiate dense thickets of bush.

They saw another armed ranger before they saw the rhinos. Samson waved and greeted the man in Shona. Hess studied the man keenly. He was more interested in the men guarding the rhinos than in the animals themselves.

The ranger scrutinised the party just as carefully, Hess noticing that he was alert and looking for signs of anything irregular. He was armed with an FN rifle, designed by Fabrique Nationale of Belgium. Hess knew the weapon well, as he had carried one during the bush war in Rhodesia. Twenty-round magazine, 7.62-millimetre ammunition. The rifle was painted with green and brown camouflage, and was probably ex-army stock. Though an old weapon, it was more than a match for the AK-47s Klaus and the poachers would be carrying, in terms of stopping power and accuracy, but not capable of pouring out large volumes of lead in a firefight. Unlike their guide, the man was dressed in a khaki dress uniform of short-sleeved shirt and pressed trousers with a yellow and green sable belt. This told Hess that the orphan rhinos did not venture far into the bush each day, or the man would have been wearing the more utilitarian green uniform.

They passed the sentry and suddenly found themselves in the midst of a herd of six snuffling and snorting young rhinos. There were two other men with the rhinos, both dressed in green overalls.

'These men look after the rhinos when they are in the bush. They show them how to feed and what is good to eat,' Samson said.

'She likes this,' one of the men in overalls said as he scratched a young rhino behind the ear. Orlov dutifully snapped off a few pictures and the rhino snorted in apparent pleasure.

'How old are they?' Orlov asked.

'They are mostly two and three years old,' the same man replied. 'But that one, she is now six.'

Hess studied the larger rhino. He noticed that she was, indeed, a female and knew it must be her the bull was sniffing around for. He also noted that none of the animals had very large horns yet, although he knew that even the stumps that these ones carried would each be worth a small fortune. Too short to be carved into dagger handles for rich Yemeni men, they would nonetheless fetch a pretty price in Asia, where ground rhino horn was a sought-after treatment for fever.

They wandered among the feeding rhinos, watching them grasp thorn bushes and leaves with their dexterous hooked upper lips and munch contentedly away. Hess knew the Zambian poachers would dearly love to slaughter these animals as well as the big bull, but he would not allow it. Not for the love of an endangered species, but because one day there would be another Orlov, perhaps from America or Germany or Italy, who would be willing to pay to bag a unique trophy.

After half an hour, Flynn asked, 'Got enough pictures, Mr Orlov?'

'Indeed I have, Flynn. Now, can we look for the bull?'

Samson briefed them on safety for the walk. 'Please stay behind me and Mr O'Flynn at all times. If we see the rhino, keep very still and quiet. Do not use the flash on your camera, please. If he is going to charge, you must climb the nearest tree immediately. As we walk, always keep looking for the tree that you will climb.'

Samson wandered over to the armed guard and spoke to him briefly before turning and addressing the party. 'This man says he saw the bull yesterday, in the distance. We may still be able to pick up his trail.'

They set off in the general direction in which the male rhino had last been seen. The sun was at its peak now and they sweated profusely in the humid air. Hess guessed the temperature was close to forty degrees centigrade, if not higher.

After a little more than half an hour Samson signalled them with an open hand to stop, then motioned them forward to inspect the tree he was standing next to. 'He has been here. See how the bark of the leadwood is rubbed away. He has been scratching himself. See his tracks in the dirt. We are not far from him now.'

They followed the three-toed tracks and the path of broken twigs and gnawed thorn bushes until the sun was nearing the tops of the tallest trees. But not once did they see their quarry.

Orlov sat down heavily on a fallen tree trunk and wiped his brow. He drank greedily from his canteen until it was empty, and tipped it upside down, letting the last drops dribble into his mouth.

'Water's low. We're all bushed,' said Flynn. 'Let's call it a day, Karl.' Reluctantly, Hess agreed, and Samson led them back to the camping ground.

'Ah, but I think there is good news today,' Samson said when he met them on the road out of the camping ground at dawn the following morning. 'I have been to the *boma* already and the night guard says he heard the bull in the evening. He was very close.'

In the lake behind them hippos honked and grunted, like fat men laughing hard at bad jokes. A gaggle of white-speckled guinea fowl crossed the road in front of them and cackled nervously when they spotted the humans.

Hess carefully framed his question. 'Are you sure the man knows what he heard? Have you asked the other guards?'

'Oh, no need, sir. There is only the one guard. He is an old man who knows the bush well. He would make no mistake, sir,' Samson said.

Hess nodded, pleased with the answer. He now knew that there would only be one sentry for them to worry about, but that the man was experienced and alert.

Flynn walked behind the armed ranger, followed by Orlov, Hess and Klaus. Hess wanted Klaus to become as familiar with the path the rhino had followed as he would be. Hess felt naked in the bush without a weapon and he imagined Klaus felt the same.

They picked up the spoor of the big bull rhino

again about two hundred metres from the *boma*. Flynn pointed excitedly to the broad three-toed prints in the red-brown dust. 'Last night, only a few hours ago,' he whispered.

Every now and then Flynn would stop and pull a small plastic puffer bottle from his pocket. The bottle had originally contained lens cleaning fluid for a camera, but Flynn had filled it with ash from a lead-wood fire. The ash was as white and fine as talcum powder, but without the telltale odour. A squirt of ash from the bottle would show them the direction of the faintest puff of wind. 'The beast is as blind as a bat, but he'll smell us a mile off, so we've got to stay downwind of him,' he said in explanation. 'Rhinos have good hearing too, so be dead quiet from now on, and remember to pick your tree in case he gets spooked and charges us.'

It was another hour before they sighted the bull and Hess could not help but be impressed by Flynn's keen eyesight when they did. He had stopped and raised a hand. The ranger peered into the dense thorn bush that blocked their path twenty metres ahead and then nodded in recognition. He turned to Orlov and Hess and motioned them to come forward, placing a finger on his lips at the same time.

The guide bent close to Hess's face to whisper and Hess recoiled slightly at the sour smell of last night's whisky. 'Ear,' breathed Flynn. He pointed into the deep shadows at the base of the thorny thicket.

Hess pulled a small pair of expensive binoculars from the pocket of his bush shirt and scanned the shadows. A few seconds later he nodded, then handed the binoculars to Orlov. Flynn was right, an ear was all that was visible, although they could make out the faint outline of the rhino as a slightly paler form in the shadows. He was lying on his stomach, asleep. Occasionally his ear would twitch involuntarily to ward off a pesky fly and it was this tiny movement that had betrayed his carefully chosen hide.

'Come on, let's get a bit closer,' Flynn whispered and motioned to the ranger, signalling they were ready to move.

'No, let's go,' said Hess, and he placed a hand on Flynn's arm to stop him moving.

That's odd, Flynn thought to himself. Hess's client had come halfway around the world to see a black rhino in the wild and no doubt paid a pretty penny to do so. Why would Hess want to leave now just when they had found one of the most elusive creatures in Africa? Flynn reckoned they could creep at least a few metres closer. Even if the animal was startled, his first instinct would probably be to scarper and that would give the tourist a chance to shoot a few more pictures. Alternatively, they could lie up where they were for an hour or so and see if the animal woke and moved of its own accord. Flynn looked at Orlov for confirmation, but he just nodded his agreement with Hess's decision.

Flynn shrugged. It was nothing to him and he assumed he would still get payment in full. There really was no figuring foreigners, he told himself, and he included Namibian Germans in that broad-sweeping categorisation. He tapped the ranger on the shoulder and motioned back the way they had come with his thumb. Samson looked as surprised as Flynn at the tourists' desire to leave.

When the order of march had been reversed, and Flynn and Samson were once again at the head of the small column, Hess pulled the GPS unit from the black pouch on his belt. The unit was on, as it had been during the previous day's trek, and he checked the screen to make sure it was tracking enough satellites to compute their exact position. He pushed the *mark* button and recorded their position, naming it simply '1'. He rarely made mistakes and when he did, he never repeated them.

When they returned to the main dirt road, Hess said to Flynn, 'Have your man strike camp immediately. Don't worry about breakfast. We have to get back to Kariba as soon as possible.'

A feeling of uneasiness had been festering inside Flynn all that morning, ever since Hess had abruptly broken contact with the rhino. Hess was no 'bunny-hugger', and by the cold glint in his grey eyes neither was his client. Flynn had watched the way the Russian handled himself in the bush. He lacked the ease that he, Flynn, and Hess had, which came from spending a lifetime in the African veldt, but nonetheless the man was no blundering, loud-mouthed tourist. He was a hunter and he'd acted like a man on the hunt.

Flynn helped Matthew lift the cool box into the boat, and then slid into his seat behind the wheel as the young African pushed off from shore and nimbly jumped onto the bow. As the engines roared to life and the boat surged back into the lake, Gerald O'Flynn was overcome by a feeling that he had just done something terribly wrong.

20

'What is this, some kind of midlife crisis in reverse?' Sam asked as clumps of grey and brown hair dropped from Mel's nimble fingers.

'You're supposed to *grow* a ponytail when you reach fifty, not cut it off,' Terry said with a belch as he crushed yet another empty Zambezi beer can.

Mike was sitting on a fold-out chair on the foredeck of the houseboat, wearing nothing but sunglasses and a pair of knee-length blue-and-white flowered board shorts while Mel snipped away a year's worth of his hair. Having a hairdresser on the trip was handy, he thought. The ponytail would have come off even if Mel wasn't around, but she was doing a better job than he would have. 'Try that fifty line again and you're going swimming without the crocodile cage, bro,' Mike said, turning to face Terry.

'Keep still,' Mel said, positioning his head with expert fingers. 'I don't know, Mike, I think long hair's dead sexy on a man. You're gonna end up looking more like a stockbroker than a safari guide when I finish with you.'

'I'm thinking of all the money I'm going to save on shampoo,' Mike said. Hess and Orlov were close, too close for comfort, and he knew both of them would recognise Sarah and himself by their most distinguishing features. He had suggested that Sarah do something to change her appearance, in case they ran into the hunters around the national park, or on the road. The roads in Zambia were as few as they were bad, and it was likely they would pass them, or vice versa.

'Yeah, I agree,' Sarah said on cue, looking up from a glossy South African women's magazine she had bought in Kariba. 'Can you give me a trim and put a little colour through mine when you've finished with Mike?'

Sarah was wearing her black bikini top and a pair of denim shorts. Sometime during the previous day on the houseboat she had found time to paint her toenails cherry red. She and Mike were speaking again, since he had relayed his conversation with Flynn to her. The animosity that she had harboured towards him seemed to disappear instantly and they had discussed several scenarios about how they might deliberately get closer to the hunters to spy on them. Mike had discounted all her wild schemes, but she was still adamant that they should find a way to discover more about Hess's plans and to thwart them.

Mike played it straight, however, and phoned in his new information to Fanie Theron. He was annoyed to get the detective's voice mail again, and left a long, detailed message. Mike had no idea whether Theron was getting the messages, let alone acting on them. He hoped the police appreciated the effort they had gone to, not to mention the pain he had suffered, and the importance of the information they were gathering.

'There's nothing more we can do,' he had told Sarah when they boarded the houseboat. Secretly, now that he was sure Orlov and Hess were the men who had killed Isabella, he hoped he would have the chance to confront them. The Browning pistol was at the bottom of the daypack he carried on to the boat, just in case.

'That's them!' Sarah had said on the first day out from Kariba, when a fast-moving speedboat overtook their sluggish floating gin palace.

Mike joined her at the railing and she handed him her binoculars.

'That's who?' Kylie had asked.

'Oh, no one,' Mike had said, pulling the baseball cap down more firmly on his head. He doubted they would recognise him from this distance, although Sarah and he had recognised them easily enough. 'Just a couple of blokes we bumped into in Vic Falls.'

That was what spurred them on to changing their appearances the very next day, along with the fact that they would be anchoring just off Tashinga for their second and final night on the houseboat. There was a good chance the hunters might be able to scan the boat from the shore with their binoculars.

After his haircut Mike ducked below deck to the bathroom to shave off his goatee. The skin around his chin was white compared to the rest of his tanned face and his new haircut conjured up memories of another life. He hadn't looked like this in over a year. The grey in his hair was more noticeable now that it was short, and the absence of his long sideburns drew attention to the crow's feet at his eyes. Still, he looked like a soldier again instead of an ageing hippie, and that was just fine. He was starting to feel like a soldier again, too.

'Jesus Christ!' is probably not the right thing to say to a woman when she shows off a new hairstyle, but that's what came out when Mike saw Sarah. Her hair was short. Very short, like a man's, and very black. The cut was stylish enough, but the transformation from soft blonde bob to GI Jane was a shock to Mike.

'That's all they had in the shop,' she said, throwing an empty cardboard box at him.

He caught it and looked at the label. A smiling African woman with frizzy jet-black hair was surrounded by the words 'Dark and Lovely'. Many African women coloured their hair, he knew, as they found pure black more attractive than chocolate brown.

'Well,' Sarah said, pursing her lips, 'how do I look?'

'Um . . . dark and lovely?' Mike ventured. Mel laughed. Sarah didn't.

'How do I look?' Mike questioned back.

'Old and grey,' Sarah said, trying hard to hold back a smile.

'I think it looks sexy,' Jane Muir said from behind him.

Mike felt long fingernails suddenly caressing his scalp.

Julie giggled and raised the old Jackie Collins paperback she was reading on the sundeck closer to her face. Sarah, Mike saw, was glaring at Julie with the same burning stare seen on lions when they're stalking.

'Time to wash off,' Mike said, and climbed up onto the safety railing that surrounded the deck.

'You've got to be joking!' Jane said with real concern.

'There're hippos and crocodiles and all sorts of stuff in there. You said so!' Mel added.

'What about the cage, Mike?' asked Sam.

The houseboat came complete with a steel cage that was lowered into the water from a small hand-cranked derrick on the aft deck. It was big enough for three or four people to splash around in while the boat was stationary. Mike had been out on boats with Zimbabwean friends in the past and they maintained that if you were in the centre of Lake Kariba, as they were now, you were safe from harm.

'It's too hard to do laps in,' Mike replied and dived off the railing. The water was cool and refreshing. It soothed the dull ache in his bruised ribs and face, and he scrubbed the annoying, itching bits of cut hair from his scalp. He struck out away from the boat in a strong overarm and then rolled onto his back to look back at the faces lining the rails.

'Sod it,' Sarah said. She stepped out of her shorts and climbed the safety rail.

Mike suddenly felt concerned for her. While it was all right for him to take risks, no matter how slight the chance of his being taken by a crocodile in deep water, he was afraid for her safety. She executed a graceful dive and swam towards him.

345

Suddenly he felt excited, seeing her swimming towards him. He imagined their warm bodies coming together in the cold water, the feel of erect nipples pressing through the flimsy black lycra of her bikini against his chest. She stopped and trod water a couple of metres away from him.

'It's great, isn't it?' she said, her smile wide, their earlier jousts forgotten.

'It certainly is,' he said.

'Race you back?'

'Good idea,' Mike said.

Sarah had about ten years on Mike and he shuddered to think what a comparison of their lifestyles and exercise regimens would reveal. She touched the boat a length ahead of him and wasn't even breathing hard when he struggled alongside her. She ran a hand through her short black hair and sent up a shower of tiny droplets. He thought the colour made her blue eyes look striking, rather than merely attractive.

He climbed the aluminium ladder that the boat captain had thoughtfully lowered over the side and instinctively reached out a hand to help Sarah aboard. Sarah looked up and for a moment it seemed to him that she was going to scorn his offer. Just as he started to pull back his arm she reached up out of the water and grasped his hand. Her grip was strong and warm. It was the first time they had touched since the kiss in the nightclub and he felt the same confusion and desire sweep through his body.

Mike handed Sarah a towel as the roar of outboard motors and the slap of a fast-moving hull on the small swell made them all turn towards shore. The houseboat was pointing towards Tashinga and Mike could just make out the A-frame camping shelters on the shore about a kilometre away. That was where the boat was coming from, loud and fast.

'Can I borrow your binoculars, please, Kylie?' Mike asked. She had been using them to watch a pair of fish eagles near the shore.

A tall man was standing in the fast-moving boat. He had blond hair. He put a hand on the driver's shoulder and the boat slowed its speed a fraction. Mike focused the binoculars and saw that the standing man was Hess. Orlov sat in the back, arms outstretched and face tilted to the sun.

The speedboat slowed and Orlov opened his eyes and stared at the larger craft. Hess and Orlov were level with the houseboat, but still about two hundred metres away. Flynn was at the helm and concentrating on the waters ahead. Travelling at the speed they were was a risky business on a lake full of submerged forests. Hess raised his binoculars, and for a moment he and Mike stared at each other.

'Thank God for the haircuts,' Sarah whispered close to Mike's ear.

Mike knew he could have turned away or led Sarah to the other side of the boat, but a part of him hoped Hess could see him, and even recognise him, though he doubted the other man would. Mike felt a burning need to get close to these men again, to exact revenge and to see fear in their eyes.

Hess turned and said something to Orlov and smiled. They were ignoring the houseboat and its passengers. Hess tapped Flynn on the shoulder and

Mike heard the outboards scream as the guide opened the throttle wide again.

'They're in a hurry,' Mike said to Sarah. She towelled her short hair while they both watched the small boat recede from view.

'Do you think they've already killed one of the rhinos?' she asked.

'I doubt that they'd travel with the horn in broad daylight if they had.'

'Scared off?' she ventured.

'I doubt it. If Flynn's as good a tracker as I think he is, he's probably found them their rhino. But I can't see him being in on the deal. He didn't strike me as being a poacher.'

'So this was just a recce and they'll be coming back later.'

Mike nodded and reached for his towel. 'Soon.'

The houseboat had a shallow draft, but even so, they could only anchor about a hundred metres from the lake shore at Tashinga that afternoon. Sarah and Mike were first into the small aluminium tender boat when the captain offered to take people ashore to stretch their legs.

Mike wanted to call Theron to update him on Hess and Orlov's latest movements, and to pass on his theory about what the hunters were up to, but they were too far from Kariba to get a signal on the mobile phone. Mike had no idea if Theron had taken any action as a result of his earlier reports, and Sarah and he decided that the only other thing they could do was try to warn the National Parks staff themselves.

'Where are you two going?' Jane asked as Sarah stepped down into the aluminium boat.

'Sarah wants to interview the head ranger here, for her story,' Mike lied. 'I'm just taking her to the Parks office. The boat will be back soon.'

Jane shrugged and turned to George and said, 'How about that game of poker then, George? The one we were talking about the other night in the club?'

George looked startled, then replied, as calmly as he could, 'What, strip poker, you mean?'

'Get us a G and T, there's a good love. I'll shuffle the cards,' she said.

Mike smiled to himself as he climbed down into the boat. Again, Sarah let him take her hand to steady her as she climbed in. He stowed her camera gear at the front of the boat, to keep it under cover.

'That woman is incorrigible,' Sarah said, as the houseboat crewman started the little motor and they cut towards shore.

'That's exactly what I was thinking.'

'And as for her daughter, well . . . It's none of my business, but is there something serious between you two?' she asked.

'Who, Jane or Julie?' Mike asked, realising his blunder too late.

'What? You slept with both of them!'

'No, no. That incident with Julie wasn't how it looked. She came into the shower, but I turned her away after you left.'

'But what, you slept with her mum?'

Mike felt his face starting to colour.

'You did, didn't you?' Sarah persisted.

'Gentlemen don't tell,' he said, turning away from her. 'Anyway, in answer to your question there is nothing serious or otherwise going on between me and either Jane or Julie Muir.'

Mike could see the boatman was straining to hear their conversation now that it had turned to sex, and he was glad when they coasted into the sandy shore. Sarah left the boat first, so Mike didn't get a chance to offer his hand again.

'So, you slept with Jane, but it meant nothing to you and you don't care about her? Is that right?' Sarah said as they walked up the sandy incline from the lake shore.

'Typical journalist, putting words in people's mouths. If you must know, it's more the other way around. She's hardly said a word to me since we . . . well . . .'

'Maybe you didn't leave a lasting impression? I don't know how people can carry on like that. What sort of example is Jane setting for her daughter?'

'Haven't you ever had a one-night stand?' Mike asked, drawing level with her.

'None of your business if I have, but I can tell you it wouldn't be on a trip with my daughter in tow. Rather than playing around like a horny teenager I would have thought she'd have been looking for a serious relationship, so she could set an example for her daughter,' Sarah said.

'Maybe she thinks she'll never be able to replace

the man she lost. She was very young when it happened. Maybe she sees sex as a substitute for true love.'

'Do you feel like that? That you'll never replace Isabella?' Sarah asked.

He thought for a moment about his answer. He hated other people reminding him about Isabella, and a couple of days earlier in the trip he would have told Sarah to mind her own business. But now he felt it was OK to talk about his lost love and that maybe Sarah was a good person to talk to. He stopped to pick up a gnarled piece of driftwood and inspect its sun-bleached surface.

'It's different for me. I found Isabella late in my life. I'd been floating around aimlessly – having a pretty good time – but I was beginning to think I'd never find someone. I'll never forget what we had together, no matter how brief it was, but the odds of me finding a love like that again are pretty long.'

Mike didn't know what, if anything, he was starting to feel for Sarah now, despite her often prickly manner. Jane's advances and their one night of sex had awoken feelings of lust in him that he had suppressed since Isabella's death.

'What about you?' he asked. 'Where does Mr Right fit into your plans?'

'Who said I was looking for Mr Right? No, I'm not where I want to be yet with my career. But when I am, maybe there'll be time for . . . I don't know, time for love, maybe even children.'

'Want some advice from an old soldier?'

'Keep your gun clean and always carry a condom?'

351

'Very funny. No, just go for life, wherever it takes you. Grab it by the bit and run with it. Do whatever you want and chase whatever goals you want, but don't try to live your life by a timetable. I had only a few years to go in the army before I could retire with a full pension, but then I met Isabella and I knew that we wouldn't have a chance if I marked time at some middle-of-nowhere army base in Australia while she waited half a world away. I made the right choice, even with everything that happened in Mozambique, and I don't regret chucking away my old job. My only regret is that I didn't do it sooner, then maybe none of that stuff would have happened.'

'You shouldn't go on like that, Mike. I believe in fate. What will be, will be, and there's no point wondering "what if". It's easy for you to talk about chucking away your career on a whim, but it's still early days for me. I'm trying to make a name for myself. I want to do well and be successful, even if that means making some sacrifices in my personal life.'

They arrived at the park headquarters. The building was green-painted, rendered brick with an array of solar panels on the roof and a tall radio mast at one end. Garbled voices chattered noisily through a veil of static from the radio's loudspeaker as Mike and Sarah entered the building.

An old ranger with tight curly grey hair greeted them from behind the polished wooden counter.

'Good morning, sir, madam. How are you?' He spoke with a whistle through the gap where his front teeth had once been.

They exchanged pleasantries and introduced themselves quickly, as Mike was eager to raise the alarm. 'Are you the head ranger here?'

'No, sir, the boss he is in Kariba for three days,' the old man said.

'We have information that some poachers will be coming to this camp, probably to shoot one of your rhinos.'

The ranger was taken aback. 'Poachers? No, sir, we shoot the poachers here.' He raised his arms, pantomiming pointing a rifle.

'No, you don't understand. There are men planning to come here, maybe tonight, to shoot a rhino.'

'How do you know this?' the ranger asked, narrowing his eyes.

Mike thought things were going badly. Not only did the ranger not believe them, but now he was getting suspicious.

Sarah tried a different tack. 'There were five men camped here last night. They tracked a wild rhino this morning, in the bush, didn't they?'

The ranger looked even more distrustful now. 'How did you know this?' he asked. He was fidgeting with a piece of paper now, but Mike couldn't read what it said.

Sarah continued. 'These are the men that the South African Police suspect of poaching. We overheard them talking about illegally hunting a rhino in Zimbabwe when we were travelling in South Africa and we reported our concerns to the police. Haven't you received any information about this?'

Mike liked Sarah's neat paraphrasing of the truth

and nodded in support. The ranger looked down at the paper again.

'As a matter of fact we have received a warning of possible illegal activity from the police. But those men who came yesterday, they were with a man who would not be involved in such things. I do not think they are the ones.'

'Gerry O'Flynn, you mean? Flynn?' Mike asked.

'Yes. That is the man. He worked here as warden in the old days. I once saw him kill a poacher. He would never shoot a rhino.'

'I know Flynn also, and I believe you. I don't think he knows what the other men were up to.'

'Let me take your name and I will make a report,' the ranger said, reaching for a large book on the counter.

Mike knew there was nothing more they could do and his exasperation must have shown.

'Don't worry, sir. We take poaching very seriously in this country and we do not need the South Africans to tell us to be vigilant. We know how to treat these people.'

Mike wasn't sure whether the man was referring to meddling South Africans or desperate poachers, but either way they had to leave it in his hands. Sarah and Mike supplied their names and addresses, and the man took a long time writing down a short version of what they had told him. When they were finished, the ranger offered to arrange a visit to where the young orphan rhinos were kept. Sarah was keen to see them and Mike realised he had no problems about spending another hour or so with her away from the group.

21

Hess looked up at the half moon. He knew they needed its light to track the rhino, but any illumination at night increased the risk of their being spotted, by a National Parks or border patrol boat, or by anti-poaching patrols on the ground.

Hess was dressed in black denim jeans and a long-sleeved black T-shirt, his blond hair covered with a navy-blue woollen watch cap. Orlov, as usual, had scorned his advice and insisted on wearing his faded old *Spetsnaz* smock. Klaus was dressed like his employer, while the three poachers wore ragged T-shirts and shorts. Hess had produced specially made boots for Orlov and himself before they left the lodge at Siavonga. They were leather hiking boots, but Klaus had fitted new soles to them.

'The tread looks like it has been cut from an old car tyre,' Orlov had said as he turned one of the boots over in his hands.

'It was,' Hess said. 'Any tracks we leave will look

like those left by African poachers wearing locally made sandals.' Sure enough, when they rendezvoused with the local poachers on a small lakeside beach just out of the Zambian border town of Siavonga, the poachers were wearing sandals cut from old car tyres.

The night air was cool on their faces as the boat skimmed across the calm silvery waters of Lake Kariba. They detoured around a couple of kapenta boats, the noise and lights from the ungainly vessels visible from far off and, as they closed on the shores of Matusadona, Hess pointed out a lone houseboat to the helmsman, the eldest of the Zambian poachers, whose name was Alfred.

Alfred nodded and gave the houseboat a wide berth. He adjusted the throttle setting at the same time to reduce the noise from the seventy-horsepower outboard motor. The outboard was already muffled, its top housing covered with an old wooden packing crate lined with hessian sacks. Hess guessed this was not the first time the three poachers had used this speedy but comparatively silent craft on the lake. They moved with no lights and, at Alfred's urging, Hess and Orlov sat with the others in a puddle of water at the bottom of the sleek, open fibreglass ski boat so as to lower their silhouette as they crossed the lake.

On his lap, Hess cradled the weapon they would use for the hunt. He would hand it to Orlov once the rhino was in sight, but not before. The rifle was an old American M-14, and it was perfect for the mission at hand. The M-14 was issued to American soldiers and Marines in the late 1950s and '60s. The rifle looked very much like its ancestor, the semi-automatic M1 Garrand rifle carried by US soldiers in the Second World War but the M-14 could be fired on full automatic. To feed the faster rate of fire the weapon had been fitted with a twenty-round magazine. The American army had swapped its M-14s for the newer, lighter, mostly plastic M-16 by the mid 1960s. The US Marine Corps, however, had held on to the trusty M-14 for most of the '60s during the Vietnam War. The rifle's heavier 7.62mm-calibre ammunition gave it a greater accuracy over long distances than the smaller-calibre M-16 and, as such, it had an extended lease of life as a sniper rifle.

Hess had bought his weapon from an ex-Marine who served in the Rhodesian Light Infantry during the bush war. Already a long and heavy rifle, Hess's model was even more cumbersome as it was fitted with a silencer on the end of the barrel and a starlight nightscope on the top. The rifle was the largest-calibre weapon Hess owned that could be silenced to an acceptable level, and that was why he had brought it along. He wanted Orlov to kill the rhino in silence and, if it became necessary, Hess would be able to deal with any rangers who stumbled into their path during the hunt in the same way.

Klaus and the three poachers each carried their trademark AK-47s, and the Zambian rogues also carried razor-sharp *pangas*, to behead the dead rhino. One of the men had an old potato sack stuffed with hessian to wrap the massive skull in and rope to sling the trophy between them.

Hess had left his Glock pistol behind, but had

given Orlov Klaus's Russian Tokarev pistol for personal protection. Klaus had taken the old pistol from a Cuban military adviser he killed on a cross-border raid into Angola. If they were stopped by the authorities from either side of the lake during the crossing, they would ditch their rifles and the old pistol over the side of the boat and claim that they had gotten lost while on a night-time fishing trip. The cover story was flimsy, but they carried rods, bait, tackle and half-a-dozen fresh-caught bream at the bottom of the boat to help substantiate it.

Orlov raised the heavy pistol slightly to catch the moonlight and, for the second time that night, eased back the metal slide to check that there was a round chambered in the breech. At that moment, Alfred swung the outboard's tiller sharply to port to avoid the top of a dead tree that only just broke the black surface of the water. Instinctively, Orlov reached for the side of the boat with the same hand that was holding the pistol. The weapon clunked against the fibreglass hull with enough noise to make all the occupants turn and stare at him. Orlov hurriedly replaced the pistol in the pocket of his combat smock. He cursed silently and was glad the darkness hid his embarrassment.

Hess masked his annoyance at the noise by kneeling lower and resting the wooden stock of the M-14 on the side of the boat. He peered intently into the M-14's nightscope. The houseboat showed as a bright, pale-green box against the darker shoreline. The low-wattage navigation light that burned dully on top of the boat's stubby mast shone like a full lime-coloured moon surrounded by a lighter, brighter halo. The nightscope magnified any ambient light it detected and had the single bulb been brighter, its luminescence might have washed out everything else in his view, and even damaged the scope. As it was, Hess could scan the decks easily, the weak navigation light helping, rather than obscuring his view. It was after two in the morning and, predictably, there was no sight of movement on deck. All the cabin lights were dark. He had no reason to fear the houseboat – the tourists on board would see and hear nothing if all went to plan. There was no sign that anybody aboard had heard Orlov's clumsiness.

The most direct route to where they had last seen the rhino would have been to beach at Tashinga Camp again and retrace their steps, via the *boma* where the orphan animals were kept. But that was also the most dangerous route. Instead, Alfred took them past the camp and the moored houseboat, and into a small cove half a kilometre further on. As they entered the cove, he cut the engine and the boat coasted noiselessly into shore and beached gently in the sand.

As they had rehearsed on the beach near Siavonga, Klaus was first out. He sprinted across the sand to where the grass began and dropped to one knee. The barrel of his assault rifle followed the sweep of his eyes as he scanned the bush in front of them. Hess followed, then Orlov, and they crouched beside Klaus while the three Zambians dragged the boat into the tree line. Alfred broke a branch from a mopani tree and returned to the water's edge. He walked backwards to the group, sweeping the sand clear of footprints and drag marks as he moved. Then he handed the branch to one of his comrades, a tall, thin man named Ezekial, who would bring up the rear from now on and follow Alfred's example as they moved.

Hess touched the third man, William, on the arm, and pointed towards the camp. William nodded and scratched the ugly, puckered scar running vertically down his left cheek. Alfred, the leader of the trio, claimed the wound had been inflicted by a leopard, which William had subsequently killed with a knife. Hess thought it more likely the injury originated in a *shebeen* brawl and that William had encountered the business end of a broken bottle.

'Disable the radio first, then watch the *boma*,' Hess whispered to William, who nodded, once again, that he understood his part in the operation. He was to break into the camp office, cut the antenna and any other leads he could find on the solar-powered radio, and then make his way to the orphan rhino enclosure, where he would maintain surveillance on the guard there. 'Only watching, OK? No shooting unless there is trouble. Understand?' Hess repeated his orders again.

William nodded once more, annoyed that the hunter was treating him like a stupid child. He crept off through the bush, the AK-47 pointing ahead of him, and followed the shoreline back towards the camp.

Hess raised his hand and pointed into the bush. Klaus surrendered the lead to Ezekial, who would take point until they reached the approximate area where the rhino's tracks had last been seen. The Zambian had hunted rhino many times before and, though his trips across the lake had been fewer and fewer in recent years, he was still able to detect the animal by sound and smell, as well as by any visible spoor.

Orlov was eager to find their prey as soon as possible. He felt acutely underpowered with only the ageing Russian pistol for protection and eyed Hess's long, ungainly M-14 covetously. The rifle was the same one with which he had shot his sable, and he had enjoyed the feel of the heavy sniper's weapon.

They crept silently, pausing every ten or twenty metres for the trackers to listen and smell the bush around them. After an hour at this snail-like pace, Hess slipped the GPS unit from its belt pouch during one of the stops. He knelt and bent over the instrument to shield the glare from the tiny screen light. The distance to the point where they had seen the rhino during the day was a mere hundred metres, but instead of heading towards the sighting point, Ezekial was now leading them away, back towards the camp.

Hess moved forward until he could whisper into the tracker's ear. 'What have you found?'

'Fresh spoor. He left the area where you found him during the day sometime, but look, see the broken branch and the footprint, he has passed back this way tonight. He can smell the woman, you understand?' Hess nodded. 'He is heading for the *boma*. We are close to him now.'

Hess reckoned they were now less than a kilometre

from the camp and the lake shore. He wanted Orlov to make the kill as far away from the rangers' post and the guarded *boma* as possible, but the lovesick rhino was making it difficult for them. 'Move quickly, Ezekial,' he whispered.

The tracker nodded, hiding his exasperation at such a foolhardy command. The money the three poachers would make from this one kill was more than they would have received if they had taken all the horns from all the rhinos in the *boma*, so he held his tongue.

A gentle breeze rustled the leaves above their head, but the wind, what little there was of it, was on their faces, so the rhino would not smell them. Hess had to admit that the Zambians knew their trade well. Of course, for them the price of sloppiness was death.

For another half-hour they continued the hunt, all the while the footprints and other evidence of the rhino's path becoming more obvious to everyone in the small column now they knew what they were looking for. Ezekial stopped, so abruptly that Klaus nearly walked into him. They all knelt. From somewhere in front of them they clearly heard a low grunt and a shuffling of heavy but nimble feet in the dry leaves. Then there was a sniffing noise. The rhino was almost as close to his prey now as the hunters were to theirs.

The tracker pointed into the gloom ahead. Hess raised the butt of the M-14 to his shoulder and peered into the starlight scope. At first he saw nothing but a fuzzy haze of glowing green vegetation. He swung the rifle a little to the right, to the exact spot where

Ezekial was still pointing, and waited. The problem with the night sight was the lack of depth in the image it displayed. Everything looked as if it was the same distance away from the observer. Hess blinked sweat from his eyes and stared hard to find meaning in the illuminated clutter.

Then he saw it. Just a shape moving among the glowing leaves, but an unmistakable silhouette. The rhino was moving into a thinner patch of thorn bush now and was clearly visible in the scope, though hardly so to the naked eye. Hess estimated the range at seventy-five metres, no more. Close enough for a killing shot.

He lowered the rifle and nodded to Ezekial, who crouched lower into the grass. Hess turned to Orlov and the Russian instinctively knew it was time. 'It's cocked,' he whispered as he handed over the M-14.

Orlov took the weapon, relishing its weight, the smoothness of the stock, the ungainly, brutal beauty of the long barrel.

Hess knelt close to the Russian and whispered, 'Remember, put as many rounds into the animal as you can. You must disrupt his internal organs, the way the poachers do with their AK-47s.'

The Russian frowned at the unnecessary advice. They had been over the killing tactics earlier in the day, and he did not need to be told how to hunt. Also, Hess's comparison of their hunt to a poaching expedition annoyed him.

Orlov squinted into the eyepiece of the nightscope and sighted the rhino immediately through the lime-coloured haze of intensified moonlight. The rifle was fitted with a folding bipod for extra stability in the sniper role, but if Orlov lay on the ground and used the supports he would not see the rhino clearly. He chose a sitting position instead, knees bent and legs spread, pointing at forty-five degrees to the right of the rhino.

He swivelled his torso slightly to the left and rested his elbows just below his raised knees. He double-checked the selector was set to semi-automatic fire. The rifle would fire one shot every time he pulled the trigger. He lifted the butt of the rifle to his shoulder again.

Hess willed the Russian to take his shot, because the rhino was starting to move again. Mercifully, the beast stopped and sniffed the wind.

Orlov had the rhino in his sights now. The animal was munching contentedly on the thorns from a head-high branch. The Russian took a breath and slowly exhaled, then he lowered the rifle without moving his elbows. Orlov raised the sight to his eye again and allowed himself a small smile – the moment's relaxation had allowed him to confirm, when he looked into the sight once more, that his whole body was aligned perfectly for the shot.

He moved the crosshairs of the sight to the spot just behind where the rhino's stubby front left leg joined the body. The thick hide was painted a shimmery luminescent green by the night sight, making the creature appear like something from a child's storybook.

Orlov wrapped his index finger around the trigger and started to squeeze.

*

Whether it was the new haircut or not, Mike was unsure, but he had started acting like a soldier again. The realisation, which came to him while he was sitting on the deck of the houseboat gazing at the silvery reflection of the half-moon on the lake, both scared and comforted him.

The poker game had deteriorated into near debauchery as the evening wore on. George had beaten Jane down to bra and pants and then resorted to taking off his contact lenses, one at a time, instead of losing his underpants when he lost hand after hand. Even Nigel seemed to be enjoying himself at last, and he, too, was down to grey-white jockeys when Sam convinced him it was time to turn in. Mike feared that if the game had gone on much longer the next phase would have been skinny-dipping in the lake – not a good idea given the number of crocodiles and hippos they had spotted within a stone's-throw of the houseboat. He had called lights out around midnight to a chorus of half-hearted boos, jeers and facetious 'yes, sir's.

Mike stuck around after the last of them had stumbled off to bed, and climbed the shaky aluminium ladder onto the top deck to look at the stars and finish the remains of his third beer of the day. He wanted to stay relatively sober, just in case Hess and Orlov were stupid enough to cruise past the houseboat and give themselves away.

From his shirt pocket he fished a crumpled packet of cigarettes and his Zippo. He lifted the lighter and flipped the cap, but something stopped him from striking the wheel against the flint. He looked out across the lake. There was no sign of anything odd, just a couple of kapenta rigs. The chug of their diesel engines and the occasional whine of a winch reeling in a net filled with thousands of tiny fish carried clearly across the water.

When he was a young soldier, and smoking was still the rule rather than the exception, he had to be very careful doing so at night when he was out in the bush on military exercises. A naked light would expose him to the enemy. 'The enemy' was a relative term. It could be some prick from a rival unit sneaking around the perimeter, or his own troop sergeant prowling around inside the perimeter looking for an excuse to kick arse. Either way, the smokers had to be a cautious lot.

Mike glanced across the water again. This would be the approach his enemy would take, if he was out there. From the shore there was nothing to fear. He padded on bare feet across the non-slip deck, around the upper wheelhouse so that he was shielded from view from the lake. As a further precaution he faced the shore and cupped his hands close to his mouth as he lit up.

Bats squeaked in the trees above the empty camping ground and every now and then a nightjar issued its repetitive call, like a mini electric motor purring away. Above the night noises Mike detected a new sound. This time it really was a motor, the high-pitched whine of a fast, smooth-running marine outboard. It wasn't loud, so it couldn't be nearby, but the sound was man-made and out of place.

He flicked the cigarette into the inky waters of the

lake, the lee of the boat concealing the glowing trail of burning embers that followed the butt. The cigarette died with a plop and a hiss and he instinctively dropped to the deck. He edged along the rough surface, using his elbows to drag himself forward until only his head poked around the wheelhouse.

The wake gave away the position of the little boat before he saw the craft itself. What surprised him at first was how close it was. No more than a couple of hundred metres away, he guessed. The engine was very quiet, though, for the fast speed it was travelling at.

The boat jinked wildly as Mike watched it, probably to miss a sunken tree. Another noise echoed across the water, this time a loud clunk of heavy metal striking a deck. The boat slowed and the wake started to settle.

Though it was closer than he had thought, the boat was still too distant for him to tell how many people were on board. More than two, by the look of it, with some bulky cargo as well. The moonlight rippled on the disturbed water and the slowing boat rocked as someone, or something, changed position.

Shadows moved in the boat and a menacing shape broke the otherwise smooth silhouette. Someone had raised a rifle, a long-barrelled rifle. The movement was over in a split second, but there was no mistaking it. Mike lowered his body even more, hoping to disappear into the unyielding deck. He pressed his face to the gritty surface, in case the comparative paleness of his skin caught the moon's reflection.

The pilot of the darkened boat revved the engine again and Mike heard it fade away. At last he risked a look. There was nothing but a shimmering wake to prove the boat had ever been there.

His mind raced as possible explanations came to him and were then cast away. Could the boat be a National Parks vessel? No, as it would have had its navigation lights on. An anti-poaching patrol, sneaking about hoping to surprise illegal hunters? Not likely, and besides, the boat was coming from the Zambian side of the lake.

He and Sarah had clearly seen Orlov and Hess in a speeding boat, a different one, earlier in the day. Had they been doing what he would have done in their shoes? A daytime reconnaissance under the enemy's nose was a ballsy move, he had to give them that, and from what Flynn had told him, it seemed exactly what the hunters had had in mind. There was no way they could hunt in broad daylight, so the night after their trip was the logical time for their return, when the trail of the rhino they'd been tracking was still fresh.

Mike got himself up off the deck with the first movement of a push-up. He may have been thinking like a soldier again, but his body had well and truly retired from the military. He grunted with the effort, and his pectoral muscles shrieked messages of protest as he stood and shook his arms.

He retraced his steps down the ladder, taking care not to make any noise. He didn't need his passengers or the houseboat crew waking up and asking questions about what he was going to do next. On the lower deck he eased open a door and padded inside. George snored as only a passed-out drunk can snore, and Jane and Julie rolled restlessly against each other in a double bed as he crept past the tiny bedroom they shared. He gingerly stepped over an unconscious Nigel, who for some reason had not made it to his bed and lay sprawled in the narrow corridor between the cabins, one white cheek poking out very unattractively from his underpants. Mike's cabin was at the end of the corridor and he gently worked the door handle.

Mike didn't want to risk using the light. He knew what he wanted and where it was. At the bottom of his daypack was the Browning, wrapped in an oily chamois cloth. The loaded magazine was inside the weapon. He unwrapped the pistol, thumbed the magazine release and caught the mag in the palm of his left hand. The deadly little brass and copper passengers were seated comfortably, so he returned them to the take-off position inside the pistol with an audible mating of metal on metal.

Something touched his shoulder and he spun around fast, his right hand rising automatically to the fire position. The black barrel stopped just centimetres from Sarah's heart.

Panic flashed in her blue eyes, but she raised a hand to her mouth to stifle a shout. Mike didn't know who was more surprised, him or her.

'What are you doing!' she whispered, dropping her hand as he lowered the pistol. 'You could have killed me!'

He shoved the Browning into the waistband of his cargo shorts. 'Keep your voice down.'

She was back-lit by shafts of moonlight bouncing

369

down the corridor through the slatted door to the main deck. The pale silver light caught the spikes of her newly shorn hair and the light, downy hair on her arms. She wore a green T-shirt, her nipples just visible as they strained against the stretchy fabric. Her smooth legs shone like pale gold. She ran a hand self-consciously through her still-unfamiliar short hair.

'I was waiting . . . I mean, looking for you,' she stammered. 'I heard a noise up top and wasn't sure what it was, so I came to tell you, and . . .'

The rest of her story hung in the air as she fumbled for more detail. Mike closed his eyes briefly to focus on his mission. All other thought had been dispelled by the confrontation he hoped was coming. Nonetheless, a vision of he and Sarah kissing in the nightclub flashed across his mind's eye. He smelled her perfume in the small and hot cabin, the same scent she had been wearing that night.

'Sarah, I . . .' He reached out to her with his hand, now free of the weapon, but she stepped back.

'What?' she hissed with annoyance, and maybe embarrassment. 'I just wanted to talk. That's all. Don't go getting any stupid ideas.'

He looked at her again. Part of him knew he could, should, take her in his arms and finish the kiss they started in Victoria Falls.

She stepped back awkwardly as he moved towards her, the resolve crumbling as he turned side-on to pass her in the narrow doorway. Mike almost expected to get a shock of static electricity as his chest came a hair's breadth from her erect nipples.

'I've got to go,' he said.

She parted her lips to speak and Mike couldn't help but notice how the moonlight glistened on the soft, moist skin. He turned his back on her and hastened silently down the corridor. He was now driven by an emotion stronger than love, lust or fear.

Revenge.

22

'Wait for me!' Sarah called as Mike untied the rope securing the twelve-foot aluminium runabout to the houseboat.

'Keep your voice down, and stay where you are,' he replied. The last thing he wanted was the houseboat's crew waking up. There was no way the captain would let him take the dinghy out for a night trip on Lake Kariba, even if he was only travelling the short distance to shore.

Mike bent to grab an oar and felt the dinghy rock. He turned around and hissed, 'Get back on the boat, Sarah, now!'

'Go to hell,' she replied, hands on hips, eyes blazing. She had pulled on a pair of faded denim shorts and sandals and tied the hem of her T-shirt in a knot, exposing a bare, flat midriff. Slung from her right shoulder was her camera, with a large flash unit attached. 'I'm coming with you whether you like it or not. It's the poachers, isn't it? They're heading back to the park. This is my story!'

Mike clenched his teeth and contemplated forcibly ejecting her from the boat. If she screamed, however, the crew would be on deck before he could get away. 'This isn't a bloody story! If the poachers I saw . . .' He realised he had given the game away.

'I knew it! They're here!'

'If it is them, they'll be bombed-up – armed, I mean – to the teeth. They kill witnesses, Sarah.'

She studied him for a moment in silence. 'You don't have a choice. I'll wake the captain.'

He sighed. 'Push us off from the houseboat and sit down.'

'Give me the other oar.'

Off to port, a hippo laughed out loud.

'No pictures, OK?' Mike whispered as they pulled the boat onto the sandy shore of the lakeside camp. Sarah nodded and followed close behind him as he moved quickly through the empty camping ground.

They were breaking too many rules to contemplate. Walking around after dark was bad enough, but Mike realised that if he were seen brandishing a pistol in a national park the rangers would shoot him on sight and ask questions later. He kept the Browning tucked under his shirt, inside his shorts.

Off to their left, somewhere along the shoreline, an elephant trumpeted crankily. Poachers and overzealous rangers aside, they were also in real danger of bumping into any of Africa's big, dangerous animals in the park, not to mention a catalogue of poisonous snakes. Mike knew he and Sarah were woefully underdressed and underarmed, but turning back to the safety of the boat was no longer an option.

373

On the far side of the camping ground they found the access road leading through the bush to the park headquarters. They kept to the shadows of the trees rather than the middle of the road, in case anyone was watching. Mike's hopes of leaving Sarah at camp headquarters were dashed when they got to the darkened building.

'It's empty,' Mike said softly as he emerged from the building.

'Loos are empty too. I checked,' Sarah said. Mike had told her to stay still in the bushes outside the headquarters, but she had ignored him. 'There's something else, as well,' she added, beckoning him to follow her.

At the rear of the building she knelt and grabbed a loose end of black cable, which was partly fixed to the rendered wall. Sarah held the end of the cable up until the moonlight caught its bright tip. 'Someone's cut this. You can see by how shiny the copper wire is that it's fresh. I imagine the radio's out of action.'

'Shit,' Mike said, scanning the ground for tracks. There was one set of footprints apart from theirs, which had partially obscured the culprit's. It looked like a pair of homemade sandals, cut from old truck tyres. 'Poacher. He's gone that way,' he said, pointing across the road back into the bush. 'Towards the rhino *boma*.'

'Where are the rangers?' Sarah asked.

'Home in bed, pissed out of their heads probably,' he said. The fact that the headquarters did not even appear to have been manned that night, despite his warning, fuelled his anger. 'Let's go. I suppose it's useless for me to suggest that you stay here?'

'Useless,' she replied.

'At least stay behind me, and stay low if the shooting starts.'

'No argument there, Major. You're the one with the gun.' She gave him a playful punch on the arm and he found her touch reassuring. He drew the pistol from his shorts and Sarah watched intently as he pulled back the slide halfway to check once again there was a round up the spout. He showed the weapon to her.

'If anything happens, pull the trigger, here, and the bullets come out of the end, there. Got it?'

'Got it.'

They crossed the road and stepped into the bush. A couple of times Sarah bumped into him when he stopped to listen to the sounds around them. She was too close to him, but he couldn't blame her. He didn't need any distractions; however, he couldn't help noticing the intoxicating smell of her perfume and her body on the light breeze that followed them.

Mike reckoned he could navigate to the rhino *boma* through the bush, but he didn't hold out much chance of tracking down the poacher who had slashed the radio cables. Neither did he want to try. The wind was behind them and anyone, or anything, would smell them coming. He decided they would stop at the *boma*, take up a defensive position, and do the job the absent rangers should have been doing. He hoped he would at least find one of them on guard duty at the *boma*, although he half expected the sentry would be asleep.

Mike judged they probably had about two to three hundred metres to the *boma*. He moved a thorn tree branch to one side, being careful not to let any of the wicked, long barbs catch his shirt, and held it to one side to let Sarah past. A rustle in the leaves made them both freeze and turn their heads.

There was more movement and, more ominously, a low growl from the base of a bush in front of them. Mike gently let go of the branch and used his left hand to support the pistol, which he held stretched out in the firing position.

He glanced at Sarah, who was looking behind herself now. 'Don't move,' he mouthed silently, checking her natural urge to turn and flee. If it was a leopard or a lion, running was the worst thing she could do. Big cats, like small cats, love to pounce on moving creatures. Slowly he crouched, and Sarah mimicked his movements. She rested a clammy hand on his shoulder.

Mike felt short of breath and a vein began to throb incessantly in his neck. The animal growled again, low and full of menace. He strained his eyes for a better look, trying to peer through the bushes ahead, rather than at them. The barrel of the pistol started to waver slightly.

The bushes shook and Sarah placed a hand over her mouth to stifle a scream. Mike took up the pressure on the trigger and the animal burst into the clearing. Mike's eyes were locked at about waist-height, at the position where a charging lion's head would have been, so he missed seeing the creature at first.

'Look, on the ground,' Sarah whispered breathlessly. 'He's gorgeous!' She giggled with nervous relief.

There, two metres in front of them, was a honey badger, a small black and grey creature not much bigger than a skunk or an undersized specimen of its European counterpart. The grey saddle of hair that ran from the top of its head to the tip of its long tail bristled with anger and it lifted its nasty squashed Pekinese-dog face to the humans in defiance. After a moment, in which it decided they were no threat, the honey badger trotted off into a thicket to their right.

'Noisy little bugger,' Sarah said in admiration.

'And ferocious. They've been known to bring down a wildebeest,' he replied, lowering the pistol at last.

'Never! How?'

'They jump up and rip their scrotum open. The animal bleeds to death. Let's get moving.'

They walked on for a few minutes and then Mike paused. He leaned against the trunk of a leadwood and wiped the sweat from his eyes with the back of his gun hand. The thick bush prevented the lake breeze from reaching them and the going was getting harder and hotter.

'Mike!' Sarah called, too late.

As he turned he felt cold, hard steel poke painfully into the tender skin behind his right ear.

'Do not move, do not speak. Place the pistol on the ground. Do not drop it. Samson, search the woman,' said the deep African voice behind Mike.

A second man emerged from the bush in front of him. He was young and dressed in the uniform of a National Parks ranger.

'Your radio is dead, and there are poachers —' Mike began.

'Quiet. I said no talking,' the man behind him whispered, pressing the gun barrel harder into Mike's head to punctuate his order.

When the man spoke, especially when he pronounced the letter S, Mike detected a soft whistling sound. He recognised the voice – it was the old greyheaded ranger they had spoken to at the headquarters, the one who knew Flynn.

Sarah fidgeted and slapped at the hands of the tall young ranger as he quickly completed his cursory search. With the little she was wearing there was nowhere for her to conceal a weapon.

The young ranger was dressed for war. He wore an olive green bush uniform and canvas web gear, including four pouches for banana-shaped AK-47 magazines slung across his broad chest. He held his assault rifle by its pistol grip, ready for action.

'Take the camera,' the older ranger said.

'Over my dead body,' Sarah hissed as the younger man took a tentative step towards her, then checked his pace. 'Touch me and you'll be assaulting a member of the press.'

'You have no right to be here at this time of night, as a member of the press or even as a tourist. I could shoot you both on suspicion of poaching. Especially you,' the senior man said, emphasising his last words with another shove of the rifle barrel in Mike's ear.

'I'm the one who warned you about the poachers. We've been to your headquarters, the poachers have –'

'I know exactly what the poachers have been up to,' he said.

At last he lowered his rifle, allowing Mike to turn

to face him. He still pointed the weapon at Mike, though. It was a long-barrelled FN self-loading rifle, painted in green and brown camouflage colours.

The old man knelt, still covering Mike with the rifle, and said in a disdainful tone, 'I don't believe you are a poacher. No one would be stupid enough to walk in the bush at night with this thing.' He retrieved the Browning pistol from the ground and stuffed it in his canvas web belt. He, too, was dressed in green fatigues, having swapped the khaki dress uniform Mike had seen him in earlier in the day.

'We warned you! Of course we're not poachers,' Mike said.

'And I thanked you for your warning. But what you are doing here, now, with this weapon, is against the law. I think there is more to your story than you are telling me, but we do not have time to talk about it now. I have poachers to catch and now three prisoners to guard.'

'Three?' Sarah asked. She had pushed the camera behind her back, and the rangers seemed to have forgotten it.

'Show the lady our new friend, Samson,' the old man said.

Samson, the younger ranger, retreated into the bushes and returned a few moments later pushing a bound and gagged man in front of him. The man wore faded blue shorts and a torn green T-shirt. On his feet were bulky homemade sandals. The soles, Mike guessed, were cut from old car tyres. Panic showed in the man's eyes.

'He is probably the one who cut the wires. We

found a knife and an AK-47 on him. Both are safely out of harm's way, but there are sure to be other poachers around. We were on our way to the rhino *boma* when we heard you blundering around behind us,' the old ranger said.

'Let us help you,' Sarah said.

'I should tie you up here and leave you until we have finished our work. That is what I should do, but if a lion or a leopard took you, Samson and I would lose our jobs. There are only two of us in the camp tonight, and I cannot spare him to guard you. You will have to take your chances with us until the poachers are caught, madam. When we get to the *boma* I will find you a safe place, but we do not want your help. Mr Williams, keep the lady company at the rear of the column. Samson, lead off. I will guard the prisoner.'

They set off again, in a straggling single file, stopping every ten or twenty metres as Samson scanned the bush and listened. Mike smelled the bitter-sweet odour of warm animal dung before he saw the rhino pens. Little grunts and snuffles emerged from the baby animals as the group skirted the clearing around the rough wooden fence that encircled the individual enclosures. They could smell the humans, but didn't seem overly alarmed.

Samson led them through the bush to the far end of the clearing, the farthest point from the lake shore and camping ground. The old ranger motioned for Mike to join him and Samson where they knelt amid a stand of low mopani.

'My name is Patrick,' he whispered and extended his right hand.

They shook, African style, and Mike said, 'Pleased to meet you, Patrick.'

'Do not be pleased, Mr Williams, for if we meet the other poachers, then all of us may not survive this night.' He pulled the Browning from his belt and handed it to Mike. 'I think, from the look of you, that I can trust you. Keep the madam safe and do not fire unless I fire first.'

Mike nodded, and accepted without comment the pistol and the trust Patrick had placed in him.

'Your position will be over there –' Patrick's whispered orders were cut short by Samson raising his right hand and then pointing into the bush ahead of them.

They all knelt and Patrick pushed the face of the bound poacher into the dirt. Samson cupped his left hand to his ear. After a few seconds they heard the sound that had alerted Samson, a deep grunting noise and a rustle of bushes, not far off.

Patrick leaned so close to Mike that his lips almost brushed his ear. His breath smelt of rotted biltong and decades of cigarette smoke. 'It is the male rhino. He has come for one of the females. The poachers may be close.'

There was a rustle of dead leaves behind the three men and they all turned as Sarah appeared at their side. 'What's going on?' she asked.

'Silence, please, madam,' Patrick whispered. 'Samson, take these people to the *boma* and wait for me there. Set up a defensive position and don't shoot me when I return.'

Samson nodded and stood. He roughly lifted the gagged prisoner to his feet.

'Samson,' Patrick said, and the young man turned to face him.

'*Yebo?*'

'Guard those animals with your life.'

23

Vassily Orlov blinked the sweat from his eye and refocused on the rhino. The big animal had turned slightly at the moment he was going to fire, presenting more of its front than its flank to him. The Russian relaxed his trigger finger and waited patiently for the animal to turn again.

Hess and Klaus scanned the bush around them, alert for the slightest noise. Hess willed the Russian to take his shot.

The rhino turned side-on again, reaching for another thorn branch. Abruptly, it stopped feeding, and raised its big head a few centimetres. Orlov watched the big nostrils flare as it sniffed the wind. He thought that the scent of a female was a good last sensory sensation for any creature. Again he took up the slack on the trigger.

Two gunshots shattered the still of the night and brilliant flashes of light robbed Hess of his night vision. Instinctively, the hunter flattened himself on the ground. The rhino disappeared from Orlov's vision.

'What have you done?' Hess hissed. His first thought was that the silencer on the M-14 had malfunctioned.

'It wasn't me!' Orlov protested. 'I didn't even get off a fucking shot.'

'To your left, *baas*,' Klaus whispered. 'Sounded like an FN. Maybe only thirty metres.'

'*Scheisse!* Put some fire on him, Klaus. Now!'

The big African raised himself to his knees, flipped the selector switch on his AK-47 to automatic and pumped out two short bursts of three rounds each. Small night creatures scattered noisily through the bush as Hess leopard-crawled through grass and dried leaves until he was next to Orlov, who was also now lying on the ground.

'Give me that,' Hess said, grabbing the sniper rifle from Orlov.

A protest died on Orlov's lips as he remembered the firefight in Mozambique. While he craved the adrenaline rush of just such a fight, he knew he had been lucky to survive the previous year's gun battle.

'More fire, Klaus! Cover me, I'm moving forward.'

One of the poachers joined Klaus in laying down a barrage of deafening gunfire as Hess raised himself up and sprinted forward.

'One, one thousand, two, one thousand, three, one thousand,' Hess chanted softly in German as he ran. Before he got to 'three' he threw himself flat on the ground amid fallen thorns and dried undergrowth. He knew that three seconds was all it took for a marksman to take aim and fire. He rolled four metres to a new spot, in case anyone had seen where he dived for cover, cradling the M-14 to his chest like a baby as he twisted. He stopped behind the trunk of a stout tree, raised himself up on his elbows and brought the night sight up to his eye.

In front of him, to his surprise, he saw the dirt road and followed it, through the sight, to the clearing surrounding the rhino *boma*. He had not realised they were so close. Movement flickered at the periphery of the night sight's fuzzy green circle. He adjusted his aim to the right and saw a man burst from the cover of the trees and run across the little clearing.

The man carried a rifle, an FN, as Klaus had guessed. 'Three seconds,' Hess whispered to himself as he followed the man until the crosshairs were fixed on a point just in front of him. By leading the running man with his aim, his bullets would intersect with the target's body by the time they reached him.

Hess flicked the safety to fire and squeezed the trigger twice. The first shot missed, but the second found its mark and the man collapsed in the dust, about ten metres short of a gate in the wooden fence surrounding the rhino pens.

Instinctively, Hess ducked his head as a burst of automatic fire, including the glowing trails of two rounds of bright green tracer, rocketed from a gap in the wooden fence. The bullets were coming nowhere near Hess, which told him the other side was laying down suppressive fire to cover the man who had been running.

The fire also meant the running ranger was not alone. Hess briefly wondered what had caused the National Parks staff to increase the number of guards on the rhinos.

He peered into the night sight again and watched the man on the ground writhing in pain. The man lifted a hand and called out to the people inside the *boma*, 'Stay inside, stay inside!' Then he coughed painfully.

Hess knew exactly what he would do if he were safe behind a wall and a comrade of his was lying wounded outside under fire from a sniper. He would stay where he was and, if necessary, put the man out of his misery. But Karl Hess knew that he was different from most other men, so he watched and waited for what he knew would happen next.

'For God's sake, what's going on?' Sarah demanded, when the first two gunshots went off.

'It is all right,' Samson said. 'The boss, Patrick, is scaring the rhino away. Our only risk is that the animal might charge his way. That is why he has ordered us in here.'

Samson had only just swung the big gate of the wooden fence shut when the gunfire began. The rhinos grunted and jostled against the wooden railings of their individual enclosures at the sound of the rifle fire.

When the AK-47s opened up, one after another, Mike, Sarah and Samson all dropped to the dusty dirt floor of the pen. Mike hoped the stout rhino-proof timbers of the fence were strong enough to protect them from the assault rifles' bullets.

Sarah huddled close to him and he wrapped an arm protectively around her. She didn't resist, and nestled even closer to Mike's side as a couple of stray rounds zinged over the top of the fence.

'The fire is coming from a long way off,' Samson said.

'Yeah. They're deep in the bush. Probably can't even see the *boma*,' Mike said in agreement with the ranger. He wasn't sure if that was right, but he wanted to reassure Sarah. He felt her start to move. 'Stay down!' he barked.

But Sarah was on her knees now, crawling to the fence and peering through a gap. 'Look, it's Patrick! Here he comes!'

Samson and Mike squinted through other cracks in the fence. They could see the old ranger sprinting like an Olympic athlete, his FN held out in front of him to keep his balance.

'Run, man, run!' Mike urged him.

Both the AK-47s had stopped firing. As Patrick moved closer and broke into the clearing they could hear the rapid thump of his feet in the sand. Small clouds of dust rose with each step.

Suddenly he fell, heavily, and Mike thought for a moment he had tripped. 'Get up, get up!' Mike willed him, but there was no movement.

'My God, look!' Sarah cried. 'There's blood on the ground, it's coming from his belly!'

Patrick was no more than ten metres from the *boma*, reaching out to the others with his right hand, clutching his side with his left. He had certainly been shot, but there had been no sound of gunfire. Mike was momentarily confused, but then the pieces fell into place.

Samson stood and cocked his AK-47. He flicked the selector to full automatic and reached up until his rifle was pointing over the top of the six-foot-high fence. He pulled the trigger and sent a burst of fire in the general direction of where the other rounds had been coming from.

'One of them must have a silent rifle,' Samson said, as he dropped down beside Mike and swapped the empty magazine on his weapon for a full one.

'And maybe a nightscope, too,' Mike added.

'You mean he can see in the dark, like the gizmos they use in the movies?' Sarah said.

'Yes, but this isn't the movies – the bullets are real. We've got to get Patrick inside,' Mike said.

'If it's not the movies then why are you talking like Bruce bloody Willis? You'll be cut down before you get close to him.' There was real concern in her voice.

Mike found her words touching, but he couldn't let a man die without trying to help him. Once again, it seemed he would be left with another person's life on his conscience. If he hadn't raised the alarm, old Patrick would probably be fast asleep right now.

'Stay inside, stay inside!' Patrick called to them from outside the fence.

'Let me go,' said Samson, as he began to stand.

Mike laid a hand on his arm and pulled him down. 'You have to look after the lady, Samson, and we'll need some firepower to get out of here.'

Sarah closed her eyes and shook her head. 'This isn't the way, Mike.' She reached out and laid a hand on his knee. 'You won't bring anybody back by getting yourself killed.'

He was surprised that she could see into his mind so clearly, but he knew what he had to do.

'I'll need *hobos* of covering fire, Samson,' Mike said, using the local word for 'lots'. 'A whole magazine at least. OK?'

'All right, but if this man has a silencer and a nightscope he knows what he is doing. We don't even know what direction he is firing from. Remember, he can see in the dark,' Samson said, as he peered through the crack in the fence at Patrick.

'Are these infra-red, these scope things? Do they pick up body heat?' Sarah asked.

Mike was getting keyed up to go through the gate and he didn't need distractions. 'No,' he snapped. 'They work on image intensification. They magnify any light that's around.'

'So light like tonight?'

'Is perfect for him. Not too dark, not too bright with only half a moon. I don't have all night to explain this, Sarah.'

'Just bloody well bear with me. Let me get this straight – too much light's a bad thing for a night sight?'

'Too much light, a very bad thing. If we had a spotlight or a floodlight and could put it on him, the light would be so intense it might damage his eyes. His scope would be whited out, overloaded, for sure. But we don't have a spotlight.'

Mike stood and turned his back on Sarah. He and Samson walked to the *boma* gate at a crouch and discussed their hasty plan.

'I'll open the gate and you lay it down, hot and

heavy, Samson. Keep it low and spray all around, OK?' Mike asked.

'OK,' Samson said with a nod. He stood by the gate, rifle raised at the ready. Samson unbuttoned one of his chest pouches, ready to reload the rifle once his magazine was empty.

Patrick coughed and groaned from the other side of the fence. Mike jogged back to where Sarah was standing, peering through the fence. Despite the tension of the moment he was sorry he had cut her questioning off so abruptly.

'I'm sorry about before. Here, take the pistol. Remember how to use it?'

'Won't you need it out there?' Sarah asked.

'I won't have time. Besides, if anything . . . if anything happens, you might need it.'

She blinked her blue eyes a couple of times and Mike wondered if she was fighting back tears. He held out the pistol, but she ignored it. For a moment they stood in silence, looking into each other's eyes.

Mike stepped closer to her and took her hand, pushing the pistol into it. As she took the weapon he reached out with his free hand and drew her body close to his. He kissed her hard on the mouth and, just when he thought she might push him away, he felt her lips part.

Samson coughed. 'Mister?' he said.

Mike broke their embrace, which had only lasted a couple of seconds, and Sarah stepped back from him, the pistol hanging heavy in her right hand.

'Gosh,' she said, confusion clouding her face. 'Good luck.'

Mike nodded, and walked to the gate.

'Mike,' she called after him.

He paused at the gate, where Samson was nervously waiting with one hand ready to lift the wooden latch from its iron brackets, and turned to face Sarah. 'Yes?'

'Hang on, I've got an idea,' she said.

Karl Hess heard the crackling of dried leaves and twigs in the bush behind him but did not turn at the sound. All his attention was focused on the little ring of bright green light and the wounded man writhing at the centre of the illuminated picture.

'Karl, is that you?' Hess heard the Russian whisper from behind him, confirming his guess.

'Be quiet and stay down.' Hess hissed back. He had lowered the folding metal legs of the rifle's bipod to give him extra stability and now he gently swivelled the weapon's barrel to the left so he could view the gate in the high wooden fence. That was where the enemy would come from, at a rush and probably with covering fire. He traversed back to the wounded man. He was safe from random fire, having edged his body behind the trunk of a stout leadwood. Only the rifle barrel and the bare minimum of his skull were exposed to fire.

'I suppose you know that we should leave now,' Orlov whispered again, ignoring the hunter's rebuke. Orlov crawled forward on his belly until his face was only centimetres from Hess's left boot.

'Where are the others?' Hess asked, blinking away

sweat that was running from under the hot woollen cap into his eyes.

'I've left them back where we stopped. The poachers have no stomach for this fight. I've told Klaus to shoot them if they try to leave without us, but we can't wait here all night, Karl.' Orlov eased himself forward further until he was next to Hess and peered around the opposite side of the tree trunk. 'Look! The gate!'

'Here he comes, stay down!' Hess said.

On cue, the heavy wooden gate swung open and a rattling barrage of gunfire spewed from the narrow gap.

Orlov ground his face into the dirt as yellow muzzle flashes lit up the night and bullets zinged in the air above him. Every now and then an arcing trail of bright green tracer flashed across the periphery of his vision, like the tail of a low-trajectory skyrocket.

Hess remained motionless amid the hubbub and allowed himself a small smile as a darting figure entered his narrow field of vision from the left, just as he had expected. It was a European man, clad like a tourist in shorts and a short-sleeved shirt. He raced to the wounded ranger and bent to grab the man under the arms.

Shifting his aim, Hess placed the crosshairs on the standing man's head and started to squeeze the trigger. Suddenly, the image in the night sight was gone, blasted away by a blinding burst of light.

Hess cursed and blinked, seeing nothing but silver stars when he closed his right eye. When he opened it, his vision was seared again by more brightly flashing lights. Confused, he rolled back behind the safety of the tree.

'What is it?' said Orlov.

'I can't see a fucking thing!' Hess replied, rubbing his eyes as he spoke.

Orlov had drawn his pistol now and thrust it out in front of him. 'Camera!' he said, and fired off two quick shots at the man who was dragging the wounded ranger closer and closer to the open gate. Gunfire started again from the gateway. The man inside had replaced his empty magazine with a full one.

'What?' Hess asked. He risked a peek around the tree and light flashed from the top of the wooden fence. Now he understood. A camera. How simple, how brilliant. He shook his head. Someone had taken a succession of flash photographs with a camera and this had blinded his view through the nightscope.

'They're inside. We've lost them. Let's go, Karl,' Orlov said, rising to his knees.

'Bastards!' Hess spat. He stood, in the cover of the tree, brushing leaves from his black shirt. 'Go back to the others, Vassily. Get to the boat and wait for me there. If I'm not there within fifteen minutes, leave without me. I'll make my own way back.'

'Karl, leave it! You've got to come now!'

Hess picked up the M-14 and folded the bipod legs back against the barrel. He slung the weapon over his head and across his back and reached up for a low branch of the leadwood. 'No witnesses, Vassily. You know the policy.'

Orlov watched as the hunter hoisted himself up into the branches, muscles rippling under his tight shirt like those of a climbing leopard. He knew it was pointless arguing and, also, that Hess was right. 'Fifteen minutes, Karl. That's all,' he said, and turned and retreated silently back into the bush.

Higher and higher Hess climbed until, at last, he could see down into the rhino *boma*. He found a position in the crook of two strong branches and unslung the rifle from his back. Through the green haze of the night sight he surveyed the compound.

Beyond the high wooden outer wall was a ring of clear, bare ground. Then there were individual pens for each of the orphan rhinos. From his perch he could hear their grunting and snuffling in the almost painful silence that had replaced the cacophony of gunfire. Here and there a rhino crashed noisily against its wooden pen, still scared by the memory of the noise.

He moved the rifle left and right, scanning the top of the outer fence. The wounded ranger and the man who had saved him must have been sitting, or lying, close to the wooden wall, because he could not see them from this angle. There were two other targets in sight, however, including the one he most wanted.

A figure backed away, crouching, from the fence into the open ring around the pens. He focused closely on it. To his surprise, he saw it was a woman: the outline of breasts and curving hips was unmistakable as she momentarily stood. She was holding something to her face. Light flashed again and Hess instinctively closed his eyes. It was the camera again, but it was pointing down and not up at him, so the effect was neither as blinding nor as surprising as it had been at first.

'Stupid bitch,' he whispered to himself and let the crosshairs linger between her breasts for a second. He was amazed that someone would be taking snapshots in the aftermath of a firefight. Was this a hapless tourist or, potentially worse, a reporter or news photographer?

He moved the rifle yet again. Though the woman was an inviting, easy target, he found the man he was looking for. Hess had been concerned about the non-appearance of the poacher who had been sent to disable the radio at the rangers' post. He assumed the man had either got lost or been captured. He had enough respect for the Zambian's ability in the bush to doubt that he would get himself lost, so he had correctly guessed the man's fate.

There he was, sitting with his back to one of the rhino *bomas*, mouth gagged and hands bound behind his back, watching whatever was going on out of Hess's sight, in the lee of the high wooden fence. Hess imagined the white man was treating the wounded ranger. Neither the ranger nor the Samaritan who had saved him were a threat to Hess, as neither would have seen his face.

Hess placed the crosshairs over the poacher's forehead. The man would be able to describe Hess and Orlov to the authorities once he was questioned. Hess had no reason to assume the miserable man would not cooperate fully with the Zimbabwean authorities in order to reduce his inevitable jail sentence. For his stupidity, for allowing himself to be caught, there could be only one verdict and only one punishment.

Hess pulled the trigger. The M-14 jerked back into

his shoulder. The only noise was the gas-operated slide chambering a new round from the magazine. Blood spurted from the poacher's forehead as his body rocked back hard into the wooden corral with an audible thud. The woman disappeared from Hess's view and he heard a scream.

'Shit, it's the sniper! He's up high!' Hess heard a man shout out in English from behind the fence. 'In the tree, Samson! That leadwood . . . about one o'clock high!' said the same voice.

Hess had a good vantage point over the compound, but no cover. Now was the time to retreat. He slung the M-14 over his head again and swung himself down from his perch to the next lower branches. With more time he could have found a safe spot in the tree and picked off the armed ranger when he broke cover, but Hess did not have time.

Two rifles opened fire, the chatter of an AK-47 on full automatic, and the slower, deeper report of a semi-automatic FN. As he swiftly descended, Hess realised the man who had rescued the ranger had retrieved his rifle as well. The odds were now two to one, another good reason to retreat.

Leaves, bark and twigs rained down on his head as blast after blast of copper-jacketed lead tore into the branches above him. Hess dropped the last six feet to the ground and landed silently, like a cat. Then he turned and ran for the cover of the bush.

Samson and Mike fired a few more rounds into the bush at the base of the leadwood where the sniper had been hiding, but they had to conserve what little ammunition they had left.

'If he is smart, he will be gone by now,' Samson said, as he swapped his empty magazine for the last full one from his chest pouches.

'Mike, Patrick's still losing too much blood. We've got to get him to safety,' Sarah said from the shadows of the wooden barricade.

Patrick had taken a bullet in his left side, a through-and-through shot a few centimetres above his hip. Mike checked him again. There was no blood coming from his mouth and no air escaping from his lungs, which was good, but the old man was losing blood and they didn't have any proper dressings to bandage him. Mike had taken his shirt off and wrapped it around him, as best he could.

Patrick lay there now, just as Mike had left him before the gunfire started, with his hand pressed hard against the wound. He was a tough old chap, but that, too, was the problem. He wouldn't let on just how bad the pain was.

Mike understood why Sarah had to get a picture of him treating the ranger – it was her job – but he was glad to see she had slung her camera again to tend to him while Samson and he were blasting away at the sniper. He respected her professionalism for doing her job under fire, but he loved her for stopping to help the wounded man. She could have gotten some award-winning action shots of Samson and him shooting, but her first concern had been for Patrick.

The smell of cordite stung Mike's nostrils and the hot barrel of the FN smoked in the cool night air. His bare shoulder ached from the recoil, but it was a good pain. Patrick was alive and hopefully they had seen the poachers off for the time being. The captured poacher was dead, though, and Mike realised all of them had been lucky to escape with their lives.

'Why would he shoot his own man?' Samson asked, as he felt one last time for a pulse at the dead man's throat.

'Witnesses,' Mike said, as he slung Patrick's rifle and reached down to pick up the old ranger. 'It's their style. Make sure no one who can identify them lives to tell the tale. We would have been next, though.'

'Give me the rifle, it'll make it easier for you to carry Patrick,' Sarah said.

'Your little trick with the camera flash probably saved my life, and Patrick's,' Mike said as he unslung the rifle and handed it to her.

She blushed and examined the weapon.

'Pull the trigger here . . .' he began with a smile.

'And the bullets come out *here*, I know,' she said with a nervous little laugh.

'You're getting good at this.' This was an absurd time to be making jokes, Mike knew, and Samson gave them a peculiar look.

'Samson, take point. Sarah, stay behind me and keep checking the rear,' Mike said as he lifted Patrick up onto his back. Patrick was almost unconscious now, probably through loss of blood.

Mike noticed how easily he had lapsed into the familiar routine of giving orders and expecting them to be obeyed. It was as though part of him had been dead for a year and was only now reawakening. He liked the feeling, although he didn't underestimate the responsibility he was taking on. This was not a training exercise. Here the enemy were firing real bullets, not blanks, and people he cared about were in the firing line.

'We'll bomb-burst out of here, on a count of three,' Mike said. Both Samson and Sarah gave him puzzled looks. He had, he realised, also lapsed back into army jargon. 'We all go in slightly different directions when we leave the gate, then meet up in the trees on the lakeside. Got it?' The others nodded.

'One, two, three!'

Samson swung open the gate and they ran out. Patrick was not a big man, but he was, almost literally, a dead weight. Burdened as he was, Mike knew he was the easiest target of the three of them, and he prayed that if the sniper was still around he would find him more tempting than Sarah.

There were no shots. They regrouped and made their way back to the camping ground on the lake shore.

'Come this way, sir,' Samson said, directing them further along the shore, away from the houseboat's tender boat and the now-blazing lights of the anchored vessel. 'We have a bigger boat, bigger engine.'

Around a small spit of land, out of sight from the main camp, they came to the National Parks staff accommodation. There were two simple brick houses with corrugated-iron roofs and a separate toilet block. All of the buildings were painted the light olive green favoured by the Zimbabwe National Parks Service. Hens clucked in a small chicken run and clothes flapped lazily on a wire washing line strung between two trees. An old woman emerged tentatively from one of the staff houses and Samson spoke quickly and reassuringly to her in their language.

The woman, bent and grey-haired, rushed forward when she saw Mike easing Patrick from his back. Mike sat Patrick gently on the gunwale of the National Parks boat. The aluminium boat was bigger than the tender, and painted Parks green. On the back was a seventy-horsepower outboard. 'Help me, Samson,' Mike said.

Samson hadn't even worked up a sweat during the run. He helped Mike shift the old ranger into the boat and together they laid him on the deck.

'This is Patrick's wife,' Samson said.

The old woman pressed against Mike to get a look at her husband. Patrick opened his eyes and tried to smile at her. She pushed Mike aside and bent over so that her face was close to Patrick's. She ran her gnarled fingers through his tight grey curls as they spoke.

'He is telling her to stay here, to look after their child. They still have a daughter living here,' Samson translated. He added, 'I must take Patrick now.'

Mike respected the younger ranger's desire to stay with his comrade, but he had duties here. 'No, Samson,' he said, laying a hand on his shoulder. 'You must stay here, protect your women and my people, over there.' Mike pointed to the houseboat, bobbing at anchor. All the lights were on now and Mike could see people lining the rails.

Samson looked hard at Mike, reluctant to leave his superior.

'Stay, Samson,' Patrick croaked in English from the hull of the boat. 'Your duty is here.' Painfully, the old man raised himself up onto one elbow, on his good side. 'This is your post. Protect these people and these animals.' Patrick gave a ragged cough and sank back down into the boat.

'Stay, Samson,' Mike said, echoing the older man's words, 'but first come with me to tell my friends that they will be safe.'

The young man nodded and Sarah jumped into the boat, taking Patrick's hand in hers. 'I'll look after him for you,' she said to the old woman who, in turn, reached out and tenderly grasped Sarah's hand. There were tears in the old woman's eyes as she waved farewell to her husband.

Samson and Mike pushed the heavy boat into the water and then jumped aboard. The craft was big enough to have a separate seat for the driver and Mike settled in behind the steering wheel. He set the gear lever to neutral and pressed the starter button. Samson took a seat on the rear bench and apprehensively watched Sarah tend to Patrick as the engine roared to life.

Mike rammed the gear lever into reverse and pulled away from the shore. Once clear of the submerged trees, he pushed the throttle to full-forward. The bow of the boat reared up like a prancing stallion as they accelerated.

'I don't suppose it would do any good to suggest that I drop you off at the houseboat with the others?' he called to Sarah over the roar of the big outboard.

'None at all,' she said, as she looked up from her

seat on the deck. She cradled Patrick's head in her lap. 'Besides, you need someone to keep an eye on Patrick.'

It was a short ride to the houseboat and the nose of the boat dropped again as Mike flicked the gear lever back down into neutral.

'What gives?' a bare-chested Sam called from the railing on the houseboat's lower deck. The captain and his mate were also awake and glaring angrily at Mike, along with everyone else from the tour group.

'Poachers, but they've probably gone now. Sam, George, jump aboard and I'll run you to shore to pick up the tender boat,' Mike said as the Parks boat drifted up to the houseboat.

'Probably gone?' Jane asked in alarm, a protective arm around Julie's shoulders. Sam and George stepped onto the boat, which rocked and dipped with the extra weight.

'Fucking hell, what's happened to him?' George asked.

'Gunshot wound. We're taking him back to Kariba.'

'Can I help, Mike?' Kylie asked. 'I *am* a nurse, remember?'

'Thanks, Kylie, but we've got no dressings and no drugs. Our best bet is to get him to a hospital as quick as we can.'

'What about us, Mike?' Jane cried. 'You've got to look after *us*!'

Mike knew she was right, but there was too much to do and not enough people. 'Samson here will take care of you,' he said, gesturing to the tall ranger now standing next to him in the boat, cradling his AK-47. 'You'll be safe with him.'

Samson slung his rifle, reached out and grabbed the railing of the houseboat. With a deft step he was aboard. Linda and Mel parted from their places at the railing next to Jane and Julie to make way for him.

Once Samson was on board Mike said to him, 'Ask the captain to let you use the houseboat's radio. Call Kariba police and tell them to meet us at Andorra Harbour, with an ambulance. OK?'

'*Yebo*,' he said. 'Take care of Patrick, please.'

'And you're just abandoning us?' Julie interrupted. 'With people firing bloody machine guns around us!'

'There's a man dying of blood loss here,' Sarah spat back angrily at the mother and daughter. 'For God's sake, stop thinking about yourselves for one minute.'

Jane looked tired and worried. 'Mike, tell the captain to take us back as well on the houseboat. Tonight!'

The captain spoke for the first time. 'I'm sorry, madam, but we can't travel at night, in case the winds pick up.'

Before Jane could reply, Mike said, 'You'll all be fine. Captain, bring the boat back tomorrow, as scheduled. I'll explain everything there. Sarah and I will meet you at the dock.' To forestall the anticipated argument and barrage of questions, Mike gunned the motor and raced into shore.

'Bring Samson back to shore once everyone on board the houseboat's calmed down, OK, lads?' Mike said to Sam and George as they closed on the beach. 'Samson's a good man. You'll be safe with him. The poachers aren't after you guys.'

'No, they're after you two, aren't they?' Sam said.

'Jump ship,' Mike said as the boat skidded up onto the sand, next to the houseboat's dinghy. When the two young men were out of the bigger boat they gave Mike a hand to push the National Parks craft back out into the lake. 'Take care,' Mike said.

'You too,' replied Sam.

24

The water's surface was etched with lines of white-topped waves as they sped into the centre of the inland sea. The swell sent shock waves through the boat's hull as it bounced across the peaks. Sarah looked up pleadingly from the bottom of the boat, concerned about the constant slamming on Patrick's body.

'Take the cushion from the back seat,' Mike suggested, then returned his concentration to the choppy water. Mike knew the rough ride wouldn't be helping Patrick, but speed was what mattered now. There was nothing they could do for the ranger on board the small boat.

Spray flew up over the bow each time they crested a wave, stinging Mike's bare torso and soaking Sarah. He was bitterly cold and he had to continually wipe water from his eyes with his free hand. His mind raced in time with the screaming outboard as the boat thudded across the lake. He had plenty of questions to mull over, but not enough answers.

Where were the poachers staying and what would they do next? Could he, or even should he, continue with the tour after what had happened tonight? Was it safe for them to complete their journey while the poachers were still at large? Where was Fanie Theron, and did he have enough information on Hess and Orlov for him or his counterparts in Zimbabwe or Zambia to arrest them?

The last question concerned Mike the most. He and Sarah had been shot at and a man was close to dying but, as far as he was aware, none of them had actually seen their assailants. The only witness who could identify the members of the poaching party, and confirm whether or not two white men were involved in the hunt, was dead. There was a frightening possibility that even if the authorities could pick up Hess and Orlov – for Mike was convinced it was they who had been hunting the rhino – they would get off through lack of evidence.

He decided to find Gerry O'Flynn again. He needed to know if Flynn knew anything about what Hess and Orlov planned to do after they left him. For all Mike knew, Flynn might have been with them on the night hunt.

Mike looked down at Sarah and Patrick, and saw the ranger was now lying on the long green vinyl-covered cushion from the boat's rear bench. His eyes were closed.

'How is he?' Mike yelled.

Droplets of spray fanned from the top of Sarah's head as she ran a hand through her short black hair. She placed two fingers on Patrick's wrinkled neck to check his pulse. 'He passed out a little while ago. He's still breathing, but his pulse is very weak.'

'Thank God,' Mike said, pointing to their front. The lights of Kariba's shoreline were now revealing the shapes of houses and other waterfront buildings. Mike saw a flashing blue light on the shore and swung the steering wheel so the bow pointed towards it. Never had he been so pleased to see a police vehicle.

'Mike! Mike!' Sarah screamed. Mike looked down.

Patrick's eyes were open now, but not focused on anything. His mouth was wide open, revealing stained yellow teeth. 'He's stopped breathing!' Sarah yelled, looking up at Mike with pleading eyes.

'We're nearly there, Sarah! Start CPR!'

'What?'

'Mouth to mouth! Do you know what to do?'

'Oh, shit! I think so.'

She rocked Patrick's head back, pinched his nose and placed her lips over his. Mike watched as the ranger's skinny chest rose and fell twice.

'Good girl!' Mike said. 'Now the compressions.'

Sarah shifted her position so that she could press her left palm on Patrick's chest. Covering that hand with her right she started compressions in exactly the right spot, at the base of Patrick's sternum.

Again she switched positions and blew more hard breaths into the old body. Suddenly, Patrick coughed. He was alive.

'Bugger me!' Sarah said, looking up at Mike with a broad smile. Blue light bathed her face, on and off. 'I did it!'

'You certainly did.' Mike cut the engine and the

boat settled in the water and coasted up to the concrete launching ramp beneath the darkened Kariba Yacht Club. A white mini-van ambulance was parked on the ramp, its back door raised, and two paramedics in green overalls pushed a wheeled folding bed down to the water's edge. At the top of the ramp waited a white Land Rover with the blue and gold stripes of the Zimbabwe Republic Police. The blue beacon that had guided them there continued to flash. Two officers dressed in khaki were waiting for them and one grabbed the bow of the boat as it nosed in.

'Mr Williams?' the taller of the two policemen asked.

'That's right.'

'We have received a message from National Parks. It seems congratulations are in order, but this is a very irregular business, as I am sure you will appreciate.'

'Irregular is hardly the word for it, mate. But we've got a badly injured man here,' Mike said.

'Of course, he will be taken to hospital immediately.'

Mike busied himself in helping the paramedics lift Patrick from the bottom of the boat. Patrick was cold and wet where the bilge water had soaked his back. As the ambulancemen laid him on the stretcher he reached out and locked a bony hand around Mike's wrist.

'Thank you,' he whispered hoarsely.

'Thank the lady,' Mike said, gesturing to Sarah with a flick of his head. 'She saved your life.'

Patrick nodded and smiled at Sarah. 'Madam . . . forgive me my rudeness earlier . . .' He coughed painfully. 'And thank you, too.'

Mike looked at Sarah and there were tears in her eyes as she took Patrick's hand in hers. The paramedics broke the contact by pushing the wheeled bed up to the waiting ambulance. 'We must hurry,' one of them said.

'Yes, of course,' Sarah said, wiping her eyes with the back of her hand.

The ambulance sped off, and Mike walked over to the policeman who had first spoken to them, taking note of his rank, as he was the most senior of the two. 'Inspector, are we going to be charged with anything?'

'Charged?' the officer asked, his face puzzled. 'No, of course not. We were told that you were tourists staying in the camping ground who had gone to the aid of Parks officers who were under fire. Your actions may not have been the wisest, but you have committed no crime.'

Mike mentally thanked Samson for neglecting to mention they had been prowling around, unauthorised and armed, after dark. 'We have information about the men who shot at us –' he began.

'Everything is in hand, Mr Williams. We spoke to the other ranger at Matusadona and we have also received some information from the South African Police Service. A watch will be put on our border posts at Chirundu and here at Kariba for some men we wish to talk to in relation to this matter,' the inspector said.

Mike was relieved that Fanie had apparently been able to make contact with the local police, but he imagined Hess and Orlov were long gone by now. If the police were already aware of the suspects' identities, there was no need to involve himself and Sarah in unnecessary paperwork. 'I hope you catch them,' he said.

'Thank you, Mr Williams. Come see us around ten in the morning, if that is convenient, and we will get a formal statement from you about the shooting of the ranger and the poacher who was killed. Now, perhaps we can give you a lift somewhere?'

Mike thanked him, and he and Sarah climbed into the back of the Land Rover. They sat side by side on a padded bench seat as the old vehicle groaned its way up from the boat ramp and then down the hill out of the yacht club. Sarah moved closer to him until their legs were touching. Mike reached out and put an arm around her.

She laid her head on his shoulder and said, 'You sure know how to entertain a girl.'

A short time later they waved their thanks to the policemen in the Land Rover and promised to see them later that morning. The bleary-eyed security guard at the camping ground let them in through the barbed-wire-topped gate and they walked over to Nelson, parked where Mike had left it at the far end of the camping area, under the high, shady branches of an apple ring acacia tree.

Mike patted the truck's yellow metal bodywork affectionately. 'Nice to be home,' he whispered. 'I need a beer,' he said to Sarah.

'I need a shower,' she replied, looking down at her bloodstained T-shirt, 'and a beer.'

'Let's combine them,' Mike suggested.

'Combine what?'

'A beer and a shower. Nothing like it.'

He walked to the back of the truck, got down on one knee and reached under the chassis as far as he could. Above the rear axle, welded to the underneath of the cab floor, was a small metal box with a lid secured by a sliding bolt. Mike worked the bolt and fished inside for the spare set of keys.

Before leaving the truck he had run an extension cord from the external power socket on the right side of the cab to a power box mounted in the camping ground. He unlocked the main door to the cab and climbed inside. The car fridge was humming away contentedly. From inside he pulled four ice-cold bottles of Zambezi Lager.

Mike snapped the lids off two of the beers and handed one to Sarah. 'One for now and one for just now. You've earned it.' He unlocked the storage locker at the back of the truck, where everyone's spare bags and backpacks were stowed.

'Mine's the light blue backpack. God, that tastes good,' Sarah said, taking a second long swig of cold beer.

Mike passed down her pack and fished a towel, soap, clean shorts and underpants from his kitbag. He took his first sip of beer and toasted Sarah. She was right, it tasted good.

He finished the first bottle before they made it to the ablution block on the other side of the camping ground. Sarah, too, upended her bottle, draining the suds as they arrived.

'See you soon,' Mike said.

'Soon,' she said.

411

He walked into the gents side of the empty block, into the first shower stall. It was an old building and there was no curtain or door on the cubicle. Mosquitoes buzzed his ankles and ears, and moths and flying ants hovered around the bare light bulb over his head. Frogs and cicadas croaked and chirped in a ceaseless night-time concerto outside the cubicle's open window.

Mike stripped off his shorts which, like Sarah's shirt and his hands, were stained with Patrick's blood. He turned on the water, leaving red fingerprints on the chrome taps. The water was still hot and the pressure was strong. Mike realised he had left the bottle opener in the truck, so he laid the edge of the cap of the second bottle on the concrete windowsill and slapped down on the top with the palm of his free hand. The bottle top jangled on the concrete floor when it struck and Mike took a long, deep swallow of the cold golden fluid as he leaned back and put his head under the water. Bliss.

'Mike?' Sarah called tentatively from somewhere nearby.

'In here,' he replied after swallowing a mouthful of beer.

'The light's out in the ladies. I'll have to use one of the showers in here, OK?'

'Sure,' he said, placing his bottle on the window ledge and reaching for the soap. He closed his eyes and rubbed the cake of soap into his hair. Blindly, he replaced the bar on the ledge and massaged his scalp hard with his fingers. He heard footsteps in the corridor and turned to face the wall as he let the water wash the suds away.

With the soap gone and his eyes clear he turned his head and looked back over his shoulder. Sarah was standing motionless outside the cubicle, staring at him. It was hard for Mike to read the emotions in her eyes, in the set of her mouth, but he knew what he was feeling.

'Are you OK?' he asked.

'I'm fine,' she said in a low voice. Still she stood there, immobile, hesitating. She held up the green bottle and added, 'I need some assistance.'

He turned to face her, completely naked. She kept her eyes fixed on his as he walked towards her. He stood, dripping water, centimetres away from her and she looked up into his dark eyes.

Sarah blinked, twice, but there were no tears there, then bit her lower lip. It was as if she was giving herself one last chance to change her mind. Mike took the bottle from her hand and sat it next to his on the window ledge. He turned back to her, wrapped his wet arms around her and pulled her to his chest.

'We're safe,' she said.

'Yes,' he whispered, stroking her short dark hair. He put his fingers under her chin and lifted her face, then kissed her. It was a long, slow kiss, passionate but gentle. The kind lovers still enjoy after years of togetherness. He could feel the heat of her through her damp, clammy clothes.

The kiss broke and Mike whispered, 'Let's get you out of these.' She raised her arms and he pulled the knotted T-shirt over her head. She ran her fingers through his hair as he bent to unzip and lower her denim shorts and pants. The woman smell of her filled his nostrils and he felt himself harden.

'Clean me,' she said, and they both stepped under the hard, purifying spray of the shower.

It was a long shower, punctuated with bouts of laughter and progressively longer, wetter kisses. They explored each other's bodies, washing and teasing at the same time.

'Not here,' she whispered, nibbling his earlobe as he ran his nails down her long smooth back to the cleft of her buttocks.

'No. Let's go,' Mike agreed.

They hurriedly dressed and he led her back to the truck, hand in hand. From the rear of the truck he pulled out two camp mattresses, a mosquito net, sleeping bag and two pillows and passed half the load to Sarah.

'Follow me,' he said. They walked to the back of the truck and he started to climb the tubular metal ladder welded to the rear of Nelson's cab.

'Up there?' she asked, surprised.

'No one will see us, and the view is unbelievable.'

The big truck rocked slightly as Sarah's torso appeared over the top edge of the back of the cab. The roof was flat and there was plenty of room. Mike laid the mattresses side by side, and Sarah spread out the sleeping bag as he tied the mosquito net to a low branch of the acacia tree.

'The stars are incredible,' she said softly and Mike turned to see her staring up through the trees.

Mike thought for a moment of Isabella and that first night of theirs on top of the UN four-wheel drive in Kruger. He looked up as well and wondered if there really was a heaven and if you ever really forget someone. He hoped he would never forget

Isabella as long as he lived, but he also realised he had reached a turning point and that he really cared for Sarah. He wanted her sexually, but there was much more to his feelings than that. He knew what they were about to do was right – as right as it had been for him and Isabella.

She looked at him, kneeling on the opposite side of the mattresses. He moved towards her, on his knees also, and took her in his arms. They kissed again, hard and passionate. He laid her down and pulled her T-shirt off, urgently, lusting to see the firm white breasts he had so tenderly caressed just a few minutes before. Now he wanted to devour them, to consume every bit of her.

Her movements were just as frantic as his as she tore at the fastening and zipper of his shorts, hands reaching roughly inside.

He moved between her opened legs, running his hands the length of her body, over her tanned arms and legs, her creamy white pelvis and breasts. He tasted her clean, soap-scented skin, from the base of her neck to the tight curls between her legs. She encircled him with her fingers, pulling hard and fast. They both needed release and she was hot and already pulsing with desire as his fingers opened her.

'Now,' she pleaded in his ears, guiding him towards her. She closed her eyes as he entered her, and bit down hard on her lower lip. Her muscles tensed for an instant, then relaxed as he slid home with a thrust that made her gasp with pleasured surprise.

There was no slow build-up to their first love-making. She clung to him fiercely, digging her nails painfully into his back, her long legs wrapped tightly around him, as he plunged in and out of her. Beneath him, she arched her back and gripped him tighter and tighter with her arms and her unseen muscles, bringing them both to the brink of climax.

'God, I need you,' he whispered breathlessly in Sarah's ear.

'Me too. I'm yours tonight.'

25

'I've got work to do today,' Sarah said, sitting upright and clutching the sleeping bag to cover her bare breasts.

'Thank you,' Mike said, as he lazily ran a finger down the ridges of her spine.

'Oh. Thank you, too,' she said, smiling brightly as she looked down at him. She fumbled under the covers for her T-shirt and added, as she pulled it on, 'Mike, I've got calls to make. Can we talk later?'

He wasn't expecting flowers or a champagne breakfast, but he could guess from the excited look in her eyes what she wanted next, and it wasn't sex or a lazy lie-in. Besides, the sun was up and campers were wandering around, to and from the shower block. There could be no hanky-panky on top of a bright yellow truck in daytime, nor any shared showers.

'I've got a friend on *The Times*, Mike. He's on the foreign desk. I've got to call him now. The story is too good to miss, and it might be my ticket out of travel magazines.'

Mike rubbed his eyes. By the time they had made love a second, slower, time, it was only a couple of hours before dawn and they had woken with the sun. He, too, had calls to make before the rest of the group arrived.

After showering, separately, they each bought phone cards at the camp shop and took turns at feeding them into a hungry payphone just outside the entrance gate. While Sarah waited for the newsdesk of *The Times* of London to call her back, Mike squeezed in a long call to Rian. Mike explained everything that had happened, from the real purpose of his meeting with Theron at the border, up to last night's mayhem.

'Christ, Mike, you could have ruined me if anything happened to the tourists!' Rian said angrily. 'Is it safe to go on? They haven't caught these people and they might track you down!'

'I know, that's why I'm cancelling the trip, Rian.'

'Cancelling it?'

'I've got no reason to think they know who I am or what I'm driving, but the other passengers will have been shaken up after last night. I'm going to drop them at Lusaka. Can you and Susie arrange for their flights to be rescheduled?'

'*Ja*. It'll cost us, but you're right – their safety has got to be our priority. There's a flight to London tonight. I know some people at BA. I'll see how many seats I can book. It was bloody foolish of you to even agree to help the police in the first place.'

Mike knew Rian was right. In truth, however, his only regret about the preceding night was that he

418

hadn't had a clear shot at Hess or Orlov with Patrick's rifle.

Mike explained to Sarah what Rian had said. She looked at him thoughtfully for a moment. 'How long will it take to get to Lusaka?' she asked.

'It's only about a hundred and thirty kilometres from here. We'll get going as soon as we pick everyone up from the houseboat. With the border crossing, probably about three hours. We'll be there by four at the latest, I reckon.'

The payphone rang again and Sarah snatched it up. She outlined what had happened to her and Mike, talking up the danger and mentioning the nationalities of everyone in the tour group. Mike listened in uneasily.

'Pictures? You bet I've got pictures! A crusty old ranger being treated for a bullet wound, hero tour guide dragging him to safety.' Sarah winked at Mike, but he didn't smile back.

She listened to the caller, nodding her head and making notes in her spiral-bound reporter's notebook. At last she hung up. 'Right, I've got an hour to write the story, then they'll call back and I'll dictate it down the line. Depending on the pics and the comments we can get from your chum in the South African Police, they may even want a follow-up and a weekend feature!'

'How will you get the pictures to them?' Mike asked.

'Um, Mike, I'll be in London.'

'You're leaving? Of course . . .' Although he had instructed Rian to cancel the tour and arrange flights home for everyone he had half expected – hoped – that Sarah might want to stay in Africa for a while longer.

'Mike,' Sarah said, placing a hand on his arm, 'this is my big chance. They've offered me a few days on freelance rates to follow up the story, but there's not much I can do from the back of a truck on the road in the middle of nowhere. If I get home and do a good job there might be a full-time position in it. Nicholas hinted as much and said they were looking to hire people at the moment.'

He didn't know or care who Nicholas was. 'What about the job you've got now? Don't you like travel writing?' he asked.

'Sure, it's fun, but I want to do hard news. I want to be sent overseas to cover coups and great events, not travelogues and advertorials for tour companies. Anyway, I'm not giving up my job right now. My magazine will be happy for me to do the stuff for *The Times* as long as they mention who I work for – it's great publicity for the mag. But if something better comes up, then I'd be mad not to jump at it.'

'I'm sure you're making the right decision,' he said. 'Now, I've got to pick up the rest of the gang from the wharf. You'd better start writing.'

He turned and walked to the truck. He allowed himself a quick backward glance. Sarah was still standing by the payphone and she was staring at him, lost in thought. He smiled and she smiled back. She turned and walked to a picnic table in the camping ground, sat down on the wooden bench and started to write in her notebook.

On his way to the wharf where the houseboat would dock, Mike stopped in at the police station, located on the top of a hill with panoramic views over the lake and township of Kariba. He gave the police a written statement on behalf of himself and Sarah, who, he fibbed, was too distraught to come to the station. Then he continued on to the wharf and found another payphone. His mobile phone still wasn't picking up a signal. He dialled Fanie Theron's number and was surprised when the detective answered the phone.

'It's Mike Williams. I'm glad I've got through to you and not your voice mail.'

'I've been trying to call you all morning. Are you OK?' Theron asked.

'I'm OK, but we cut it close last night,' Mike said. He talked Theron through the events in Matusadona National Park.

'I heard about that. I've been on the phone to the Zimbabweans this morning.'

'How did you find out so quickly?' Mike asked.

'I can't go into that now. Did you see Hess or Orlov? Can you stand up in court and testify that they were in the park after hours, with weapons?'

Mike hesitated as the thought of lying crossed his mind. Perjury seemed a small crime compared to the trail of blood Hess and Orlov had left in their wake, but he could also imagine the difficulties of mounting the case against them. 'I'm sorry, Fanie. It was dark, and they were the ones with the night sight, not us.'

'*Ja*, I understand,' Theron said.

Mike could hear the disappointment in his voice.

'Anyway, it's over for now, Mike.'

'What do you mean?'

'They're leaving. Orlov is probably on his way back to Russia right now.'

'How do you know?'

'Again, I can't say, but trust me – it's over. Look, I can't talk now. Contact me when you get back to South Africa so I can debrief you in more detail. Goodbye.' He hung up.

So that was that, Mike told himself. No thanks for risking his life, and no chance of catching the men who had killed Isabella and nearly finished off Sarah and him. He was disappointed and angry, but he had other people to worry about now.

Everyone spoke at once as they hopped off the moored houseboat and onto the concrete dock.

'Quiet, please!' Mike called above the hubbub, raising his hands for silence. He made his apologies to the stern-faced captain of the houseboat, and shepherded the group into the back of Nelson for some privacy from the labourers and deckhands milling around the wharf. When the tourists were seated, he repeated the long story he'd told Rian.

'Anyway, the upshot is,' Mike said in conclusion, 'that the tour is cancelled. My boss is arranging flights for everyone from Lusaka in Zambia, and those of you who can't get out immediately will be put up in a hotel until we can get you on a flight.'

'You endangered us, Mike. I can't believe you'd do

that!' Jane Muir said when he had finished. She had one arm wrapped protectively around Julie's shoulders. The daughter, too, regarded Mike with an accusing stare.

'It's not his fault,' Sam said, rising to Mike's defence.

As much as he appreciated the young American's words, Mike knew he was not entirely correct. 'No, Sam, it is my fault. I could have stopped the tour earlier or told the cops to shove their request for help.'

'What will happen to you?' Mel asked.

'I'm taking the truck back to South Africa.'

'Will you be OK? Won't the poachers still be looking for you?' Kylie inquired.

'The cops tell me the poachers are bugging out. Don't ask me how they know, because I don't know the answer. It seemed they were scared off after the action last night, and at least they failed to kill a rhino.'

Mike climbed into the driver's cab, alone, and started the engine. Above the noise of the diesel engine he could hear murmured conversations from the rear cab punctuated by the occasional angry outburst. He felt frustrated and restless as he drove back to the camping ground to pick up Sarah.

He fished a cigarette from his pocket and lit it as he drove. He should never have agreed to help Theron in the first place, he told himself. Worse still was the fact that Hess and Orlov had escaped, unscathed. He had risked his job and many lives for no result at all, in a fanciful search for revenge.

During the night, as they had sped across Lake

Kariba in the dark, the adrenaline still clouding his mind, Mike had thought of revisiting the safari guide, Gerald O'Flynn, to see if he could account for his clients' whereabouts during the shooting spree. Now, in the sober light of day, he couldn't be bothered with any more amateur detective work. However, he'd relayed his suspicions about Hess and Orlov to the police and given them Flynn's name as a possible lead.

Now, as should have been the case all along, his first priority had to be the tourists under his care. He had to get across the border and into Zambia as soon as possible. His head ached from a lack of sleep and the cigarette was not helping. He needed a dozen cold beers and as many hours' sleep.

26

'Karl, what a surprise,' Gerald O'Flynn said as he opened the front door of his dilapidated two-bedroom house, leaving the screen door locked.

Flynn's house was set in a quiet spot, just the way the bushman liked it, on the side of a hill overlooking Lake Kariba, off the road that led to the Cutty Sark Hotel and Marina. Mopani and leadwood trees surrounded the house, and wildlife, including lion and leopard, occasionally strayed out of the bush onto the unfenced property. But here stood the most dangerous predator Flynn had ever seen.

'Not going to invite me in, Flynn?' Hess asked, baring his perfect white teeth.

'Tell me why I should, Karl?' Flynn asked from the other side of the holed flyscreen door. 'The police called this morning. Said they're coming around to interview me later today. Why would that be, do you think? And why are you here again? You crossed over to Zambia yesterday, didn't you?'

'So I did, but I had some unfinished business to take care of on this side of the lake.' Hess was dressed in a stone-washed, short-sleeved khaki shirt and matching trousers. 'You tell me why the police would be after you.'

'Something about an incident that happened over in the Matusadona last night after we left. Maybe you can tell me about it?' Flynn asked.

'I don't know what you're talking about, Flynn,' Hess said, though this was exactly what he had feared.

Orlov had argued with him earlier in the morning, pleading with him not to return to Zimbabwe, and for them both to get to Lusaka airport as soon as possible. The Russian had telephoned British Airways and brought the date of his flight forward, eager to be out of Africa. But Hess wanted to make sure there were no loose ends that could incriminate them.

Hess needed to know who had tipped off the Parks authorities the night before. It was possible, he conceded, that the only reason the hunt had been foiled was because that fool of a poacher had allowed himself to be captured by the park rangers. However, on their reconnaissance Hess and his team had been told there would be only one armed guard looking after the rhinos at night. As it turned out, there had been two, plus the unknown man and woman who had been with the rangers. He had no idea who they were and could not place them from the brief glimpses he had caught of them through the rifle's nightscope. On Hess's orders, Klaus had organised one of the poachers to ferry the hunter across the lake by high-speed motorboat. Now Flynn had confirmed that the authorities believed that he and Orlov, Flynn's clients, had been involved in the night's failed hunt.

'Who else knew you were taking my colleague and me to the Matusadona? Had you been talking around town?'

The change of tack confused Flynn momentarily. His mind, still foggy from last night's whisky, turned laboriously as he scanned his memory of the preceding few days. 'You worried other people might know you're in town, Karl?' he asked, buying himself more time.

Hess smiled again, an attempt at charm that reminded Flynn of a crocodile basking on a mud bank. 'Come now, Flynn, we're old friends. You know my clients demand a certain amount of discretion. Who else knew about our trip?'

Flynn remembered now. An Australian, a long-haired fellow. He had been at the bar when Hess called to change his plans. He recalled writing Hess's name and the date and time of his arrival on a beer mat. The Australian had asked about rhinos, maybe even about Hess at the time.

Hess saw the unmistakable look of recollection in the safari guide's eyes.

When Gerald O'Flynn had seen the speedboat pull into the shore below his house and Hess step onto land, he had quickly pulled his old British Army Webley revolver from its usual resting place under the yellow-stained pillow on his unmade bed. He had stuffed the heavy pistol in the waistband of his baggy green shorts and it rested uncomfortably at the base of his back now.

Flynn turned, looking back down the narrow corridor behind him, considering running instead of fighting. Hess reached around himself with his right hand to the small of his back and unsnapped the cover of the short, wickedly sharp hunting knife in its pouch.

'Karl, there was no one, no one else knew,' Flynn stammered. He started to turn, reaching behind his back as he did.

Hess glimpsed the wooden grip of the old firearm and his arm flashed in an arc, faster than a striking mamba. The knife's curved stainless-steel blade pierced the ragged flyscreen and then the shirt, skin, muscle and heart of Gerald O'Flynn.

The pistol fell from Flynn's grip and clattered to the floor. Hess punched his free hand through a tear in the flyscreen and grabbed Flynn's collar, holding the older man up and twisting the knife deeper in.

'Bastard . . .' Flynn gasped.

'Tell me, you stupid old fool, who did you blab to?'

Gerald O'Flynn, soldier, hunter and big-game guide felt his life force draining away. Many times during an existence of danger and adventure, he had wondered what this moment would feel like, and what final words he would utter when his time came.

With the last reserves of energy available to him he forced a smile. Then, in silence, he died.

27

Sarah was brimming with excitement as they crossed the border into Zambia and started the long, tortuous climb up the escarpment on the other side of the Zambezi River. Unlike the Zimbabwe side, where elephant, buffalo, zebra and various antelope species were often seen around town, the Zambian bush was devoid of wildlife, thanks to decades of unchecked poaching. She busied herself in the back of the cab, taking portrait shots of the other travellers and making notes of their names, ages, occupations and backgrounds.

He could already imagine the break-out stories being picked up by wire services around the world: 'American tourist in African firefight' or 'New Zealander narrowly escapes injury in battle with poachers'. That sort of thing. Mike cringed at the thought of his photo being beamed to newspapers everywhere, and he wondered how Rian would react.

Mike was surprised by how much his brief fling with Sarah – for that was how he was determined to remember it – had meant to him. Jane had reawoken the sexual feelings he had suppressed after Isabella's death, but Sarah had rekindled something else. After they made love he had drifted off to sleep with the thought that from now on there could be nothing better in the entire universe than to lie down next to this woman every night and wake up next to her every morning, no matter where in the world they were.

Once they reached the top of the escarpment and the countryside levelled out, they made better time. The road to Lusaka was in good condition for a Zambian road, and they raced on through the hot, slanting mid-afternoon sun, past the turn-off to the spectacular Kafue Gorge, where the river of the same name cut its way down to the Zambezi.

Mike longed to slow down and show these beautiful places to Sarah, to stop at roadside fruit stalls and buy newly ripened bananas, to sip cold Zambian Mosi beers while watching a lingering sunset. He wanted the pair of them to giggle at the antics of shy African children pushing toy cars made out of wound fencing wire along dusty side tracks, to introduce her to African music and to have their fortunes told by a village *sangoma*. But she was going back to her world, to a world of deadlines and airports and faxes and computers and e-mail. He lit another cigarette and tried to let the whine of the engine drown out his thoughts.

Lusaka was a seething mass of suicidal taxis and blind pedestrians, all determined to raise Mike's ire and force him continually to bip Nelson's horn. They stopped and started along the main street, Cairo Road, a wide boulevard split by tree-lined median strips. The street might have been attractive once, he thought, before the build-up of blue-black smoke that blanketed the traffic.

'Fuckin' idiot!' he yelled out the open window to the driver of a brand new Mitsubishi Pajero. The man gave Mike the finger as he cut in front of the overlander, forcing him to stand on the brakes.

They crawled up to a big roundabout and Mike followed the sign to the airport, turning right on to the Great East Road. The buildings dropped in height as they slowly headed back into the flatlands. They passed a big single-storey shopping centre that was surrounded by a high fence and patrolled by an army of security guards, including two at a checkpoint on the gate.

Too soon, much too soon, they were through town and turning off towards the airport. Mike found a parking space in the half-full car park and turned around to face the group in the rear cab.

'This is it. Last stop.' His heart was heavy but his tone belied it.

'Not a chance,' Nigel said.

'What do you mean? Trip's over, mate,' Mike said.

'Bullshit,' Nigel said. 'A few of us have taken a vote and we're coming with you. We've paid for this trip and we're not ready to go home yet. Tell your boss to shove his airfares and hotel rooms.'

'We wouldn't miss the rest of this trip for the world, mate,' George said. 'I joined the Territorial Army back home for a bit of action, but I've never seen anything like last night.'

'Better than *Match of the Day* . . . well, almost,' Terry added.

'Count me in too,' Kylie said. 'As long as there's no more gunfire,' she added with a nervous laugh.

'We're staying, right?' said Linda, looking at Mel, who was sitting next to her.

'Right,' Mel confirmed.

Mike held up a hand. 'Listen, all of you, I'm touched, but I shouldn't have even let you come this far.'

'But you said the cops had told you the baddies have left,' Mel said.

'That's true, but –'

'Then it's settled,' Sam said. 'Most of us are in, Mike.'

Mike nodded, grateful for their understanding. He resolved to make it up to each of them by ensuring they had a fun, safe holiday for the rest of their time together. But not everyone was happy with the way things had panned out.

'Come on, Julie, let's go,' Jane said, edging her way between the seats. Julie cast a quick glance at Mike as she followed her mother down the steps, but he couldn't read the emotions in her face. 'I can't stand any more of this musketeer bullshit.'

'Sorry,' said Sarah, with a little smile. She bit her lower lip, and then bent her head out of sight to retrieve a daypack from under her seat.

Everyone else filed out behind Jane and Julie, including Sarah, and the guys helped unload the backpacks and other bags of those who were departing. Hazy waves of baking heat wafted up from the tarmac of the car park and in the distance Mike heard thunder. Black clouds gathered along the horizon and the air was pregnant with moisture. He felt his shirt stick to his back as he climbed down from the driver's cab.

Jane and Julie hugged and kissed all the members of the group, including Nigel, but not Sarah, who would be travelling on the same BA flight as them back to England that night. Mike stared idly at the long, three-storey terminal building of Lusaka International Airport. To the left were offices and a dark-brick air traffic control tower bristling with radio aerials. The white concrete section to the right of the building housed the arrival and departure halls and an old-fashioned observation deck, where friends and lovers could wave goodbye. They wouldn't be staying for lingering farewells, though, as they would have to get back on the road in order to reach a camping site before nightfall.

Jane had dressed in a matching short khaki skirt and sleeveless blouse for the trip home. She walked towards Mike but stopped out of arm's reach. 'Julie's all I've got, Mike, and she means more to me than anything . . . any man. You put us in danger, and I can't forgive that.'

She turned her back on Mike and started walking away. He realised she was right. He could have told her that he would miss her, but that would have been lying.

'Have a safe flight,' he said, as she and Julie walked off.

Sarah had her backpack on and was saying the last of her goodbyes to the people she had finally got to know, too late to make an impact on them, and vice versa. Except for Mike. Mike was aware of other eyes on them as she walked across to him, stopping close to his chest.

'You'll take care of yourself, won't you, Mike?' she asked, looking up at him and blinking.

'I'll stay off the main roads for a few days, watch my back, just in case. But I can't imagine Hess and Orlov would be stupid enough to hang around after last night,' Mike said.

He couldn't put his arms around her while she had her pack on, so he put the fingers of both hands under her chin and raised her face to his. She blinked again and he glimpsed a tear in the corner of each eye.

'I've got to go, Mike . . . I'm so sorry. I . . .'

Mike lowered his face to Sarah's and kissed her on the mouth. Her lips parted and he tasted the salt of her tears running down her cheeks and into their mouths. Behind them, he was aware of some hooting and whistling. Sarah encircled his neck with slender arms and pulled him closer.

'Bye, Mike. I'll write,' she said after a few seconds as she pushed herself gently away.

Mike started to speak, but a Boeing 767 screamed over their heads on its final approach, drowning him out.

'What?' she asked, as the roar passed over them.

'Nothing. Nothing at all. Have a safe trip.'

Vassily Orlov was angry and bored. He paced the hall idly looking in the windows of the few duty-free shops in the departure lounge of Lusaka International Airport. His mind was not on cheap cigarettes and whisky – he controlled a large percentage of the distribution of both in Moscow, anyway – it was on the previous night's debacle in a Zimbabwean national park.

Hess, who sat calmly in a plastic chair in the open bar area smoking a cigarette and reading a news magazine, had relayed all that he had learned from his brief trip back across the border into Zimbabwe that morning. While Orlov fretted that the police may be tracking them at this very moment, he reminded himself that apart from having been in a national park with a weapon – a crime no one had seen him commit – he had broken no laws. It had been Hess who had engaged in a running gun battle and wounded, or possibly killed, a park ranger. And still there was the nagging question of how much the authorities actually knew about their identities and their plans.

Orlov was concerned at Hess's report that Gerald O'Flynn had been contacted by the police, but satisfied that the Namibian had dealt with that problem in his own inimitable fashion. The death of the guide was another good reason for them both to part company as soon as possible.

After checking in on the ground floor of the terminal at their respective airline counters, the two men had turned right and passed through Zambian immigration and customs procedures and then headed upstairs to the departure hall without incident. Although neither would admit it to the other, both had feared that at any second armed police would emerge and detain them for questioning. When they had passed through all the checks Orlov had thanked God. Hess had thanked African bureaucracy. At Hess's insistence they had left all their firearms, even Orlov's personal hunting rifle he had brought from Russia, with Klaus in the Land Cruiser.

Orlov was booked on a British Airways flight to London. Hess had purchased a ticket to Nairobi and would later connect to a flight to Windhoek, where he planned to lie low for a week or two before crossing back into South Africa by road at a quiet border post. Klaus would return the four-wheel drive to Jo'burg, ship the hunting rifles to their respective owners and then make his own way back to Hess's game ranch.

'Relax, Vassily,' Hess said as the Russian joined him at the table. 'Let me buy you a drink.'

Orlov didn't need anyone to tell him to relax, but he accepted Hess's offer. 'Yes, thank you, Karl. A scotch.'

Hess nodded and walked to the bar. Orlov noticed three women, all of them slim and attractive, enter the departure hall. One of them had short dark hair, and carried a notebook and an expensive camera. He didn't get a good look at her face, as she disappeared through a door that read 'Private, National Airports Corporation Staff Only', which struck him as odd. The other two women walked towards the bar.

Both women were blonde, one slightly older than the other. They might have been related, he thought. He was mildly jealous when the elder of the pair struck up a conversation with Hess.

436

Hess saw the two women approaching in the mirror behind the bar as he waited for the elderly African barman to finish serving a man at the far end. The barman finally arrived, but looked to the two women to take their order, even though Hess had been waiting first. Hess bridled at the man's inefficiency, if that's what it really was.

'Gin and tonic and a Bloody Mary, please,' the older of the two women said in an English accent. 'Oh, sorry, I think you were first,' she said, noticing Hess standing nearby.

'No, it's fine, carry on,' Hess said.

'Thanks.' The woman fumbled in a daypack and produced a packet of cigarettes. To the barman, she said, 'Do you sell matches?'

'No, sorry, madam, we have run out,' the barman said as he reached for two glasses.

Hess noted the woman's obvious annoyance. 'Please, allow me,' he said, and pulled a gold lighter from his shirt pocket and struck the flint. The woman leaned close enough for him to smell cheap perfume.

'Ta,' she said, exhaling smoke. 'You really are quite the gentleman, a change from the company we've been keeping lately!'

She smiled, and Hess had the distinct and vaguely discomforting feeling that she was looking him over as she waited for the barman to finish pouring their drinks. The younger of the two women peered around the older and stole a look at Hess as well.

'My pleasure,' he said, pocketing the lighter. 'You haven't had an enjoyable experience in Africa?'

'Hardly,' said the older woman with disgust.

The younger of the pair leaned around again and said to Hess, 'We were shot at last night!'

'You don't say. Where was that?' Hess asked, raising his eyebrows in genuine surprise.

'Zim-bloody-babwe on Lake bloody Kariba somewhere,' said the older woman.

'Amazing. Who would shoot at a couple of pretty ladies like you two?'

Hess noted that the older woman smiled at the compliment. 'A couple of hunters – one of them a mafia boss, no less! It's a long story,' she said.

'I've got a couple of hours until my plane leaves,' Hess said. He thought quickly. He could not introduce the women to Orlov, whose Russian accent was too thick to mask. He ordered a beer for himself and invited the women to join him.

'Yeah, why not,' the mature woman said. 'Grab us a table, Julie.'

As they seated themselves around the small table, Hess caught Orlov's look of confused indignation from across the room. He dismissed his employer with a curt shake of his head. Hess reopened the conversation. 'So, who was shooting at you?'

'Well,' the younger one, Julie, began, 'they weren't actually shooting at us, they were shooting at our tour guide.'

'Your tour guide?' Hess prompted, sipping his drink.

'Yeah, there's these two guys, right, a Russian and a German – a Namibian, actually – and they were in this national park trying to poach a rhino. Where are you from, Mr . . . ?'

'Swanepoel, but call me Piet. I'm from South Africa.'

'Anyway, our tour guide knows these guys because they killed his girlfriend and so he was recruited by the South African Police to try and track them down and –'

'Bloody dangerous stuff, if you ask me,' the older woman said, smiling. 'I'm Jane, by the way, and this is Julie.'

Bloody dangerous indeed, thought Hess as he said, 'You're sisters, right?'

Sarah had been told to expect a fax from *The Times*'s foreign desk when she arrived at the airport and, after being shunted from one airport official to another, finally discovered that her fax was waiting for her in the National Airports Corporation office in the departure hall. She found the office as soon as she, Jane and Julie emerged from customs and immigration.

An overweight female secretary handed the fax to her when she entered the office and introduced herself. Nicholas had been nice enough to send her a proof of the story, which had already been placed, on page one. The story was below the fold, on the bottom half of the page, and there was white space around it where other breaking stories would be placed as the day wore on, but she had made it. Front page of *The Times*, with her by-line.

On the cover sheet of the fax were a couple of questions Nicholas needed answers to in order to sell the idea of a follow-up story and a possible weekend feature to the news editor. There were also orders for her to report at the offices of *The Times* as soon as she landed. Nicholas had spoken to her magazine editor and her freelance assignment was confirmed. Sarah was ecstatic.

'You work for *The Times*?' asked the secretary. 'That is very impressive.'

Sarah didn't explain she was only working as a freelance journalist. Instead, she said, 'May I please use your fax machine to send a reply?'

'I shouldn't really allow you to send an overseas fax without authority, but I'm sure we can make an exception just this once,' she replied with a conspiratorial wink.

Sarah wrote down the answers Nicholas needed on a blank sheet of A4 paper, and then placed it in the machine and dialled the number. There was a portable radio on the bookshelf behind the secretary's desk and Sarah strained to hear the last of the news while the machine attempted to bridge two continents. To her relief there had been no mention of a shooting or possible poaching incident in Zimbabwe. She would have hated to be scooped.

The news finished and the announcer switched to the weather: 'The first heavy rains of the season are expected within the next twenty-four hours, with storms forecast for the Lusaka area and the eastern part of the country, including Petauke and Chipata . . .'

Checking her watch, she saw it had been nearly half an hour since she parted company with Jane and Julie Muir. She didn't relish spending any more time than she absolutely had to with the pair. It was an embarrassing situation, to say the least. She and Jane had slept with the same man and she was surprised how jealous she suddenly felt. Thinking about Mike also made her sad again, but she was determined to let nothing get in the way of the next, enormous, step in her career. When she thought of what she was doing in those terms, however, she felt miserable all over again.

She rationalised her feelings away, though, as she watched the paper click slowly through the fax machine. She would have left Africa at the end of the overland trip anyhow, and she and Mike would probably never see each other again. The previous night had been the best sex she had experienced in a long time, fuelled as it was by the incredible excitement and danger that preceded it. As she thought of Mike again, with his big hands and mature, muscled body, she found herself feeling both aroused and, once more, depressed that she was leaving him behind.

Nicholas Charters, the assistant foreign desk editor who was sticking his neck out to help her make the jump from second-rate magazine to national newspaper, paled, literally, in comparison with the bronzed Australian tour guide. She had met Nicholas at a party and they had dated a couple of times. He was intelligent, and tall, but he had a weedy build and his skin was so white he sometimes looked anaemic. When he had dropped her home after an expensive dinner at a French restaurant and asked if he could come upstairs for coffee, she had to say no. She felt no physical attraction to him at all. He never asked her out again, and Sarah thought he had been childish and arrogant in his expectations so early in their friendship. She wondered if his newfound interest in her career would manifest itself in other ways. She would cross that unpleasant bridge when she came to it, she told herself.

The fax transmission was completed and the secretary was standing behind her desk now, jacket on and handbag in hand. 'I'm sorry, but it is time for me to go home now. I must close the office. I hope that is not a problem,' she said.

'No, I understand completely. Thank you so much for your help. I must get back to my friends, anyway,' Sarah said. Except they weren't her friends and she didn't want to spend the next two hours making small talk with them.

Sarah was shown out, and she and the secretary said their farewells. Sarah shook her head when she saw that Jane and Julie Muir were entertaining a man at their table. She didn't regard herself as a prude – she'd had a couple of one-night stands with handsome strangers in her time – but Jane Muir seemed to have turned the come-on into an art form.

She reluctantly walked across the polished linoleum floor of the departure hall towards the bar. The man the Muir girls were chatting up had his back to her. Sarah noticed he had wavy blond hair and was solidly built.

'Oh God,' she whispered. She slowed her pace and raised a hand to her mouth.

The man turned his head slightly as he addressed a comment to Julie, showing a little of his profile. Sarah took in the tanned skin and the aquiline nose, and froze. She scanned the rest of the hall until she found who she was looking for. Vassily Orlov sat at a table at the far end of the bar's lounge area, by himself, glancing at Karl Hess and Jane and Julie Muir over the top of a magazine he was clearly not reading.

Panic rooted Sarah's feet to the floor. A loudspeaker crackled to life and an African woman announced something about a flight to Johannesburg. She looked around and saw the secretary starting to disappear through the door that led back downstairs to customs and immigration. Sarah took a deep breath and walked as quickly as she could without attracting attention to herself. When she was out of sight of the bar area, she broke into a run.

'Thank God I caught you,' she gushed.

The African woman looked startled at first but then smiled when she recognised Sarah. 'You gave me a fright.'

'This is terribly important. I can't find my friends and I must speak to them urgently, can you take me to someone who can page them for me?'

The woman nodded and led Sarah back downstairs to another office near the customs and immigration desks.

'Will Mrs Jane-i Muir and Miss Julie Muir please report to the customs desk immediately,' said the deep African voice over the loudspeaker. The announcer repeated the message once more.

'Mum, that was us!' Julie said.

Jane looked at the three empty gin-and-tonic glasses in front of her and giggled. 'Sorry, Piet,' she said, using Hess's alias. 'Duty calls. Don't go away,

443

though, I'll be back,' she added, reaching under the table and patting his knee with her hand.

Hess nodded, pleased for an excuse to be rid of the two women now he had learned all he was going to. He had the distinct feeling that if he stayed any longer he would end up being dragged off to a dark corner of the terminal and sexually assaulted by the older woman. The younger one, too, seemed to be openly flirting with him as if in competition with her mother, which Hess found disgusting.

The women hurriedly drained the last of their drinks and teetered off towards the stairway that led to the customs desks. Hess beckoned Orlov over as soon as they were on the stairs and out of sight.

'Hello, you get called too?' Jane Muir asked when she saw Sarah standing near a vacant customs desk.

'Jane, come here,' Sarah said, leading Jane and Julie to one side of the narrow passageway where they could talk in relative privacy. 'What were you talking to that man about?'

Jane bridled at the question and a red flush coloured her cheeks. 'What's it to you, nosy?'

'Jane, stop it. Listen to me! That man you were chatting up –'

'Chatting up! How dare you, you snooty bitch!' Jane huffed.

'Sorry, sorry,' Sarah said, holding up her hands in apology. 'That man you were talking to is Karl Hess. He's one of the poachers who was doing all the shooting last night!'

'No, he was a South African . . . Pete something or other,' Julie chimed in, in her mother's defence.

'That's just an act. I've met him before and I'll never forget his face,' Sarah insisted.

'Neither will I,' said Jane, nudging Julie with an elbow.

'Jane, listen. This is very serious. What have you told him?'

Jane stared at Sarah in silence for a few moments. 'You're serious, aren't you?' Sarah nodded. 'Well, I haven't told him anything he doesn't already know,' she went on defensively, 'only that Mike knows who he is and that the cops are on their tail.'

'Oh Christ,' Sarah said, touching a palm to her forehead. This was a bloody nightmare.

'I haven't done anything wrong, have I?' Jane said, and started biting her thumbnail.

'Did you tell them we were on an overland truck? Who Mike was working for?'

Jane looked at the floor.

'Shit,' Sarah said.

Behind them, Sarah heard the clump of heavy male feet on the staircase. She looked around and saw the legs of two men appearing. She recognised their voices immediately.

'Stay cool,' she whispered hurriedly to Jane and Julie. She fished a baseball cap from her daypack and jammed it on her head. Sarah walked a few paces closer to the staircase, away from Jane and Julie, and turned to face the wall, pretending to look for something else in her pack as she eavesdropped on the men's conversation.

445

'Karl, let's go. Let's board our flights and get out of here,' the Russian said in his heavily accented English. The two men had halted midway down the last flight of stairs. Sarah could hear them clearly, but could not see their faces.

'Vassily, the man knows too much. You are going back to Russia. I live on this continent, remember?'

'What are you suggesting?' the Russian asked.

'I'll get Klaus to round up the men from last night and meet us in Lusaka tomorrow. The man will not get far in that relic of a truck he drives. The woman said the tour group is heading for South Luangwa National Park. They won't make it there tonight and we will catch them on the road tomorrow.'

'And air support?' Orlov was still vacillating, but at the same time he felt a growing sense of electric excitement pulsing through his body.

'I'll call the helicopter pilot again and tell him to stay in Zambia and that the mission is back on again. He doesn't need to know what we're hunting, though.'

'It's a risky plan, Karl.'

Hess laughed out loud. 'Of course it's risky. It's also why you keep coming back, isn't it? It's the ultimate trophy, Vassily, and this one I might let you have!'

There was a moment's silence, as if the Russian were weighing his options one last time. Then Sarah heard the footsteps start again and the men continuing on their way downstairs. She turned as Hess and Orlov passed her, neither man noticing the woman behind them.

The colour had drained from Jane Muir's face, for she, too, had heard their conversation.

'Bye-bye,' Jane said shakily as she brushed past Hess.

Hess stopped, and put a hand on Orlov's forearm to check his pace. The two women from the overlander truck were starting to walk up the stairs again. There was a third woman behind them who had averted her face as she passed the men.

'What is it, Karl?' Orlov asked.

'There's something about her,' Hess said.

'Who?'

'That woman, with the short dark hair.'

'Come, Karl. If we are going to catch that truck we must hurry.'

Hess knew Orlov was right. There were too many loose ends on this job. He could stay and check out the woman who had joined the other two, perhaps learn some more information, or he could get some payback from the man who had ruined this latest safari.

'OK, let's go,' he said to Orlov. 'She's not important.'

'Jane, we've got to do something!' Sarah said, once they were back in the departure hall.

'That was them . . . the killers,' Jane murmured in comprehending horror.

'We've got to get after them,' Sarah said.

'You've got to be joking! Come on, Julie, let's get back upstairs.'

'Jane, help me, we've got to stop them. You heard what they said. They're after Mike. These people don't take prisoners, Jane, they kill all their witnesses!'

'I know, and that's why my daughter and I are getting on that bloody plane as soon as it's called.' Jane led Julie by the hand to the stairway.

Sarah watched them, not knowing what to do. She could call the police, but it would take an hour to explain the whole story to them. Besides, she had no proof that Hess and Orlov had committed a crime.

'Shit!' she said aloud. Then she had an idea. She followed Jane and Julie up the steps, taking them two at a time.

The hall was much fuller now, thronged with passengers waiting for the flight to London. Some of the African women wore brightly coloured traditional wraparound dresses and turbans, others smart casual European clothes. Well-heeled tourists in uniform beige and khaki waddled the length of the hall carrying bulky camera bags, searching for last-minute souvenirs and duty-free gifts. A baby cried noisily, not quite drowning out a group of hard-looking sunburned miners in short sleeves and jeans who were drinking at the bar.

At the end of the crowded hall Sarah saw a payphone on the wall. She bought a phone card from the bar and fished the creased sheet of paper with Mike's contact numbers from her bag. She made the call and tapped impatiently on the wall of the booth while she waited for a connection. At last there was an answer, but her heart sank as she heard Mike's voice on his recorded voice mail message.

'Mike, this is Sarah,' she said. 'Hess and Orlov are coming after you! They haven't left the country. If you get this message call me on . . .' Sarah scanned the information plate mounted above the payphone and then read the number into the mouthpiece.

Dejected, she walked over to a table in the bar area where Jane and Julie Muir had ordered fresh drinks to still their frayed nerves.

'No answer?' Jane asked.

Sarah shook her head.

'Mobile phone reception's crap in this country,' Julie said. 'I haven't had a signal on mine since we left Zimbabwe.'

Sarah tried calling Mike five more times in the ensuing hour, exchanging barely more than a few sentences with the other two women in between calls.

A series of musical chimes from speakers in the ceiling heralded an announcement. 'Good evening, ladies and gentlemen. British Airways would like to welcome all passengers travelling to London Heathrow this evening.'

The female announcer droned on with more information about first and business class passengers and mothers with small children, but Sarah wasn't listening. The time had come for her to make her decision.

She tried Mike's mobile phone once more, but only received the frustrating recorded message. She knew that by tomorrow he would be well and truly out of range of the Lusaka phone towers. The remaining passengers were called to board, and Jane and Julie Muir stood holding their daypacks and shopping bags crammed with duty-free cigarettes and alcohol.

'You're not coming, are you,' said Jane. It was a statement, not a question.

Sarah looked at the boarding pass in her hand and then screwed it up. She shook her head.

'Is he worth it?' Jane asked.

'They'll kill him, and maybe all the others if I can't warn them first,' Sarah said, but she knew what Jane was really asking.

'I can't stay, Sarah. I'm not made for it.'

'Mum, isn't there something we can do to help?' Julie pleaded, switching her gaze from Sarah to her mother.

'No, love, there isn't, I'm afraid. I said it before, I can't put you at risk. Mike knew what he was in for when he agreed to spy on these men. Are you all right for money, Sarah?'

Sarah nodded.

'Right then, we've got to go. Good luck,' Jane said. Two women in the red, white and blue of British Airways were impatiently watching the trio from a desk near the door at the end of the departure lounge.

No hugs or kisses were exchanged, and Sarah gave a little wave. 'Jane,' she said, as the pair were about to disappear through the door which led to a staircase and the airport apron below.

Jane turned around. 'Yes?'

'I think he is . . . Worth it, I mean,' Sarah said.

'Me too. Take care of him, girl,' Jane said, then hurried through the door to catch up with her daughter.

28

After leaving the airport, Mike made a quick stop at a big supermarket just outside Lusaka for provisions and then headed eastwards. Sam sat up front next to him, in Sarah's old seat, and made small talk as the hours droned on. The diesel engine whined and the temperature gauge red-lined as Mike floored the accelerator. He knew he should have stopped somewhere just out of Lusaka, but he wanted to put as much distance between them and the airport as he could.

The tarred road out of Lusaka was in good condition as far as the bridge over the Luangwa River, about two hundred and fifty kilometres to the east, and it was there that they would camp for the night. Mike pulled off the main road and drove down a gravel track to a small camping ground run by a company that organised canoe trips down the Luangwa River to the Zambezi. It was after nine o'clock at night. The passengers were exhausted and subdued now that the excitement of the previous evening had worn off.

Mike was tired too, bone tired. As soon as the tents were up he crawled into his sleeping bag in the back of the truck. He dreamed of Sarah, and of pulling old Patrick from under the nose of the sniper. In his dream he saw the wild flashes of light from Sarah's camera and heard the rattle of Samson's AK-47 as he dragged the wounded ranger through the dust. The dream was vivid and he awoke with a start to see flashes of light illuminating the truck windows. A gunshot echoed outside and he looked around, confused. It took him a couple of seconds to realise he was safe and that a violent electrical storm was raging in the night sky above. There was no rain as yet, just peals of thunder and garish streaks of lightning.

The next morning they set off for the town of Petauke on a steadily deteriorating road.

'The first pothole always takes you by surprise,' Mike said to Sam after the truck jumped like a 747 hitting severe turbulence. 'You slow down a little, getting cautious, but when you haven't seen a pothole for twenty or thirty kilometres you press a little harder on the accelerator, shift up into top again and then, bang, another pothole.'

In some places the road was so bad that drivers had started a track along the dirt verge. Many of these little detours were also potholed, so there was no escape from the suspension-pounding dips.

They were heading into real Zambia now. Away from the bustle of Lusaka and the big commercial farms that lined the road between the capital and Livingstone, there was little sign of wealth or prosperity on the long drive eastwards. Out here people still lived in mud huts with thatched roofs, their only visible wealth a flock of troublesome goats or maybe a few scrawny cattle. The vehicles, when they saw one, tended to be thirty- and forty-year-old Land Rovers held together with fencing wire and prayer.

'Mostly, people get from point A to point B on foot and wherever you drive in this part of the country, at whatever time of day, you are guaranteed of seeing people walking on the side of the road,' Mike said. He pointed out a woman on the roadside with a twenty-litre water container balanced on her turbaned head and three tiny children in tow. 'It's a damned nuisance when you need to stop and find somewhere private to go to the toilet.' On several occasions he swerved violently to miss goats and cows, but after a while he was driving like a local, honking the horn, planting his foot and praying the livestock scattered.

Petauke itself was a ramshackle collection of markets and trading stores, old colonial administration buildings, a couple of banks and a service station or two. Mike thought the town was simply there because it had to be there. A traveller could only go so many hundreds of kilometres before he or she needed somewhere to shop, to barter, to drink, to screw or to be screwed by bureaucrats. There were patches of colour here and there. Local women on their big shopping day out clad in bright floral wraps, and a travelling theatre troupe performing a noisy musical play on the back of a truck.

'What's the play about?' George asked.

Mike answered, 'Toothpaste. Although most people out here don't have a radio, let alone television or even electricity, advertising companies will always find a way to get their message across.'

They stopped for Cokes at a shop that seemed to sell nothing but soft drinks and oversized skin-toned bras that only a grandmother would wear. The grizzled old grey-haired storekeeper insisted they consume their soft drinks on the spot because he didn't want to risk losing his empty bottles. Mike's bottle had been cleaned and reused and shipped so many times the glass was frosted with scratches, but the Coke tasted good.

Mike sat on the concrete step of the shop and lit a cigarette. He wished again that Sarah was there to share the trip with him. At least Hess and Orlov were off their tail, he told himself, and while that should have been a relief to him he still felt strangely uneasy.

Kylie and Mel wandered off towards the market, cameras in hand, but Mike wasn't interested. From his experience of Zambian markets he knew they wouldn't find much more than a few undersized tomatoes, bald tyres and more enormous bras. The rest of the group gathered around him as he laid a map out on the step.

'The highway continues east to the border with Malawi,' he said, tracing the line of the route they had been following from Lusaka. 'I'm sorry to say, the road doesn't get any better along the way.'

Linda groaned and said, 'Those potholes are murder on my bum. I think I've done myself serious spinal damage!'

'Massage?' Terry queried.

'Bite me,' Linda replied.

454

'What I suggest is that we take this short cut,' Mike said, pointing to the unsealed road that branched off from where they were, running north-east to South Luangwa National Park. 'It won't be a comfortable ride, and it won't be a fast one, but it should be fun.'

'Fun?' said Mel, her eyes bright and white in her dark face. 'Fun, as in the other night, with blokes shooting at us and all?'

'The Petauke Road is not much more than a dirt track over bad terrain, through thick bush. I've only ever heard of one other overland truck making it through, and that was a Bedford, just like ours,' he said, looking for a reaction from the group.

'Brilliant,' said George. 'Like trailblazers – sort of.'

'Sort of. The views when we get to the other side of this ridgeline and start our descent into the Luangwa valley again are superb, and we might see some game on the way. It's a part of Africa more primitive and inaccessible than any other we're likely to see on the trip.'

'I'm up for it,' said Terry.

'Me too,' said Mel, hesitantly.

'Have we got enough fuel, enough supplies?' asked Kylie.

'Yes. Nigel, what do you think?' Mike asked.

'I didn't come here for air-conditioned comfort,' Nigel said with a breaking grin.

'Go for it,' Sam said.

The rain started as soon as they boarded the truck and Mike almost turned around then and there. The sky had been dark all morning and they had heard thunder in the distance, but Mike had expected a few more days of rainless electrical storms before the deluge began in earnest. He was wrong. The rain engulfed them like a hot, wet blanket. In the back, the crew rolled down the furled clear plastic windows and lashed them shut. This made the rear cab hotter than ever. Mike knew it would not be pleasant when they started to bump and slide up and down the coming hills.

Nelson's tiny windscreen wipers were next to useless at shifting the waves of water from the glass in front of him. Mike rolled down his window to stop the windscreen fogging up, and his right side became drenched as a result.

The first stretch of road wasn't too bad, as they started the long climb from Petauke up into the mountains. The road surface was good: wide, graded dirt, with only a few potholes. However, it steadily deteriorated. The surface became rutted and the corrugations deepened to rivulets with the sudden onset of the storm.

As they got farther from the town, the foliage on either side of the road started to thicken and they saw fewer goats, cows and people. Soon it seemed as if the bush was gradually closing its bristling green jaws around them, swallowing their vehicle. Leaves and twigs brushed the sides and top of the high rear cab. Mike didn't tell his crew, but he'd heard that the passengers in the other Bedford that had made this same trip had to get out and cut the bush away on the sides of the road in order to pass.

He felt the wheel spin in slick mud a couple of times as they chugged up steep slopes or rounded tight bends. Mike had the Bedford in four-wheel drive, however, and he was reasonably confident they wouldn't get bogged if he could keep the momentum up.

They crested a high ridge in first gear, so high and steep, in fact, that someone had actually laid a hundred metres or so of concrete in two narrow, parallel ribbons over the peak on both sides. The concrete gave them the traction they needed to struggle over the top of the hill, but once on the other side the truck started to slide left and right as the strip road ran out. Mike wrestled with the steering wheel and Sam gripped the dashboard in front of him.

'Put your seatbelt on!' Mike barked as he wiped furiously at the fogged windscreen. 'Everybody hang on!' he yelled into the back of the cab as they fishtailed down the hill. He tried hard not to overcorrect, but at times the steering wheel was spinning so hard and fast it would have snapped his wrist if his hand had been caught inside it.

As the slope started to bottom out Mike regained some control. His arms ached with the effort of steering, but they were not even halfway through the trying journey. He wiped the windscreen again. 'Shit,' he said, as the bubbling mass of dirty brown water came into view. At the bottom of the valley, a dry riverbed had come alive in a flash flood. The Bedford was picking up speed now and he knew that if he slammed on the brakes, they could end up sliding sideways into the river.

'Fuck it,' he said to himself, and put his foot down. The truck ploughed into the river. Someone yelped in the back as twin rooster-tails of water gushed up alongside them.

'All right! You can do it. Gun it, man!' Sam said, thumping the dashboard.

The water nearly reached the top of the truck's wheels and Mike could feel the force of it trying to push them sideways. He shifted down and revved the engine hard and Nelson forged ahead, fighting the force of the water, its wheels occasionally slipping on wet rock or sand.

'Look out – tree!' Sam shouted, and Mike glanced to the left. A broken branch, maybe five metres long and as thick as a man's leg, was careening down the river towards them. Momentum is everything in a river crossing, he knew. He could have hit the brakes, but if he did they might get bogged mid-river or even swept away.

Mike kept the pressure on the accelerator and gripped the wheel hard, bracing his arms for the impact. The branch slammed hard into the left front mudguard, just in front of Sam's door, and then bounced along the side of the truck as they continued on. Mike heard a screeching noise and felt the steering wobble.

At last they forded the river and rolled up onto the far stony bank, water gushing from a hundred pockets under the chassis. 'Everyone all right?' Mike called into the back.

There was a chorus of exultant hoots and people were laughing with relief. Mike knew, however, that there would probably be more close calls. Instead of rising again, the track stayed flat as they crossed a narrow flood plain that in all likelihood would soon be flooded. Rushes and thickets of tall grass brushed the side of the truck and Mike could feel the wheels starting to slip again.

They began to slow down, though not because he had eased his foot from the accelerator. 'No, baby, no!' he said to the truck. They were slowly sinking as the big wheels tore twin gashes deeper and deeper into the sludge of the flood plain. Instinctively, stupidly, he floored the accelerator, but that only lessened what little traction they were getting and, eventually, they stopped.

'Unscheduled pit stop, folks,' Mike called into the back cab. The cheers of a few moments before turned into groans.

The rain had eased, but it was still falling steadily. Mike opened the door and jumped down from the cab. His feet immediately sank past the ankles into a molasses of cloying, wet black-cotton soil. His shirt was drenched within moments and he wiped running rainwater from his eyes.

The situation was bad. The truck was stuck fast in the evil-smelling muck, right up to the axles. Nelson creaked and rocked as the passengers jumped down for a look. Mike trudged slowly around to the passenger side of the driver's cab, the mud sucking at his sandals and almost pulling them off with each step. The left-hand panel around the wheel arch had taken a direct hit from the floating log and the buckled metal was now rubbing against the tyre. The rubber was scored where the metal had come into contact with it and Mike knew the tyre would blow if they didn't fix the damage soon. But first they had to get out of the mud.

Mike took off his mud-caked sandals and tossed them inside the cab. He walked to the back of the truck and opened the tool stowage area. 'Any volunteers?' he asked. All of them said yes or nodded, which pleased him. He handed out his store of tools.

'Nigel, take the bow saw and the axe up there to the tree line, and cut as many logs and branches as you can, not too big, but no twigs, OK?' The trees started about a hundred and fifty metres away, where the land started to rise out of the flood plain.

'Terry, George, you two and I have got some digging to do – around the wheels and in front of them, where we'll lay the wood for traction. Sam, you can spell us on the shovels, and in the meantime get a crowbar on that bent panel and see if you can bend it back off the tyre. Right, let's get to work!'

'What about us?' Linda asked, hands on hips and green eyes glaring as she stepped in front of Mike to block his path. Behind her were Mel and Kylie.

'Mel, go with Nigel and carry back the wood he cuts.' It would be heavy work and hot, even with the rain, but Nigel would be dog-tired and blistered after an hour's wood chopping.

'I'll take that, shall I?' Linda said as she snatched a shovel from Terry and plunged the head hard into the mud in front of a rear tyre. Her green tank top was plastered to her skin and her hair hung in a wet ponytail on her back. The muscles in her slender arms stood out as she heaved a clod of earth up and over her shoulder.

Mike realised Linda was in excellent physical shape – much better shape than the overweight Englishman he had assigned the job to.

'Terry, get the gas cooker out of the back and get a brew going, please,' Mike said.

'What about me?' Kylie asked.

'You're our doc, Kylie. Get the first aid kit out and keep it somewhere handy and dry. I want everyone to take it easy, and be careful and keep their wits about them. Also, Kylie, I'd like you to sit up on the roof and keep a lookout over that adrenaline grass,' Mike said, gesturing at the high brown grass that stretched away on either side of the truck. 'Take an umbrella up with you.'

'Why do you call it "adrenaline grass"?' Kylie asked.

'Because there are lots of things that hide in there that get your adrenaline going if you bump into them.' They were still a good seventy kilometres from South Luangwa National Park, but there was no fence around the park and animals don't recognise lines on a map. The grass could have been hiding elephants, buffalos, maybe even grazing hippos or the odd big cat. 'Let's get to work, people!'

It took them the best part of an hour to dig out the mud from around the bogged wheels and to lay the fresh-cut green logs in front of them. As Mike had predicted, Nigel's hands were red-raw with blisters from the saw. Mel's bare arms were chafed from carrying the logs and her hands pockmarked with splinters. Linda and George sat side by side in the mud at the side of the track, oblivious to discomfort and rain. They compared blisters and strained muscles as they drank steaming tea. Terry was spattered with mud from his spell on the shovel. Kylie was bandaging Sam's left hand where he had cut it on a jagged piece of the truck's front guard.

Timber cracked and splintered as Mike started the engine and the wet, muddy tyres struggled to find purchase on the branches. Nelson strained at the mud's grip and, ever so slowly, started to inch up the crude wooden ramp. The logs had not been as thick as Mike would have liked, but he had not chastised Nigel, who had worked as hard as anyone else. Nelson crawled along, up and out of the mud, but Mike could feel the smaller branches starting to give. He increased the speed a little, but he felt the wheels starting to spin again.

'No!' Linda cried in horror as Nelson's rear started to slide. The land had dipped slightly again where the track crossed a shallower watercourse, yet to be flooded. Here the ground was even softer than before and Mike tasted bitter bile in his mouth as he felt the Bedford's big wheels spinning in place. The small logs could not hold the weight and cracked as Nelson sank again.

Mel started to cry, and Linda walked over and put her arms around her. Sam turned away angrily and picked up a shovel. He started to dig the churned mud from under a rear wheel.

Nigel spat on his hands and rubbed them together.

'Who's for more tea?' asked Terry from the back of the truck.

Mike laughed and took up another shovel. 'Let's get dirty again.'

Mike checked his watch and had to hold it close to his face to see the time. Condensation beaded the inside of the glass, thanks to the humidity and constant rain. It was after four. He had thought they might have completed the track by early evening, but there was no chance now. They would have to camp somewhere in the bush.

Bush camping, he knew, was not the safest activity in Africa, given the widespread crime problem in most of the continent, but in remote areas like the Petauke Road it was sometimes the only option. They hadn't passed a village for more than twenty kilometres and Mike doubted they would come across another for at least the same distance in the direction they were heading. Besides, everyone, including him, would be in need of a rest as soon as they were clear of the mud.

'Crocodile!' Kylie screamed from her vantage point on the roof. Those of them near the truck turned to stare in the direction she was pointing. 'There, look, coming out of the river. It's enormous!'

The crocodile was walking slowly up the muddy bank, very close to where they were stuck. His beady eyes blinked at the sound of Kylie's voice and he stopped and lifted his broad snout a little to sniff the air. He looked like what he was, one of nature's perfect killers – green-brown camouflage skin, wicked yellow teeth and a tail that would knock a grown man down with one flick.

The crocodile turned away from the road and the truck, and sauntered off into the high adrenaline grass. 'They leave the rivers when there's a flood on the way, same as the hippos,' Mike explained to Terry and George, who were standing nearby, leaning on their shovels.

Mike thrust the blade of his shovel into the mud, but stopped at the sound of vehicle engines and turned back to the direction they had come from. Two late-model Land Rovers, one white and one red, were crossing the swollen river, which now threatened to fill the first churned hollow they had just freed Nelson from. The trucks had South African plates and each sported a heavy-duty aluminium roof-rack with a folded roof-top tent, green plastic cargo boxes and bright-blue gas bottles. Seeing the mess in the road and the bogged Bedford, the driver of the lead vehicle swerved boldly into the adrenaline grass as he cleared the river, forging a new road alongside the rutted track, a tactic Mike wished he had tried in the first place.

'Hey, man, looks like you're stuck!' a middle-aged man with blond hair and beard, a rugby forward's bulk and a thick Afrikaans accent said with a grin.

Mike resisted the urge to hit him with his shovel and smiled instead.

'Need a hand?' the man offered.

Mike doubted the Land Rover could pull the Bedford free because the truck was too heavy, and he explained as much. 'Where are you headed?' Mike asked as an afterthought.

'Flatdogs. You know it?'

Mike nodded. A flatdog is African slang for a crocodile and Mike knew the camp of the same name was a popular spot for travellers. The camp was located on the banks of the South Luangwa River, at the entrance to the national park.

'I'd appreciate it if you'd tell them at the camp that we're on our way. We should be there by tomorrow evening,' Mike said. At least that way if something else went wrong and they didn't show up, the authorities would know where to look for them.

'No problem, *boet*,' the South African said, using the word for 'brother' in his own language. 'I'll mark your position here, just in case you can't get out, and give it to the camp staff.' He reached across to a GPS unit mounted on the dashboard of his Land Rover, between him and an equally bulky redheaded woman, and punched some buttons with a meaty finger. 'Done,' he added with finality.

'Thanks, mate,' Mike said. 'Tell them we'll make camp on the first high ground we come to on this side of the river.'

'Good luck, man,' the South African said.

Tired and sore, the rest of the team managed only limp waves as the two Land Rovers trundled off on their way. Mike cast another look at the river, which was still swelling. They would have to be quick.

465

29

Sarah Thatcher slammed her palm down on the steering wheel of the rented Mitsubishi Pajero hard enough to hurt her hand. 'Shit!' she said as she took another glance at the map of Zambia spread out on the empty passenger seat. She looked up and swerved hard to miss a tree branch that had fallen across the slick muddy track. The rear of the white four-wheel drive slewed drunkenly. She got the vehicle back on track, and risked taking one hand off the steering wheel to fish for the cigarettes and matches in her daypack.

For the twentieth time in as many minutes she wondered if she had taken the wrong road. Standing in the rain at a service station in Petauke she had studied the map and remembered one of the last things Mike had said to her before he kissed her goodbye. It was something about watching out and taking the back roads. There was only one back road between Lusaka and South Luangwa National Park, and that was the dirt road heading north-east from

Petauke. On the màp it looked fine, almost like a short cut, but no road Sarah had ever driven in her life had prepared her for what she had experienced in the previous few hours.

After trying Mike's mobile phone from her room at the Holiday Inn over and over again with no reply, she'd finally called reception and asked for the numbers and addresses of nearby car rental companies. Before leaving the hotel she also phoned Nicholas, at *The Times*.

'Where are you? Heathrow or Gatwick?' he had asked. 'The line's shocking.'

'Africa,' she said.

He had been furious when he learned the truth. Sarah had managed to placate him by explaining the reason for the delay and hinting at the possibility of a second run-in with the poachers.

'They could be after the tour guide and everyone in the truck, Nicholas. These people have a reputation for killing witnesses.' Even as she spoke the words she regretted them, and felt sick with fear and shame that she might somehow capitalise on the danger faced by people she had come to care for. 'The story isn't over, Nicholas.'

There was a long pause at the other end of the crackling international line. 'All right,' he said at last, and she could picture him scratching his weak, hairless chin, the way he always did when he was pissed off, 'I'll cover for you. But if you don't come up with something better than the feature we *already* had you set up to write, you can kiss a job here goodbye – no matter what there was between us in the past.'

Sarah bit her lip to stifle the reply that almost sprang to her lips. There had been nothing between her and Nicholas, but he obviously remembered their relationship differently. She hated to think she had sold her story on the basis of a failed affair, and Nicholas's remark only made her more determined to deliver an even bigger scoop than she already had.

She had telephoned the police in Lusaka, but they had insisted that unless she wanted to report a crime there was nothing they could do.

'But these men shot at my friend in a national park!' she said tersely to the policeman on the phone.

'Which national park?'

'Matusadona. They were trying to kill a rhino.'

'Ah, but madam, Matusadona is in Zimbabwe, not Zambia,' the policeman had said.

Sarah had slammed the phone down in its cradle. She did not have a number for Mike's police contact, Theron, and, although she considered calling the South African Police, she had no idea what part of the force the detective worked in.

The rain blotted out the afternoon sun and the thick, dripping bush on either side of the road made the muddy track even gloomier. She found the headlight switch and flicked the lights on, but all that did was illuminate the curtain of pouring rain that shrouded the vehicle. She had breakfasted at the hotel and bought a chicken pie for lunch at a service station in Petauke town, and the only food and drink she had with her in the car was three under-ripe bananas and half a litre of tepid drinking water. She realised she was woefully under-equipped to spend a night in the African bush.

Black diesel smoke belched from the back of the four-wheel drive as she geared down and floored the accelerator to climb a steep hill. Suddenly the wheels hit solid ground, a pleasant surprise after kilometres of treacherous mud. Through the rain she could make out twin ribbons of concrete passing beneath the tyres. 'That's more like it,' she said to herself, although the smile on her face quickly returned to a hard-set grimace as she coasted over the hill and saw the concrete tracks disappear into the mud.

Looking down into the valley she saw a fast-flowing muddy river bisecting a flat plain of long grass. On the far side of the grass a flash of colour caught her eye, then the Pajero passed under the low branch of a leafy tree and she lost sight of the bright object. Cursing, she stopped the four-wheel drive in a long wet skid when the view into the valley cleared again. She rubbed the misty windscreen with a tissue plucked from the courtesy box in the console between the seats, and stared hard.

There, partially obscured by long grass, was the unmistakable garish yellow of Nelson. 'Oh God, hold on!' she cried. She released the handbrake and gunned the engine and the Pajero lurched forward like an ungainly child on new ice skates. Sarah wrestled with the steering wheel. Her vehicle was almost broadside to the road and she was scared it was about to roll, as the angle of her descent became steeper. She took her foot off the accelerator and let go of the wheel momentarily, knowing she could not straighten the vehicle by trying to overcorrect. The Pajero slowed and nosed into some bushes at the side of the track. She reversed and turned the nose back down the road, and resisted the urge to accelerate.

She could see people, three or four at the back of the yellow truck. They were holding their arms high now, tools in hand, as if in celebration. The Bedford started to move forward, gradually disappearing into the long grass. 'No, no, no!' she yelled as the Pajero careened down the hill. She felt the hill start to bottom out, and the truck slowed as the cloying mud became softer and softer. She switched the transfer lever into low-range four-wheel drive to increase its traction and plunged on towards the swollen brown river. Down low she could see, in the distance, that the truck had stopped just short of where the trees started again, and the last of the people were climbing aboard. She stabbed the vehicle's horn, but doubted it would be heard over the noise of the fast-flowing river and the rain.

Water cascaded over the bonnet of the Pajero as Sarah stood on the accelerator and entered the river. She gasped with alarm as she felt a cool wetness on her foot. Water was seeping into the cab from around the door seals. Still she leaned on the horn, but the truck was almost completely out of sight and showed no sign of stopping.

Sarah was nearly halfway across the river when the engine started to cough and chug. 'Come on! Come on!' she willed the vehicle. The engine shuddered sickeningly then died. The Pajero came to a halt in the middle of the raging river.

'Mike!' Sarah screamed uselessly as the truck finally vanished into the thick trees ahead. Something bounced off the side of the Pajero with a loud clang and Sarah willed herself to calm down and think. She tried the engine again and again, but there was only the painful screech of the starter motor.

The Pajero rocked with the force of the raging river and Sarah looked down to see water over her ankles. She curled her legs under her and knelt on the driver's seat, still sounding the horn. She could swim, though not strongly, and she debated with herself whether she would be safer staying with the vehicle or trying to reach the far shore. After weighing the options she decided to stay inside the vehicle, and that as long as there was no danger of the Pajero being washed away this was the safest spot for her to await rescue.

There was a creaking, grating noise beneath her and the four-wheel drive started to slide sideways.

Spirits were high in the truck as Mike drove up the incline away from the river and its boggy bank. He was only mildly annoyed when Nigel called out for him to stop.

'Sorry, Mike, but I think I left my shovel back in the mud when we got on board,' he said, poking his head into the driver's cab.

They were all soaked and filthy and those with tools had simply thrown them into the passenger cab in their eagerness to get moving again, away from the cloying mud. The cab floor was slick and stinking with the ooze and its cargo of decaying plant and animal matter.

'OK, Nigel,' he said, 'out you get, and be quick about it. I can't drive back, in case we get stuck again.'

Nigel nodded and leapt down from the truck. Mike shook a wilting cigarette from the crumpled pack in his damp shirt pocket and after several attempts managed to light it. The smoke flowed grudgingly into his lungs as he watched Nigel in the wing mirror, running down the track. He closed his eyes for a moment and savoured the feeling of sore hands, tired muscles and nicotine. He felt like he was twenty again, back in the army.

When he opened his eyes a couple of seconds later he could just make out Nigel. He had stopped in the track, facing away from the truck. He was waving his hands over his head, but at what Mike couldn't make out.

'Jesus Christ, what now?' he muttered. Mike watched the reflection for a couple more seconds and then saw Nigel turn and start running back towards the truck, empty-handed. Mike stubbed out the cigarette in the truck's ashtray, opened the door and jumped down.

'Mike!' Nigel screamed as he ran.

Mike took a few paces towards him.

'It's Sarah!'

Mike was running now, and as they met, the words sprayed from Nigel in excited gasps.

'Stuck in the middle of the river . . . her car's starting to slide . . . we've got to get her!'

'Get the tow ropes out of the locker in the back. And bring everybody else. Hurry!' Mike ordered.

Mike ran as fast as he could in the sucking mud,

losing a sandal on the way and nearly falling twice. He was gasping for air as he reached the water's edge. There was a white Pajero in the middle of the river, turned at an angle three-quarters to the direction of the roadway. It was stalled and starting to slide. Sarah sat on the sill of the open passenger side window. She was soaking wet. Her hands were on the roof of the vehicle, constantly slipping as she tried to find purchase on the polished metal. 'Hang on!' Mike called.

He looked over his shoulder and saw everyone from the truck running down the hill. Nigel and Terry, who had started out on the trip as enemies, were side by side, joining the metal snap hooks of Nelson's two yellow nylon tow ropes together to make one long line as they ran.

'Mike, it's moving!' Sarah yelled, as the force of the churning water pushed the Pajero's nose even further around. The stricken vehicle was almost facing downriver.

'Give me that,' Mike said to Terry and took the free end of the tow rope. He wrapped it over one shoulder and under the other arm, and fixed the snap hook onto the rope. He shrugged off his other sandal and ran as far upstream from the submerged crossing as the rope would allow. He charged at the river and dived in.

The water was colder than he expected and the current snatched viciously at his body as he struck out overarm towards the Pajero. Mike struggled to keep his head out of the filthy water, but the speed of the river and a fierce undertow dragged him down after every few strokes. He watched, enraged, as he was pulled downstream past the Pajero, still fifteen metres short of Sarah. He rolled onto his back to conserve his strength and waved one arm.

'Pull me in!' Mike hollered, and felt the rope tighten painfully around him as Nigel, Terry, George and, eventually, all the other members of the crew started pulling. He waded out of the river as his feet touched the muddy bottom.

'No good,' Mike said, bending, hands on knees as he spat out foul water. 'Let's go further upstream. Run down with me as I swim across, OK?' There were nods all around and they jogged along the river bank.

'Hurry!' Sarah cried.

Again Mike dived into the torrent and struck out hard. The crew – his lifeline – ran down the bank, playing out the rope. This time they had the angle of interception right and he could see the Pajero in front of him. He was going to make it.

Suddenly, he felt the rope go tight, pulling him to a halt. He glanced quickly over his shoulder. Sam was gesticulating madly at the river and Mike realised with dread that the rope was too short. The current had him now and he was hurtling downriver. He turned to face upstream and struck until his arms felt like they were about to fall out of their sockets. He was breathing so hard that he took in a mouthful of brown water in every few breaths. He was about to stop, give up and let the current take him back downstream, where he could be retrieved, when he felt the line slacken again.

Mike looked over to the bank and saw that all of the crew had linked arms and were wading into the river. Terry, the heaviest by far, was the anchor man, his legs wide apart and his feet planted as far as he could thrust them into the soft mud. At the end of the human chain was the lightest of the women, Linda. She had looped the other end of the rope around her body the same as he had. The human chain had given them the extra reach they needed to get to Sarah, but Mike knew it would take a hard toll on all their bodies once he had Sarah in his arms.

He swam towards the Pajero again, summoning his last reserves of strength. He was within an arm's length of the four-wheel drive when it lurched and violently slid downstream.

'Jump!' he yelled. Mike stopped swimming, and let the current fling him towards Sarah and the slipping vehicle. Sarah lifted a foot to the windowsill and pro-pelled herself out towards him. At that moment the Pajero bobbed up as it came free of the underwater ford and was snatched away by the river like a piece of driftwood.

Sarah's arms flailed as she tried to reach Mike and he swam hard, with the current this time. He smashed into her with the force of a breaking wave, knocking her underwater as he reached for her. Mike grabbed the lapel of Sarah's shirt and heaved her head above the surface. Water streamed from her mouth and nose, but she was alive and breathing. She wrapped her arms around him and he felt the tow rope bite into his flesh as it was pulled tight.

Mike held Sarah in a lifesaver's grip, one hand under her chin to keep her head above water as he paddled with his free arm. He looked up at the bank and saw faces straining as the human chain was dragged down-stream with the weight of two people on the end of the line. The girls at the end of the chain were sitting or kneeling in surging water up to their necks. Linda's face was red, her mouth open and contorted with pain as the rope cut into her slim, wiry body. Mike flailed for the shoreline, to relieve the strain on the others as quickly as possible. Sarah kicked her legs hard, which helped them inch towards shore.

Mike's feet touched bottom and he dragged Sarah to a point where she could finally stand. The water was still at his chest and her neck, but the pull was less now as they had swung around into the lee of a small spit of land, which had not yet been sub-merged. He felt relief as the lifeline around him went slack again.

The rest of the team gathered around them, Nigel and Terry supporting Linda, who had taken the strain of the tow rope biting into her body as they pulled Sarah and Mike into shore.

Sarah's hand was in Mike's as they waded ashore. Once on land he took her other hand and looked into her eyes. 'What are you doing here?' he asked.

She coughed, then said, 'I had to warn you. Hess and Orlov . . . they're on their way. They're looking for you.'

Mike was shocked, but also amazed, proud and touched that she had made it through to warn them. He pulled her close and wrapped his arms around her.

'I'm scared, Mike,' she whispered as she buried her face in his chest.

30

'They're coming. The poachers. They're look-ing for Mike,' Sarah said to the circle of people surrounding her. Her hands were wrapped around a steaming hot mug of tea and a sleeping bag was draped about her shoulders. She had changed into one of Mel's sweatshirts and a pair of Linda's tracksuit pants.

As chilling as the news that she brought was, it lifted Mike's heart to see her again. Sarah had already told him, as they drove up the track looking for a campsite for the night, about how she had overheard Hess and Orlov at Lusaka airport. He marvelled again at her bravery and her decision to abandon her flight to come and find him. He guessed that part of the reason she had turned back was because she was a reporter in search of a grand finale to a good story, but he also knew it would have been very easy for her to cut and run with what she already had.

With the news that the poachers were on their trail he had selected a campsite not only for its ease of access, but also for its tactical advantages. He had stopped just below the crest of a hill, on a fairly level area that might have once been a stores dump or truck parking place when the track was first cut through the virgin bush. The level patch was set back about fifty metres from the road and surrounded on three sides by tall trees. The once-cleared land was now covered with low scrubby trees that grew to about the height of a man's chest, interspersed with waist-high grass. Mike had knocked a path through the bush with Nelson and they then cut down just enough saplings to make a cosy clear patch.

As soon as the campsite was set up George and Terry made a fire, mostly using dry charcoal from one of the bags Mike kept in the truck. The fire was warm and glowing, but didn't give off much smoke once the charcoal was alight – another advantage if someone was tracking them.

Mike wanted everyone to know exactly what Sarah had learned. His days of keeping secrets from the people around him, people who depended on him and who had just saved his life, were over. As she sipped her tea, Sarah relayed everything she had told Mike to the rest of the group.

'What do you mean, "they're looking for Mike", Sarah?' Linda asked.

'I mean they want to kill him,' Sarah said. 'These people do not like witnesses. Isn't that right, Mike?'

It sounded like a melodramatic summation, but it was a true one. Mike nodded.

'Well, it's not like any of us can just pack up and leave, is it?' Mel said.

'Not yet, anyway,' Mike said. 'But as soon as we get to Mfuwe, near South Luangwa National Park, everyone is flying out. No arguments this time. I'm not going to risk anyone's life on this trip.'

'So what happens between now and then?' Kylie asked, rubbing tired eyes. The sun was setting behind the clouds and it would be dark in a matter of minutes.

Mike stood and, while there was still light, kicked some grass aside to make a clear patch on the ground. He took a stout stick and sketched a crude map of the triangle made by the main road from Petauke to Chipata; the road from Chipata up to Mfuwe; and the long side of the triangle, the track they were on from Petauke to Mfuwe.

'The bad guys have probably stuck to the main road, via Chipata, and are possibly in Mfuwe already. They'll have been looking for us and asking about us as they drove. There aren't that many towns and service stations on the way and Mfuwe itself is nothing more than a couple of shops, half-a-dozen goats and a petrol pump. They'll soon know we haven't arrived.' Mike paused and sipped on his mug of steaming coffee.

He continued. 'What they'll do then is have a look at the map and work out that we've taken this road, through the bush, from Petauke. They can either wait for us in Mfuwe, or come looking for us.'

There was silence in the circle of faces around him. Silence and fear.

Mike remembered the South African tourists in the Land Rovers. They had taken a GPS reading of the place where the truck had been bogged. With so few vehicles taking the long, arduous track from Petauke there was a chance Hess and Orlov would meet them. Mike didn't voice his fears to the others. They were scared enough.

'Our advantage,' Mike said with as much force and assurance as he could muster, 'is that we have a pretty good idea where they are, we'll be able to see them coming, and we can get ready for them.'

'Can't we turn around and go back to Lusaka? Surely we'd be safer there?' Nigel ventured.

'We would, if we could make it back across that river behind us. There's no way now we can cross until the river drops, and that could be a day or two. We're closer to Mfuwe than we are to Petauke and Lusaka and, as I said, the closest airport's at Mfuwe.'

'What about pushing on to Mfuwe now, Mike, tonight?' George asked.

It was a valid question. 'I've thought about that, but we just can't risk any more river crossings in the dark. Besides, if we can't cross a river to get out, Hess and Orlov can't cross a river to get to us. We wait until morning and travel then.'

'So we stand and fight,' Sam said.

'Let's hope it won't come to that,' Mike said, looking at each of their faces. 'But in case it does, this is how we'll be ready for them.'

The last job of the night, for it was pitch-black and nearly ten o'clock by the time they had finished the preparations around the campsite, was to set up an

OP – an observation post. Also, Mike wanted to arrange a welcoming present for their expected guests.

Everyone else would sleep together, but two people would have to be their eyes and ears, keeping watch on the most likely avenue of the enemy's approach. Mike picked George and Terry to man the OP, mainly because he remembered George saying he was a soldier in the Territorial Army, Britain's reserve military force. Weekend army training was better than no army training for the job he needed George to do.

He led them through the bush, to the crest of the hill above the campsite, and over the other side. They walked downhill for a while, Mike in the lead holding back springy branches and pointing out burrows and other holes in the ground so nobody got a whack in the face or twisted an ankle. Mike carried the axe over his shoulder and had a machete in a scabbard attached to an old army web belt around his waist. He kept the machete for clearing grass around camping sites and for protection against invading snakes. In addition, he had the Browning stuffed in the waistband of his shorts and the box of spare ammo in his shirt pocket. He thought he must have looked like a bedraggled pirate, but no one was laughing. Terry carried the bow saw.

'What do you do in the Territorial Army, George?' Mike asked softly. He didn't think there was anybody out in the bush listening, but he wanted the two young men to get used to whispering from now on.

'I'm in the Parachute Regiment,' George said.

'I'm impressed. What's your rank?'

'Private,' he said, stepping over a fallen log Mike had just pointed out to him.

'Rifleman, medic, machine-gunner?'

'Cook,' George whispered.

Mike stopped, and George nearly bumped into him. 'A *cook*?'

'Yes, a cook.'

'Is this a joke?'

'No,' he said defensively, 'I'm a chef.'

'I thought you said you were a lorry driver?' Mike said.

'I am, in my civilian job. I'm trying to get a job as a chef, but until then the TA's the only chance I get to do what I really love.'

'But you *are* a para, right? You did P Company, right?'

'Yes. Of course I did. We all have to do P Company to get our wings. And infantry training, so I do know what I'm doing, OK?'

Mike believed him. P Company was the British Army's gruelling training course for would-be paratroopers. It involves long-distance running and marching with brutally heavy packs and weapons, punishing obstacle courses and navigation exercises. There is a high drop-out rate, making those who get through some of the toughest soldiers in the world – including the cooks. Mike knew enough about the course to respect anyone who had passed it.

He put a hand on George's shoulder. 'Think back to your basic infantry training, George. Try and remember everything you were taught.'

Mike had been out for a walk earlier in the evening

482

by himself to reconnoitre the surrounding area, and he pointed out to George and Terry the position he had chosen for the OP. It was two large trees, leadwoods, growing close together. The trees were set back a few metres from the road. From their base there was good visibility down the hill where the track crossed a small creek and then rose again to a lower hill across the valley. The trees were taller than any in the immediate area and Mike would be able to pick out the position from the crest of the hill that the rest of the group were sheltered behind.

Before setting up the OP, though, he led Terry and George to the bottom of the hill and halfway up the side of the opposite knoll. They walked along the edge of the track.

'This should do it,' Mike said, slapping the trunk of a tall tree at the edge of the road. Its trunk was about two feet in diameter. He spat on his hands, hefted the axe and cut a notch on the side of the tree closest to the road. 'Terry, you start on the other side with the saw. George, take a walk up the road to the top of the hill and keep watch for vehicles or people.'

Mike figured that at this time of night it was unlikely there would be any legitimate traffic on such a treacherous, isolated road. By blocking it he might buy them some time if Hess and Orlov did show up. It would take the poachers time and energy to find the overlander, although Mike didn't believe they could hide from them completely. At the very least, they would be hot and tired by the time they climbed the steep hill and discovered the camp. Also, by then the boys in the OP would have had a chance to get a good look at them and report back on their numbers and weapons.

Mike was sweating heavily when the tree at last began to creak. They stood back as it crashed across the muddy road. He gave a low whistle and a couple of minutes later George was back with them. George took the lead on the walk back up the hill to the lonely place where he and Terry would spend most of the night. Mike brought up the rear, dragging a leafy branch from the fallen tree behind him to obscure their tracks.

'You stay as a pair and you never leave your buddy, OK, Terry?' Mike whispered as they crouched at the base of the twin trees. The big man looked nervous. They were all soaking wet, but he could still make out beads of perspiration on Terry's forehead. 'If you have to shit or piss you do it here, and you bury it. OK, now cam up.'

Camming up, as Mike explained to Terry, was slang for 'personal camouflage'. George was already thinking about concealment. He had worn a green T-shirt and dark grey shorts and had borrowed a black baseball cap from one of the girls to hide his bright ginger hair. He'd organised for Terry to wear green and khaki as well – everyone on the trip carried neutral-coloured clothing in case they went on an organised walk in one of the national parks. They had been warned that whites and bright colours that draw attention to the wearer are dangerous around wild animals. George took a lump of charcoal he had selected from the camp fuel supply and rubbed black smears on his friend's pasty white face. He then did the backs of his own hands and made Terry blacken his face for him.

'Remember what I said before,' Mike said, and they both nodded, their faces now blackened like commandos. He repeated his instructions anyway. 'I need to know how many of them there are and what weapons they're carrying. George, you should be able to identify their guns. Pay attention to how they are dressed and what kit they're carrying. Let me know if anyone stays with the vehicle or vehicles, and try and work out who is giving the orders. If they start heading this way, we've got to assume that they'll find our camp.'

'What do we do then?' Terry asked.

George answered for him, for they had already gone over this part of the orders. 'We pull on the communication cord – two tugs for bad guys approaching. Remember, Terry?' George held up a stick to which he had tied the free end of a reel of fishing line. Mike would keep the other end of the hundred-metre line near him or tied to him if he slept.

'That's right, two tugs,' Mike said. 'Then, if you can, get back here without being spotted or heard. If you can't get back –'

'We cover ourselves with bushes and leaves and lie still here,' Terry said, remembering the rest of the plan.

'Good man,' Mike said, clapping him on the shoulder. 'Remember, guys, one sleeps, one awake at all times, OK?'

They nodded. Mike unbuckled his belt and handed the machete to George, who accepted it with a solemn nod. Mike thought the weapon provided more of a psychological benefit than a serious means of self-defence. If the likes of Hess and Orlov or their cronies got close enough to George and Terry for them to unsheathe the machete, then things would already have gone horribly wrong.

Mike had considered leaving the pistol with George and Terry, but there were six other people under his care back at the main camp. This was one of those unenviable times when, as a commander, he had to leave two men out on their own, to their own devices, for the greater good of the group. While it was not fair on Terry or George, there was no other option.

'And chef . . .'

'Yeah?' George said, as he slid the machete half out of its scabbard and tested the sharp blade with his thumb.

'No heroics.'

Hess and Orlov were dressed for war. Hess wore a dark green bush shirt and matching trousers. He took a twenty-round magazine from a pocket on his green canvas hunter's vest and clipped it to his M-14 rifle. He pulled back the cocking handle and then let it fly forward, chambering a round. His Glock pistol was tucked under his left armpit in a shoulder holster. On his belt he carried a water bottle and a hunting knife with a carved bone handle and a wicked twenty-five centimetre blade. The knife scabbard was tied to his right thigh to stop it from catching on low-lying branches. Again he wore the black woollen watch cap to camouflage his blond hair. He jumped on the spot a couple of times to double-check that nothing in his vest or pockets would rattle and betray his position in the bush. He was ready.

Orlov worked the bolt action of his hunting rifle, smiling at the satisfying snicker of oiled metal on metal. He carried spare bullets in elastic loops on his vest and a hunting knife at his waist, along with the old Makarov pistol he had taken on the ill-fated trip across to Matusadona. Beneath his vest he wore his faded Russian camouflage smock.

The memory of the failed rhino hunt burned in Orlov's mind. As a businessman and, before that, as a soldier, failure had never been an option for him. He had come to Africa to hunt big game and he had been cheated. Tonight's action would be his source of revenge and satisfaction.

The thought of imminent battle had another effect on him. As he blackened his face with charcoal from a lightning-shattered tree he thought of sex, of a desire as primal as the need to kill. He felt his loins stir as he remembered the young black girl he had ravaged at Hess's hunting lodge. The way she had felt, the way she had fought, the way she had screamed. He knew there would be female tourists on the overland vehicle. Hess, in his usual blunt manner, had explained that while the object of this mission was to eliminate two witnesses – the man and woman who had tracked them down at Victoria Falls – they could not afford to leave more people alive who could identify and incriminate them. How and when the others were killed, Orlov decided, would be a decision he would make.

Hess had programmed in the coordinates for the last known position of the yellow overland truck into his GPS unit, the location having willingly been given by the burly Afrikaner tourist in the Land Rover. He had flagged the two South African vehicles down as they neared the Mfuwe end of the Petauke Road. He explained to the driver of the first vehicle that he was very concerned he had not yet met up with his friend, an Australian tour guide driving a big yellow Bedford, who should have been at Mfuwe several hours earlier.

Hess had spoken to the helicopter pilot again on the satellite telephone. He ordered the man to fly to Mfuwe airstrip and remain there on standby through the night, although he didn't tell him the exact nature of their illegal mission.

Klaus had driven at breakneck speed from Lusaka back down to Siavonga on the Zambian shore of Lake Kariba, and recruited the remaining two poachers, Alfred and Ezekial, who had accompanied them across to Tashinga. It had been easy to convince them to join forces with the two white men again. They faced the same risk of imprisonment if their part in the rhino hunt was revealed and, on Hess's authority, Klaus had promised them all the spoils a raid on an overland truck would bring. The impoverished poachers were more than happy to kill for a sackful of cameras, watches, jewellery and foreign currency.

What Hess had not told Klaus was that he planned to kill the two poachers as soon as the job was done. There would be saturation coverage in the media of the violent deaths of a group of tourists and this would bring a high-level investigation. Hess could not afford to have any of their accomplices picked up and coerced into revealing the identities or descriptions of the white men who had organised the attack.

For now, though, he treated the men like loyal foot soldiers. He gathered them around him in a circle where they stood, on the edge of the dirt road just outside of Mfuwe. 'Tonight we will find the people who killed your comrade, William, at Matusadona,' he said forcefully. 'Tonight is your chance for revenge, and for money.'

The poachers smiled and gathered their meagre belongings – AK-47s and crude shoulder bags stuffed with a little food and spare magazines of ammunition. They had no reason to doubt Hess's story that their friend had been killed by a lucky shot from a ranger's rifle in Matusadona.

Hess reached into the front of the Land Cruiser and pulled out a detailed topographical map. He unrolled it on the bonnet of the vehicle, weighing one side down with his pistol and the other with a magazine crammed with burnished brass and copper bullets.

'Gather around, gentlemen. Here is where the truck crossed the river,' he said pointing to the wavy blue line. 'According to our helpful South African tourist friends the river is probably in complete flood by now, so the overland truck will not be able to retreat from us. Notice these two hills on this side of the river? If we have not found the truck by the time we get to the first of these hills we will dismount, camouflage our vehicle and patrol through to the river. Everyone understand so far?'

'Yes *bwana*,' said Alfred. Ezekial and Klaus nodded.

Hess smiled at the old poacher's use of the Swahili term of respect. It would be a shame to kill him, but there was no other way. 'When we find the camp we do the job quickly and we do the job properly.'

A lifetime spent in the African bush had taught Karl Hess how to drive in any condition. Through deep sand, glutinous mud and innumerable creek crossings he kept the Land Cruiser travelling at a speed that killed conversation among his passengers. Orlov sat beside him in the front, with Klaus and the poachers crammed into the back seat. All the passengers had rifles resting across their knees, and Hess had removed his Glock from its holster and placed it in his lap.

'We're only a few kilometres from the two hills now, Karl,' Orlov said, using a shaded flashlight to relate the coordinates on the illuminated screen of the GPS unit to Hess's map. 'Beyond the hills is the river where the tour truck was bogged.'

Hess switched off the headlights, leaving only the parking lights on, and slowed the Land Cruiser. Eyes stared hard into the shadows flashing by. Hands tightened on the pistol grips and stocks of rifles. After a few minutes, Hess cut the lights completely and slowed the vehicle to a crawl. They had started to climb the second-last hill from the river. He noticed a break in the vegetation on the right-hand side, possibly an old elephant trail, and swung the Land Cruiser off the road.

'Cut some branches,' he said to the poachers and opened his door. 'Cover the vehicle with them.'

Once the vehicle was hidden from sight of the road Hess called the men together and said, 'Alfred, you take the lead. We move in an arrowhead formation. We will spread out on either side of the road, but nobody walks on the road. Do not lose sight of the man on either side of you. No noise.'

The night was eerily quiet, except for the occasional chirp of an insect or screech of an owl. The five heavily armed men moved slowly, searching the ground for any spoor, watching the bush ahead and to their sides for their quarry. The wet leaves and sodden earth helped deaden what little sound their movements made. They reached the top of the first hill and slowly descended the other side.

Alfred raised his left hand, and everyone stopped and crouched.

Hess, who was behind and to the right of the poacher, moved to him. 'What is it?'

Alfred pointed to the fallen tree across the road and they moved forward to the stump on the right-hand side of the track. He rubbed a finger on the white stump, then raised it to his lips, tasting the sticky sap. 'This has not been cut for long, *bwana*. Maybe only a few hours.'

Hess peered up the slope of the second hill in front of them. The fallen tree was a man-made obstacle. From his military training he knew that obstacles, by themselves, were of no use to a defender. The point of an obstacle is to slow an attacker, and allow the defender to observe or fire upon the attacker while he tries to bridge or destroy the barrier. 'They are probably watching us. Alfred, when we move forward, keep an eye on the side of the road for tracks and other signs.'

'The rain has been heavy, *bwana*, it will be hard to read tracks.'

Hess clapped a hand on the black man's thin but muscled shoulder, smiled, and said, 'If they see us before we see them, Alfred, I will kill you.'

He crept back along the line of advance, kneeling close to each man and whispering in his ear, 'They are not far, probably at the top of the next hill. Stay low and stay quiet.'

They moved forward again, even slower than before. Every few metres Alfred would stop, standing against the trunk of a tree or crouching next to a low bush so as not to be silhouetted. He would look and listen, and then move again. The tracker searched for fresh spoor along the edge of the road and in the bush around him, but the heavens rumbled above him and he knew more rain would come again soon, washing away what little remained of their enemy's trail.

An eerie, mournful howl sounded off to their left. The advance stopped again. Alfred turned to Hess, behind him to the right, and mouthed, 'Jackal.' Hess nodded impatiently, for he reckoned he had probably seen more jackals in his lifetime in the Namibian bush than even the old Zambian poacher had.

*

492

'What was that?' Terry whispered in alarm at the weird animal sound off to their right. George rolled over on the carpet of sodden leaves and mud, and clapped his right hand hard on his friend's mouth. He felt Terry struggle beneath his grip, but held firm until the bigger man calmed his frantic movements.

George pointed to the road, in front of them and slightly off to their right. Terry's eyes widened in fear and recognition. There was an African man bent in a half crouch near the edge of the road, not ten metres away from where they lay at the base of the twin trees. Terry scanned the bush around him and then clutched the sleeve of George's rain jacket. He pointed to the left of the black man, to a spot further back. A European wearing a dark watch cap was moving silently through the bush. 'Look. It must be them,' Terry whispered, his lips almost brushing George's ear.

The men were moving forward now, closer and closer to their position with every step. George felt sick with fear and anger. The men that he and Terry were there to spot in advance of their arrival were almost on top of them. He wondered what had happened to their vehicle, how he could possibly warn Mike and the others in time. George had been awake, but he had not seen or heard the men until just now. Terry had been sleeping, snoring, in fact, and George had decided that he had to wake his friend because he was making too much noise. George realised he had at least done something right, because the men gave no sign that they had noticed the OP yet. But that couldn't last. His right hand clenched the wooden handle of the machete so hard he felt his knuckles start to ache.

Slowly, a centimetre at a time, he moved his left arm down beside his body. His arm had been in the same position, his hand resting under his chin, for about half an hour and it hurt as the blood slowly started to circulate again. He would have only seconds to find the communication line and warn Mike before the men were literally on top of them. He found the stick they had tied the fishing line to and he yanked on it as hard as he could. Awkwardly, he wound more line around the stick to increase the tension on the line, to make sure that Mike felt the signal at the other end.

Terry, worried that George's movement would be noticed, laid a hand on George's arm to still the movement. Blood pounded in Terry's ears and his vision went blurry. He pressed his face hard into the mud and leaf litter, like a child who thinks he can hide by covering his eyes. He shook with fear, and worried that he would lose control and wet himself.

George made out the distinctive silhouette of the lead poacher's rifle – an AK-47. He risked a final glance at the white man wearing the black beanie and noticed a very long rifle. The weapon had a magazine, which meant that it had to be semi-automatic, if not fully automatic, and it looked familiar, but he couldn't place the design – probably American. He noticed the huge sight mounted on top and recalled that Mike had said the men who had shot at him had used a night sight. George could have screamed at the frustration of not being able to pass this vital information on to Mike in time for him to use it. He could only hope that Mike had got the frantic signal. Now he, like Terry, lowered his face into the muck as the faint footsteps came closer.

Suddenly, without a warning clap of thunder or a flash of lightning, the clouds opened and Terry and George felt fat drops of rain spatter their backs. George thought of all the wet, cold, miserable weekends he had spent in the field with the Territorial Army, and how much he despised getting wet. Now he smiled grimly into the puddle forming in front of his face.

There was the swish of a leg rubbing against a low bush and the slosh of a boot in water beside him, close to his face. George tilted his head ever so slowly to the right. The man was beside him, just on the other side of the tree trunk. If George had stretched out his arm, he could have touched him.

31

Mike was dreaming he was on Manly Beach, seven miles from Sydney and a million miles from care, as the old tourist slogan said. The sun was shining, children were laughing and splashing in the shallows. He was out in the surf and a beautiful, long, perfect wave of liquid-green glass rose up behind him. He pushed off the sandbar and the wave lifted him, propelling him, and for a moment it felt like he was flying. He slid down the face of the wave, arms rigid beside him as he bodysurfed all the way into shore.

Sarah was there, on the beach. Standing and waving. Her hair was back to her natural blonde again, and she was wearing that simple sexy black bikini. Her body was tanned, her teeth white, her eyes sparkling. She walked towards the water, hips swaying slowly, hypnotically. He stood in the shallows and shook the water from his long hair, then he started to jog towards her. He wanted her so much he could barely breathe.

He reached for her. She giggled and they were almost touching, at the line of the sea's furthest reach, where water meets land, wet meets dry, dark meets light. Their fingers were so close he could practically feel the heat radiating from her sun-drenched body. Then someone, somewhere, grabbed his left arm, painfully, and pulled him back. He fell and landed in the water, on his side. Water filled his mouth. Sarah faded from his sight.

Mike coughed and rolled, aware immediately of a dull ache in his hip from sleeping on the bare ground, and a sharp pain in his wrist. His arm jerked like a puppet's as he sat up, and his head knocked against something hard and dirty. He had been sleeping underneath Nelson, away from the others. The water was real, because his face was cold and wet. As his eyes slowly became accustomed to the gloom he noticed that a puddle had formed around where his head had been. The baseball cap he had been resting his head on was sodden. He squeezed as much water as he could from it and placed it on his head.

The pulling on his arm was the signal from the boys at the observation post that Hess and Orlov had arrived. The ferocity of the tugging alarmed him. They had agreed two tugs, but his arm still jerked, the fishing line digging painfully into his skin. He reached for his pocket knife and cut the line. The line had served its purpose and if it proved to be a false alarm he would retie it after he had found out what was going on. He had to assume, though, that either George and Terry were about to arrive or, if things had gone wrong, the poachers were about to come over the hill and find them.

Mike had slept under the truck in order to be ready to put his plan into action. Also, he couldn't have slept in a tent or sleeping bag as that would have prevented him from feeling George and Terry's signal. The rest of the group was at least dry, if not completely safe from danger. In the small clearing they had made next to the vehicle were the group's green canvas dome tents, arranged in a horseshoe pattern, with the open end facing the tarpaulin they had rigged up to cover the eating area. At the border of the little clearing, half under the extreme edge of the tarp's shelter, were the remains of the fire. Fortunately, the brief shower hadn't extinguished it completely. Mike stood, joints stiff and sore, and walked to the fire. He knelt and blew hard on the embers. He was able to coax a red glow from a few sticks and a narrow column of smoke snaked its way up.

He reached in his pocket for his cigarettes and lighter, and lit one as he opened the driver's side door and climbed into the cab.

Hess passed the M-14 rifle across to Orlov and pointed to the direction in which he wanted him to look. From their vantage point on the crest of the hill they could plainly see the yellow overland truck. The rain had eased, but there were no stars or moonlight to assist the night sight's image intensification equipment. When Orlov raked the truck with the sight, however, the lack of ambient light made the two pinpricks of illumination even more obvious than they would have been.

The first was on the ground and, as Orlov squinted hard in concentration, he made out the glowing embers of a campfire. That meant there were people there, in the campsite, who were now sleeping in the open circle of dome tents. When he shifted the sight onto the cab of the truck, as Hess had instructed, he saw only blackness.

'Wait,' whispered Hess.

Orlov held the crosshairs on the cab and, a few seconds later, broke into a grin when the interior suddenly flared a warm bright green. He trailed a tiny bright speck of light, like a green firefly, from a point high up in the cab, to down below the dashboard, out of sight again. There was a person in the cab, smoking.

The Russian could not comprehend such stupidity. Their quarry had taken the precaution of posting a sentry in the vehicle – a ridiculously obvious location in any case – but had allowed the person to give his presence away by smoking. When the tip of the cigarette flared bright again, Orlov picked out the man's silhouette. He was wearing a baseball cap and sitting in the driver's seat. Hess reached for the weapon.

'No,' Orlov said. 'Let me take the shot.'

Hess lowered his hand and looked at the Russian, who stared back at him. Hess saw the desire in Orlov's eye, the look of a hunter who has been cheated of his prey and then given another chance. The professional soldier in him wanted to ensure the job was done properly and, in Hess's book, that usually meant doing it himself. But he understood Orlov's frustration, particularly since the man had spent a small fortune on organising the expedition.

He touched Orlov on the arm and said, 'Of course, Vassily.' Hess motioned for Klaus and the two poachers to join them at their vantage point.

'Listen in. Alfred, you and Ezekial go in first – quietly. I will give you five minutes to be in position. That should be plenty of time. As soon as the man in the truck is dead, you do as we discussed before. Klaus, you stay here in reserve with us. Understood?' Everyone nodded.

The two poachers disappeared into the darkened bush below the crest of the hill as silently as a pair of mambas in search of prey. Orlov used the time it would take for them to get into position to prepare himself for the crucial shot. He unfolded the bipod legs under the end of the rifle barrel, and cleared away grass and a fallen branch that obscured his view from the crest. He lay down on his stomach and lifted the butt of the weapon to his shoulder, caressing the oiled wooden stock with his cheek as he lowered his eye to the night sight. The man in the cab drew on his cigarette again, illuminating the outline of his head and hat. Orlov was sure that even if the cigarette went out he would still be able to make the shot with the little ambient light present.

Hess checked the luminescent dial on his watch and tapped Orlov on the shoulder. 'Thirty seconds.'

Orlov centred the crosshairs of the glowing sight on the dark mass of the head under the baseball cap.

'When you're ready, Vassily.'

Orlov had to will his hands to stay steady, such was his excitement. His heart pounded against his rib cage and his throat went tight. He took a deep breath, held it, then expelled half of the air in his lungs. His finger curled around the trigger and he squeezed.

The rifle bucked against his shoulder. There was a slick mechanical noise of sliding metal as the rifle automatically chambered another round. Through the sight he saw a baseball cap sail out the driver's side window of the truck's cab. Orlov smelled burned cordite. The windscreen of the truck had shattered into a crazed spiderweb, with a tiny hole at its centre where the bullet had smashed through on its deadly path. Of the figure inside the truck there was no sign.

Hess picked up the ejected brass cartridge, which had landed next to his face. He held it up for Orlov to see. A thin wisp of smoke curled out of the empty end of the hot casing. 'Good shot, Vassily.' Orlov nodded.

The bark of automatic rifle fire tore the night apart. Orange-yellow flashes from the two AK-47s momentarily illuminated the two poachers as they charged into the middle of the tents. With each burst of fire they stitched ragged holes in their flimsy canvas. The men's rifles were pointed downwards, aimed at unseen sleeping inhabitants inside each of the tents.

The lead poacher, Alfred, raised his rifle and took aim at the driver's side door of the truck. The last three bullets in his rifle's magazine punched through the yellow metal and ricocheted wildly inside the cab, one exiting through the roof with a whining buzz. There was an audible click as his weapon emptied, the cocking handle locked rearwards. Smoke rose from the rifle's barrel and the open ejection port as he reached up for the door handle. Ezekial, the other poacher, stood a couple of metres away, his rifle raised to cover the interior of the cab. His eyes were wide and wild with the thrill of killing. He nervously shifted his weight from foot to foot.

Alfred opened the door and jumped back. The body inside tumbled down.

Hess could just make out the shadowy forms of the poachers. Through the night sight he saw something fall from the truck's cab when one of the men opened the door. The night was still – even the insects were hushed in the eerie silence that followed the shooting.

'Come, Vassily, Klaus. Let's get down there,' Hess said. All three were on their feet now, running towards the truck and the bullet-holed tents.

'By the sounds of it, none of them has survived,' Orlov said between gasps as he trotted along at Hess's side.

Hess caught the note of disappointment in the Russian's words. Hess himself would not have minded if the man or woman who had been following them had survived the initial onslaught. He could then interrogate one or both of them to find out who they were, what they knew about him, and why they had so doggedly followed him and Orlov.

But it was quiet. Dead quiet.

*

'Don't move,' Mike said. 'Lower your guns. Now!'

He held the Browning out, left hand cupping right, the barrel pointed at the head of the man in ragged clothes who had just opened the cab door.

The man's eyes were wide in stupefied amazement. When he opened the door a tangled mass of arms and legs had fallen on him, and he had instinctively jumped back. Now, even though Mike's pistol was pointed at him he still stared incredulously at the crumpled, lifeless form at his feet.

'Meet our friend Britney,' Mike said.

'Not a girl, not yet a woman,' said Sam from behind Mike.

The inflatable girl had been sitting in the driver's cab of the Bedford ever since Mike had sent the passengers to bed. After he woke to the tug on his arm from the OP he had climbed into the cab with his cigarette. Unseen in the gloom he had crawled into the back of the truck and perched just behind the doll. He had placed his baseball cap on the head to add to the illusion. Sitting behind Britney he was able to draw repeatedly on the cigarette and occasionally hold it near her gaping red-lipped mouth, exposing himself as little as possible to what he expected to be the poachers' line of fire. It had taken three cigarettes before the attack came. Mike had hoped that the poachers would have been preceded by George and Terry, but the enemy had arrived first, which left him very concerned about the fate of the two young Englishmen.

When the shot came, it had nearly taken his hand off. He sneaked out of the truck via the main door to the passenger cab, which was out of sight of the shooter, and hid under the vehicle. Sam was waiting there for him. Nigel was squatting out of sight in the bushes, somewhere at the rear of the truck.

The elder of the two poachers looked up at Mike now and held out his AK-47, away from his body. Mike could see the breech of the rifle was locked open, which meant he was out of ammunition. The poacher knew it as well, and he dropped the rifle in the mud. Mike shifted his aim to the second man. As he did, the man started to move, his body swivelling as he swung the barrel of his rifle.

Mike saw the poacher's face beyond the black metal nub of the pistol's foresight. His eyes were wide and wild. Mike pulled the trigger twice, quickly. The man's head snapped backwards, like he'd been king-hit, and his body landed with a splash in a puddle.

The old poacher dropped to his knees and crawled toward the younger man. Mike was still locked in the firing position. Smoke curled from the hot barrel of the pistol.

The man was dead. He lay half on his side, one leg bent underneath his body. The first bullet had entered his right eye and torn out the back of his head, the other had pierced his neck. Blood pumped from the throat wound, then slowed. Mike could see grey brains and stark white skull fragments in the puddle, and he swallowed hard.

The old man was crying, deep sobbing moans, as he cradled the younger man's pulped head in his lap. Mike guessed he was the dead man's father. At another time, as an innocent bystander, he would have felt for the old man, no matter what crime his son had committed, but he was no mere witness to this shooting. The young man had tried to kill him and he had replied in kind. There were more men out there in the wet darkness who would kill him and his passengers if he did nothing.

'Shit,' Sam said, hovering near Mike, peering at the dead man and his tear-racked companion.

Sam carried the axe from the truck loosely in his right hand. His face, like Mike's, was blackened with charcoal.

'You OK?' Mike asked.

'Sure. He was going to shoot us,' Sam said.

'Now you get the picture. Let's get this guy out of the way.'

Sam and Mike dragged the keening old man away from the body and Mike relieved him of the cloth bag he wore around his neck. While Sam bound the man's hands behind his back and gagged him with duct tape, Mike retrieved the fallen AK-47 from the mud and wiped it down with the tail of his shirt. The weapon had a reputation for being able to take rough treatment and still fire under appalling conditions. Tonight would be a good test. Mike removed the empty magazine from the rifle, tossed it into the bush, and fished a fresh magazine from the poacher's bag. He fitted it to the rifle and let the cocking handle fly forward. There were still two full magazines inside the cloth bag. He picked up the dead man's rifle and slung it over his shoulder.

'Where's Nigel, Sam?' Mike asked.

'Don't know,' Sam said, biting off the last strand

of tape as he secured a strip across the poacher's mouth.

'Help me . . .' came a voice from the rear of the truck.

Mike jogged around Nelson and saw Nigel lying at the base of a tree. There was blood all over his left shoulder and his face was ivory white.

Nigel opened his eyes. 'It hurts, Mike. Christ, it fucking hurts, man,' he said. Blood welled from his lower lip where he'd bitten it to stop from crying out.

Mike was touched by Nigel's bravery. If he had screamed or cried out, the ambush would have been blown.

He knelt and took Nigel's right hand, and clasped it hard. 'You did good, mate.' Gently, Mike raised him to the sitting position and inspected the wound. 'It's gone straight through, but it doesn't seem to have hit your lungs. Believe it or not, you'll live.'

Mike fished in his top left pocket and took out a handful of tampons. He had asked the girls to surrender any spares they had. 'Sam, remember what I told you? Take a few of these and pack them around the entry and exit wounds. Cover them with that piece of plastic shopping bag I gave you and tape it down. We'll take him to Kylie, but you'll have to help him walk.'

Kylie, Sarah, Mel and Linda were a hundred metres behind them, hidden deep in the bush. Mike had found a natural strongpoint in the forest, made by two fallen trees with trunks wide enough to stop a bullet. One tree had knocked the other over when it fell, making a barricade with the point of the two trunks facing the way the bad guys would most likely approach. They had tied the spare tarpaulin across the fallen logs to provide shelter and then covered the whole thing with fresh-cut trees. Mike made everyone empty their backpacks and stuff them full of food and water bottles. His plan was to run a fighting retreat from the log fort, as they had christened it, or, if too many of them were wounded, to make their last stand there.

Nigel winced as Sam finished applying the crude bandage. Sam's hands were red and sticky with blood, and he stared at them.

'Good job, Sam. Here, take this,' Mike said as he unslung the dead poacher's AK-47 and handed it to Sam.

'What'll we do with him?' Sam asked, pointing to the bound and gagged poacher lying on the ground.

Mike pulled the pistol from his belt and walked over to the prone man.

'You're not going to . . .' Sam said, his eyes wide.

Mike shook his head, bent over and clubbed the man hard on the back of the head with the butt of the pistol. 'Drag him under a bush. He'll wake up eventually.'

'It looks like you've got a spare gun. I'll take it,' Sarah said. She had arrived silently behind them.

'What are you doing here?'

'I've come to help, and you look like you need it,' she said.

'I told you to stay back at the fort, with the –'

'I *know* what you told me. Back with the *girls*. That's what you were going to say, wasn't it?' Her eyes burned with barely suppressed anger. 'I know you

507

have trouble accepting that women can do more than make the tea, but you seem to be short of able-bodied men, now, don't you?'

'I killed a man tonight, Sarah,' Mike said. 'I didn't want to do it, but he was going to kill me if I didn't. Believe me, you don't want to do what I've just done.'

'Spare me the patronising chauvinist bullshit! Sam's got to carry Nigel, and get him back to Kylie. I'll tell you right now that he's too big for me to carry, but I can fire that gun of yours!'

'Lucky you showed up, then,' Mike said to Sarah, and handed her the pistol and the spare magazine. 'Everyone ready?'

Nigel's face was even paler as Sam pulled him to his feet, but he managed to stand and lean on Sam's shoulder. They set off, as quietly and as quickly as Nigel could manage. They headed straight back from the truck through the bush towards the log fort. Mike was hoping to keep the truck between them and the remainder of the poachers. With George and Terry missing he had no idea how many others they faced. The poachers would soon know their initial raid had failed.

There was a sound like the ripping of canvas, followed by a thump that could have come from the back room of a butcher's shop. Nigel and Sam were knocked to the ground. Someone cried in pain.

'Sniper!' Mike yelled. 'Everyone down!'

Mike grabbed Sarah's wrist and pulled her to the ground. He hugged her to his chest and rolled down a slight slope, four, maybe five times, their bodies alternately riding on and crushing each other until they came to rest against a stout tree trunk.

'Christ, Nigel's been shot again,' Sam cried.

The American lay on his stomach a metre away from Nigel. Low ferns hid him from view, but Nigel was lying in a patch of clear ground. He stretched an arm out to Sam, and Mike saw Nigel's fist opening and closing in a futile attempt to reach him.

'Nigel, where are you hit?' Mike called.

'Leg . . . It hurts. Mike, it hurts!'

'Sam, get behind some cover before you get shot.'

'I've got to move Nigel. We can't leave him out there!' Sam said.

'No! Stay where you are. The sniper wants you to go into the clearing. He's waiting for you, Sam. Nigel, can you hold on for us, mate?'

Nigel coughed. 'I think so,' he croaked.

Another silenced bullet slammed into the mud next to Nigel's face, sending up a geyser of black water. The shooter was toying with them. Undergrowth and tree limbs obscured his view, but Mike guessed the sniper was close, probably just on the far side of the shot-up tents.

'Sam, I'm going to swing around to the right, back to the truck. I've got to get up high where I can see these bastards, but I need a diversion. You got the cocktails?'

'Yeah, I got them with me,' Sam replied.

'I'm coming with you,' Sarah said.

Mike could have argued, but he supposed that at least if she was with him he could try to protect her. He didn't bother replying to her since nothing he could say would have made the slightest bit of difference. He simply nodded.

'Give me three minutes, Sam. Remember the plan – aim for the tents,' Mike said.

'What about Nigel?' Sam called back.

'Three minutes, Sam, that's all he has to hold on for,' Mike said.

Nigel coughed and Mike saw how his body shook with the pain. He had both hands pressed on the wound on his thigh, and the blood had stained them crimson. Another bullet whizzed low over his head and split a narrow branch behind him. 'Come on,' Mike said to Sarah, 'the shooter's going to get tired of this game soon.'

They headed along the ridgeline towards the log fort, keeping to thick bush out of the sniper's line of sight, and then hooked across their intended path and turned back to the truck. Mike checked his watch and motioned for Sarah to stay close.

He could see Nelson through the bushes. The windscreen was shattered and the bodywork riddled with bullet holes. Mike whispered to Sarah what he wanted her to do. The plan sounded insane, but Sarah nodded. They crept along the side of the truck, careful not to make a sound. Sarah climbed the steps up into the passenger cab, pausing for a second when her weight caused a spring to creak. She continued on inside. Mike went to the back of the truck, slung the AK-47 he was carrying, and climbed the external ladder up onto the roof.

Mike checked his watch again and saw by the ticking luminous green second hand that he and Sarah had reached their positions with just twenty seconds to spare. Those last seconds, however, were ticking by with agonising slowness.

As the sweep hand passed the ten-second mark, Mike heard a whoosh of displaced air as the sniper fired another silenced shot. The second hand passed the final mark and Sam screamed, 'Take this, you motherfuckers!'

A bright trail of burning orange sparks arced out from where Sam hid towards the nearest of the bullet-holed tents.

'Now, Sarah!' Mike yelled.

Nelson's headlights flicked on, followed by the extra driving lights, and the horseshoe of tents was bathed in stark white light. The whisky bottle Sam had lobbed hit one of the tents and exploded, shards of broken glass and burning petrol shooting out in every direction. The tent burst into flames. A rolling cloud of oily black smoke danced upwards and momentarily shrouded the glare of the headlights as the petrol ignited.

Mike always kept a jerry can of petrol in the truck to clean the diesel engine's air filter and he had used it all tonight on the last of his surprises for the poachers. They had doused the tents with fuel and made Molotov cocktails from empty spirit bottles.

There was movement between the tents. Mike recognised the tall black man who had attacked him in Victoria Falls. The man was dressed in a khaki bush shirt and trousers, and armed with an AK-47. He hesitated as the tent next to him caught fire. The man raised his rifle to his shoulder, and Mike swung the barrel of his own weapon around and thumbed the safety catch.

Klaus fired first and Mike felt the truck shudder

beneath him as a long burst of ten or fifteen bullets raked the front. Bullets penetrated the panels and ricocheted off the solid engine components, but two found their mark, and one of the headlights and one of the brighter driving lights were snuffed out with a spray of broken glass.

A heavy-bore hunting rifle joined the din, crashing as fast as the new marksman could work the weapon's bolt action. Mike couldn't hear the hiss of the silenced rifle above the din, and he hoped the weapon's night sight had been blinded by the headlights and the glare from the flaming tent.

Mike pulled the trigger of his AK-47 and Klaus dived to his left as three bullets ploughed harm-lessly into the earth where he had been standing. He fired again, but the mud-caked rifle jammed. Mike swore aloud as he snapped the magazine from the rifle and worked the cocking handle back and forth furiously. A live round tumbled from the breach and he banged the butt of the weapon down hard on the roof of the truck, causing dried mud to flutter from the working parts. He fitted the maga-zine back onto the rifle and yanked on the cocking handle.

Klaus raised his rifle to his shoulder and aimed at the roof of the truck, where Mike was lying. Mike rolled to one side as he pulled the trigger. Bullets punched through the thin skin of the walls and roof of the cab beside him, buzzing and whining as they carried on into the black sky.

Mike rolled back onto his stomach and saw the other man taking aim again. There was no way Mike could get back into a firing position and take aim before his enemy got another burst away.

From Mike's left another AK-47 started firing, its bright muzzle flashes giving Sam's position away in the dark. 'Come and get me, you cocksuckers!' he cried.

Klaus swung to face the new threat. Mike brought his weapon up to fire again, but a flicker of light to his left distracted him. Klaus was crawling for the cover of an unburnt tent. He also looked up at the sputtering wick sailing through the damp night air.

'No!' Klaus shouted as the bottle fell towards him. He held up the rifle in his right hand to ward off the Molotov cocktail, but the bottle shattered with a whoosh when it struck the barrel of his weapon. Klaus was sprayed with burning petrol and his clothes erupted. He stood, and the fire engulfed him like a torch. The big African staggered from side to side, his arms waving uselessly. He stumbled and fell into another of the petrol-soaked tents and this, too, blazed into a consuming funeral pyre. His screams were muffled as the burning canvas enshrouded his body.

Somewhere nearby, another shot rang out. It was not the heavy-calibre rifle or the chatter of a Kalashnikov but the flat report of a pistol, puny in comparison with the other weapons, but just as deadly. Sarah, Mike thought with rising panic.

The hunting rifle boomed and one of the two remaining lights on the truck shattered. Mike fired a wild burst into the night in the general direction of where he thought the shot had come from. He realised he was a sitting duck now, and that he had to get himself and Sarah away from the truck. The heavy-calibre rifle echoed again and the truck shook as Mike shimmied down the ladder at the rear of the cab. With the last of the headlights now out, the only light in the clearing came from Klaus's burning body in the tent. The sickly smell of burnt flesh filled the air around the campsite. Mike swallowed hard and looked under the truck, where he had told Sarah to hide.

There was no sign of her.

32

'It is over!' Hess called from the bush beyond the flame-lit clearing. Sarah cried in pain.

Mike peered around the tree he was sheltering behind and saw Hess stride into the centre of the camp. One side of his body was bathed in flickering orange light from the guttering fire. On his dark side he had his left arm wrapped around Sarah's neck. His right hand held an automatic pistol to her temple.

Mike was consumed with a mixture of rage and helplessness. Hess was doing it again, taking away someone he cared about – someone he loved. This had become a personal war between the two of them. Mike forced himself to control his emotions. Hess was a cold-blooded killer. Mike had killed once that night. He could do it again.

'Come out!' Hess said, standing still. He smiled. 'You know I will kill her if you don't obey. Shall I start the count? One . . . two . . .'

'Wait,' Mike said, emerging from the darkness.

'And the other one. The one who throws the

515

Molotovs. I want to meet this man who calls me a "cocksucker".'

'If the name fits.' Mike shrugged.

'A funny man, eh?' Hess pushed the barrel of the pistol hard into Sarah's skin and she cried in pain.

'Sam,' Mike said, 'come out.'

A few seconds later Sam strode from the other side of the clearing, his rifle pointed at Hess. Mike's weapon dangled loosely in his right hand, the barrel pointed down.

'Place the weapons there, three metres from me. Do it now. Both of you,' Hess said.

They did as he ordered, then Hess said to Sam, 'Lie down, on your stomach, hands locked behind your head.' Sam dropped to the ground. 'You,' he said to Mike, 'stay standing. I want you to have a good view of everything that goes on.'

Mike noticed Hess's left hand was bleeding and the hunter caught his gaze.

'A fine souvenir, don't you think?' Hess said, holding up his hand, covering Sarah's face. The little finger was missing and he had wrapped a handkerchief around the stump. Hess grinned as he held the bloody wound close to Sarah's eye.

'She is a fighter, this one,' Hess said, looking at Sarah. 'She saw me approaching your position and took a potshot at me with her pistol. The little finger I don't think I'll miss, but she destroyed my fine rifle with that carelessly aimed shot. If I still had that weapon you would all be dead now.'

'It didn't do you much good at Matusadona,' Mike said.

'Ah, good. I am glad that was you in the national park. I would have hated to have gone to all this effort to kill the wrong man. I like your new haircut, by the way, but my colleague liked the lady better as a blonde, I'm sure.'

Orlov jogged into the clearing, then stood, panting, next to Hess, his hunting rifle levelled at Mike. 'So,' he said with a grin, 'we meet again. I didn't recognise the lovely lady at first. I think we have some unfinished business from Victoria Falls.'

'Pig,' Sarah said. She turned her head and spat at the Russian, but Hess silenced her by tightening the grip on her neck.

'Who are you working for?' Hess asked Mike.

'Read the sign on the side of the truck. I'm a tour guide.'

'My instinct is to kill you right now and then hunt down the rest of your little tour group. Answer my questions and I promise you that they will all die quickly. However, if you refuse I will allow my colleague here to have some fun with the women first.'

'Let her go, Hess. It's me you want.'

'Of course it's you I want – and her. Now, I ask you one more time, who are you working for?'

'I work for a tour company.'

Hess glared at Mike, then pushed Sarah away from him, towards Orlov. 'Tie her hands, Vassily. Use your rifle sling, that way the bitch won't scratch you when you fuck her.'

Orlov grabbed Sarah by the hair, and forced her to her knees. He unclipped the sling from his rifle and started wrapping it around her wrists, behind her back. His rifle was lying on the ground while he used both his hands. Sarah struggled and Orlov slapped her hard across the cheek with the back of his hand.

'Stop!' Mike roared. He took a pace forward, but Hess bought his pistol up between Sarah's eyes, stopping Mike cold as Orlov tied the canvas sling tight. Sarah's eyes were wide with fear. 'I'm working for the South African Police.'

'I thought as much,' Hess said. 'Who is heading the investigation?'

Mike wavered, unwilling to name Theron. He knew that if he identified the detective he may as well have put a bullet in his head himself.

'Take her, Vassily. Loosen her tongue for us, and whatever else takes your fancy,' Hess said, turning his pistol on Mike again.

Orlov pushed Sarah hard in the chest and she fell heavily, twisting to one side to break her fall. She was on her back now, knees raised and together, her hands pinioned beneath her. Orlov dropped to his knees beside his discarded rifle. He took a long-bladed hunting knife from the scabbard at his belt and held it to her slender throat. Hess smiled as Orlov reached out with his free hand and tore open the front of Sarah's shirt. Orlov stared at her pale breasts, mesmerised for a second, and Sarah hawked and spat at him. The Russian laughed as he wiped his face. He slapped her face again and forced a knee between her legs.

Mike heard his own blood pounding in his ears as the rage boiled up from deep inside him. From the corner of his eye he noticed a tree branch move and had to will himself to keep his gaze locked on Hess. Sam, lying on the ground to his left, had raised his head, but Hess was staring at Mike, down the barrel of his Glock pistol.

'They told me you were a soldier, Hess. Don't soldiers believe in honour?' Mike asked.

'Yes, I was a soldier. I've fought in many wars and I can tell you that terror, not honour, is what wins wars. Now, tell me, who was the policeman who sent you?'

Hess was distracted for a moment by a noisy hiss of radio static. With his bloodied left hand he reached into a pocket of his hunter's vest and pulled out a multi-channel walkie-talkie with a flexible rubber aerial. He returned his piercing stare to Mike as he spoke into the radio in Afrikaans. A broken voice at the other end answered in the same language, but Mike had no idea what they were talking about.

Mike looked over at Sarah, and saw she had turned her head away from Orlov and was staring out into the gloom beyond the burning body in the tent, apparently resigned to her fate. Orlov grappled awkwardly with the belt on her shorts with his one free hand, reluctant to lay down the knife.

'So you don't struggle now? You want this, I think,' Orlov chuckled as he finally undid Sarah's belt.

'You're not a soldier, Hess,' Mike said. 'I bet you don't even clean that pistol of yours.'

Hess looked at Mike, puzzled at the last remark, and shook his head. 'Cleaning my weapons? What are you talking about? I think you must be losing your mind. Perhaps I'll kill you now and be done with it.'

Mike searched his eyes for some sign of comprehension, allowing Hess a couple of seconds for his words to sink in, but he gave no sign that he understood the real meaning of the question. The bush moved again and Sarah turned her head towards Mike.

'George Terry!' Sarah said loudly.

Hess turned to face her, but kept the pistol trained on Mike. 'What?'

'George Terry. That's the man you want. But he's armed and ready for you,' Sarah said. She glanced at Mike and he read the silent message in her eyes.

'Shut up, bitch,' Orlov said, and slapped Sarah hard across the face once more.

Mike looked to the darkened bush past where Orlov grappled with Sarah and saw a figure emerge stealthily from the long grass.

'Now!' Mike bellowed. He lowered his shoulder and charged directly at Hess, his body tensed and waiting for the shot that would come. To Mike's left he heard a wailing war cry and George and Terry burst from the trees where they had been hiding.

The machete in George's hand reflected the orange firelight as he brought it down in a wide slashing arc from above his head. Orlov raised his knife hand high in a futile attempt to ward off the blow. Crimson blood gushed from the stump as Orlov's right hand, still grasping the knife, sailed through the air in the wake of the swinging machete.

There were noises behind Mike, words of warning screamed by young women. Sam was on his knees now, slipping through the mud as he scrambled towards his dropped rifle.

Hess fired his pistol at the moment Mike hit him, hard, in the chest, with his lowered shoulder. Hess toppled back under the force of the charge and the left side of Mike's body erupted in pain as he fell on top of his quarry. Awkwardly, Hess twisted his right hand inwards and thrust the barrel of the pistol hard into Mike's stomach. Hess pulled the trigger again.

Nothing happened.

There was confusion in Hess's eyes as Mike grabbed the lapel of his shirt with his left hand and smashed his right fist into his nose. Mike felt a hot spurt of blood on his knuckles and then landed another blow on Hess's jaw.

'Good soldiers clean their weapons,' Mike hissed at him as he reefed the watch cap from his head and took a hank of his wavy blond hair in one hand.

When Mike had searched Hess's room at the Victoria Falls Hotel he had risked detection to ensure that the next time Hess used his pistol he would get off no more than one shot. If Hess had cleaned the pistol since then there was no way he could have missed the round Mike had reversed in the magazine.

While Mike knew that Hess would manage one shot, he had consoled himself with the thought that even if he was killed, George and Terry, who he had seen creeping through the bush, and Sam would be able to overpower Orlov and Hess before the latter had time to clear the blocked pistol.

Hess was down and bloodied now, but that just made him more dangerous. While his pistol wouldn't fire again, it still made a good weapon. He jammed the barrel hard into the deep open furrow his bullet had gouged just above Mike's left hip. Mike yelped like a kicked dog and instinctively clutched his side.

Hess thrust up with his butt and his hips, throwing Mike off to one side. Mike tried to stand, but the pain had taken his breath away, and he pitched over on his face a second after making it to his knees.

'Freeze!' Sam yelled.

Hess raised the useless pistol. Sam, not knowing the pistol was jammed, dived forward into the mud, firing the AK-47 wildly as he fell. The bullets flew wide of Hess, who nimbly leapt to his feet and sprinted away as Sam struggled to his knees. The rifle wavered as Sam took aim at the running figure. He fired twice, but neither bullet found its mark and Hess disappeared into the trees.

Orlov lay in the mud on his side, tears streaking his blackened face as he clutched the spurting stump where his right hand had been. Mike struggled to his feet, his left hand pressed against the wound in his side. The pain stopped mattering as he walked slowly towards Orlov. The blood was beating in his ears again.

Everyone from the crew was gathered in the clearing now, the girls alternating their gaze from the stinking, burning body, to Orlov's bloody stump. They all turned to Mike as he approached.

'Give me his pistol,' Mike said to Terry, who had pulled the weapon from Orlov's belt.

The Russian was on his back now. Kylie had wrapped a clean T-shirt around the stump and tied a belt on Orlov's forearm as a tourniquet. Her hands were dark with his blood. Sarah stood over Orlov, her torn shirt knotted together at the front to cover her breasts.

George handed Mike the pistol, butt first. He cocked the weapon.

'Stand back, all of you,' he said, as he thumbed the safety.

Kylie looked up at him, horrified. 'Mike?'

'No, please, I beg of you! No!' Orlov wailed.

'You pathetic piece of shit,' Mike said. 'You fucking coward.' He straightened his arm and pointed the pistol between Orlov's eyes.

'Don't do it,' Sarah said.

Mike looked across at her. 'They killed her. They killed the nuns. They killed the workers at that mission. I saw what was left of the place, Sarah.'

'And he tried to rape me, Mike. But this isn't the way. You'll be as bad as them.'

'It wasn't me,' Orlov cried. 'I was unconscious, I killed no one. It was Hess.'

'Get out of the way, Kylie,' Mike said.

Kylie looked at Sarah, then at Mike, but did not move. 'For God's sake, I'm a nurse, Mike,' she protested. 'Sarah's right.'

Mike dropped to one knee and pressed the barrel of the cumbersome Russian pistol hard into Orlov's temple. He heard a gurgling noise and looked down to see a spreading dark stain on the man's trousers. Mike was close enough to him to smell his urine.

His hand started to shake as his finger tightened on the trigger. He felt a gentle touch on the back of his neck and looked up into Sarah's serene face. She was beautiful, he thought. His face was contorted in pain, but it wasn't from the oozing wound in his side.

Mike lowered the pistol and stood. He looked down at the pitiful, bleeding figure below him. He couldn't kill him, no matter how much he despised him. Mike believed Orlov when he said he had not been responsible for the deaths in Mozambique, but the fact was that Isabella had died because of him. Orlov was guilty and would be held to account.

Mike looked around and saw everyone was staring at him. Nobody spoke. He noticed for the first time that Nigel wasn't there.

'Where's Nigel?'

'We carried him back to the log fort,' Mel said. 'The bleeding's OK, but he's dreadfully pale, Mike.'

Mike knew he had to check his emotions and take charge again. He also realised that Hess was getting further away with every second he wasted.

'Sam, get everyone in the truck and get it started. George, Terry, take the AK-47s and ride shotgun. I'm going after Hess. He probably left his vehicle on the far side of the hill and that's where he'll be heading. Once you're out on the road, head for Mfuwe. Pick me up on the road if you see me. If you don't, send someone back for me tomorrow.'

Mike picked up Orlov's hunting rifle and worked the bolt to open the breech. The weapon was still loaded. He looked around for another weapon and saw Orlov's severed hand. He picked it up.

The flesh was cold now and the white fingers, with their chunky, crass gold rings, still gripped the hunting knife. Mike slung the rifle over his shoulder and turned so that Orlov could see what he was doing as he prised the knife from the lifeless fingers. He slid the knife into his belt. The colour drained from Orlov's face.

'Need a hand?' Mike asked, as he tossed the cold hunk of flesh into his lap.

Orlov screamed, then passed out.

33

Sarah hastily washed Mike's wound, and packed and dressed it with tampons, a handkerchief and tape.

She wrapped her arms around him, ignoring the mud and blood that caked his body. After a moment he returned the embrace, holding her as closely and tightly as the painful wound in his side would allow.

'I've got to go,' he said to her.

'I know. Be careful,' Sarah said.

They kissed, and he said, 'Stay with the others. Come get me when it's done.'

She nodded and turned her face away. She wanted to be strong for him, but she was so worried for his safety. He broke their embrace and left.

Mike's face felt sticky where he had wiped away sweat with his bloody hands. The pain was a dull, constant throb, but he found he could keep up a slow jog. He carried Orlov's hunting rifle, a round in the chamber, ready to kill. He could have taken one of the AK-47s, but he needed to make sure the people on the truck had enough firepower to get past Hess if the Namibian killed him and then tried to take them out.

If Hess was smart, Mike thought, he would run as fast as possible to his vehicle and get away from the overland group – and away from Zambia. Mike hoped Hess wasn't that smart, and was sticking around waiting to finish him off.

He was almost at the edge of the road when the first shot rang out. The bullet tore through the skin of his left forearm, halfway between his wrist and elbow. Mike pitched forward into the mud and couldn't stop himself from crying out in pain. He felt like he needed to throw up and he could see bone shining white through the ragged exit hole under his arm. Dragging his left arm uselessly beside him, he crawled to a fallen log and propped the barrel of the hunting rifle on the wet trunk. He scanned the road and the bush along its verge, but couldn't see Hess. Another bullet zinged over his head and he ducked back behind the log.

The next sound he heard was at once familiar and ominous – the dull *whop-whop* of helicopter rotor blades – a sound that could signal death just as easily as it could salvation. Mike looked up and caught sight of a bright light fighting to penetrate the cloud cover above the horizon. Hess darted from the bush into the middle of the road, waving his rifle high and speaking into a walkie-talkie. Hess had assumed he had put Mike out of action.

Mike could see the helicopter now. The pilot had the nose down to pick up speed as he followed the muddy road over the two hills towards Hess. The chopper's spotlight was lowered and the beam swept a path along the road in front of it. Mike shifted the barrel of the hunting rifle until Hess was in his sights. He tried to steady the stock with his left hand, but couldn't bend his arm enough to get a proper grip. His arm was slick with blood from the fresh wound. He centred the crosshairs of the telescopic sight on the centre of Hess's body and pulled the trigger. Without the support of his left hand the barrel jumped and crashed down again on the log, but he saw Hess slip and fall.

Mike was on his feet as quickly as his injuries would allow. The hunting rifle was useless to him now – with only one good hand he couldn't work the bolt action, let alone aim it accurately. He pulled Orlov's knife from his belt and wished he'd brought one of the pistols with him. Pain coursed through his arm and side with every jarring footfall. As he ran he saw Hess roll onto his side and start to get up.

As Hess straightened, he raised the AK-47, which was still clutched in his right hand. Mike guessed he had wounded him in the left arm, evening the odds a little, but Hess could still manage the lighter automatic rifle with one hand.

The helicopter was behind Hess now, not more than a hundred metres away, and the beam of the landing light picked Mike out like a trapped rabbit. He held up a hand to shield his eyes as he stumbled on. The AK-47 rattled from the blackness beyond the cone of light that imprisoned him. Bullets split the air on either side of him, but he could tell Hess was having trouble steadying the bucking rifle. Mike lowered his head and slipped in the mud, crying out as his left arm hit the ground.

Hess was screaming into the walkie-talkie in Afrikaans. The chopper was close enough for Mike to feel its rotor downwash. Loose stones and drops of water stung his face as he looked up. The pilot was flaring back for landing, the nose rising up like a prancing warhorse.

The landing light was now on Hess. He was pointing the AK-47 at Mike, one-handed, from less than twenty metres.

'Goodbye, Mr Williams,' he yelled over the whine of the turbine engine. 'Say hello to your Portuguese doctor for me.'

Mike rose unsteadily to his feet. He gripped the knife tightly and readied himself for one last lunge. The helicopter rocked forward, its nose dropping back towards the ground as the pilot pushed the machine forwards. Hess was looking at Mike, not at the aircraft behind him, so he didn't see the tip of the right skid coming closer and closer to him.

Hess pitched forward as the skid slammed into the back of his neck. He fell, arms thrown wide, and landed hard in the mud. As he dropped, his finger jerked on the trigger of the rifle and two rounds slammed into the ground no more than a metre in front of Mike. Above them, the helicopter pilot wrestled with the controls of his aircraft, desperately trying to compensate for the sudden change in the machine's altitude.

'Mike!' Sarah called from behind him.

Mike glanced back and saw she was on the road.

Orlov's hunting rifle, which he had discarded, was in her hands. He ignored Sarah and closed on the prostrate Hess. He stood over the hunter and stabbed down at him with the knife. Hess was quick to recover, though, and parried the slash with the barrel of his AK-47. Steel rang on steel.

'Get down, Mike!' Sarah called.

This time he dropped and rolled away from Hess, aware that he had lost his temporary advantage. Mike heard the crash of the rifle, and Hess instinctively turned and pointed the AK-47 towards Sarah. The round from the hunting rifle whined harmlessly over Hess's head.

Mike pushed himself up again and staggered back towards Hess, hoping to draw his fire and give Sarah a chance to reload. He lunged at Hess, shoulder down, aware of the flash of orange flame from the muzzle of the AK-47 and the din of the shot in his ears. Though he steeled himself for the shock of another hit, Hess had missed. As they fell to the ground, Mike heard the repeated click of his finger on the trigger. Hess was out of ammunition.

Mike slashed wildly with the knife, and felt it tear through fabric and slow as it met flesh. Hess grunted as he grasped Mike's right hand with his left and punched his wounded left arm with his free hand. Mike's eyes watered with the pain and in an instant he found himself on his back. Hess's next blow caught him on the jaw and hot, salty blood flooded his mouth.

The helicopter settled on the road near them, its main and tail rotors still spinning at high speed, ready for immediate take-off. Hess had one hand on Mike's throat, and gouged at his wounded arm again with the other. The knife fell from Mike's hand, and Hess scooped it up and raised the wicked blade above his face, ready to strike.

As Mike tried to roll out of the knife's path he heard the sickening thud of wood on flesh. Hess toppled over, his knife hand hanging harmlessly at his side. Mike twisted his body to avoid being crushed by the hunter and looked up to see Sarah silhouetted in the glare of the helicopter's light. She was holding the hunting rifle by the barrel and had wielded it like a club.

Sarah dropped to her knees by Mike's side and reached out for him. Suddenly Hess twisted and rose behind Sarah, the knife still clutched in his hand.

'Sarah, look out!' Mike cried, too late.

Hess moved behind Sarah and wrapped an arm around her neck. She dropped the rifle when she felt the sharp point of the knife press against her throat.

'I am getting on that helicopter now,' Hess said. Blood dribbled from the gash on his right temple where Sarah had struck him with the rifle. Her eyes were wide with fear. 'It is over,' he said as he dragged her to her feet.

'It'll never be over, Hess,' Mike said, spitting blood. 'Go, but you can't kill both of us. You've only got a knife and there'll still be one witness.'

'You think I'm an idiot? You're coming with me, or I'll kill the woman now in front of you.'

'You'll kill her anyway, you cold bastard.'

'That is true, but it's up to you whether it is quick

or very slow. I'll take the chopper up and out of small-arms range, and drop a piece of her out the door every ten minutes until you change your mind.'

Above the noise of the whirring rotor blades Mike heard the chug of Nelson's diesel engine. The truck wasn't in sight yet, and he didn't want the boys with the AK-47s opening up indiscriminately on the chopper when they arrived.

'Last chance,' Hess said as he backed towards the open cargo door of the chopper, dragging Sarah with him.

'Save yourself, Mike. Get to the police,' Sarah said, but the point of Hess's knife silenced her and a trickle of blood welled from a tiny puncture.

Hess looked back over his shoulder at the pilot, who nodded and gave a thumbs-up to show the helicopter was ready for take-off. Hess dragged Sarah backwards and into the cargo compartment after him.

Mike sprinted to the helicopter, just as the skids started to leave the ground. He jumped in and saw Hess was sitting in the nylon-webbing troop seat opposite him, his back to the pilot. Hess still had Sarah in an arm lock with the tip of his knife pressed against her blood-streaked neck.

The pilot was focusing his attention on the control panel in front of him, and both his hands were on the aircraft's controls. They lifted off in a vertical hover and, when they were above the tops of the trees, he held the rudder stick between his knees and passed an automatic pistol back over his shoulder, nudging Hess in the back of the neck with it. Hess quickly stuffed the knife into an empty ammunition pouch in his vest and took the pistol from the pilot.

'Is it loaded?' he yelled back at the pilot. The pilot gave a thumbs-up and then returned his free hand to the stick.

Hess slid to the far end of the troop bench, dragging Sarah with him. He raised his arm and pointed the pistol at Mike. Mike figured that from his new position Hess was sure he could shoot him without hitting the engine or other vital parts of the helicopter through the padded bulkhead behind him. Hess smiled at Mike, who grinned back at him like a madman.

Hess pulled the trigger as Mike leapt across the narrow gap that separated them. Sarah was wide-eyed with surprise and fear.

'No, Mike!' she screamed.

Hess was open-mouthed in disbelief as he pulled the trigger again and again, but there was no noise, no bullets. Mike smashed his forehead into the Namibian's nose and Hess wailed with pain. He reached for his face with his hands, and Sarah, seeing her cue, rolled off the troop seat and onto the floor. The helicopter bucked with the sudden displacement of weight and Sarah hit her head on the corner of the metal frame of the troop seat. She got to her knees, swayed, and then collapsed on the floor of the cargo compartment.

Mike dragged Hess off the seat with his good arm and straddled his chest. The knife slipped from the unbuckled pouch on Hess's vest and skidded across the floor away from them. Again and again Mike slammed his closed fist into Hess's face, but he was weak from loss of blood and each blow was weaker than the last. Hess ignored the pain in his face and reached up for Mike, pushing him out of reach.

Hess stabbed two fingers into the bloodied makeshift dressing on Mike's side, causing him to lurch backwards. Hess slid from under Mike and got to his knees. Mike lunged again for him and they became locked in a frantic embrace.

Hess punched Mike's wounded arm, and then pushed him onto his back and along the metal floor until Mike's head and shoulders were sticking outside the open cargo door. The slipstream tousled his hair and blew hard and cold on the cuts on his face. Mike was furious that he had allowed Hess to get the better of him again.

Hess gripped the wrist of Mike's good arm, keeping it away from him. With his other hand he grasped the belt on Mike's shorts and pushed him farther and farther out the door. Something hit the helicopter with a loud zing and the pilot threw the machine violently onto its side. Green tracer arced past them and Mike realised the boys in the truck were firing at them. They must have thought Hess had made his escape and decided to try to down the helicopter.

The pilot's evasive action had saved his machine from taking another hit and also given Hess more leverage. The whole upper half of Mike's body was in the slipstream now. His back was arched painfully. As soon as Hess chose to let go of him, he would fall.

Suddenly, Hess was lying on top of him. Mike struggled to sit up and saw Sarah standing behind Hess's prostrate body. Her face was sickly white and she was holding onto a webbing strap on the bulk-head to steady herself.

Then Hess was on his knees again, his hands reaching frantically behind his back, his face contorted in agony. With the Namibian's weight and hands off him Mike used his legs to slide himself back inside the helicopter cabin. As Hess twisted his torso Mike saw the leather-bound handle of the hunting knife protruding from the centre of his back, where Sarah had stabbed him.

Hess twisted again to get a grip on the knife handle and, as he did so, Mike pushed himself to his knees and then stood. He kicked Hess in the side mercilessly.

'That's for Isabella,' he said.

The chopper pitched again as the pilot circled and Hess teetered on his knees on the edge of the open cargo cabin. As he was about to topple into space, Hess stopped trying to grab the knife from his back and reached out with his right hand for Mike instead.

Mike was too slow to back away and Hess snatched his wrist in an iron grip. Worried that the hunter would pull him out if he fell, Mike dropped suddenly to the floor of the chopper, landing hard on his chest and stomach. Hess slipped and fell out the door anyway as the helicopter lurched again, but he did not release his grip on Mike.

Mike felt as though his arm was being pulled from its socket, as Hess dangled in space below him, kicking his legs as he tried to gain a foothold on the skid. The helicopter was still high, the pilot circling at altitude to avoid mist-shrouded hills and the possibility of more ground fire from the truck.

'Help me!' Hess screamed, staring up into Mike's eyes.

The pilot looked over his shoulders and yelled, 'Pull him in. Now! Pull him in!'

If Mike had been holding onto Hess, instead of the other way around, he would have let go, then and there. Mike wanted Hess dead more than anything else in the world, but there was nothing he could do while Hess gripped him. Mike was using his free hand to help keep himself inside the helicopter by gripping a strut supporting the troop seats. 'Help me, Sarah,' he called.

She grabbed hold of Mike's belt and started to drag him back across the cargo compartment floor. Slowly, painfully, they hauled the struggling Hess upwards. Eventually, he was able to hook a leg over the helicopter's skid and pull himself to a sitting position.

Mike sat back on the aircraft floor, drained by the effort. Hess stood on the skid, one hand holding the roof to support himself. He smiled at Mike again as his right hand reached behind his back.

'Mike, look out!' Sarah screamed.

He saw the flash of steel as Hess pulled the blood-stained knife from his back. Mike dropped onto his back as the blade arced down towards him. He drew his knees protectively up to his chest. He avoided Hess's killing stroke, but the point of the knife scored a bloody trough down one of his shins.

Mike kicked out, ankles together, and caught Hess in the stomach with both his feet. Hess lost his grip on the roof and sailed backwards, arms windmilling. Mike couldn't see the ground below and guessed they were three or four hundred feet above the blackened bush. Hess didn't scream, but Mike knew he would never forget the wide-eyed look of surprise on the Namibian's face as he fell.

Sarah knelt beside Mike and wrapped her arms around him as he sat up.

'It's over,' she said.

The pilot settled the helicopter into a hover with the stick between his knees and removed his helmet with his free hand. He turned and looked at them over his shoulder.

'Sarah, meet Captain Fanie Theron of the South African Police Service,' Mike said.

'Did you have to do that?' Theron shouted. He was trying to look stern, but Mike saw the hint of a smile at the corners of his mouth as he shook his head.

'Yes,' Mike replied.

Epilogue

Michael Williams had found a quiet piece of Africa where he could recuperate. He was ready for some peace.

Over the past few mornings he had watched two old bull elephants drinking from the Zambezi River, casting dark reflections on the water like black irises in shining blue eyes. Crocodiles basked lazily on golden spits of sand in the middle of the day and the hippos came out to graze in the afternoon, as the sun set.

The only sounds in his refuge came from nature, not from man. Last night he had heard hyena calling and the night before that it was a lion.

Three months of eating, drinking and fishing had cured the worst of his wounds, including a bout of bilharzia, which he had probably picked up from the flooded river when they rescued Sarah. The gunshot wounds had turned to pink puckered scars. The memories and the dreams were taking longer to go away.

The house where he had been living, if one could call it a house, was a two-room fishing shack on the Zambezi near Chirundu, in the far north of Zimbabwe. The place wasn't much to look at, but the big concrete verandah was well shaded by a cracked asbestos roof, and the fridge worked.

Mike had left his job, mainly to escape the glare of publicity that followed his last overland trip. Despite what some people said, he hadn't been sacked. In fact, bookings actually increased and Rian had begged him to return after a rest at the shack, which was owned by some Zimbabwean friends of his.

He had decided that he wasn't going back, though. Forward, maybe, but not back. He had made pretty good money working for Rian on the overland trips and, with all his food and expenses covered by the job, he had managed to put some cash away. Lately he had been thinking about buying some land, perhaps setting up a small game farm and a lodge. The proposition would be more attractive if he could find a partner, although not necessarily a financial partner.

An old African caretaker also lived in the fishing shack. Moses had kept Mike company over the long, hot summer months on the river. They would fish for bait together in the mornings and then go out on a boat to drift lazily in the current in the hope of bagging a tiger fish or two in the afternoon. Mike never caught many of the tenacious fighting fish, but that was fine with him. He found no great thrill in hunting, fishing or killing.

Rian and Susie forwarded get-well cards and postcards from the other members of the tour group, and just the other day he had received a letter from Nigel. He and Nigel had been flown out of Mfuwe airport on an air ambulance to Lusaka as soon as Fanie Theron had touched down in the helicopter. They had missed the chance to say a proper goodbye to everyone else.

Nelson, the truck, was still plying the highways and dirt roads of southern Africa. According to Rian, the new driver, a young American guy called Sam, loved showing the female travellers where the bullet holes were patched. Rian had told him the rules when he took him on as a driver, but Mike had told him that some rules were made to be broken.

Sarah left for England the day after Mike was flown to Lusaka. Susie regularly pulled Sarah's stories from *The Times* off the internet and sent hard copies to Mike in the post.

A raid by Russian police on Orlov's mansion outside Moscow unearthed a huge pair of elephant tusks which, with the help of the South African authorities, were positively identified as having once belonged to Skukuza. There was no direct evidence linking Orlov to the killings in Mozambique, mainly because there were no witnesses. However, the South Africans had enough on him to extradite him from Zambia. Orlov hadn't actually killed anyone in Zambia, except for an inflatable doll, of course. A string of firearms charges, while proved by a Zambian court, weren't enough to keep him in jail in Zambia for very long; however, the South Africans took poaching seriously and it looked like Orlov would be in prison for a couple of years at least.

Susie had kept in touch with Sarah via e-mail and they had corresponded intermittently. She posted copies of the messages to Mike, but the mail took weeks to arrive. There was no phone at the fishing shack and the payphone in Chirundu rarely worked. He'd tried a few times to call Sarah, but on the one occasion he had been able to get through to her work, he was kept on hold so long waiting to talk to her that his money ran out.

Mike was grown up enough to realise that Sarah's future was a world away in England in pursuit of her career, which seemed to have really taken off in a very short space of time. He was pleased for her.

The shack came with its own vehicle: a beat-up, roofless old Land Rover. Moses and Mike mainly used it to go shopping and to pick up the mail. This morning was Moses's turn to pick up their beer, canned food and mail from the postbox at the general store.

'Letter for you, *bwana*,' said Moses.

Mike had given up telling Moses to stop calling him '*bwana*'.

'Thanks, Moses.'

'From the lady,' he added.

Mike's mail was almost always from Susie, and Moses could recognise her large, girlish handwriting. He looked at his watch and saw that it was after eleven, so he relieved Moses of one of the cold bottles of Castle beer in the carry bag and knocked the top off with the opener on his pocketknife.

'Sundowner already, *bwana*?' Moses cackled.

'I'm on holiday.'

541

'You been on holiday more than any man I know, *bwana.*'

Mike sat down in his favourite deck chair and slit the envelope with the blade of his pocketknife. Inside was a single sheet of paper and he saw it was a photocopy of a one-paragraph item from *The Times*.

The beer bottle slid from his fingers as he read the lines. Moses wore a disapproving scowl as he emerged from the kitchen and saw the broken glass and spilt beer.

Mike read the item again.

Times reporter Sarah Thatcher has been appointed as this newspaper's new Africa correspondent. Ms Thatcher, who will be based in Johannesburg, won two major media awards for her first-hand coverage of an armed attack on a tour group in Zambia and the subsequent arrest of a Russian national on poaching charges.

At the bottom of the photocopied page was a handwritten message giving the date and time of arrival of a British Airways flight from London to Johannesburg. The aircraft was due in a few days' time. After that she had written: 'Do you know a good safari guide who could show me around and not get me killed? Love, Sarah.'

'Moses,' Mike said, 'how much fuel's in the Land Rover?'